C000132487

ARTHUR'S WAR

Alan Reynolds

Fisher King Publishing

ARTHUR'S WAR
Copyright © Alan Reynolds 2022
Print ISBN 978-1-914560-38-5
Epub ISBN 978-1-914560-39-2

All rights reserved. No part of this publication may be
reproduced or distributed in any form or by any means, or
stored in a database or electronic retrieval system without
the prior written permission of Fisher King Publishing Ltd.
Thank you for respecting the author of this work.

This is a work of fiction. Names, characters, businesses,
places, events and incidents are either the products of the
author's imagination or used in a fictitious manner. Any
resemblance to actual persons, living or dead, or actual
events is purely coincidental.

Published by
Fisher King Publishing
The Old Barn
York Road
Thirsk
YO7 3AD
England

fisherkingpublishing.co.uk

A huge thanks to Rick Armstrong for his
unstinting support, guidance, and friendship,
also to Samantha Richardson and Rachel Topping
at Fisher King Publishing.
My thanks also to my very talented niece, Karen Paxton
for her superb cover art work and to Jane Wheater
and all at Artus Digital Marketing for
editorial and proof-reading support.

Dedicated to my family and friends, and to all
those who have supported me in my writing –
your encouragement has been inspirational.
Much love

Also by Alan Reynolds

Before my eyes shadowy figures creep
Whilst ghostly creatures break the need to sleep
Fear envelops like a corpse's shroud
But least we've done our King and country proud
The phantom shells that burst above my head
The only sound you hear before you're dead
Trench life 1915

Chapter One

Saturday, August 8th, 1914.

Just four days into the war, and in the West Yorkshire mill town of Keighley, there was little evidence that anything had changed – except everything had changed.

The Malt Shovel, the meeting place for so many mill workers over the years, was devoid of the usual bonhomie associated with the establishment. The old men were still there, some reminiscing about earlier conflicts in faraway lands to anyone who would listen. Many of the pals had signed up, some voluntary, some not so, pressganged by dint of the local magistrate.

One such victim was Arthur Marsden, the nineteen-year-old master-baker, whose shop was just a few doors up James Street from the alehouse. A regular visitor, he had been caught up in one of the many protests a few weeks earlier and arrested with three of his drinking pals. They were conditionally discharged; the condition was that they signed up for the army. The alternative was a spell in Armley gaol.

Back at the bakery, his mother Mildred had taken charge. Recently widowed and unexpectedly the beneficiary of a significant fortune in her husband's will, she had used some of the money to buy a substantial property in the nearby village of Oakworth. For now, however, the bakery had her undivided attention. People needed bread.

With Arthur now on his way to serve his country, Ivy Stonehouse, the butcher's daughter, had taken over the breadmaking. She had only recently been recruited and had taken residency in the upstairs living quarters, looking after Arthur in lieu of rent, a responsibility she had undertaken with more diligence than was really necessary.

Mildred was serving behind the counter with two of her four daughters, Grace and Agnes. Grace was still suffering from the emotional turmoil of discovering the young man she had been courting was her stepbrother, a fact that had only come to light after Mildred's husband had died. Freddie Bluet, the object of Grace's affection, signed up for the army when he found out the truth of his parentage to escape from thoughts of Grace.

"I'll just go and check on Ivy," said Mildred in a break from the seemingly endless queue of customers.

Ivy was in the baking shed mixing her second vat of dough of the morning.

"Hello, Mrs Marsden," said Ivy as she noticed Mildred entering from the corridor which separated the shop from the baking shed.

"Hello, Ivy, I've just come to see how things were."

"Aye, 'appen I'll finish this mix and that'll see us till we close."

"What did Buxton's say this morning?"

"T'miller? Nowt much, the price hasn't changed. I paid him for the three bags we needed. Have you heard owt?"

"About the war? No, nothing yet. I'm going to call at the newsagents shortly and get a copy of this morning's Times; that will have the latest."

"I'm so worried for Arthur," said Ivy, breaking off her mixing.

"Yes, me too, Ivy, but when faced with life's challenges, one must put on a brave face and carry on. Life doesn't stop."

"Aye, tha could be right, but I can't stop thinking about him."

She looked at Ivy with a degree of admiration. Drafted in at the last minute to serve in the shop and now single-handedly in charge of the baking.

"What will you do about the flat upstairs?"

"Well, if it's all the same, I'd like to stay. I can keep it tidy for when Arthur gets back and it's handy for baking."

"Yes, of course, if your mother's happy with that arrangement."

"Aye, 'appen she'll be happy enough."

"What about the butchery? How is your mother managing?"

"Well, with Wilfred gone, Phyllis and Ernest have been learning; they can cut most meat now. Phyllis can even bone a rabbit."

"And the others, what are they doing?"

"Glynis, Lillian and Ronald are in the shop; they seem to be managing."

"That's good. I will call in on the way to collect my paper and buy something for this evening. Is there anything you need?"

"Nay, 'appen I'll be alright, ta."

"Anyway, I better let you get on."

Ivy checked on the oven then went back to the mixing vat. Mildred walked back down the corridor to the shop. There were a few customers but Grace and Agnes seemed to be coping.

"I'm just going to collect a paper," she shouted to Grace.

Her coat and hat were in the parlour in the first floor living quarters and she ascended the stairs. It seemed strange seeing the old room that had been her life for over twenty years looking so different. The clutter of five children had gone. Ivy had done an excellent job in tidying the place; she couldn't imagine Arthur contributing anything in that direction.

Out of curiosity, she went into the two bedrooms. The dividing curtain in the children's room had gone and so had one of the beds. Her former bedroom had similarly been transformed. She noticed Ivy's nightclothes were hung over the back of the chair. The bed hadn't been made and both pillows appeared to have been used. Mildred quickly put two and two together and smiled.

She left the bakery and walked up James Street, which was busy this Saturday morning, though not with the panic-buying of earlier in the week. She passed Nugent's the greengrocer's and the butcher's, which were both doing a good trade.

On the corner of James Street and the High Street was Granger's Grocery Emporium, an establishment that had been in that prime position for over seventy years. Unfortunately, there had been some looting earlier in the week following the announcement of war and there was now a police officer stood outside. Mildred collected her newspaper from the tobacconist's next door and then entered the grocer's. George Granger, the proprietor, was at the cheese counter and noticed Mildred.

"Mrs Marsden, it is indeed a pleasure. How are things in the new house?"

"Well, thank you, Mr Granger. I'll take some of the Wensleydale, please, half a pound."

"Aye, right you are."

The grocer picked up a slab of cheese and cut it to the appropriate size to within less than an ounce difference, demonstrating his skill in cheese cutting. He wrapped it in paper and handed it over.

"Would there be anything else?" asked the grocer expectantly.

Mildred reeled off a list of requirements which Granger supplied.

"What's this I hear about you being looted?" asked

Mildred as she was paying for her items.

"Aye, Tuesday, it were terrible. Had to call in the constabulary. It was in t'news."

"Oh? I didn't see it; I don't get time for the provincials these days. I take The Times, it's much more relevant, I think."

Mildred's gentrification was progressing well, a point not lost on the grocer, who had known Mildred since she married Albert over twenty-two years ago but kept his council. 'Nowt but a baker's wife,' he would say to the gossipmongers.

"Can you get one of your boys to deliver them to the bakery when you have a moment?" she said on seeing the three large carrier bags of produce.

"Aye, I'll get young Jimmy to drop them down directly."

Mildred had one more stop before returning to the bakery.

The butcher's shop was busy. Mildred recognised three of the children working behind the counter. Phyllis, the second eldest, appeared to be cutting away on a shin of beef, separating the meat from the bone. Just then, Violet Stonehouse appeared from the back and noticed Mildred. She was also a widow, but with seven children.

"Hello, Mrs Marsden, how are you settling into Oakworth?" she said as she approached the counter.

"Hello, Mrs Stonehouse. Very well, and I wanted to say thank you for the excellent cleaning you did after we left on Tuesday. The rooms look very tidy."

"Aye, our Ivy will keep it as such an' all. She's been brought up to be so."

"Yes, indeed."

"Did you want something?"

"Yes, I'll take two pounds of your pork sausages, please."

"Aye, I can do them today, but have you heard about the shortages?"

"Yes, we've had problems with flour deliveries, too, but they seem to be satisfactory this morning according to Ivy."

"How is Ivy getting on?" asked Violet as she cut a number of sausage links and weighed them on the scales.

"Well, I have to say, she has done a remarkable job. She's a quick learner and I know Arthur was very impressed."

"Aye, Wilfred said she was doing well."

Violet Stonehouse had put the sausages into a paper bag and placed them on the long glass counter. Plates of various cuts of meat were on display below. Other customers were being served further along.

Violet looked down. Mildred could see tears starting to roll down her cheeks.

"Now, Mrs Stonehouse, I share the pain you're feeling, but we women have to be strong and support our sons."

"Aye, 'appen you're right, but seeing Wilfred go like that this morning… It went through my mind that I may never see him again."

"Yes, I know, I do understand. I had a similar feeling saying goodbye to Arthur last evening."

Violet pulled a handkerchief from her apron pocket and dabbed her eyes in a dainty fashion.

"I watched him and Arthur from the window. They took a cabbie to Bradford," said Violet, trying to compose herself.

"That's good, at least they're both together."

"Aye, Arthur's been a good pal for Wilfred."

"Yes, indeed. Well, they have been friends since they were at infants' school."

Mildred handed over the money for the sausages.

"Stay strong, Mrs Stonehouse, stay strong," she said as she picked up her purchase and left the store.

It was midday and just an hour before the half-day closure. Mildred walked the short distance to the bakery. It was a bright morning and to her right in the park many people were taking in the opportunity of the clement weather. A trolleybus passed her brimming with customers, its power-feed cable snaking up to the overhead wires which shook as it went by.

Seeing that the shop was quiet, Mildred decided to return to the parlour and read the newspaper, which was neatly folded under her arm. She took the sausages into the kitchen; she would take them back to Oakworth for dinner. She took off her hat and sat at the table, the broadsheet almost covering the entire surface. As she scanned the illustrious newspaper, she was amazed at the activity that was going on.

There was an article that attracted her straightaway headed 'Five Months' Supply of Breadstuffs', which she read avidly. The panic-buying in London had eased since Tuesday, much the same as Keighley, although many shops and the large departmental stores had imposed rationing on certain produce. One or two stores, including Harrods, had closed in order to be able to deal with orders by post. The important news was that the supply of grain appeared to have stabilised and the price of flour fixed; that would help no end. She must tell Arthur directly, she thought. Then came the realisation; there would be no informing Arthur. She sighed.

She turned the pages and there was another article pondering the question of how long the war was going to last. Some commentators suggested three weeks while others, more pessimistically, five months. Few envisaged it extending for longer than that. It gave Mildred a glimmer of hope that Arthur would be safe. Maybe, just maybe, it would be over before he had completed his training. That was something to hold on to.

Earlier in Bradford, master-baker Arthur Marsden and butcher Wilfred Stonehouse arrived at Bradford Town Hall to report for duty. It was mayhem as the taxicab pulled up in front of the building with upwards of two hundred men milling around, seemingly lost. A number of lorries were lined up at the side of the building. Men in military uniform were in urgent discussion; an officer appeared to be directing matters.

Eventually, all those who had already signed their papers were ordered into the waiting vehicles. Arthur and Wilfred found themselves in truck three with ten others crammed in the back. Wherever they were going, the journey was not going to be comfortable.

A uniformed private, complete with rifle, was the last to get on board. The truck was a fairly flimsy affair with just a tarpaulin cover placed over five metal stays. Inside there were two long benches against each side. The passengers were facing each other, six to a bench, with no personal space. The soldier was seated on the running board facing behind with his legs dangling over the edge. The driver cranked the starting handle and the engine sprang into life with a cough and a splutter. The lorry lurched forward trying to take the weight of the cargo. There was a great deal of gear-crunching and then gradually it moved ahead.

As the convoy laboured through the streets of Bradford, it was greeted by shouts of encouragement and good wishes from bystanders who were about this early morning. Inside truck three, there were anxious faces among the passengers.

"Has anyone a thought on where we're going?" asked the child opposite Arthur.

Arthur had his head down staring at his feet, locked in his own world. He looked up at the enquirer, fresh-faced and looking much younger than the eighteen years qualifying age.

"Nay, can't say I have." There were similar dissenting voices.

The squaddie was still sat with his back to the rest of the group, holding onto a hanging rope to prevent him from falling into the road and being hit by the following vehicle.

"Eh up, soldier, dos tha know where we're heading?" asked Arthur, shouting across two other volunteers. The private turned his head.

"'Appen tha'll find out when us gets there," he replied, which killed off that line of enquiry.

Arthur looked at the child opposite who had posed the original question and shrugged his shoulders.

"I'm Arthur… Marsden, baker from Keighley," he said to the lad.

"Joseph Tandy, accountant's clerk, from Barker End," replied the lad. The others repeated the introductions.

Arthur was surprised. He had expected mill workers and labourers, cannon-fodder for the generals, but most were from professional backgrounds; clerks, bankers and agents, the products of local grammar schools, fired by the desire to serve their country.

Over recent months, Arthur had become increasingly bitter at the treatment of the working class; he had seen poverty at first hand as wives bought bread by the ounce. He had joined the Labour Party which he felt shared his ideals. He had also supported the recent strikes which had so badly affected the town and its working community. It was his involvement in one of the protests which led to his arrest and subsequent court appearance. His views had caused friction and arguments within the family and he had flatly refused to move to the new house, preferring not to benefit from what he believed to be 'tainted' money.

The truck continued bouncing and lurching for almost two hours. Arthur looked outside the back of the lorry and noticed the scenery had changed significantly. The road had narrowed to just a single track and every so often the truck had to stop in a passing point to allow other trucks to pass; all appeared to be being driven by military personnel. They were surrounded by hills, white drystone walls creating patterns on the landscape. Sheep wandered freely – another reason for the unscheduled stops.

They pulled up outside a wire fence that stretched as far as the eye could see in both directions.

"Looks like we're here," said Arthur to Wilfred, who was just staring blankly at the floor.

Wilfred turned and looked out of the back of the truck. The squaddie had gone and was now talking to another soldier. Arthur could hear orders being shouted. Then the soldier approached.

"Right, lads, everybody out and line up in pairs," he shouted.

One by one, the lads dropped down from the truck carrying their belongings and started stretching their legs and backs. There were six other trucks disgorging their passengers. The first group moved off escorted by a uniformed private and the second followed.

"Right, lads, follow on," barked the soldier.

The group from truck three marched in pairs and caught up with the others. Arthur noticed a sign, 'Breary Banks', hanging from a post.

As the recruits marched through the gates, Arthur was taking it all in. To the right there was a guard hut and then a long tarmac drive before the path forked. They took the left-hand track and reached a number of huts. In front of the first, a more substantial construction than its neighbours, was a large open area with a flagpole in the middle. There were dozens of military personnel milling around and also others, not in uniform, who just seemed to be idling.

A sergeant major came out of the hut and watched as the men from the trucks were lined up. A corporal then shepherded them into some sort of order. Six other soldiers carrying clipboards assembled in front of the building. An officer appeared at the hut entrance, followed by another.

The sergeant bellowed his first order.

"Atten... shun!"

There was no coordination, but the men stood up straight and stared ahead.

The first officer stood on the steps of the hut and looked down at the seventy or so new arrivals.

"Good morning, gentlemen. My name is Major Foster, in charge of Colsterdale Camp. You will be based here for your initial training for a few weeks before your operational deployment. This is Lieutenant Hoskins, who has just joined us today from the officer training college." The other officer stepped forward. "He will be responsible for allocating your accommodation and duties. Carry on, Lieutenant."

The major walked back into the hut and the lieutenant looked at the men staring at him.

"Right, when your name is called, report in and you'll be taken to your accommodation."

The first private stepped forward and read names from a sheet of paper. After fifteen were called, he marched away, leading the recruits to one of the huts.

The next group were called and the next, following the same procedure. The fourth soldier called Arthur and Wilfred's names. Two other familiar names were read out; Samuel Tanner and Henry King, two of Arthur's drinking pals from the Malt Shovel. They were also arrested with

Arthur and Wilfred during the protests and had suffered the same fate. Arthur was pleased to see them and anxious to catch up.

With the rest of the fifteen assembled, the soldier in charge, a corporal, marched the men away from the parade ground. Arthur caught a glimpse of the lieutenant; his name was familiar.

To the right, there were more huts in rows; over a hundred, they would discover later. To the left in what was a vast open field, men – some in uniform, some in civvies – were constructing wigwam-fashioned tents. The group stopped at a hut with the number '43' stencilled beside the entrance door in white paint.

"Right, lads, this is your hut," said the corporal. "Stow your gear then report to the cookhouse in one hour." There were looks of confusion. "It's next to the officers' mess," he explained.

There were two rows of eight beds either side of the long hut with a small set of drawers separating them. One bed had already been taken; the remainder were allocated to the fifteen. Once ownership of the sleeping quarters had been completed, Arthur and Wilfred joined Samuel and Henry for a catch-up. Henry had a reputation for being a snazzy dresser and today was no exception with his smart three-piece suit and cap.

"'Ow do, Henry, Samuel," said Arthur as the pals shook hands enthusiastically; it was good to meet up again.

"Eh up, Arthur, Wilfred, t'is good to see tha."

"Aye, you an' all," said Arthur. "What is this place?"

"One of t'lads on truck said it were an old navvy camp for them building the dams."

"Aye, that sounds about right," said Arthur.

"I heard one of the officers saying there's more coming

today on t'train," said Henry.

"Aye, I can imagine. There were hundreds of lads at t'recruitment centre in Bradford. Do tha reckon there's a pub here? I could murder a pint," said Arthur.

"I think tha's had tha last pint for a while," said Henry gloomily.

"Aye, tha could be right, Henry."

Back in the bakery, it was approaching one o'clock and closing time. Grace and Agnes had already started cleaning down the shelves. There were just two loaves and a few small baps left which Mildred would claim if not sold. Ivy came in from the baking shed.

"Shed's all done," she said, wiping her hands with a towel. The shop was empty.

"'You've done a grand job with bread, Ivy," said Grace. "Customers were happy enough."

"Aye, thank you. There's a sack of flour left which'll start us Monday till miller turns up."

Just then, there was the customary 'clang' of the front door as a man, flamboyantly dressed in a green suit with brown squares and sporting a bowler hat, came in. Agnes looked up from cleaning one of the shelves behind the counter and recognised him straightaway.

"Mr Delaney! My, what a surprise," she said, wiping her hands on her apron and straitening her maid's bonnet. "You must excuse my appearance, sir; I've been working today," she added in as refined a voice as she could manage.

Grace and Ivy looked at the colourful visitor then at each other. Grace shrugged her shoulders. He doffed his hat in Agnes's direction.

"No matter, Agnes, my dear. I was wondering if I could speak to you on quite an urgent matter."

"Why, of course. Please wait a moment while I tidy myself."

Agnes took off her apron and went through the beaded curtain which separated the bakery from the corridor to the baking shed. She turned left up the stairs and headed for the parlour.

"Hello, dear," said Mildred seeing Agnes walk in.

"Mr Delaney's here… the promoter."

"What, from the theatre?"

"Aye, and he wants to speak to me. I've not a change of clothing."

"No matter, a quick touch of rouge will suffice."

Mildred opened her handbag and took out her small makeup bag while Agnes was fussing with her hair.

"Don't worry, dear, you look perfectly acceptable."

She applied a little makeup to Agnes's cheeks. Then Agnes exchanged her working headwear with the bonnet she had worn from home earlier and headed back downstairs.

In the shop, Ivy had locked the front door and Mr Delaney was stood at the counter in convivial conversation with Grace.

"Ah, Agnes, I was just telling your sister here how much we admire your singing."

"Thank you, Mr Delaney, that's very kind."

"Shall we go for a walk? It's a fine afternoon; I don't want to disturb your work."

"Aye, of course; we can go to the park."

Agnes was feeling anxious, unsure of the meaning of the surprise visit by the promotor.

They left the shop. As the man had said, it was a bright day and James Street was bustling with people. They waited for a trolleybus to go by before attempting to cross the thoroughfare. They passed the cabbie stop where two taxis were parked waiting for custom, their drivers tugging on cigarettes, chatting amiably.

"How are you, my dear?" asked Delaney, making conversation.

"Aye, I'm well enough, thank you," replied Agnes, still recovering from the visit of the famous promoter.

"Let's sit here," said Delaney, seeing an empty bench. They made themselves comfortable. "I expect you are wondering why I've chosen to visit you rather than put pen to paper?"

"Aye, it was a surprise."

"Well, I have had some exciting news this morning and I wanted to share it with you before you received more offers."

"More offers?"

"Yes, I assumed you would have continued with your auditioning, London even."

"London, nay, although I would welcome such a venture."

"Well, let me get straight to the point. I received a telephone call this morning from a military man, Captain Henderson, who's leading a recruitment drive for fighting men here in the North, and he's asked me to arrange a variety show at very short notice."

"You have a telephone?" asked Agnes. Delaney was momentarily distracted.

"Yes, of course, my dear, it's essential in my line of work."

"A variety show, you said."

"Yes, I don't have all the details, but we'll be touring around the north of England attracting men to sign up to serve their country. Nothing too spectacular, there won't be time, but with a touch of glamour. I've already spoken to Mr Tooley, you remember, the pianist."

"Aye, of course."

"He's going to arrange a small accompanying band. Luckily, the army doesn't need our more mature musicians. I have in mind using you as the headline act. What do you say?"

Agnes sat there unable to speak. Noticing the hesitation, the promoter continued.

"Don't worry, I will pay the same as I promised before, a pound a night, and I'm writing to Miss Lloyd today to see if we can use some of her songs. They are doing similar shows in London."

"Marie Lloyd?!"

"Yes, I was hoping you could finish the show with some of her songs. What do you say?"

"Well, you've fair taken my breath away, I don't know what to say. When do we start?"

"I need to work on a few things, there are a lot of arrangements to be done. This Henderson fellow will be letting me know the venues next week, so I just need to concentrate on the programme. I do have one or two acts I can call on who will be available. I would think we should be ready to start rehearsing a week on Monday and the tour to start in early September. What do you say?"

"Aye, of course."

"That's good, I will have my assistant draw up a contract. The army are paying, I'm glad to say."

Agnes was still taking everything in.

"You might want to call on Mr Tooley in the week and talk to him about arrangements; I will be discussing suitable songs. I have asked him to provide a gramophone so you can listen to them."

"Aye, that will be grand," replied Agnes, still in a dream.

"Very well, I'll speak to Mr Tooley this afternoon and arrange for you to call on Tuesday. What time can you be available?"

"'Appen about three o'clock."

"Three o'clock Tuesday then. I will, of course, write to you with more information as I have it."

"Thank you, Mr Delaney."

"It's Cameron, you can call me Cameron, all my artists do."

"Aye... Cameron, very well."

The promoter got up and bid farewell with an exaggerated doff of his hat. He would walk in a different direction to return to his office in the Hippodrome.

Agnes was walking on air as she returned to the bakery, a heady mix of excitement, nervousness, and anxiety. Grace and Ivy had finished scrubbing the shelves. Ivy, seeing Agnes approach, opened the door of the bakery; the 'clang' reverberated around the shop.

"Eh up, Agnes, what were that all about?"

"'Appen Mr Delaney wants me to star in a new show."

Grace was stood behind the counter. "What's this?"

"Aye, it's true enough. I need to speak to Mam."

The three girls went up to the parlour where Mildred had prepared some sandwiches.

"Hello, girls," greeted Mildred as they entered the room

"Agnes has got some news, haven't you, Agnes?" said Grace excitedly before Agnes could say anything.

"Aye, Mr Delaney wants me to be in a music hall show he's arranging, to help recruit men for the war."

"My, that's wonderful. Come and sit down and tell us all about it."

Agnes related the conversation.

"How are we going to run shop with Agnes gone?" asked Grace.

"Well, we did know that was a possibility."

"Aye, but that was before they took our Arthur off to war," replied Grace.

"I might know someone," said Ivy.

"Who might that be?" asked Mildred.

"Betty Granger, she works at the grocery store sometimes."

"I didn't know George Granger had a daughter."

"Nay, he's her uncle. She was at school with me. 'Appen she's good with customers."

"Yes, that sounds ideal. Very well, do you know where she lives?"

"Aye, I do."

"Good. See if she can call on Monday and we can see how she fares. She could do a morning's work if she's willing. I'll pay her for her time."

"Aye, Mrs Marsden, I'll call on her later."

With her staffing issues seemingly resolved, Mildred was anxious to return home; she had things to do. She looked at her daughters in turn.

"If you're ready, we need to leave. We can take a cabbie back to the house."

A few minutes later, Mildred, Grace and Agnes were heading back to Oakworth, the small village about seven miles away. Ivy was tidying up the parlour before calling on Betty Granger to discuss possible employment.

It was three o'clock as the taxicab drove up to the front of Springfield Hall, the magnificent mansion Mildred had bought with some of the proceeds from her husband's will. There was one issue she was keen to resolve. Freddie Bluet, the object of Grace's affection, had just taken over the role of gardener when he learned the truth of his mother's indiscretion and subsequently joined the army. This had left

Mildred with a vacancy. Daisy Jessop, the wife of the local store proprietor, had taken on the role of housekeeper and was in the kitchen when the three returned from the bakery. She left her chores and greeted the arrivals.

"Hello, Mrs Jessop," said Mildred seeing her in the kitchen doorway. Agnes and Grace went to their rooms to change. "I'm glad I've caught you before you'd left, I wanted to ask you a question."

"Of course, Mildred," replied the housekeeper. "Would you like some tea?"

"Yes, thank you, that would be most welcome."

Mildred took off her hat and followed Daisy into the kitchen. Daisy was straight to the sink to fill the kettle, a luxury unimaginable only weeks earlier.

"I've been giving some thought to the position of gardener now Freddie is no longer available. Do you know if that Jed fellow would still be interested?"

"What, Jed Dewhurst?"

"Yes, the one who used to work here," Mildred clarified.

Daisy put the kettle on the gas stove and lit the burner.

"Well, I can certainly call and ask him. I can't imagine he will have joined up; he'll be too old."

"Excellent," replied Mildred.

Sunday morning, five-thirty. Back at the camp, the sound of a bugler playing reveille roused the residents of hut forty-three. There were groans of protests.

27

Following their arrival at the camp the previous evening, the four pals had teamed up and started to look around their new surroundings. It was surprisingly well-appointed with a cookhouse, canteen, shower facilities and its own post office. There was electricity and running water courtesy of Leeds City Corporation. The camp even had its own narrow-gauge railway to ferry supplies and materials from the railhead at Masham. Unfortunately, troops and recruits arriving by train were faced with a six-mile march from the station.

There were hoots of protests at the early call, then the corporal who had delivered them to the hut the previous day entered hut forty-three. The group stared at the new arrival; most were still in bed.

"Right, lads, we weren't formally introduced yesterday; my name's Corporal Dorkins, fall-in at the parade ground at oh-six-hundred."

There was little urgency in the hut; a couple of the lads started to go back to sleep, but they were in for a rude awakening. Suddenly, the sergeant major entered.

"Right, you lot, fall in – now!" he barked.

There was a scramble to get out of bed. Most of the lads were still in their underclothes. He prowled up and down the hut like a panther on the hunt. The recruits lined up next to their respective beds.

"My, my, my, is this the best that Yorkshire has to offer? Bloody shower, look at you. You want to kill Germans? You lot couldn't kill a bloody fly." He paced along the hut, looking at each recruit in turn.

"Dear, dear, dear, the Kaiser's gonna eat you for breakfast," he bellowed as he reached Wilfred. "What's your name, lad?"

"Stonehouse."

"Stonehouse? Shite-house, more like. A stick of wind and you'll be away, and it's Sergeant Major... remember, Sergeant Major Stafford, right?"

"Yes, Sergeant Major," said Wilfred nervously.

He continued marching up and down. Arthur wasn't the only one needing the toilet.

The sergeant major reached the door and turned.

"Well, have no fear, lads, we're going to change all that. Right, five minutes on the parade ground. Go!"

There was a mad scramble as the recruits dressed. Most had no change of clothes, and with no uniform, it was a case of putting on what they had taken off the previous evening.

The lads piled out of the hut and were joined by others making their way to the parade ground. The number of recruits had swelled significantly to around seventy; to maintain effectiveness, they were split into squads based on their huts, which also served to aid the bonding process. Each squad was allocated a trained soldier; in hut forty-three's case, it was the corporal who had awakened them earlier. The fearsome Sergeant Major Stafford was overseeing the whole exercise.

There followed an excruciating ninety-minute drill training, laboriously marching in lines, then pairs, form fours, and about turns. At eight o'clock, the group were dismissed and ordered to the cookhouse for breakfast. There was a hubbub as the recruits queued for their food, many complaining about their feet. Footwear was a big problem. Many had bought new boots while others were relying on totally inappropriate shoes. Most of the recruits seemed to be complaining about blisters.

Arthur and Wilfred were in the queue.

"I thought they sent us here to kill Germans, not march up and down all day," said Arthur.

"Aye, tha's not wrong there; me feet are near shredded," replied Wilfred. He looked down at his shoes.

Henry was just behind them. "Aye, I reckon we've not seen the last today, an' all."

"When're we going to get us stuff, uniform and the like?" said Wilfred.

"I've no idea," said Arthur, "'Appen they've got too many recruits and not enough kit. I don't know what us supposed to kill Germans with."

"Aye, chuck bloody stones at 'em," said Henry.

"Well, they're going to need to come up with something quick if they want us over there fighting."

Just then, Corporal Dorkins walked past carrying a tray of some unidentifiable food.

"Hey, Corp, when're we going to get uniforms and summat to fight with?" asked Henry.

"Your guess is as good as mine, they don't tell me owt," he replied and moved on.

The buzz of conversation continued. One or two recruits were limping. Arthur's boots at least had been worn in for a couple of weeks and had not caused too much discomfort. However, after another two hours of 'square-bashing', his feet eventually succumbed. By lunchtime, the recruits were in no state to fight anybody; fatigue and poor footwear had taken their toll.

Sunday morning in Oakworth, and Mildred and the girls were dressed for church, but not the usual Methodist church in Cavendish Street where they had been part of the congregation for many years. There were no trolleybuses and Mildred could not order a cabbie. She had decided that, as she was now a significant member of the community, she would attend the local one.

It was a pleasant morning as the family left the house and headed along the lane to the place of worship. It had rained during the night and there were puddles in the potholes, but the clouds were white and high. The chat among the family as they walked was dominated by Molly, who was excited about starting her new job with the seamstress. Agnes was full of her new concert tour. Grace, however, was still brooding over her lost love and was locked in her own world. The youngest, Freda, just tagged along happily.

Mildred had passed the chapel a few times but had not had chance to venture inside. From the outside, it was quite a formidable building, not church-like at all – more resembling a bank. Set back off the road, there was a substantial stone wall about four feet tall surrounding the property with two pillars holding the black metal gates at the front. The façade was austere in appearance, its grey stone quite drab, though the entrance with its three supporting Doric columns was nevertheless impressive.

The family walked through the main entrance; several others were heading in the same direction. The two entrance doors were open, allowing easy access. It was a large building with a capacity for almost a thousand worshippers, but today it would be far less. Inside it was quiet as many of the parishioners engaged in private prayers. The service was being conducted by the Reverend James Conrad, a white-haired man in his sixties.

After the service had finished, Mildred waited for the hundred or so worshippers to leave before escorting the family out of the church; she was anxious to announce herself to the new vicar. He was stood in the narrow narthex at the church entrance greeting parishioners. Mildred waited for the queue to go and then approached the vicar.

"Good day, Reverend. A nice service, thank you. Mildred Marsden, newly moved into Springfield Hall."

The vicar's eyes lit up. "Ah, so you're the new owner. Yes, there's been much talk around the village."

"I'm sure there has," replied Mildred, trying to weigh up the vicar. He seemed a man of good cheer and comfortable with people, judging by the attentive way he addressed his congregation, and seemed dedicated to his vocation.

"So do you plan to become active in our community?"

"Why, yes, indeed I do."

"Well, that is so good to hear. I'm afraid the previous incumbent was less than participative. He was not a churchgoer to my knowledge. Spent most of his time locked away in that house, counting his money, by all accounts."

"That is certainly not my intention; I have too much to do running the bakery."

"You have a bakery?"

"Yes, Marsden's on James Street."

"Well, I must call in when I'm next in town, although Mr Jessop usually looks after our needs."

"Yes, indeed, most convenient."

"And this is your family?" observed the vicar, looking at the four girls behind Mildred. They appeared impatient to leave.

"Yes, oh, and my son, he's just answered the country's calling."

"Has he indeed? That's very brave of him. Not that I condone this war, far from it. It must be very hard for you."

"Yes, it is… Anyway. I must let you get on. You must join us for tea one afternoon."

"Yes, that's most kind."

Mildred shook hands with the vicar without finalising

any arrangements and left the church. The four girls nodded politely to him as they walked past.

Twenty minutes later, the family had reached the house. As they walked down the drive, they could see a man pacing up and down in front. He approached the group. He resembled a tramp; worker's overalls, worn boots, his face weatherworn. He had a tatty jacket and a flat cap that had also seen better days. He looked painfully thin; his cheeks were hollow and gaunt.

"Can I help you?" said Mildred as the man approached and took off his cap.

"Aye, 'appen so. Jed Dewhurst, Mrs Jessop says tha's looking for a gardener."

"Oh, er, yes," replied Mildred, slightly taken aback by the man's appearance. She handed the front door key to Grace. "You carry on, dear; I'll see to Mr Dewhurst."

The four daughters went inside as Mildred turned to the man.

"So, Mr Dewhurst, I understand you worked here for the previous owner?"

"Aye, that I did, fifteen year it be, all told."

"I hear he was not an easy man; how did you get on with him?"

"He were alright wi' me, left us alone most've the time."

"I see… So, how many hours did you work?"

"Four hours most days, 'cept weekends, of course."

"Hmm, not sure I will need that many. Shall we say five hours, three days a week?"

"Aye, whatever tha says."

"What did Sir James pay you?"

"Sixpence an hour."

"Hmm, no wonder he kept you on for all those years. I believe in paying a fair wage for a fair job, Mr Dewhurst. I will pay you one shilling."

His eyes lit up. "Aye, thank you, thank you; that's very kind of you."

"Very well, you can start tomorrow, ten o'clock sharp, one month's trial. Does that suit?"

"Aye, 'appen it suits well enough. Thank you, Mrs Marsden."

"Tomorrow morning then."

"Aye, I'll be here."

"Well, you know where everything is. I'll give you the key to the shed tomorrow."

"Right you are, Mrs Marsden."

The man put on his cap and turned to walk away. Mildred called him.

"Have you had breakfast this morning, Mr Dewhurst?"

He turned around. "Nay, ma'am, I can't say I have. I eat tonight."

"Well, we can't have that, can we. We're just about to have something, you're welcome to join us."

"That's very kind, but I don't want to be troubling you."

"Nonsense, it's no trouble; come in," replied Mildred and headed towards the front door. The man stood back. "Come on, Mr Dewhurst, we won't bite you."

Mildred walked in but the gardener seemed reluctant to enter. Grace was in the kitchen with Agnes.

"Grace, can you make something for Mr Dewhurst?" Mildred shouted. "He can join us for breakfast." Grace acknowledged.

Mildred turned; the man was stood at the door and looking at his worn boots.

"Don't worry about the boots, come in."

There was a metal boot-scraper and coir mat just outside the front porch. He scraped any excess mud and then vigorously wiped his feet on the mat. Anxiously, he walked slowly through the lobby, clutching his cap like a comfort blanket, and into the hall. He looked around with an expression of amazement.

"What's the matter? You must have been in here before?" said Mildred.

"Nay, ma'am, can't say I have."

"What, in fifteen years, you didn't once venture inside?"

"Nay, t'weren't allowed."

"Not even in the kitchen?"

"Nay, ma'am." The man continued to look around the Great Hall; his eyes appeared to be scanning every nook and cranny.

"Come on through," said Mildred as she removed her hat and placed it on the hall table.

Mildred walked into the kitchen where Grace and Agnes were at the range frying eggs and sausages. The man followed, checking his footwear was making no marks on the floor.

"Grace, Agnes, this is Mr Dewhurst; he's going to be our new gardener."

Grace's expression changed; in her mind, that was Freddie's job.

"'Ow do," said the man.

Up close, the man's condition appeared even worse. Then his stomach growled quite audibly, triggered by the smell of cooking.

"Be seated, Mr Dewhurst. Agnes will make us some tea."

The man sat down at the kitchen table facing the window. The sun had now appeared and the lawn was looking fresh following the rain shower during the night. Jed took an interest.

"Someone's done a good job on t'grass."

"Yes, we had a gardener but he's answered the country's calling. Such a brave young man."

Mildred looked at Grace; she smiled.

"So tell me, Mr Dewhurst, do you have a family?"

"Aye, 'appen I do."

"You have children?"

"Aye, two daughters and a son."

"And how old are they?"

"The girls are eleven and ten, the boy eight."

"What about your wife?"

"She's not been well; the consumption nearly took her the winter last. It's left her weak in spirit."

"Yes, I can imagine."

Agnes made the tea and started pouring a cup for Jed, who continued to reveal his desperate family circumstances.

"So, what have you been doing since you left Sir James's employ?"

"Just odd jobs, like, when I can get 'em."

Grace and Agnes completed the breakfast and served up a plate of eggs, sausages, and fried bread. They were joined at the table by Molly and Freda. They watched as Jed devoured his meal as if it were his last.

"My, Mr Dewhurst, you seem hungry."

"Aye, 'appen there weren't enough for everyone last night."

"Oh dear, well, we can't have that, can we?"

Jed finished his breakfast, which included another round of bread. Mildred, meanwhile, had gone into the pantry in the scullery and retrieved some potatoes, a cabbage, green beans, six eggs and a bag of flour. She placed them in a hessian carrier bag and returned to the kitchen.

"Take these, Mr Dewhurst. You can return the bag tomorrow."

Jed stood up and took the produce. "That's very kind of you, Mrs Marsden, very kind indeed."

"Have you far to go?"

"Slad Cottages, near t'mill, twenty minutes with a good stride."

Mildred saw Jed to the door and watched him walk down the drive.

By two-fifteen, lunch at the camp had finished and the recruits were ordered back to the parade ground. With muscles having stiffened and blisters taking their toll, most of them had difficulty standing, never mind any serious drill. They lined up, seven rows of ten, with the sergeant looking at the group menacingly. The lieutenant came out of the main hut.

"Atten-shun," bellowed the sergeant. The call to attention was more a shuffle than the crisp coordinated sound more associated with the command. The officer stood in front of the group.

"This afternoon you will be issued with your Small Book and allocated your duties while you are here at the camp. Those of you needing medical attention should report to the medical orderly. For the moment, you can return to your hut and you will be called when required. You will report back here at sixteen-thirty hours. Dismissed."

"Dismissed," bellowed the sergeant major.

The group dispersed, almost half heading to the medical hut to get treatment for blisters and other feet-related problems.

"What's this about a small book?" asked Wilfred as the pals walked back to their hut.

"I've no idea," replied Arthur, "But 'appen us'll soon find out."

There was little chat as the occupants entered hut forty-three; fatigue and low spirits had overtaken the men. Two were missing, having decided to seek medical attention for their feet. Arthur lay on his bunk staring at the ceiling. He suddenly thought of Ivy and wondered what she was doing, then fell asleep. It was only a quick nap before he was awoken abruptly by the corporal.

"Right, lads, report to the admin hut... now!"

The recruits slowly left their bunks and shuffled out of the hut.

The administration centre was situated between the officers' hut and the mess hall. The medical centre was immediately behind, a sign above the door indicating its presence. It was a busy area with recruits and uniformed soldiers everywhere. The group lined up outside and waited while another hut was being processed, then after ten minutes they were called inside. There was a long counter and behind that two uniformed men and the lieutenant, who appeared to be supervising the activity. They were called forward one at a time, their names checked against a manifest and ticked. Arthur reached his turn.

"Name?" enquired the squaddie.

"Marsden, Arthur Marsden." He was handed a compact booklet. On the front was printed the words 'Name', 'Number' and 'Corp', then the title 'Soldier's Small Book'.

"Make sure you fill that in and read it," ordered the lance corporal. The lieutenant suddenly took an interest.

"Marsden, Arthur Marsden?" he enquired.

"Aye."

"The baker on James Street?"

"Aye, that's me."

"It's Norman, Norman Hoskins, a friend of your sister, Agnes."

"Oh, aye, I remember, the solicitor. Aye, she talked of you."

"Really?"

"Aye, 'appen tha asked her to marry tha."

The lieutenant looked down. "Yes, I did, but she said she wasn't ready for marriage."

"Aye, that sounds like Agnes, but 'appen she'll come round."

"Tell me, how is she?"

"Aye, she were right enough when I left. Maudlin about her singing getting cancelled."

"Cancelled, you said?"

"Aye, cos of t'war."

The lieutenant looked at Arthur.

"I see…" He appeared to drift momentarily then focussed. "We need to find you some suitable duties while you're here for when you're not training. We could certainly use a baker in the cookhouse."

"Aye, I can do that."

"Excellent, report there tomorrow at oh-eight-thirty after breakfast."

"Aye. What about Wilfred here?" said Arthur indicating behind him. "He's a butcher."

"Yes, very well."

"What about our kit and something to fight with?"

"Hmm, good question. Well, we're expecting more deliveries of kit and supplies Wednesday or Thursday. I'm afraid weapons may take a little longer. Every available piece is being sent overseas at the moment. For the time being, we are having to improvise."

Arthur picked up his booklet, left the hut and waited by the entrance for his three pals. He started flicking through the pages. Wilfred, Samuel, and Henry were eventually processed and met up with Arthur.

"Says here how to look after your feet," said Arthur, showing the lads the appropriate page.

"Bit bloody late now," said Henry looking at his boots, the laces undone and flapping about.

"So, what'll you two be doing?" asked Arthur.

"They've put us on maintenance on account of the work at mill."

"Aye, that makes sense, tha's good with machines and stuff," observed Arthur.

Back in the hut, the men had removed their shoes. All fifteen had blisters; one had lost a big toenail. They passed around cotton wool and alum to harden the feet, procured from the medical centre.

Arthur had filled in his details in his Small Book with a pencil. Mildred had bought him three, together with some writing paper to write letters home. Arthur handed Wilfred one of his spares.

"Eh up, has tha seen this at t'back?" announced Arthur to anyone who would listen. He was still engrossed in his copy.

"What's that?" answered Wilfred.

"There's only a bloody will. That don't fill tha with too much confidence, does it?"

Wilfred and the others close by flicked to the back.

"Eh, tha's not wrong, Arthur. What'll us write?"

"'Appen tha'll have to think about that."

Arthur *was* thinking. If anything happened to his mother while he was away, he would be in line for a sizable inheritance. Then there was the bakery that his mother was in the process of transferring to him. There was a lot to consider.

"Well, I don't have owt," said Samuel, who was in the next bed to Wilfred.

"Well, tha'll have nowt to think about," said Arthur.

Monday morning at the bakery, Ivy was waiting for the miller to arrive. The oven was lit and she had made a start mixing the dough using the sack of flour left over from Saturday. Hearing the lorry pull up in the yard, she left her chores and went to greet the man.

"'Ow do, Ivy, how's tha managing?" asked Edward Buxton, the jovial miller, as he descended from his cab.

"Aye, fine thanks, Edward, there's a lot to learn but 'appen Arthur was a good teacher."

"Aye, have tha heard owt from him at all?"

"Na, he'll be busy just now. I hope he'll write, though; he's been on my mind."

"Aye, well let me knows when tha hears from him... How many bags're tha wanting?"

"I don't rightly knows. What does Arthur usually have?"

"Well, I can do tha three today."

"Aye, that suits, I reckon," said Ivy, rummaging in her apron pocket. "Mrs Marsden's given me the money."

"Aye, and there's some good news."

"What's that?"

"Tha's not heard?"

"Heard what?"

"Government have fixed price of flour to stop the profiteers and black market."

"What's that?"

"Black market? It's people selling stuff at high prices."

"Ah, I see... Well, that's good then."

The miller took the money from Ivy, unloaded the three sacks, and took them into the baking shed.

"I'll bid tha a good day, Miss Ivy, and tha must let me know if tha hears anything from young Arthur."

"Aye, Mr Buxton, I surely will."

By seven-forty-five, Ivy had finished baking the first batch of bread and had loaded it into the large wicker carrying baskets. There was activity in the shop and Ivy heard footsteps coming down the corridor.

"Hello, Ivy," said Grace. "Nice morning."

"Aye, 'ow do, Grace, bread's ready."

"Good, I'll just change, there are one or two people waiting already. Did tha manage to contact your friend?"

"Aye, I did. She'll be here anytime; I said we started at eight o'clock."

"Oh, that's excellent… Well, Agnes is here, too, so we'll be able to show her what to do."

"What about tha mam?"

"No, she's decided to stay at home today. She's taking Molly to Kitty's; she's starting working for her today."

Just then, there was a knock on the front door. Grace took one of the baskets of bread through to the shop, Ivy following with the other. There was a 'clang' as Agnes opened the door. The waiting customers stood to one side to let through a smart-looking girl with a fresh face and flowing ringlets.

"Hello, you must be Betty."

"Aye, Ivy told me you're looking for an assistant. She said to start this morning."

"Aye, that's right, come through."

Agnes led Betty behind the counter where Grace was starting to stack the loaves.

"Grace, this is Betty," said Agnes.

"Hello, I'm Grace. I think I've seen you before; you work at Granger's."

"Aye, that's my uncle's shop. I work there when he's busy."

"Hmm, very well, Agnes'll show you what to do. I'll find

you an apron and bonnet."

Since moving to the hall, both Agnes and Grace had started losing their accents; it was not deliberate but more an indication of their newfound position and reflecting their mother's dialect.

With Betty suitably kitted out, the door opened and the battle for bread started again. The queue on this Monday snaked up the street almost to the greengrocer's. It was going to be a busy morning.

Back at Springfield Hall, Mildred was preparing for her visit to the seamstress. Kitty Bluet had, perhaps surprisingly, become a close friend since the discovery she had had a child, Freddie, by Mildred's late husband. With both Freddie and Arthur now serving their country, that bond had become even closer.

Just before nine-thirty, the delicate ringing of the front doorbell echoed around the hallway. Mildred was in her bedroom.

"Don't be long, Molly, we need to go shortly," she said as she passed her daughter's bedroom on her way to open the front door

"Hello, Mrs Jessop," said Mildred as she reached the door to greet her housekeeper. "Fine morning."

"Yes, it is. I've brought you the newspaper you wanted. I'll get Oswald to put one by for you each morning and bring it with me."

"That's most kind, Mrs Jessop."

"And can we dispense with 'Mrs Jessop'? It's Daisy, please, and can I call you Mildred? It is much less formal."

"Yes, er, Daisy, I don't see why not."

Mildred took her copy of The Times from her while Daisy put on an apron.

"Have you anything particular you need me to do today?" asked the housekeeper.

"No, not especially, but Mr Dewhurst the gardener's due to start this morning. I'm expecting him around ten. Would you be so good as to let him in and give him the key to the shed? I've left it on the kitchen table."

"Oh, that *is* good of you. Yes, of course… I know his wife has not been well of late and work's been very difficult to find since he left Mr Springfield's employ; he was telling Oswald just last week."

"Well, I've given him a month's trial, so I hope that will ease things for him."

"Oh, yes, that will indeed," replied Daisy.

Just then, Molly came down the stairs in her working overalls but looking very smart. She was carrying her needlework box and a carrier bag.

"Now, we really must go. Molly is starting her new job this morning."

"Hello, Molly," said the housekeeper. "What's this about a new job?"

"Aye, 'appen Mrs Bluet is giving me a chance to learn to be a seamstress."

"Oh, that's lovely. I'm sure you will be very good."

"Yes, she does show a talent," interrupted Mildred. "Show Daisy your embroidery."

Molly opened her carrier and pulled out an example.

"My, but this is exquisite, Molly… and from someone so young."

"Aye, thank you."

"She's hoping she can sell some to help pay for her materials."

"Well, I'm sure Oswald will take some to sell."

"That's very kind of you, Daisy," replied Mildred.

Mildred put on her bonnet and she and Molly left the hall. It was just a twenty-minute walk to Blossom Cottage where Kitty Bluet resided. Molly talked excitedly on the walk, nervous at her first proper job. They reached the long box-hedge and walked down the crazy-paved footpath to the front door. To the left and right, the product of Freddie's labours; row upon row of vegetables of every description. Canes with runner beans, their red flowers starting to fade now and giving way to the developing vegetables, potato plants, turnips, parsnips. Mildred suddenly thought who would be looking after it all with Freddie away.

Kitty had seen them approach and was at the door before Mildred had chance to knock.

"Mildred, it's good to see you," said Kitty and they exchanged cheek-kisses. "And Molly, lovely to see you, too."

"Good morning, Mrs Bluet," said Molly.

"Kitty, please call me Kitty. Come through. I've made some tea. I thought we could catch up before we start."

"That's most kind, Kitty."

They went through into the sitting room where a tray with a teapot and milk jug was standing with three cups and saucers. They sat down and Kitty started to pour the tea.

"How are you?" asked Mildred.

"I don't honestly know, Mildred, to be quite honest with you. I keep expecting Freddie to come in at any moment. I miss him so much."

"Yes, I am sure you do."

"What about you… and Arthur?"

"Well, yes, of course, but you just have to get on with things, don't you? I find moping serves no purpose."

"Yes, you *are* right, of course, but I do find it hard. I don't know what I'm going to do about the garden. It needs a lot of attention and I just don't have the time with my orders."

"Yes, I noticed that as I walked down the path. Actually, I may have a solution. I've just employed a new gardener myself, used to work for Mr Springfield."

"Jed Dewhurst, you mean?"

"Yes, you know him?"

"Of course, you get to know everyone in the village in time. I'd forgotten about him, I must admit. Do you think he might be interested, until Freddie gets back?"

"I believe he will. I just need him three days a week so I'm sure he'll have the time. Would you like me to ask him to call?"

"Oh, yes please. That will be so kind."

They continued catching up as good friends do. Kitty was glad of the company; it was clear that Freddie's departure had hit her hard.

After half an hour's discourse, Mildred excused herself and left. She wanted to call in at the village store to order more supplies to replace those she had given the gardener the previous day. Kitty took the tray into the kitchen then led Molly to the studio. Molly was anxious to start her new job.

"I've brought these," said Molly. She opened the carrier bag and took out the embroideries she had completed. Kitty examined them with an expert eye.

"My, these really are excellent, Molly. I think you and I are going to make a great team."

Monday morning at Colsterdale Camp and again the bugler was wakening the camp at five-thirty. There were shouts of protest, but remembering the visit by the sergeant major the previous day, the residents of hut forty-three were soon up and dressed. The corporal entered at ten-to-six and gave the group their standing orders for the day.

"Right, lads, it's down to work today. Report to the parade ground at oh-six-hundred for drill training. Breakfast is at eight-hundred and then you should report to your squad leader for your duties. Have you all been allocated a work detail?"

"Aye, Corp," said the group in unison.

"This afternoon after lunch, you will report at the parade ground for more training. Everybody clear?"

There were a few mumbled replies.

"I said, is everybody clear?" shouted the corporal.

"Yes, Corp," shouted the group.

"Right, get your arses together and report to the parade ground."

Chapter Three

Mildred returned to the hall and decided to spend a few minutes catching up on the war news in The Times. Daisy made her a cup of tea and Mildred sat in the sitting room overlooking the garden drinking it. She could see Jed Dewhurst walking up and down, appearing to be assessing what needed to be done. It was a fine day now with no threat of rain. The sun streamed through the window, bathing the room in bright light. Daisy had lit the fire to heat the water, so the room was hot. Mildred opened the patio doors to let in some air. The gardener detected the movement and waved; Mildred acknowledged.

She picked up the newspaper and started browsing. The news highlighted the defence of Liege, the Belgian town that had been besieged by the Germans. There were some harrowing tales of bloodshed with many casualties on both sides. Suddenly the war seemed real and Mildred thought about Arthur. She decided to skip the war news, it was too distressing, and instead turned to the political news. She became drawn to an article on a new Act of Parliament that had been passed; the Defence of the Realm Act.

Reading through the various commentaries, the act, as the name suggested, was designed to aid the country in the time of war. It banned flying kites, starting bonfires, buying binoculars, feeding wild animals bread, discussing naval and military matters, or buying alcohol on public transport. Alcoholic drinks were to be watered down to discourage drunken behaviour and alehouse opening times were restricted to noon until three p.m., and six-thirty p.m. until nine-thirty p.m. Whilst some of these measures seemed trivial, a great deal of power had been seized by the government, including the right to take over factories to produce items needed for war. Some food prices had been fixed as the miller had mentioned to Ivy. The Act also banned strikes, and Mildred couldn't help thinking how that would be received in the mills. Arthur would have objected strongly. Her son came into her mind again from nowhere.

She put down the newspaper and went to the open door. The gardener spotted her and approached.

"'Ow do, Mrs Marsden, fine day."

"Hello, Mr Dewhurst, it certainly is."

"My wife told me to say thank you for the vegetables you sent yesterday. I left the bag with Mrs Jessop."

"Thank you, Mr Dewhurst, please pass on my regards to her."

"Aye, that I will."

"So, what have you got in mind for the garden?"

"There's not much to do; it's been well attended."

"Well, I do have an idea. We don't know how long this ghastly business is going to last and I think we should make an effort to grow our own food. What do you think?"

"Aye, makes sense. Tha wants me to dig up the lawn?"

"Goodness, no. Not yet, anyway, but there's quite a bit of land next to the orchard which we could use. Wait there while I put on some suitable shoes."

Mildred walked through the hall into the kitchen. Daisy Jessop was busy baking and Freda was watching her, knelt on a kitchen chair.

"I want to learn to be a cook," she said as Mildred entered.

"Do you indeed? Well, I'm sure Daisy will be only too pleased to show you."

"Yes, it will be a pleasure; it's good to see a youngster taking an interest."

"Indeed... I'm just going to talk to Mr Dewhurst about

the garden."

Mildred walked through into the scullery where she had several pairs of shoes on a long rack and found a suitable pair. The gardener was still stood on the patio in front of the sitting room.

"Right, let me show you what I mean," said Mildred, striding across the lawn and through the gap in the hedge on the right.

Immediately before them was the apple orchard. The boughs were bent, heavy with unripe fruit. There were several apples scattered across the ground, the result of windfall. Some had shown evidence of being chewed by birds or small mammals. Jed looked at the trees.

"Should be a good crop this year. I were telling Mr Springfield before he passed. Tha can always tell by blossom."

"Yes," said Mildred. "I don't know what we will do with them."

"Mr Springfield used to sell them to the store."

"What, Mr Jessop?"

"Aye, got a good price for 'em, an' all."

"Well, we'll have to see... Now, that's what I was thinking," said Mildred, pointing to a plot of land to the left which ran down to the border fence and a stream. It was about the size of maybe two football pitches, perhaps a bit bigger.

Jed pushed his cap back on his head and scratched his forelock, or at least where it would have been if he had any hair. The ground was meadowland and had not been cultivated for years by the appearance.

"Did Mr Springfield have no use for it?" enquired Mildred.

"Nay, 'appen he left it up to me. I just left it fallow, like."

"Yes, I can see that, but with these changing times I think we should make the most of what we have. Don't you?"

"Aye… 'appen you're right. Mind you, it'll be a big job to get it ploughed and seeded. We're gonna need a horse and maybe a couple more hands."

"I'll leave it to you, Mr Dewhurst. Do whatever you need. Do you know anyone who can help?"

"Aye, 'appen I might, if they've not joined up."

"How are you going to get a horse on there? I can't have one trotting across the lawn."

"It won't be a problem; there's a gate down yonder." Jed pointed to the left; sure enough, there was a five-bar gate leading to an adjoining lane.

"Well I never, I hadn't noticed that. Mind you, I've had little time to explore properly."

They left the field and returned to the house. The gardener stopped at the shed.

"Oh, I nearly forgot. Do you know Mrs Bluet? Blossom Cottage."

"Aye, 'appen I do."

"Well, I was speaking to her earlier and it seems she has need of a gardener. I thought you could work there when you're not working here."

"Aye, that I can, much appreciated, Mrs Marsden. I don't know how to thank you."

"There's no need. Do a good job on the garden is all I ask."

"Aye, that I will. I'll call on Mrs Bluet when I've finished here."

Mid-morning at the bakery and the queues had shown no sign of relenting. Betty Granger had taken to the role like a duck to water; it wasn't dissimilar to her uncle's shop –

even the cash registers were the same. One or two of the customers had recognised her and commented. Just then, Grace noticed a very smart-looking woman easing herself to the front of the queue, to much protest.

"It's alright, I'm not buying," she remonstrated.

Then Grace recognised her. It was Minnie Glyde, the local secretary of the Suffragette movement, of which Grace was an enthusiastic member.

"Miss Glyde," said Grace on seeing her barge to the front. "What brings you here this morning?"

"Just wanted to let you know there's an emergency committee meeting tonight at the hall at seven-thirty. I hope you can be there."

"Yes, of course," replied Grace.

"Very well, I'll see you later. I can see you are busy."

The woman turned and left the shop to stares from the waiting line.

Over at the camp, the recruits had endured another two hours of gruelling marching.

"Well, one thing; if we meet any Germans, we'll be able to march 'em to death," said Arthur as they made their way to the canteen.

"Aye, tha's not wrong there," said Henry, who was still limping.

They walked into the hut to be greeted by the smell of cooking and cigarettes; most of the men seemed to be smoking. The pals took their turn in the line of recruits waiting to be served. Eight o'clock; the bakery would be opening now. Arthur found his mind was elsewhere as he collected his breakfast and found a seat. He wondered how Ivy was coping. He would write to her today.

He wasn't the only one who was quiet. Arthur snapped

out of his retrospection but noticed Samuel seemed locked away in his own world. In fact, he had been quieter than usual since they reached the camp. He was seated opposite Arthur, next to his best pal Henry.

"Eh up, Samuel, what's up wi' tha?"

Samuel looked up from his oatmeal. "Nowt much."

His eyes narrowed. His spoon was in mid-flow to his mouth and it stopped, dripping oatmeal back onto his dish.

"I don't know what we're supposed to be doing here and my bloody feet're killing me. There's no kit, the food's shit, and we do sweet Fanny Adams 'cept march up and down all day. I thought we was supposed to be fighting the Germans."

"Aye, but apart from that," countered Arthur.

The group howled with laughter; even Samuel saw the funny side. "Aye."

"Well, as I see it, the longer we spend here, the better; at least we ain't being shot at. Tha never knows, 'appen the war might be over by Christmas and we can all go home," said Arthur.

"Aye, tha could be right," said Samuel and carried on eating, still locked in his own thoughts.

Wilfred, too, was not his usual self. He and Arthur had been friends since junior school, but with his large family, he was not used to spending so much time on his own.

"'Ow's tha feet, Wilfred?" asked Arthur, trying to engage his pal.

"'Appen me blisters have got bloody blisters. I don't know how they expect us to do any marching. Up and down, up and bloody down; it's all us does. What's that got to do with any killing?"

Arthur had never heard Wilfred use any profanity before; he was clearly not himself.

"Have tha seen medic?"

"Nah, have tha seen queues?"

Further discussion was interrupted by the corporal, who stood at the front of the canteen and announced that all recruits should report to their respective work detail, or words to that effect. There were moans of protest, but gradually the recruits piled out of the hut. Directly outside, there were two delivery wagons filled with what looked like tents. Several men walked towards the trucks.

"Eh up, looks like we're gonna get more arrivals. Glad we're in hut; I wouldn't want to be sleeping out in one of them," said Henry before the men went their separate ways.

Arthur and Wilfred headed for the cookhouse to report for duty.

Just after six o'clock back in Oakworth, Grace was taking the trolleybus into town for her hastily arranged meeting with the local Suffragettes committee. It was unusual to have an extraordinary meeting and Grace was intrigued as to its purpose. She was ready for any direct action, although her previous month's experience had made her more cautious. Her bruises had faded but her treatment at the hands of the constabulary still made her angry.

It was another fine evening as she rode on the upper deck, taking in the early evening activity. Suddenly, as she scanned the green fields, her mind was transported back to her times with Freddie, how he held her and kissed her. She was bitter at the world for giving her these moments only for them to be taken away so cruelly. What if no-one had discovered the truth? They would still be together. Wherever he was now, she hoped he was safe.

She got off the trolleybus in the centre of town and made her way to the meeting hall. She would take a cabbie back; Mildred had given her the fare.

There were more attendees than she was expecting. As well as the executive committee, there were about another thirty women sat in front of the stage. At precisely seven-thirty, Minnie Glyde, the local chair, stood and addressed the group.

"Thank you all for coming. I have a sad announcement to make…" She paused dramatically. "Earlier this morning, I received a message from H.Q. that Mrs Pankhurst is suspending the Suffragette movement."

There were gasps and howls of protests from the gathering. Ms Glyde put her hand up to quell the rancour.

"It appears the executives have been in discussion with the Government about the present situation and, as a result, all Suffragettes presently in prison are to be released and militant action taken by our members will cease…"

More hoots of derision and, again, Ms Glyde called for order.

"Let's be clear; this is not the end of our struggle in the women's movement. Our aim is now to support the country and get behind our brave soldiers. With so many of our menfolk called to arms, there will be a need for women to step up. Now is the time to fight for our country as we fought for the vote. We believe that this will serve our cause well." There were more murmurs.

"What about Mrs Pankhurst, what is she going to do?" shouted one of the members.

"I have been told that Emeline is presently in Paris, but she is returning to support the recruitment campaign."

Grace looked at the person next to her; there was a look of confusion, which Grace mirrored.

There followed a long debate on what the decision meant in practice. Actually, it made sense, Ms Glyde explained. With the country now at war, the Government could not afford a national movement of disruption and disobedience.

"To continue the protest would risk harm to achieving our aims. Now is not the time for division but unity," she exalted to shouts of support from the floor. There would be plenty of opportunities for women to show what they were capable of, especially undertaking jobs traditionally done by men.

Grace felt inspired. Others around her were applauding. It was food for thought.

The meeting had finished by nine o'clock and Grace found a taxicab to take her back to Oakworth with a lot on her mind. She had an idea.

Back at the house, Mildred was in the sitting room reading when Grace returned. Agnes, Molly and Freda were in their rooms. She heard the front door open then close. Grace appeared at the sitting room door.

"Hello, dear, how was your meeting?"

Grace took off her hat and jacket. The room was hot; Daisy had lit the fire to heat the water, but the coals were now just embers.

"It was inspiring, Mam. 'Appen Miss Pankhurst has stopped the women's movement because of the war."

"Has she indeed. Well, how's that going to help women?"

"She says we need to get behind the country; there'll be plenty of things for women to do here with men away at war."

Mildred rested her book on her lap. "Hmm… Do you know, now you come to mention it, I think you're right. I wonder how the mills will cope with all the men gone. Mr Jessop at the store was telling me that several of them have been ordered to start making military uniforms."

"Really?"

"Well, according to the newspaper, they've already

enlisted thousands of men. They're going to need uniforms."

Grace sat down opposite her mother. "I've been thinking; I want to do more."

"But you *are* helping, in the bakery. People are going to need bread."

"Aye, that's right enough, but I can do more, I know I can... I had a thought while I was in the cabbie; can we get a motor car?"

Mildred looked at Grace. "I don't know, I hadn't thought. Why would you want one? We've managed perfectly well without."

"I want to learn to drive. I would be better able to help the war effort."

"But women don't drive, my dear."

"That's precisely why."

"Well, I will need to speak to Mr Drummond and take his advice. I know nothing about making such a purchase."

On Tuesday morning at six-thirty a.m., Mildred, Grace, and Agnes were having breakfast.

"I have been thinking more about your proposal last evening, Grace, and I intend to visit Mr Drummond this afternoon. I have drafted a letter requesting an appointment at two-thirty. We can then all return home by cabbie. Can one of you deliver it? If he is unavailable, I can do some shopping; it's of no consequence."

Agnes looked at Grace with an air of expectancy. "What proposal is this?" she enquired.

"Grace wants to learn to drive to help the war effort. I want to discuss getting a car with Mr Drummond. I have no knowledge of such matters."

"Aye, 'appen you can take us into bakery," said Agnes with a smile.

"I think I can do more than that," replied Grace.

Grace took the letter then went to finish getting ready for work.

Breakfast time at Breary Banks. Arthur, his three pals and the rest of the recruits had endured another hour and a half of 'square-bashing'. The vast majority were still experiencing difficulties with their feet, but complaints were more aimed at the lack of 'real soldiering'. The camp had only a limited supply of weapons and those were dating back to the Boer War. It meant that drills were completed using walking sticks, which many of the recruits were using for their intended purpose.

The banter in the canteen mess hall was starting to get livelier as the men became more accustomed to their surroundings; even Samuel seemed brighter. The previous evening, Arthur had kept his promise and decided to write to Ivy. Others had also written to loved ones. Arthur was not good with words; he was a practical and physical person and not blessed with the orator's art.

'Dear Ivy, we are in a camp. I am not allowed to say where but I am still in England. We are safe, the traing (sic) is hard but nessy (sic) if we are to beat the Hun. I am working in the cokouse (sic) with Wilfred. I am making bread for the camp. Wilfred is well and cuts meat. I hope you are well and Grace and Agnes. You can write to me at the army post office, my number is 22077, Bradford Regiment. I wait for your reply, your good frend (sic), Arthur.'

There was a post office on camp, which was the busiest hut after the mess hall. Arthur found himself looking forward to hearing from Ivy.

Back at the bakery, it had been another busy morning, but with the supplies of flour being maintained they had managed to keep up with demand. The new recruit, Betty Granger, had proved to be excellent with people; she was bright and chatty, and customers loved her, so the immediate staffing issue had been resolved. Agnes would be free to pursue her musical career without impacting on the business.

Grace had delivered Mildred's letter to the solicitor and he had confirmed the appointment. The thought of acquiring a car had lifted her spirits. Agnes was also in a buoyant mood with her pending visit to the music shop to see George Tooley.

Such was the demand for bread over recent weeks, the queues at opening time stretched up James Street almost to the greengrocer's, and by lunchtime the shelves were almost empty. The afternoon trade tended to be very light and most days the bakery was shut before three o'clock. Agnes had taken the opportunity to use the lunchtime break to freshen up and change clothes ready for her meeting with the music shop proprietor. She had brought her best dress with her in a large carrier bag together with some makeup. Betty and Grace would be very capable of managing the shop in her absence.

Just after two-fifteen, Agnes made the short walk up James Street. It was a dry day but cloudy; rain was forecast for later. She waited while a trolleybus went by before crossing the High Street and turning left into Colston Lane. It was a cobbled road and covered in horse manure, which Agnes avoided with skipping movements.

The store was empty of customers, its musical instruments in the window display positioned to entice potential purchasers. Agnes could see the proprietor seated at the piano with another person, whose back was turned, stood watching him. She entered the store. Immediately, the pianist stopped playing and the two men watched her approach. Agnes recognised the other person straight away.

"Why, Mr Delaney, er, Cameron," she exclaimed, remembering his preferred address. He was wearing his usual flamboyant suit with a white rose protruding from his jacket buttonhole.

"Agnes, might I say how wonderful you look." The promoter spoke not in a local accent but one more associated with London and its environs.

"Thank you, you're very kind."

"Hello, Agnes," said the pianist.

"Hello, George," acknowledged Agnes.

"It's lovely to see you, Agnes, and I'm so pleased you were available to join the show. I was afraid someone else may have acquired your services," added the promoter.

"No, sir, I've not been singing," replied Agnes.

"That's such a waste; you have so much talent... Well, we will soon remedy that. I was telling George here that I have received more details from the army and what they're looking for. As I explained, the tour will travel across the North supporting the recruitment campaign, so we'll be having a military theme. We've also been assigned an officer from their recruitment centre to accompany us during the tour. I'm arranging for some soldiers' uniforms for the men in the cast, and we'll find something suitable for the ladies that will attract attention, something gay and uplifting. How does that sound?"

"Aye, it sounds fine."

"Good, good... I have also spoken to Miss Lloyd's musical director and managed to obtain some of the music for her songs. She's doing a similar programme in London; I think I mentioned."

"Aye, that you did." Agnes was trying to take in everything. Singing her idol's songs would be a dream come true.

"Some of these are quite new and you may not know them, so I've asked George to play the songs for you so you can learn them. I think five will be sufficient for your spot; how does that sound?"

"Five…? My, yes, of course."

"These are the ones we have chosen; they are the ones they use in the London production. They are not all Marie Lloyd songs, but I think you will be able to give them similar treatment."

"Aye, I'll try."

Agnes flicked through the five sets of sheet music: 'We Don't Want to Lose You, but We Think You Ought to Go', 'Now You've Got the Khaki On', 'Kitchener's Boys', 'All the Boys in Khaki Get Nice Girls' and 'I'll Make a Man of You'.

"But I don't know any of these," said Agnes, looking concerned.

George looked at her and smiled. "That's alright, Agnes, don't worry; we have time. I've arranged for a phonograph to be delivered tomorrow so you can listen to them. Then we'll go through each one, you'll soon learn them," he added.

Cameron picked up the energy. "And I've managed to put an orchestra together; not too large, mind, too expensive, but enough for the theatres. They will join us for the final rehearsals… Will you be available to start next week?"

"Aye, I can," replied Agnes, still trying to take in everything.

"That's most excellent. I'll get my secretary to send you the contract and you can return it to me on Monday."

"And this is in Bradford?"

"Yes, the new Alhambra Theatre, it's near the city centre. I'm sure you'll find it. We'll be using the rehearsal rooms;

I've reserved them for the remainder of the month."

"What time shall I need to be there?"

"Hmm, about ten o'clock," said the promoter after a moment's thought.

"Actually, I'll be driving over, Agnes; why don't you let me take you?" said George.

"I don't want to be no trouble."

"You won't be any trouble. We can confirm arrangements at the weekend."

George Tooley was an impressive man. Tall with dark, swept-back hair starting to grey, his moustache neatly trimmed. Agnes thought he looked like an officer. His fingers reflected his craft; long with well-manicured nails and showing no signs of having done any manual labour.

"Well, I need to get back to the office; I just wanted to say hello and answer any questions," said Cameron and extended his hand. "I'll see you on Monday, but if you have any concerns, please let me know. I do have a telephone," he added.

"Aye, I will," replied Agnes.

The promoter left the store, leaving Agnes and George Tooley discussing the five songs.

Meanwhile, Mildred had made the journey from Oakworth and crossed the park from the trolleybus stop. She decided not to call in the bakery as the journey had taken longer than usual; there had been some problems with the vehicle, apparently.

She arrived at the solicitor's just after the allotted time and was greeted by the matronly secretary, who for some reason appeared to have taken a dislike to Mildred and was abrupt in her greeting.

"Oh, it's you... I'll let Mr Drummond know you're here."

She stood to one side to allow Mildred to pass and returned to the back office without further discourse.

A few moments later, the solicitor appeared, as obsequious as ever.

"Mrs Marsden, how delightful to see you again. I hope everything is going well at the hall, please do come in. I have prepared some tea for you." Actually, the solicitor had not been near a teapot; his secretary had been called into service.

Mildred took her seat in front of the magnificent desk and removed her gloves, a completely superfluous item of clothing given the current temperature outside, but fashionable in gentry circles. The solicitor started pouring the tea.

"So, this is a business call, I believe? You said in your letter you needed my advice."

"Yes, Mr Drummond, I do… My daughter Grace has got it into her mind that she wants to learn to drive. She thinks she can help the war effort, but I'm not sure how."

"Well, I am sure there are many ways your daughter can help…" He steepled his fingers to his chin. "Actually, it is most fortuitous you mention this to me today. I have been in discussion with the Dowager Lady Garner. Do you know her at all?"

"No, Mr Drummond, we are not acquainted."

"She lives in Coltswood Manor, a great benefactor… and a supporter of the women's movement."

"Really? I wonder if Grace knows her. She's on the local committee, or was till it was stopped."

"No, she wasn't an active member due to her position, but she did donate quite large sums."

"So, how does this help Grace?"

"Have you heard of FANYs?"

"Fannies…? I can't say I have."

He looked at Mildred in a studious way, like a teacher to a pupil.

"It stands for First Aid Nursing Yeomanry. They help with giving first aid and support to the field hospitals. Lady Garner is hoping to recruit more women to assist the war effort. Only yesterday she was talking to me about providing a motor ambulance."

"That sounds excellent, I know Grace will be interested. She asked about buying a car so she could learn to drive."

"I see… hmm, that may be difficult. Cars are being requisitioned for war service, but I can certainly put you in touch with Herbert Pease at the car emporium. I'm not sure if he can sell you a car, but I know he provides lessons on how to drive one."

"Oh, that will be most kind, Mr Drummond."

"Very well; I will write to Mr Pease directly and ask him to write to you, if you are content for me to disclose your address."

"Yes, of course, that will be most acceptable."

"And I'll speak to Lady Garner; she has a telephone, you know."

With arrangements made, Mildred left the solicitors and walked through the park to the bakery.

As Mildred approached the shop, Archie Slater, the youthful newspaper seller, was in his usual spot trilling the latest news trying to entice potential sales. Since the war started, there had been a thirst for news and he had been in great demand. There was a board next to him leant against the bakery with the headlines. It just said, '*War Latest*'. She nodded to the lad and let herself in.

Upstairs in the parlour, Grace and Ivy were chatting, with Ivy expressing her feelings for Arthur. She missed him a great deal, she told Grace, and would write to him as soon as she had his address. Mildred climbed the stairs and entered the parlour.

"Eh up, Mam," said Grace. "How was your meeting with the solicitor?"

"Fine, dear. I have some information for you." Mildred sat down and recounted the information she had received from Mr Drummond. "Do you know a Lady Garner? She's an important benefactor to the women's cause, according to Mr Drummond."

"No, I'm not familiar with the name, but I know someone was donating large sums of money; Miss Glyde mentioned it but said the person wanted to remain anonymous."

"I expect that will be her."

Mildred explained the role of the FANYs and her involvement. Grace could not hide her excitement.

"That's exactly what I should be doing."

It was two days later when two letters arrived at the house, both addressed to Grace. One was in flowing script on a high-quality velum envelope, and the other in what was clearly a man's hand; there were dark marks staining the envelope which appeared to be oil.

Grace had returned from the bakery with Agnes around four o'clock after another hectic day. Daisy Jessop was just leaving having finished her work and welcomed the girls as she was parting.

"There's some tea just brewing and I've made some scones," she said as she left the house.

The girls acknowledged with gratitude.

Mildred heard them; she was in the sitting room and went to greet them.

"Hello, girls, how was your day?" She greeted them both with a cheek-kiss.

"Aye, very busy, Mam," said Grace. "And Betty's coming

on very well; she's been a great help and customers love her."

"And what about you, Agnes? How were the rehearsals?"

"Well, Mr Tooley was very complimentary. He played me the recordings on his phonograph again, which helped immensely. At least I know the tunes now. We were working from nine o'clock this morning, my throat is quite dry."

"That's excellent news, but you must look after yourself. Make sure you drink plenty of water," said Mildred.

"Aye, Mam," said Agnes, holding her throat.

"Are you still interested in learning the piano?"

"Aye, but I'm not going to have time for the moment with the concert tour and all, 'appen I'll wait until it's finished."

"Yes, that makes sense." Mildred turned to Grace. "There are two letters for you. I think one might be from Lady Garner."

Chapter Four

Mildred handed over the two envelopes. The three walked into the kitchen and Mildred poured the teas while Grace opened the letters. The first was on elegant headed notepaper: *'The Lady Garner, Coltswood Manor, Laycock'*. Grace started to read.

'Dear Miss Marsden, I understand from Mr Drummond that you would be interested in joining my plans to support the war effort. He tells me that you have been active with the women's movement of which I am a keen supporter, and it is that energy and commitment that I am seeking. I would be so delighted to meet you on Saturday at the Manor around four o'clock. I do hope that is convenient. Best wishes, Jane Garner'. Grace passed the letter to her mother.

"She wants me to visit on Saturday… at the Manor."

"Where is it?" asked Agnes.

"Laycock," replied Grace.

"Well, Laycock's not so far," replied Agnes.

Mildred looked up. "No, it's about three miles, but the road's very narrow. You should not be walking it."

"Well, I don't have much of an option," replied Grace.

"Let me speak to Daisy, maybe her husband can take you if I reward him appropriately."

Meanwhile, Grace was opening the second letter. There was a heading which looked like it had been made with a rubber stamp and inkpad; there were more brown marks on the letter. *'Herbert Pease Automotive Services, Bradford Road, Keighley'*. The handwriting was that of someone not skilled in the craft.

'Dear Miss Marsden, I have been advised by Mr Drummond the solicitor that you would like to learn to drive. I am giving lessons here at the garage. I have a nice Wolseley which is good

for learning on. I have free time on Friday afternoon if you're interested. The charge is half a crown for one hour. Yours, H Pease, proprietor'. Grace showed it to her mother.

"My, that's quite expensive."

"Aye, but it will be worth it if I can drive."

"Very well, I will give you the money. Do you know the place? It must be fairly new; I can't remember a car emporium down there."

"No, but I can take a cabbie, it's not far. I think they call them garages now."

"Really? My, how everything is changing," said Mildred and sighed.

Grace was buoyed by the recent developments; they had given her a new focus, and thoughts of Freddie were gradually starting to fade into the background.

Back at the camp, the daily schedule continued. Five-thirty, reveille; six-thirty to eight o'clock, 'square-bashing'; eight-thirty to midday, work detail; two-fifteen to four-thirty, more drill; four-thirty to six o'clock, work detail; six-thirty to seven-thirty, evening meal; and ten o'clock, 'lights out'. The upside to this regime was that it gave a sense of order and routine for the recruits, and most were settling into the new world. Relationships were starting to form as well as cliques, which in time would cause problems, but for now, morale in the camp was reasonably good.

Numbers had swelled considerably since Arthur's arrival and the new bell tents, which had been hastily erected in the long field south of the huts, were now mostly populated. There were many complaints from the inhabitants, particularly about the quality of the blankets, which were rough and uncomfortable. It was still reasonably mild but there were concerns about the coming autumn and subsequent winter, and how they would keep warm. The constant traipsing up and down the paths to the tents created quagmires after the smallest shower, another area of complaint.

There was some piece of positive news; just after the midday meal, the corporal announced that the recruits were to report to the quartermaster's store. They would be called in hut order to save a long queue. The afternoon drill session had been cancelled, to many cheers from the ranks.

It was turned three o'clock before hut forty-three was called.

"Eh up," said Arthur. "'Appen we're gonna get us kit, I reckon."

Wilfred was alongside him as they walked towards the stores.

"Aye, let's hope so. Another day of square-bashing and these shoes are gonna fall to pieces." He looked down and raised his disintegrating footwear to confirm.

They reached the hut and joined a queue. Men were coming out carrying kitbags bulging with clothing.

"Told tha so," said Arthur.

Inside the hut, the place was heaving with people, but for all that, there still seemed a semblance of order. The presence of Lieutenant Hoskins, Norman, was partly the reason; respect for officers was total at this early stage of the campaign. He looked very smart in his officer's uniform, which, of course, he had to provide for himself. Corporal Dorkins was acting as the liaison and was shepherding the recruits into their respective places.

Several of the regular troops were stationed behind a long counter, each with an item of kit. The recruits were issued with the standard 1902 Pattern Service trousers and dress tunic. This was a thick woollen jacket dyed khaki. There were two breast pockets for personal items and their pay book, two smaller pockets for other items, and an internal pocket sewn under the right flap of the lower tunic where the First Field Dressing would be kept. Rifle patches were sewn just above the breast pockets to prevent wear from the webbing equipment. Then came the accessories; vest, webbing, puttees, caps, boots and, finally, a large kitbag to carry it.

"Eh up, 'appen we'll look more like soldiers now. Just need us summat to fight with," said Arthur, seeing the piles of clothing and other items stretching back on more tables at the rear of the hut.

The lieutenant spotted Arthur and nodded; Arthur acknowledged.

There were many jocular remarks as they lined up to be given their new uniforms. Most of the men accepted the advice from their more experienced colleagues to choose boots a size larger than their shoes and wear additional socks. This would help with blisters and protect their feet when the weather changed.

After ten minutes, hut forty-three had been given their clothing and returned to their quarters to try them on. There would be a drill in the morning in full kit.

"What are these things?" said Wilfred, sat on his bed holding up a length of thin leather.

Henry looked at him. "They're tha puttees."

"Puttees?"

"Aye, me dad had 'em in South Africa; tha wraps 'em round ankles, stops 'em getting wet. Helps with marching, an' all, by all accounts."

Wilfred lifted up the item with a look of uncertainty.

"Don't tha worry, I'll show tha," said Henry.

There was a great deal of banter and hilarity among the hut. It was quite noisy but gradually all the recruits had managed to dress appropriately. There was going to be a dress inspection at seventeen-hundred hours. Arthur was particularly pleased with his new boots, which gleamed in the sunlight that streamed through the hut window. With some free time, he decided to write to his mother.

'Dear Mam, Me and Wilfred are still at traing (sic) camp, just got us kit. We are both well. I hope you and my sisters are well and the bakery. You can write at the army post office, my number is 22077, Bradford Regiment. Your loving son, Arthur'.

Arthur couldn't think of anything else to say but he had promised his mother he would write once he had settled in. He had assumed Ivy would have shared the contents of his earlier letter. He addressed the envelope to the bakery; he still could not bring himself to acknowledge the new residence. He would post it on his way to the mess hall.

Friday morning at Springfield Hall and there was a great deal of excitement as Grace and Agnes got themselves ready for their day. Grace's motivation had returned since her decision to learn to drive; she was more like her old self. She was looking forward to her visit to the car emporium later. Agnes and Grace would ride into town together, even though Agnes was not due to visit the music store until ten o'clock. She would help in the bakery; there was plenty to do.

They took the early trolleybus and, as it was a fine morning, rode on the top deck. As they approached the town centre, it was noticeable how the place had changed despite the fact that the war had yet to make any significant difference to the majority of people. It would be usual to see young men hanging around the street corners chatting or having a smoke before their shift started, but there were very few now. That was the difference.

The girls walked across the park to the bakery. Agnes couldn't help looking across towards the solicitor's office. She still thought about Norman and wondered how different her life would have been if she had accepted his proposal of marriage.

Inside the baking shed, Ivy had finished the first batch of bread and was loading the loaves into the two large baskets for transporting to the shop. This morning, she felt her energy levels were not as high as usual, which she put down to the early hour. She greeted the girls as they arrived. The distribution of flour had continued without interruption and the miller was more optimistic that supplies would continue as normal for the foreseeable future. This did not stop a queue forming outside the shop by eight o'clock. Betty Granger arrived in time to change into her serving attire and prepare the shelves for the customers.

Agnes helped in the shop until nine-thirty when she went up to the parlour to change ready for her rehearsal with George Tooley at the music store.

With the shelves empty, Grace closed the bakery at two-fifteen. Betty offered to complete the cleaning to allow Grace to leave for her driving lesson. She was feeling slightly anxious and excited at the prospect of entering what was ostensibly a man's world; very few women drove. She went up to the parlour, changed into her smart daywear, and returned to the shop.

"I'll be returning in an hour or so to wait for Agnes," Grace explained to Betty as she walked through the door.

She walked across the road to one of the cabbies waiting at the taxicab rank and gave the driver the destination. It was not an area of town she was familiar with; she was not a regular visitor to Bradford, the large city some ten miles or so distant.

The journey took less than ten minutes. Grace could have walked it in twenty, but appearances were everything. The cabbie parked in front of the establishment and Grace paid the driver. She looked at the building. It was a fairly recent brick construction with a green sign; the words *'Herbert Pease Automotive Services'* were scrolled in yellow script. There was a service bay with a single petrol pump outside.

The forecourt was black with congealed oil and small puddles of petrol with their technicolour surfaces. She could see all manner of tools and equipment within the service bay; it looked very drab and grimy. To the right, a small showroom with a large picture window and space for probably three cars. It was functional rather than decorative, its white paintwork surround peeling in places. It was also empty.

A man in overalls appeared from the bowels of the garage and approached Grace, wiping oil from his hands.

"'Ow do, can I help tha?"

"Yes, hello, I'm Grace Marsden, I wrote to you about driving lessons. I hope it's convenient now; there was no time to reply."

"Aye, 'appen I have an hour or two. Let me clean up and I'll be with tha."

He left Grace outside the showroom, feeling a little self-conscious as the traffic went by. She noticed one or two people looking in her direction from passing trolleybuses.

A few minutes later, the man returned in a suit and white shirt. He was a working man, medium build and height, with a ginger moustache and fading hair. Despite having washed, his fingers were ingrained with oil, his nails black and grimy.

"Herbert Pease, at your service, miss. Just down here."

Grace followed the man past the service bay to an adjacent side lane. It was a cinder track and not the easiest terrain to negotiate in her booties.

"Just down here," repeated the man.

They were at the back of the garage block and in a large yard. There were two cars parked. A Ford Model T had its engine cover raised to allow access; the other was a new-looking Wolseley Stellite. They walked towards the Wolseley.

"We'll use this one; it's easy enough to drive and reliable. I've not long had it." He gave the car a look of pride. "I'll show tha around before we do any driving."

The car was a popular model, the proprietor explained. This particular style had a fold down soft-top, which given the clement weather was retracted, enabling greater visibility. The pair walked around; it was an impressive vehicle with a shiny gold-coloured radiator grill and large headlights either side. There was a wooden running board, four spoked wheels, and a spare strapped to the side. Grace looked inside at the various levers and dials.

The man continued to explain the exterior, extolling its many virtues. The large steering wheel dominated the driving position. There was a hooter which was sounded by depressing a hollow rubber globe next to the steering column. The car man depressed it making a loud honking sound and laughed.

"My, it seems so complicated," said Grace.

"Nay, miss, it's very easy once tha gets used to it."

Herbert Pease spent the next hour explaining the workings of the vehicle and the method of giving it forward propulsion. Steering was the least of the problems, Grace realised, as he explained the workings of the three gears and the process of double-declutching.

The proprietor started the engine with a sharp turn of the starting handle, which he had inserted into the front of the engine. This was a new but fascinating world. There was just enough time for Grace to sit behind the steering wheel and slowly drive around the yard in a wide circle.

Grace experienced an amazing feeling of exhilaration and couldn't wait for her next lesson, which they arranged for Monday. She paid the man for the hour's tuition and in return he drove her back to the bakery, giving her a running commentary of his actions during the short journey.

Earlier at the hall, Mildred was in the kitchen when there was a knock on the scullery door.

"Hello, Mr Dewhurst," said Mildred, seeing the gardener stood clutching his cap.

"'Ow do, Mrs M. Just so tha knows, I've got three lads and a horse working on t'field as tha wanted. 'Appen it'll take a few days, like."

Mildred reacted slightly to the informal address but let it pass. She quite liked it.

"Yes, of course. Let me know how much you need when you've finished."

Jed went back to supervising the ploughing of the meadow. Mildred, meanwhile, had an errand to run. Well, not so much an errand, more a proposition; she needed to speak to the vicar.

Just after lunch, she changed into her 'Sunday best' and walked into the village. She called into the village store and spoke to Oswald Jessop. He was happy to take Grace to Laycock the following afternoon for her meeting with Lady Garner. Mildred agreed to pay the cabbie rate to recompense.

Mildred continued her perambulation and reached the church a few minutes later. She had no appointment but fortunately the vicar was working in the church and greeted her enthusiastically.

"Mrs Marsden, what a wonderful surprise," he said as he saw her enter the nave. He was quick to greet her.

Mildred was wearing her white gloves and accepted his handshake.

"To what do I owe this pleasure?"

"Good morning, Reverend. I have an issue I would like to discuss; well, not really an issue, more a proposal."

"Of course, Mrs Marsden. Would you like to come through to the office?"

The minister walked back down the church aisle, turned left behind the pulpit, and led Mildred through a heavy wooden door.

"Please take a seat."

Mildred looked around; the vestiges of church work were everywhere. It looked incredibly messy and untidy with pamphlets, files, and other paraphernalia in small piles around the room.

"Please excuse the mess; my wife usually helps with the tidying but she has been unwell."

"Oh dear, I'm sorry to hear that. Nothing serious, I hope?"

"The doctor said it's her heart; she has to rest. She's not enjoyed the best of health over the past year or so."

"Well, I'm sorry to hear that, Reverend," she repeated. "I do hope she improves swiftly. Please pass on my regards."

"That's most kind, Mrs Marsden. You wanted to discuss some business with me? A proposal, I think you said."

"Yes, Reverend. I've been thinking how I could best serve the war effort and it occurred to me that many of the families around here will be struggling with their menfolk called to war."

"Yes, that's very true. I've already been approached several times for help but, of course, the church can only do so much."

"Well, I want to set up a committee and start a fundraising campaign to help those in need in the village. What do you think?"

"I think that's an excellent idea. How do you propose doing this?"

"Well, if you could announce it on Sunday at the family service, that would be a start, and see what response we have. We can get some posters printed and ask people for donations – spare food, clothes and such – then we can deliver them to those in need."

"Yes, yes, indeed." The minister's spirits appeared raised; Mildred could see a likeminded supporter.

They continued debating possibilities with mounting enthusiasm, concluding with agreement that the vicar would make an announcement from the pulpit and pass the message around his wealthier contacts.

Mildred left after almost three-quarters of an hour fired up with ideas. She would speak to her daughters when they returned and elicit their support.

It was late afternoon when the girls arrived back from town. Grace was gushing with her experience at the car emporium; she couldn't wait until Monday for her next lesson. Agnes was similarly fired by her rehearsals with George Tooley. He had even given her a spare leather briefcase to carry her music. She too was looking forward to Monday; she would continue her practice over the weekend. Mildred informed them of the plan to raise money for the community and both agreed they would help the cause in any way they could.

A little later, Molly returned from her work with the seamstress. Daisy the housekeeper had left and the family were in the kitchen enjoying some tea and scones that she had made with Freda's help.

"Hello, Molly, how was your day?" asked Mildred as she joined the family.

"Aye, it were good; Kitty seemed very pleased. Look, she's given me some money." Molly opened her purse and proudly showed the contents to the rest of the family.

Mildred looked on with pride, watching the banter as the girls recounted their experiences to each other. It was Arthur, though, where her thoughts lay. She had been reading the papers and things had deteriorated in Belgium. Chances of a short war seemed to be receding; she just hoped he was safe. If only he would write.

Her meanderings were interrupted by a knock on the scullery door. She left the kitchen to answer it; she had a good idea who it would be.

"Ah, Mr Dewhurst, come in. Would you like a cup of tea? It is fresh."

He looked down at his boots, which were caked in mud.

"'Appen I best not, ma'am. I just called to say that t'lads have cleared most of t'meadow. Have tha had thoughts on what to grow?"

"Well, no, not really. Vegetables, I think, things people need to eat. Potatoes and the like."

"Aye, I can see to that. Not sure 'ow much we can plant for this year but should be able to get some turnips and potatoes, and maybe some cabbages and beans."

"Oh, yes, that would be wonderful. You must tell me what you need."

"Aye, ma'am, I'll see to it."

Friday lunchtime at the camp and there was some exciting news. Not only had the kit arrived but a small supply of rifles and ammunition had been delivered. They were old, reconditioned weapons dating back from the Boer War and not considered of suitable quality to be used in battle. Nevertheless, there was a great buzz around the camp that, at last, the recruits could practise real fighting.

The mood had lifted considerably with the receipt of the uniforms; even the early morning drill was taken with more enthusiasm than of late. New boots irritated recently healed blisters, but that was a small price to pay; they looked the part. The announcement that weapons training would start that afternoon was greeted with a great deal of enthusiasm. With the scarcity of weapons, the recruits were to be called to the rifle range hut by hut.

Corporal Dorkins called at hut forty-three just before three-thirty and marched the lads past the parade ground towards the main entrance. The left-hand turn led behind the huts. On the right, there was an open space which had been converted into a shooting range. Six targets were placed about a hundred yards away and, behind that, a small hill which would catch any stray bullets, of which there would be many. There was a small flagpole with a red flag attached indicating the range was in use.

Other huts were already practising, each with their own instructor. The corporal led the group to one of the vacant shooting alleys.

"Right, lads, gather round."

There was a table with a long wooden box on top. He opened it and inside were six Lee Enfield 300 rifles, which looked well used. He picked one at random and demonstrated how to load the ammunition, then he handed out the five others for the recruits to emulate his actions.

"Eh up, Wilfred, tha's doing it all wrong," said Arthur, watching his pal struggle with the mechanism. Having gained sufficient prowess, he helped Wilfred master the exercise.

Once he was satisfied that the recruits could load the ammunition, the corporal walked them across to the firing position. There were bales of straw for resting the rifle and behind them matting on which to lie. Again, the corporal lay down and demonstrated the correct posture for firing. In the distance – a long way in the distance, it seemed – there was a post about a foot wide with a cardboard target attached, white with three black rings.

"Now, lads, there's a pint for anyone who can hit the bullseye in the middle," said the corporal.

The sense of competition together with the promise of alcohol was a huge stimulus and there were arguments on who would go first.

There was one hut member who Arthur did not really get on with: Harold Dace from Skipton. He was a large man, a collier by trade and strong as an ox. Few would argue with him and he was starting to bully one or two of the less confident hut members. Arthur had intervened on one occasion when he started making fun of Wilfred's shoes.

Naturally, Harold barged to the front. "Eh up, Corp, give us it 'ere, 'appen I can take tha money."

Dorkins handed Dace the weapon together with three bullets and supervised the loading. Private Dace concentrated hard and squeezed the trigger. There was a significant kick which wrenched at his shoulder and the noise was much louder than he was anticipating, but he was not about to show any sign of discomfort. He reloaded then fired the remaining two bullets. It was difficult to make out, but one seemed to hit the post and the other two missed. There followed a range of expletives that Arthur was not familiar with.

"Bloody useless, 'appen sights are all over t'place. Tha'll never kill Germans with one of these," Harold remonstrated with the corporal.

"Well, it's all we've got, Dace, so make the most of it. Who wants to go next?" reposted the corporal.

There were chuckles among the group seeing the collier fail, and his reaction.

Henry went next and fared little better but managed to hit the target with one shot. The rest of the group took their turns. Wilfred was reluctant to try, but with some encouragement from Arthur, took the rifle and lay down. He looked awkward and the corporal had to help him into the correct position. He eventually fired but all three bullets missed the target; in fact, they missed the post by some distance. The corporal raised his eyes to the heavens.

"It looks like there's a bit of work to do, Stonehouse. Fall in."

Wilfred got up and handed the rifle back to the corporal.

"Right, Marsden, let's see what you can do."

Arthur took the rifle and assumed the position.

"Very good," said the corporal, watching Arthur manoeuvre the rifle into his shoulder.

There was a calm assuredness in his actions. He squeezed the trigger. He felt as though someone had punched him in the shoulder as he felt the kick, but the bullet sped away, slamming into the centre of the post. There were murmurs around the group.

"Good shot," said the corporal.

"Bloody lucky shot, more like," said the collier, watching with an air of disdain.

Arthur took his time and fired again. The same result, the bullet hitting dead centre.

"Come on, Arthur," hollered Henry. There were more shouts of encouragement from the team. Private Dace seemed incandescent.

Arthur took his time and concentrated; he took aim and squeezed the trigger. The third shot again hit the target. There were hoots and cheers from the hut members – all except Private Dace, that was, who appeared disinterested.

"Well done, Marsden, where did tha learn to shoot like that?" said the corporal.

Arthur got up and handed the rifle back to him.

"'Appen I've never seen a rifle in my life afore, let alone fired one," replied Arthur.

"Aye, like I said, lucky," said Dace.

With the shooting practice completed, the group marched back to the hut where they had some free time until their work duties at four-thirty. Back at the hut, Arthur's right shoulder was starting to stiffen as a result of the rifle's recoil and he was exercising it.

"Eh up, Arthur, that were impressive," said Henry, sat up on his bed next to Arthur.

"Ta. Don't know why, t'were first time I've seen a rifle," said Arthur, who was sat on his bed cleaning his boots.

Henry shouted across to Wilfred who was the other side of Arthur. "What happened to tha, Wilfred? Tha couldn't hit a barn door!"

"Aye, 'appen I could, if I could see it."

"What tha mean?" said Arthur, whose attention had been drawn to the remark.

"I couldn't see target; let alone hit it," said Wilfred despondently. "They told me my eyesight was poor at medical. 'Appen I shouldn't be here."

"Well, there's nowt to be done now. Tha's got to make the best of it," said Arthur.

Wilfred lay back on his bed and stared at the ceiling.

Saturday at the bakery and the queues for bread were

unrelenting. Grace and Betty were serving while Ivy was busy in the baking shed mixing the second batch of the day. The postman pushed through the waiting women and dropped a letter on the counter; it was addressed to Ivy. Grace picked it up and thanked the man. In a break between customers, Grace went through to the baking shed and handed it to Ivy.

"From our Arthur, judging by the writing," said Grace and walked back to the shop.

Ivy left her mixing and went outside where the light was better. Her heart was pounding as she opened the letter. It was briefer than she had hoped, just a couple of lines to say he had arrived in a camp somewhere. It was also not that easy to read, the handwriting and wording not that conducive to comprehension, but it was from Arthur and that was all that mattered. Now she had his address, she would write to him today. She put the letter in her apron pocket and continued with her bread making but with her mind elsewhere.

As usual, it was a half-day on Saturday, though lately most of the bread was already gone by lunchtime. Grace closed the shop at one o'clock and helped Betty finish up. Ivy was cleaning down the baking shed. She felt tired again; her energy levels had dropped and she was clammy from the exertion. It was taking all her willpower to complete her chores. She would have a lie down after she had finished and read Arthur's letter again.

Agnes was taking a break from her rehearsals and stayed at home to rest her voice. Grace had decided to take the two o'clock trolleybus back to Oakworth, which would give her plenty of time to get ready for her visit to Lady Garner. With the housekeeper on her day off, Mildred lit the fire in the sitting room for the water so Grace could have a bath.

Despite not officially his workday, Jed the gardener had

decided to continue working on the meadow, which had now been ploughed and was ready for planting. There was still a great deal of work to be done and he had enlisted the help of two of the men who had done the ploughing earlier in the week. Mildred had agreed to pay for the additional hours.

At three-fifteen, the sound of Oswald Jessop's delivery van echoed around the front of the house. Grace was ready and just putting the final touches to her makeup. She was wearing her best frock, the one that Kitty had made for her. She was feeling a little nervous for some reason; she was keen to make a good impression. Mildred was at the front door to send her off.

"Do I look alright, Mam?" said Grace as she was about to leave.

"You look very fine, my dear. I hope you have a wonderful time. I will expect a full report of the Manor on your return."

"Aye, Mam," replied Grace.

Oswald Jessop held the door open for Grace to get in, then turned the van in a large circle and back down the drive.

"You don't mind if I watch how you drive?" she asked as they reached the road.

"Nay, 'appen that's fine. What's tha interest?"

"I want to drive ambulances... to help the war effort," she explained.

"Nay, but that's a man's job. Why would tha be wanting to do that?"

"You don't have to be a man to drive, and you certainly don't have to be a man to drive an ambulance," countered Grace assertively.

Oswald decided not to proceed with this line of conversation; it was an argument he would not win, he realised.

The road to Laycock down Mackinstone Lane was

not conducive to motorised transport. It was wider than a bridleway, but not much, and was frequented in the main by pony and trap, evidenced by the copious amount of horse droppings on the road, an additional hazard. They reached the cricket ground where there was a fork in the road. A game was in progress. Oakworth had a strong team this year and had won their league. There were a few spectators dotted around the boundary edge watching.

Grace was distracted momentarily from Oswald's driving as she watched the players in their whites, the bowler running in and delivering the ball as fast as he could, the batsman clubbing it as hard as he could, and the fielders chasing after it as nimbly as they could to prevent any run. There was something quintessentially English about a cricket match on a warm sunny summer's afternoon; maybe that was something worth fighting for. Grace mused for a moment until the ground was out of sight.

Chapter Five

It was nearly twenty minutes before they approached the village. Once or twice the van had to stop for horse-drawn traffic and the last half a mile was spent following a herd of cattle, which slowed the journey down to a walking pace and covered the lane with cow pats. Oswald was cursing at the need to clean his van.

It was just before four o'clock when they reached Coltswood Manor. There was a wide four-bar gate at the entrance to the drive. It was open and the van drove through.

"My goodness," exclaimed Grace as the stately manor appeared before them.

The drive quickly opened onto a large, yellowed gravel area bordered by neatly trimmed lawns. The house was everything and more than one could imagine. In ochre-coloured stone, the façade seemed to be in two separate parts connected together in the middle, with small rectangle windows, typically Tudor, dotted in line across the frontage. Seven oblong brick chimneys with ornate flues protruded from the grey-orange roof tiles.

Grace got out of the van and thanked Oswald for the ride, hardly able to take her eyes off the magnificent building. To the right she could see outbuildings of a similar vintage and, in front, a wooden dovecote which looked well-used judging by the amount of bird droppings surrounding it.

Just then, the heavy wooden entrance door opened. Two Red Setters came bounding out and ran up to her, licking her hands as she made a fuss of them.

"Hello, you must be Grace."

At first, the sun impaired Grace's vision and she put her hand to her forehead to shield the rays.

"How do you do, ma'am," replied Grace.

The woman moved closer and Grace was able to see her clearly. She was much younger than she had imagined. Grace had always associated the word 'lady' with a more elderly person.

"Oh, do call me Jane; it's so tiresome all this 'ma'am' business. Come inside, I've asked Bartholomew to make some tea."

Grace followed her ladyship and the dogs towards the entrance, assessing her new acquaintance. The way she strode, almost bounded, towards the house suggested a woman of purpose, of energy. She had auburn hair coiffured in a low-pompadour style, much the fashion, her long rust-coloured dress tailored and the height of chic. She was wearing comfortable leather booties which one would normally wear indoors.

They entered the manor house into a large wood-panelled gallery with pictures and portraits covering almost every inch of the available space. There were various coats of arms and shields with swords.

"My, this is beautiful," said Grace, trying to take in the splendour.

"Thank you, yes, but it's a devil's own job trying to keep clean. Come through to the sitting room."

They walked along a short corridor into a large room with a high ceiling at the back of the house. Grace tried to take in the splendour. Beautiful oak panelling and several life-sized paintings of distant relatives aesthetically positioned with wall lights providing illumination. The two cloth-covered three-piece suites were tasselled and fussy, but nevertheless, the height of taste. The tables, adorned with porcelain knickknacks, and chairs looked as though they may have come from Mr Chippendale's workshop.

The centrepiece was a large stone fireplace, which was not lit, with an enormous bell-shaped mirror above. Grace noticed the candlestick telephone next to the doorway on a beautiful mahogany table which looked like it had been manufactured specifically for that purpose.

They sat down on one of the three-piece suites, Her Ladyship on one of the chairs while Grace was directed to the sofa.

"I do like your dress, Grace. Tell me, where did you get it?"

"Thank you, it was made in Oakworth by Kitty Bluet."

Lady Garner moved closer and examined the stitching. "Quite exquisite, you must let me know where to find her. I would certainly like to pay her a call."

Just then, a man appeared in a butler's uniform carrying a tray.

"Your refreshments, m'lady."

"Ah, thank you, Bartholomew. This is Grace; she's interested in joining the FANYs."

"Ma'am," acknowledged the man to Grace with a respectful nod.

Between Grace and Her Ladyship was a low wooden table adorned with a beautiful marquetry pattern. The tray was duly unloaded onto it and the butler poured the tea into delicate bone-China cups.

"That will be all, Bartholomew," said Lady Garner and he left the room. The dogs tried to enter but the butler shooed them away and closed the door. She picked up her cup, took a sip of tea and looked at Grace.

"Do tell me a little about yourself. Mr Drummond says you own a bakery."

"Hmm, not exactly, but I do work there. My mother owns it, although my brother will take over ownership when he returns. He's joined the army."

"Has he indeed? That is so brave of him. You must be very proud."

"Yes," replied Grace before taking her first sip of tea. "I am."

She was starting to relax. Her Ladyship was doing a fine job of making her feel at ease. Grace already had a most favourable impression.

"It's why I want to help in some way," added Grace.

"Yes, I understand. And you were a member of the Suffragettes, I believe."

"Yes, I was."

"And did you become actively involved?"

"Aye, I was on the local committee… and I got arrested," she added with some pride.

"When was this?"

"Last month."

"What, the Annie Kenny rally?"

"Yes."

"Hmm, terrible business. Miss Kenny is a personal friend; she was so distressed to hear of the outcome. So, tell me, were you gaoled?"

"No. I was ready to but my mam paid my fine."

Her Ladyship smiled. "You clearly have a caring mother."

"Aye… yes, I do." Grace corrected herself; she needed to speak like a lady.

"Tell me, what do you know about FANYs?"

"Nothing very much at all, but I would like to do something to support my brother. I thought I might drive an ambulance. I've already started taking lessons to learn to drive."

"You have? My, that's excellent." Her Ladyship took a sip of tea then continued. There was something refined and measured in the way she spoke. Grace listened intently.

"Well, let me give you some background. FANY stands for First Aid Nursing Yeomanry; we're known as 'Fannies' by the troops. It's been going for about four years now run by volunteers. I started getting involved last December; one of my good friends is a member and told me about it. We supply first aid nurses to support the Medical Corp in the field, stretcher-bearing and, yes, ambulance driving. Now we're at war, our services are going to be needed a great deal more, there's no doubting that."

"Yes, I believe that will be so."

"Do you ride at all?"

"No, I've never had the chance."

"Hmm, it might be useful if you could; motor ambulances are still very scarce at the moment and you will need to be able to get around." Lady Garner paused in thought and took another sip of her tea. "I know – you must visit here again next week; I will teach you. I have horses here in the stables."

Grace was beginning to feel overwhelmed. "Yes, that would be most acceptable."

"This war is going to change everything, Grace, you mark my words. I think it's going to be a fine opportunity to show those men in power what women can really do."

Lady Garner spoke passionately from the heart and Grace was being carried along by her rhetoric.

"Yes, I am certain of it."

The tea had been consumed and Lady Garner picked up a small hand bell on an adjacent table and rang it. The butler appeared.

"Yes, m'lady."

"We've finished with the tea. Can you tell Cook to prepare an extra meal?" She turned to Grace. "You *will* join us for dinner, won't you? I would welcome your company."

"Yes, I'd be please too," said Grace.

"Good, that's settled. Come on, let me show you around."

The butler entered the room and took away the tray and teacups. Lady Garner got up and Grace tagged along. She listened closely as she was given a guided tour of the interior.

"It's magnificent," said Grace as they left the house and entered the back garden. The two dogs bounded over and Grace bent down to stroke them in turn. "What lovely dogs. What are their names?"

"That's Bella, that's Sheba," replied Her Ladyship, indicating the respective names. The dogs followed slowly behind, their tongues hanging out as if they had been expending energy.

There was a raised patio and a footpath beyond them flanked by small yew trees. Lawns stretched either side to the boundary wall where numerous shrubs and rhododendron bushes were in flower.

"How long have you lived here?" asked Grace.

"I moved in with my late husband when we got married. I come from Derbyshire originally. That would be, let's see, about ten years ago."

"How long have you been widowed?"

"Over three years now. My husband was... how can I put this? Much older than I. His family wanted me to produce an heir, so I was told later, but unfortunately my husband was impotent."

"Oh, I'm sorry, how awful."

"Yes, I didn't find out until my wedding night... Do you know, I have never told anyone that. I don't know why I should be telling you."

"I would never repeat such a thing," said Grace.

"No, I know that."

"It can't have been easy."

"No. Frankly, it was dreadful, but you learn to adjust, don't you?"

"But you could get married again?" It was a half question, half statement.

"Yes, that's true enough; we'll have to see. I'm not in a hurry to be someone else's flummery. I'm more wary of men and their motives these days. Come, let me show you the stables," said Lady Garner, quickly changing the subject, and put her arm around Grace's shoulder.

They continued to the bottom of the footpath and turned right. There was a gate which was unlocked and Lady Garner walked through. There was a small paddock with six wooden stables on the other side. Horses' heads peeked over the top of each stable door, inquisitive to see the new arrivals. There was a lad carrying some used straw to a pile at the end of the stables.

"That's Peter, my groom. He's talking about going to war, I don't know what I will do if he leaves. In fact, getting reliable staff these days is a real problem."

"How many do you have? Staff, I mean."

"Not as many as when my husband was alive; I let some go. I didn't trust them. There were legal issues after my husband died; his sister contested the will. Luckily, the case was dismissed. That was when I met Mr Drummond. He was my legal representative and did a fine job, too." She looked at Grace, who was absorbed by her host, and returned to the thread. "The other thing is… staff are quite expensive. Now I just have Cook, Bartholomew, whom you've met, and the housekeeper. Then outside there's the groom, who looks after the horses, and the two gardeners."

They returned to the house and the sitting room where

they continued their discourse. The butler had thoughtfully placed glasses of lemonade at their disposal on the table.

"Would you like some lemonade, Grace? It is homemade."

"Yes, thank you."

Lady Garner did the honours. "So, let me ask you a question. Are you prepared to serve overseas?"

Grace looked at Her Ladyship and answered with assertion. "Most certainly, although I have no knowledge of what I will need to do."

"Please pay no heed to that, I will take care of everything, but you will need to have some training. I will speak to my good friend Lieutenant Ashley-Smythe, Flora. She's the C.O. of the camp down in Surrey where we train recruits. It will give you a chance to see if it suits you. Not everyone takes to the life; it's hard. I can arrange for you to join them."

"Yes, yes, I would be grateful for the opportunity."

"Don't worry, they are looking to take on new recruits, especially now the war has started. They will need dedicated people like yourself. I will cover your expenses."

"Thank you... Jane. I don't know what to say."

"No, it's me who should be thanking you."

It was almost nine o'clock before Grace left the Manor. Her Ladyship insisted that Bartholomew would take her home, and as she opened the front door and said farewell, the butler was sat on a pony and trap waiting.

"Thank you so much, Jane, for everything." There was a mutual hug.

"You have been good company, Grace, and I look forward to seeing you on Tuesday for some riding lessons. I may have some news for you about the camp by then, too. I'll call Flora on Monday."

The butler assisted Grace onto the trap and they were away. Grace turned and waved to her host and then reflected on her visit as the horse slowly clip-clopped along the narrow road back to Oakworth. It had been the most inspiring meeting she could ever remember. She shared Her Ladyship's views and ideals and felt a kindred spirit. She couldn't wait for her next visit.

It took over twenty minutes to arrive back at the hall.

"Thank you, Bartholomew," said Grace as he helped her down from the carriage.

She watched as he expertly turned the trap around and headed back. It was starting to get dark and the return journey for the butler was potentially hazardous with the possibility of oncoming motor traffic.

Mildred was in the sitting room and the girls in their bedrooms as Grace entered the house.

"Hello, dear," said Mildred. "Have you eaten? There is some supper in the kitchen if you are hungry."

"No, I'm fine thanks, Mam, Jane invited me to stay for dinner."

"Jane, is it? My, you are honoured."

Grace spent the next ten minutes telling Mildred about her visit, the house, the meal, and of her intention to join the FANYs and what it would entail. She also explained about the riding lessons.

"I will need to be able to ride to get around, it seems," said Grace.

Mildred had mixed feelings; having already lost Arthur to the war, she was now about to lose Grace.

"Oh dear, so when will you have to leave?"

"I'm not sure, Jane's speaking to the commanding officer of the training camp. She has a telephone."

"Has she indeed?" commented Mildred, who was deep in thought. "What about the shop?" she suddenly interjected, breaking Grace's enthusiastic recall. "If you leave, there will be no-one there from the family at the bakery."

"I don't know, Mam, but I was never going to spend my life serving in a bakery."

"I wish Arthur were here. I'm not sure what's to be done," said Mildred.

"Well, Betty's an absolute gem and Ivy, too; her bread's equally as good as Arthur's."

"Yes, that's as may be…" She thought for a moment. "Very well, on Monday we'll need to make some enquiries and find another assistant."

Saturday morning at the camp and the lads in hut forty-three were given some welcome news; they were being allowed an evening's pass. It was their first opportunity to leave the camp since they had arrived and there was a great deal of anticipation. The spirit in the hut had lifted considerably.

There was also the first pay distribution; one shilling and one penny a day for new recruits. The paymaster had set up a temporary cashier's office in the spare hut next to the admin centre and troops were again called by hut number to claim their pay. Most of it would be spent by the end of the day either by gambling or drinking.

To avoid swamping Masham, the local town where most of the recruits would be spending their leave, the commanding officer had agreed that five huts per evening would be allowed off base. It would also reduce the risk of trouble. With only three trucks available, the troops would be ferried into town on a shuttle basis.

The first convoy was due to leave at seven o'clock and the members of hut forty-three were waiting for their turn. There was already some raucous ribaldry, much aimed at Henry, who had brought a bottle of cologne with him and was wearing it liberally in the hope of attracting a member of the fair sex. He was by far the best presented in his smart suit, shirt, and tie. Arthur and Wilfred had no such pretences; they were just happy to be going off base.

The parade ground was packed with recruits and there was a rush to the wagons as they parked in front of the admin centre. Arthur, Wilfred, Henry, and Samuel managed to get on the third truck, clambering into the back in a most ungainly fashion.

Masham was a small town with just over a thousand inhabitants. Since the opening of the training camp, the railway had become very busy and the branch line from Northallerton saw regular traffic bringing materials and new troops. Supplies for the camp were ferried direct on the narrow-gauge railway. More staff had been taken on at the station to supervise the comings and goings. Despite its size, Masham was also home to two breweries including Theakston's, makers of the popular 'Old Peculier' beer, and as the recruits were dropped off in the town square, the smell of hops hung on the breeze.

Arthur and his pals jumped down from the back of the lorry. Arthur breathed in deeply.

"Eh up, lads, can tha smell that? It'll be like nectar," he said as the trucks pulled away.

They would return at ten-thirty and there would be a six mile walk for anyone not making the pick-up; all troops had to be back at base by midnight or face a charge.

The lads took in their bearings. Market Square was dominated by St Mary's Church, which looked on serenely in the evening sunshine. The lads headed for the first pub they could find.

The King's Head was just opposite the drop-off point. It was an old coaching house with rooms to let and held a dominant position in Market Street. Several of the other men were heading in the same direction and there was an undignified scramble towards the entrance. The bar was soon full of soldiers waiting to be served, many spilling over into adjacent rooms. It seemed to take the landlord by surprise to be suddenly inundated with customers, but it was not the first time and he dispensed ale with jocular efficiency. With the bar heaving, other soldiers from the second run attempted to enter but decided to seek alternative hostelries, of which there were many.

Arthur and his three pals managed to find a space in the corner and were savouring their first beer for two weeks. The bar was different from the Malt Shovel, the local alehouse back home; it was more homely. There was an impressive stag's head on the wall opposite the counter and below it a fireplace which wasn't lit. The bar itself contained a reasonable display of ale and spirits; Theakston's seemed to be the dominant beer. There was not much in the way of decoration, just a yellowy paint, although this colouration could have been caused by tobacco smoke. The room quickly filled with a blue haze as most of the men seemed to light up. Arthur and Wilfred didn't smoke; Henry and Samuel did. There were a few locals in the pub as the recruits arrived but, seeing the numbers, they quickly drank up and left; it usually meant trouble.

By ten o'clock and several pints of beer later, the atmosphere in the alehouse could have been described as lively. Several had left and wandered off to try other establishments, but it was still busy. Arthur and his pals had found a table and were sat chatting when an altercation started on the other side of the room. It appeared Harold Dace was in the thick of it. It started with raised voices, then some pushing and shoving, then some swinging arms, most of which failed to land due to the state of the protagonists.

The landlord quickly confronted the melee and ordered them out of the pub with the threat of a report to the commanding officer. Others intervened on the landlord's behalf, explaining such action would certainly mean confinement to the barracks. The warning seemed to calm the tempers and those involved slunk out of the alehouse.

A little later, Arthur noticed the clock behind the bar indicated it was time to meet the transport.

"Eh up, lads, 'appen we best go, have tha seen the time?"

After six pints, he and his pals struggled to stand up, but once in the fresh air the inebriation lessened and they managed to lurch to the awaiting transport. It was a comical scene as they tried to clamber aboard the second truck. Wilfred was still struggling after two attempts and in the end had to be assisted by two other lads, who pushed him unceremoniously on board. Others staggered out of the alehouses and crossed the square towards the vehicles. Many were being sick in the roadway.

With the three trucks full, they pulled away from Market Square and headed for the camp, leaving others to wait for the second run. There would be some facing a long walk and others facing a charge having missed the deadline.

After about five minutes, one of the group called out from the back and stood up.

"Eh up, lads, I need a piss," he said and barged to the back of the open truck, unbuttoned his trousers, and proceeded to urinate while holding onto the canopy. There were hoots of laughter as the following truck drew back to avoid being showered.

They arrived back at the camp without further mishap, all worse for wear but all benefiting from a chance to let their hair down. There would be some sore heads in the morning.

Sunday morning in Oakworth, Mildred and the girls were dressed ready for church. Jed Dewhurst had already arrived to continue his efforts to prepare the meadow ready for planting. The various seedlings were being delivered the following day. It was a drizzly morning with an accompanying drop in temperature as the family left for church wearing coats and carrying umbrellas. As they made the journey, there was a sweet-scented smell of flowers in the air brought on by the rain.

Reverend Conrad conducted the service. Before closing, he made the announcement that they were looking for volunteers to help raise money for families in need due to the war. Several women stayed behind to get more details, as the reverend had requested, and were gathered in the first two pews. Mildred suggested the girls head home as she joined the small group of volunteers.

"Ah, Mrs Marsden, so lovely to see you." He turned to the group. "This is Mrs Marsden from Springfield Hall; it is she who has suggested this initiative."

Mildred suddenly felt a burden of responsibility. "Thank you, Reverend."

She looked at the small group – six, she counted, all women – and explained her idea of trying to raise money for local families. There was an enthusiastic response. At Mildred's suggestion, they agreed to meet at the hall on Tuesday afternoon to form a committee and discuss actions.

After they had gone, the reverend joined Mildred. "I think this is a wonderful idea of yours, Mrs Marsden, and, of course, you will have my unstinting support."

"Thank you, Reverend. I have suggested a meeting at the hall on Tuesday afternoon, if you care to join us."

"Yes, I can do that, I should be free around three-thirty."

"Excellent. We will see you then."

Monday morning and more challenges lay ahead for the Marsden family. It was Agnes's first day of rehearsals at the new theatre in Bradford, and with the pending departure of Grace to help the war effort, staffing issues were on the forefront of Mildred's mind as she prepared breakfast for the girls. Although she wasn't meeting the music store proprietor until nine o'clock for her lift to Bradford, Agnes had decided to travel into town with Grace on the early trolleybus.

"Now, you mind yourself, Agnes," counselled Mildred as the two girls were leaving the house to walk to the trolleybus stop.

"Aye, Mam, I will," replied Agnes and kissed her mother on her cheek.

"Have you got your music?"

She lifted the briefcase that the music store owner had given her.

Mildred turned to Grace. "And don't forget to ask Betty if she knows anyone to help in the shop."

"Aye, Mam, don't fret; I'll see to it."

Mildred watched the girls walk up the drive to the road with a sense of pride, but also of concern. She had lost Arthur and now she was about to lose Grace and Agnes, too. The situation at the bakery was a worry. She had no intention of returning there to work – that would be a last resort – but with no family in situ, there was the running of the business to consider, not just the breadmaking and shop. Checking the takings and banking, paying suppliers; it would all need to be considered. She needed a business manager, and there was someone who sprang to mind. It would mean a trip into town.

Agnes and Grace arrived at the bakery at seven-forty-five, just as Ivy was finishing the first batch of bread. Grace walked down the corridor to the baking shed to see her.

"'Ow do, Grace," said Ivy seeing her enter the shed.

"Hello, Ivy, how are things?"

"Not bad. Miller says grain's getting through and now price is fixed, there's not the problems before war started."

"Well, that's something, and how are you? You weren't feeling yourself on Saturday."

"Aye, 'appen I feel a bit sick this morning, but I'll be fine in a day or two, I've no doubt. Can tha give us a hand with the baskets?"

Betty Granger arrived just as they were transporting the bread into the shop to be put on the shelves ready for sale. Agnes had gone up to the parlour to practise her songs. Betty put on her apron and joined Ivy emptying the baskets. Grace called them.

"Betty, Ivy, now I've got you together, I need to let you know I will be leaving the bakery shortly. I'm going to help the war effort."

Betty looked at Ivy. "But what's going to happen to the shop? We can't manage on our own."

"No, I know, and I need to ask if you know anyone of good character who would like to work here."

The girls thought for a moment.

"All us family are in the butcher's," said Ivy. "I don't know of no-one else."

"What about you, Betty?" said Grace.

Betty was thinking. "'Appen I might know someone." She looked at Ivy. "Tha remembers Ruth Danby?"

"Aye, from draper's."

"Aye, I were talking to her just last week; she were saying about going to work at t'mill. 'Appen she were looking for summat different. I could ask her."

"Yes, that would most kind. We can start her straightaway if she's willing."

"Aye, I'll see her this afternoon after work. She'll be working today, I warrant."

In the parlour, Agnes was putting on her makeup. Mildred had bought her a collection of lipsticks, eyeliners, mascara, and creams, which she kept in a small box that she had brought with her in her briefcase along with her music. She had applied more than usual, which she thought would be appropriate for a performer, but recognised her appearance might be misconstrued; she didn't care.

Just before nine o'clock, she descended the stairs to the shop. Grace and Betty were busy serving the queue. Agnes said farewell.

"Well, don't you look mighty fine," said Grace seeing her sister. "Mind you take care of yourself. I hope everything goes well."

"Thank you," said Agnes, who was starting to feel anxious.

Heads turned in the shop followed by murmurings as she lifted the counter flap and left.

She walked the short distance up James Street. The noise coming from the distant mills and foundries echoed around the valley – not obtrusively, but part of the tapestry of the town. Agnes would not notice it. The earlier rain which had kept her and Grace in the downstairs compartment on the trolleybus had cleared and the sun was starting to dry the pavement. The smell of horse manure was everywhere.

Agnes crossed the high street and turned left into Colston Lane. There was a small black car parked outside the music shop with the name 'Ford' in white script across the front grill. Agnes approached the entrance to the store just as the proprietor was locking the front door.

"Hello, George," said Agnes, which made him jump.

"Oh, hello, Agnes, I didn't see you there. Do you have

everything?"

"Aye, yes, I think so," she said nervously and showed the man her briefcase.

"My, you look very fine, if I may say so," said the man looking at Agnes more closely.

"Thank you, you're very kind, and for driving me to the theatre. I would have had to take a cabbie."

"It's my pleasure." The pianist walked around to the passenger door and opened it for Agnes to get in, feeling most ladylike.

They set off for the ten mile journey to Bradford which would take them at least thirty minutes given the volume of traffic. Buses determined the journey time because, with little opportunity to pass, following one meant constant stops to pick up and let off passengers. They spent the journey chatting and Agnes learned a lot about her companion and his musical career.

They reached the magnificent theatre before ten o'clock and parked close to the stage door. The building was on a fork in the road and trolleybus wires branched in both directions. Agnes was still feeling anxious as George opened the door for her to alight. She looked at the exterior and its distinctive domed architecture. There were notices of forthcoming productions in the windows including the Recruitment Touring Party for the following month. Her stomach did somersaults at the sight; that would be her, she realised.

"Have you got your music?" said George. Agnes showed him the briefcase. "Good, follow me. I'll show you where we are."

It was a surreal experience as Agnes followed George through the door and down a corridor. There were other people walking around. They reached the rehearsal rooms where there was a buzz of conversation and laughter coming

Alan Reynolds

from the end room.

"We're in here," said George as he opened the door.

Agnes couldn't believe her eyes as she saw twenty or thirty people engaged in conversation. There was a giant urn which appeared to be dispensing tea. Cameron Delaney, the promoter, stood next to it chatting to a couple of people. He noticed Agnes's arrival and went to greet her.

"Agnes, my dear girl, how are you? You look absolutely divine," he said effusively and put his arm around her shoulders in a fatherly way. He shouted to make himself heard above the general hubbub. "Can I have your attention, ladies and gentlemen? I want to introduce you to our new star… Agnes Marsden."

The group went quiet and looked at her. Agnes wanted the ground to swallow her up.

104

Agnes waved rather self-consciously. "Hello," she said, hardly above a whisper, looking around the room at the pairs of eyes staring at her.

"Come, my dear, let me introduce you to a few people," said the promoter.

It was a large room; sunlight was streaming through the four windows, the rays reflecting in the tobacco smoke from numerous cigarettes. George Tolley left Agnes and headed towards the piano in the corner. Other more mature men carrying instrument cases followed him.

Small groups had started to form and the promoter led Agnes to each in turn to introduce her. They reached an army officer dressed in military fatigues accompanied by a sergeant.

"Agnes, this is Captain Henderson and Sergeant…"

"Evans," confirmed the soldier.

"Yes, sorry, Sergeant Evans. Captain Henderson is coordinating the tour… he's also paying for it, so we have to look after him," said Cameron and chuckled.

"Quite," said the officer. "Pleasure to meet you, Agnes. I've heard a lot about you."

"Thank you," said Agnes and dropped her gaze demurely.

There was a brief conversation before Cameron moved on.

After a few minutes, the introductions were over and the buzz of conversation continued. Cameron Delaney retuned to the tea urn with his arm still around Agnes's shoulder.

"Would you like some tea, my dear?"

"Yes, please, my throat is quite dry," replied Agnes.

"Well, we must look after that, mustn't we?"

There was a selection of white cups and saucers neatly stacked next to the urn. The promoter filled one and handed it to Agnes. Her hands were shaking as he handed it to her.

"I can see you are a little nervous, my dear. Please don't be concerned; it's natural. You will feel so much better once we get started."

"Thank you... Cameron." She still hadn't got used to calling him by his first name.

The promoter moved away and Agnes was joined by other cast members eager to make her acquaintance. A woman with heavy makeup and what looked like a blonde wig was first. She looked much older close up.

"Hello, Agnes, I'm Gloria... Davison, speciality act. Cameron has been gushing frightfully about your singing, I can't wait to hear you."

"Thank you," said Agnes, "Do you sing?"

"Goodness no, they would close us down if I were to attempt such a thing. No, I do clubs."

"Clubs?" replied Agnes, intrigued.

"Yes, dear, I juggle them," she said and laughed.

"Oh, lovely," said Agnes.

They were interrupted by the promoter, who was now standing in the middle of the room with a blackboard and easel. It had a sheet over it. He was dressed in a different suit but still garish and distinctive; he was one of those people who was quite comfortable being centre stage. He clapped his hands to gain attention. After several attempts, the conversations subsided.

"Thank you, ladies and gentlemen. I think everyone is here. I want to introduce you to Captain Henderson who would like to say a few words." The captain joined the promoter next to the blackboard.

"Thank you... er, Cameron. Firstly, I would like to thank

you all for rallying to the cause, as it were." He chuckled nervously. "As you know, this concert tour is an important part of the army's recruitment drive. We've already started running a similar tour in London; it's proving very popular and very successful. We are using a similar format here but with a few slight changes to appeal to Northern audiences. I'm looking forward to working with you all and putting on a really good show." He was expecting some applause, but with none being forthcoming, he turned to the promoter. "I'll hand you back to Mr Delaney to explain in more detail."

Cameron moved forward and removed the sheet. "This is the running order for the programme."

There was a delay while everyone took in the contents. Agnes was amazed to see she was the last act before the singing of 'Land of Hope and Glory' and the National Anthem.

"We have other rooms along the corridor where you can rehearse your individual acts and then we will meet again at two o'clock for the first run through. Agnes, you can stay in here and rehearse with the orchestra."

Agnes's heart went to her mouth, but she was quickly joined by George Tooley.

"Come and meet the boys," he said, and before she had time to think, he led her across the room where the musicians had set up in a circle around the piano.

The word 'orchestra' was probably an exaggeration; two violins, a viola, double bass, a clarinet, saxophone and a percussionist. All had music stands with a selection of arrangements.

"Boys, this is Agnes, be gentle with her – this is her first time with an orchestra."

There were smiles and 'hellos' from the collective musicians. The term 'boys' was fairly loose and not really applicable. None were under fifty. Agnes smiled back anxiously. George sat down at the piano and vamped a few chords. Then there was a minute or two tuning up.

"Have you got your music?" asked George, "You can read the words while we run through, if you like."

"I know the words, thank you anyway," she replied.

The room had cleared and it was just the musicians. The two army personnel and the promoter were at the other end of the room in deep discussion.

"What would you like to start with?" asked George.

"I don't mind," replied Agnes.

"Well, I've worked out an order in which I think they will be best received by the audience; let's follow that. We'll start with 'Kitchener's Boys'."

There was some rustling of music as the band members chose the arrangement. It was a march tune with a rousing chorus.

"When you're ready, Agnes, I'll give you a four-bar introduction and then you come in, like we did at the shop," he clarified.

Agnes was battling the nerves and just nodded.

Then they were off. The orchestra were seasoned musicians and familiar with the song. George played the introduction and Agnes started singing. She was using the three men at the far end of the room as her focal point and noticed them stop and listen as she started singing.

After the first few notes, it was like she was floating on air or in another world. The song flowed from her very soul and the whole room was bathed in her voice. There was even a nod at choreography, which she had rehearsed in her mind, and did standing marching actions into various parts of the song. At the end of the routine, the musicians started applauding. They were joined by Cameron and his two army companions. The scene was set.

"That was excellent," said George with a look of pride.

Earlier at Springfield Hall, Mildred was in discussion with Daisy Jessop the housekeeper about the requirements for refreshments for the inaugural committee meeting of the Oakworth Christian Welfare Association, the name she had decided for her new venture. Daisy agreed to bake some cakes and provide other refreshments for the seven guests that were expected the following afternoon.

In the meadow, Jed was again being assisted by two young local lads in the task of planting the vegetables that would see the family and many of the community over the winter. Mildred had agreed to fund the project and had provided them with breakfast on their arrival.

At around eleven o'clock, she left the hall for her trip into town to try to resolve the bakery dilemma. She had arrived by midday and called in to the bakery to see how they were coping. There were the usual queues, but everything seemed to be running well enough. She greeted Grace and Betty and decided to go to the baking shed to see how Ivy was managing. With the mixing completed for the day, Ivy was cleaning the shed and didn't see Mildred walk through. Mildred could see that Ivy seemed to be struggling.

"Hello, Ivy, are you alright?"

Ivy appeared startled and turned around. "Oh, 'ow do, Mrs Marsden, tha fair made me jump."

"Sorry, Ivy. I thought I would just drop by and see how you are."

Ivy sat down on the stool in the corner; she seemed out of breath.

"I've been better, Mrs Marsden, I have to admit."

"What's the matter?"

"I don't know, I've been feeling not meself for a few days and I keep feeling sick, but nowt comes up."

"Well, leave that cleaning for the moment. Come on, I'll take you to the chemist and see if we can get something to help."

"Thank you, Mrs Marsden, 'appen I'll be well enough with a rest."

"Nonsense, I insist. Change your shoes and we will see what has to be done."

The pair walked back down the corridor into the shop.

"Just going to the chemist, I'll be back shortly," said Mildred to Grace, who was in earshot. The bakery was still busy.

It was less than ten minutes' walk along James Street to the pharmacy, close to Granger's store on the corner of the High Street. There were two other customers waiting before Mildred and Ivy were served by a man in a white overall.

"I need something for this young lady; she's feeling nauseous," said Mildred to the man's enquiry.

"What are your symptoms?" asked the man, directing his question to Ivy.

She explained her malady to the man. Mildred listened with more than a passing interest; having had five children, she was more than familiar with the early symptoms of pregnancy.

"Oh dear," she said under her breath.

The pharmacist returned with a bottle of pills which he placed in a paper bag. "Take one of these three times a day and before you go to bed with a little warm water. That should see to it."

Mildred handed the small package to Ivy and paid for the medicine.

Outside, Mildred was in deep thought. "Let's walk

through the park it's a fine day," she suggested, "The fresh air will do you good."

"Aye, 'appen it might," replied Ivy.

They crossed over James Street and entered the park. The trees had recovered from the storm the previous month and the leaves were at their peak, with many others taking the air on this fine lunchtime.

"Here, let's take a seat, Ivy. I need to talk with you."

Ivy grimaced as she sat down as though every movement was an effort.

"Ivy, can I ask you a question? And I need you to tell me the truth. Don't worry, I won't be angry… Did you and Arthur sleep together before he went away? Only I noticed your nightclothes were on the bed when I visited last."

Ivy looked down sheepishly. "Aye, Mrs Marsden, 'appen we did; but I do love him, I really do."

"I see… And did you… engage in… mm… intimate behaviour?"

Ivy looked at her. "Aye, Arthur was going to war."

"Well, I think you might be with child."

"What? No, that can't be."

"Yes, it can, and having had five children myself, that would explain why you are feeling the way you do."

Ivy looked horrified and immediately started crying. "Oh, Mrs Marsden… I'm so sorry." Ivy paused for a moment to take in the news. "What's to be done?"

"Please, don't concern yourself, my dear. If you are with child, and we'll know soon enough, we will look after you. I don't want my grandchild to suffer. What about your mam?"

"She will probably disown me," sobbed Ivy.

"No, she won't; I'll see to that… Say nothing until you are certain and then we'll see what needs to be done. For the moment, we need to give some thought to the baking. You won't be able to continue for much longer in your condition."

Ivy composed herself, still taking in the enormity of her situation. Mildred couldn't help thinking about Kitty the seamstress and how she would have felt all those years ago. Society had changed in the intervening years but there was still a significant stigma to having a child out of wedlock.

They walked together to the end of the footpath next to the cabbie stop opposite the bakery.

"I need to speak to your mother on another matter. Don't worry, I won't mention our discussion."

Ivy looked at Mildred, her face drawn and anxious. "Thank you… and for your kindness."

They walked across the road to the bakery together. Mildred left Ivy to return to her duties and then walked back up James Street to her next port of call.

Like the rest of the businesses along the street, the butcher's was busy and there were a number of customers waiting. Mildred attracted the attention of Glynis, who had just finished serving.

"Hello, Glynis, is your mother available?"

"Aye, 'appen she might be, I'll just check."

A few minutes later, Glynis returned and opened the entrance door.

"You know where to go?" said Glynis and went back to her customers.

Mildred ascended to the first floor. The layout was very similar to the bakery and at the top of the stairs was a door which she knocked. Violet Stonehouse was in the parlour and opened the door.

"Oh, hello, Mrs Marsden, what a nice surprise, we weren't expecting you… Do come in; I'll make us a cup of tea. How are you settling into your new house?" She was quite a large woman and moved to one side to let Mildred pass. "Do take a seat."

"Very well, thank you, and I'm sorry to call unannounced." Mildred entered the parlour and sat down on the settee.

"It's of no concern, always a pleasure... Won't be a moment. I'll just see to the tea."

Mildred looked around the room; it evidenced the domestic upheaval caused by numerous children. A few minutes later, Mrs Stonehouse returned with a tray holding a teapot, milk jug, sugar bowl, and cups and saucers.

"So, what can I do for you? I assume it's not a personal call," she asked as she started to pour the tea.

"Well, no, it's a business matter. You may have heard Grace is going to be leaving shortly, she wants to help the war effort. It means that I'm going to have no-one to look after the business, the money, accounts and so on. Arthur's at war, Agnes has started her theatre work, and Molly is with the seamstress. And I don't want to ask Freda; she's got another year at school and I don't want her to miss that."

"I see," replied Mrs Stonehouse. "And you would like me to take over this undertaking, a bookkeeper?"

"If it were possible. I need someone who I can trust and has experience in such matters. I assume you do the same for the butchery."

"Yes, that I do."

"I'll pay you, of course."

"That you will, Mrs Marsden."

Mildred put on a forced smile and took a sip of tea. "I don't think it will be troublesome in time. Grace sees to it usually at the end of the day. It's only a question of counting the coins and making sure there's money to cover the flour and yeast. Ivy usually pays the miller when he delivers in the morning."

"And how is Ivy? She called in yesterday, she was

looking very tired."

"She's doing very well. Grace was saying her bread is as good as Arthur's."

"Hmm… very well, but I do have a favour to ask in return. Ivy was saying that she feels lonely in the bakery on her own. Perhaps Glynis could stay with her to keep her company? It would be a great help to me. As you can see, we don't have much room and the children are growing up so quickly."

"I don't see why not. I have no idea when Arthur will return, but until then, she is more than welcome to stay… as long as they keep the place tidy."

"Aye, there'll be no problem in that regard, I can assure you of that."

There was a silence as they both sipped their teas, each in thought.

"When would you like me to start?"

"Wednesday, if that's convenient. Grace can show you what needs to be done."

"Very well, I will call at the shop Wednesday afternoon."

The women concluded their business and Mildred returned to the bakery where the shop was now closed for lunch. Ivy had finished her cleaning and had returned to the parlour. Grace was also there and Mildred was able to explain Mrs Stonehouse's new role as business manager. In turn, Grace told her mother about a possible recruit for the shop. Betty would be meeting her contact after work.

"Oh, that is good news," said Mildred, "And I know Ruth from the draper's, she would be perfect."

"Oh, I near forgot; postie brought a letter for you, Mam. It looks like it's from our Arthur," said Grace.

Grace handed over the envelope from her apron pocket. Mildred quickly slit it open with her fingers and started to read. Ivy was on the sofa resting but was alerted by Arthur's name. Mildred read it.

"Yes, it seems Arthur is settling in; he's not said much." She gave the letter to Ivy.

"Aye, 'appen he's a man of few words. I got one an' all; said same," said Ivy having scanned the letter. "I do hope he's safe."

"I think Ivy is fair smitten by our Arthur," said Grace and smiled.

"Aye, 'appen I am," replied Ivy. Mildred looked at Ivy.

"Your mother asked if Glynis could stay with you, keep you company. Is that what you want?" asked Mildred.

"Aye, 'appen company will be most welcome," replied Ivy.

On Monday afternoon at Colsterdale Camp, Major Foster had decided that there would be an inter-hut shooting competition. The objective was two-fold; to raise morale by fostering team spirit and to improve shooting skills. In hut forty-three, there was a discussion on their nominee, but given Arthur's prowess, he was unanimously selected as representative. Due to the number of huts, the competition would be phased over two afternoons. Hut forty-three would be competing today.

The mood in the hut had improved considerably since Sunday morning, when church parade was conducted to a congregation that was, by and large, still drunk from the previous evening; most had been nursing hangovers. Harold Dace was sporting a black eye but otherwise the recruits were in reasonable shape considering the amount of ale that had been consumed. The publicans of Masham would be wringing their hands, delighted with their evening's takings.

Any inebriation was soon expelled by a day that consisted

of more drill followed by a cross-country run. News of the shooting competition had prompted a great deal of excitement in the camp and a former bookmaker, stationed in an adjoining hut, was taking bets on the outcome. There was also a barrel of ale for the winning team. Those who had any money left from the purchase of ale on Saturday were quickly placing bets on their favourite and some serious money was involved. This was, of course, completely against regulations, but a blind eye was turned.

After lunch, the men from those huts who were participating were escorted down to the shooting range. Watching the men marching in pairs, completely coordinated and their kit immaculately turned out, it was difficult to believe these were the same men who just a week ago were rambling around in worn-out shoes and ill-fitting suits.

Six targets had been set up for the purpose of the competition. They were a few yards further back than the practice sessions and around eighty recruits looked on as the shooters took their turn. Lieutenant Hoskins was given the task of overseeing the event and ensuring fair play. Two of the regulars had brought a truck to the range and set up a large blackboard to record the scores. Each participant was given three attempts with five rounds each.

The event lasted all afternoon with great interest in the outcome from the spectators. It was soon Arthur's turn, and as he walked onto the range, he was cheered by his pals from hut forty-three. Corporal Dorkins had taken charge of the weapons and he handed Arthur a rifle and five bullets. Arthur lay down on the matting behind a large hay bale as before and made himself comfortable. He loaded the first bullet and felt a serene calm, unusual for someone often 'on edge'. He checked the wind direction and took careful aim. His hands were steady; he fired. He reloaded and repeated four more times. The target was checked. All five had hit the spot with two 'inners' scored. The result was welcomed by huge cheers and even some begrudging applause from his rivals. Lieutenant Hoskins was full of praise.

"I never knew you could do that, Marsden," he said as Arthur handed back the rifle.

"Aye, me an' all, sir," replied Arthur.

The afternoon's competition was finished by four-thirty and Arthur was declared the winner by some margin. He would face the winner of the following day's tournament on Wednesday to decide the overall victor. The bookmaker was doing good business.

By six o'clock at Springfield Hall, Mildred, Grace, Molly and Freda were around the table in the kitchen where most meals were eaten. Grace was explaining her latest driving lesson with some excitement.

"Mr Pease let me drive all over town; it's quite easy once you know how."

"And will you be having any more lessons?" asked Mildred.

"Aye, Thursday, and he's going to explain how to change a wheel, which is very important, he said. I think I'd like to be a mechanic; it's so interesting what goes on under the bonnet."

"Well, don't forget Wednesday," said Mildred, bringing Grace back down to earth. "I've asked Mrs Stonehouse to call after the shop's closed to see how we manage the books. She won't have a lot of time."

"Aye, Mam, I won't forget; it won't take long."

"I wonder how Betty got on with her friend."

"Well, Betty says she's sure she'll be interested. I told her she could start tomorrow if she has a mind."

"Well, yes, the sooner the better." Mildred sighed. "I don't know, everything's changing around us. I think we'll need a new baker soon, too."

"Oh, why do you say that? Ivy's doing a wonderful job. People like her bread."

Mildred quickly backtracked. "Oh, yes, well, I was talking to her today; I think she's finding the stress a little too much."

"Really? She said nowt to me, but she's not been herself for a few days, now you mention it."

"No, no, with everything that's going on, I don't think she wanted to trouble you. Don't say anything, will you? The chemist gave her a tonic; that might do the trick."

The conversation was interrupted by the sound of Agnes's arrival. She joined the family in the kitchen.

"Agnes!" shouted Freda excitedly.

"How was it, dear?" asked Mildred as Agnes took off her bonnet and kissed the family in turn.

"Oh, Mam, it was magical. George and Cameron were most complimentary, and I was singing with an orchestra; it sounded so wonderful. I sang my five songs but there's still much to do. I need to have my costume fitted."

"An orchestra, my," said Mildred.

"And there are so many different acts, not just singing. One lady is a juggler, she was very good."

"And this starts next Monday, the tour?"

"Yes, at the theatre where we're rehearsing in Bradford. There's already a poster outside."

"Really? Well, that doesn't give you much time."

"No, but Cameron says we'll be ready."

"Well, I hope you can provide us with tickets; we will want to be there on your first night."

"Yes, I can ask Cameron. I am sure he will provide some."

Tuesday was going to be a busy day in the Marsden household. Grace and Agnes took the early trolleybus and arrived at the bakery around seven-forty-five. Ivy was ready with the first batch of bread. Betty was preparing the shelves with someone the girls did not recognise. Betty turned hearing the 'clang' of the front door.

"Hello, Agnes, Grace, this is Ruth. I went to see her yesterday and she said she would like to work for you. I told her you had a good reputation… and I'm enjoying working for you." She smiled.

Grace raised the wooden hatch and she and Agnes went behind the counter to introduce themselves.

Ruth Danby was young-looking, quite tall and willowy. She was wearing a fashionable outfit which Grace had seen for sale in the draper's. The store had a good selection of ladies' fashions.

"Agnes is a singer," said Betty to Ruth. "She's going to be famous."

"Oh, I don't know about that, Betty; you flatter me too much, I think."

Grace went to find Ruth an apron and cap just as Ivy struggled into the shop carrying one of the wicker baskets. Agnes took it from her.

"Here, let me take that; you look tired."

"Aye, 'appen I didn't sleep too well last night."

"Will you be well enough to work?"

"Aye, I'll manage," said Ivy and walked back to the baking shed.

Agnes showed Ruth where everything went and then how to work the cash register.

"Aye, we have one at draper's same."

Back at Springfield Hall, Molly had gone to work with

Kitty the seamstress and Freda was in the kitchen, watching Daisy Jessop making fairy cakes for the afternoon inaugural committee meeting. Mildred had been reading the latest news in The Times. She was interested to learn about the growing number of recruits; ten thousand in London alone over the weekend, it reported. She thought of Arthur and would post his letter later, but there was another pressing matter on her mind; what to do about Ivy and the bakery. She was mulling this over in her thoughts. She went into the kitchen to make a hot drink.

"My, those smell fine," said Mildred as Freda took out a tray from the oven.

"I'll make the tea," said Daisy, taking the kettle from Mildred and filling it with water. "How is Jed getting on in the meadow?"

"He's nearly finished the planting. He's hoping for a good crop before winter."

"Oh, that's excellent, he is a good worker, is Jed."

"Yes, he is, I've been most pleased... I do have another issue which is on my mind. I'm concerned with Ivy at the bakery. She seems to be struggling with everything. I think I may need to look for someone to replace her."

The housekeeper looked at her. "A baker... you're looking for a baker?"

"Well, yes."

"You might just be an angel sent from heaven, Mildred. My brother Charles... Ainsworth, used to be the baker at Lockwood's."

"What, the mill?"

"Aye, before it burnt down. He'd been there over twenty years. Of course, after the fire they were all sacked. He's been doing odd jobs ever since."

Mildred's eyes lit up. "Really? Do you think he would be

interested?"

"I'm sure he will."

"Can you enquire? I would be most grateful."

"Yes, of course; he lives in town. I'll go and see him after I've finished here."

"Well, why don't you go after luncheon? I will be busy this afternoon."

"What about the clearing up?"

"Don't worry, I'll see to that; Freda can help me."

"Very well, I will go directly."

Mildred went to her purse and took out a shilling. "That will cover the trolley and you can take a cabbie to return; you are doing me a great favour, Daisy."

Daisy left just after lunch leaving Mildred to finish preparing for her meeting. Freda was at home and lending a hand.

The Reverend Conrad was the first to arrive for the meeting around two-fifteen, followed by the six volunteers over the next few minutes. The final visitor arrived in a horse and trap around two-forty, the coachman helping the woman from the carriage.

It was clear from their clothes and their method of arrival that four of the six were women of some wealth. There were three vehicles parked in front of the house, their drivers chatting to each other. The reverend made the introductions as they grouped together in the hallway – Jean McPherson, of Scottish descent and wife of a mill owner; Margaret Longmore, whose husband was an accountant; Helen Stewart, a widow; Evelyn Jacobs, whose husband was a mill supervisor; and Rachel Howarth, also a widow.

Mildred was desperately trying to remember their names as she led her guests into the sitting room. The sun was shining through the patio window and the lawns looked immaculate.

"This is a beautiful house, Mildred," said Lucy Hamilton, the late arrival.

The reverend had introduced her as the 'Honourable' Lucy Hamilton as her husband was a gentleman farmer, a term used to describe significant landowners, most of whom did little farming but employed managers. Her father was a viscount.

"Thank you, you're very kind... Please, everyone, make yourself comfortable. I'm just arranging some refreshments and we can start."

The six women and the reverend were duly seated while Mildred returned to the kitchen where Freda was arranging the cakes on a large plate. This was Mildred's first venture into socialising on this scale; she was feeling a little anxious and was fussing to make sure everything was in order. Less than two months earlier, this afternoon would have been unthinkable.

While Mildred and Freda were in the kitchen, the guests entertained themselves. Some were stood up looking out of the window. The reverend was keen to cement his relationship with the Honourable Lucy and was in deep conversation with her as Mildred and Freda carried in the scones and teas.

"This is Freda, my youngest... my housekeeper has the afternoon off," Mildred proudly announced.

There were nods of acknowledgement as the group helped themselves.

After a few minutes of further discourse, Mildred called the group to order and outlined her vision for the Oakworth Christian Welfare Association. She explained the sole aim was to provide support for struggling families in the village and surrounding areas while husbands served their country.

Mildred had a notepad and pencil and had made an agenda which she was following.

A committee was formed with Mildred appointed chairwoman, the Honourable Lucy as secretary, and Margaret Longmore, the accountant's wife, as treasurer. Reverend Conrad's role was not formally defined but he had offered to raise the profile of the group around the community via his weekly sermons and many contacts. Among the suggestions put forward was a village fete and garden party, and there was a great deal of energy behind it. Mildred's position in society had taken a significant upward trajectory.

Chapter Seven

Later that afternoon, Grace returned from the bakery and was getting ready for her reunion with Lady Jane. Bartholomew the butler would be arriving at four o'clock with the horse and trap. Mildred was still in the sitting room ensconced in her meeting.

As Grace was in the hallway putting on her bonnet ready to leave, Mildred excused herself to see her daughter out.

"Will you want anything to eat, Grace dear?" she asked.

"I expect Jane will ask me to stay for supper, but if not, I'll find something when I get in."

Grace opened the entrance door just as the sound of horses' hooves could be heard coming down the drive. Mildred said her goodbyes and returned to her committee.

It was a cloudy, bright day but with no threat of rain, making it a pleasant journey to the Manor. It was just a two-seater trap and Grace was sat next to the butler.

"Fine day, ma'am," he said as he steered the carriage towards the cricket ground.

It was much brighter than their return journey on Saturday evening and Grace was able to appreciate the wonderful views. They continued chatting amiably for the remainder of the trip. Bartholomew was an authority on the local area and pointed out places of interest with appropriate anecdotes.

It had taken just over twenty-five minutes with the road mercifully quiet; only once did they meet any motorised traffic, which fortunately was travelling slowly enough not to pose a threat of a collision.

Lady Jane was waiting at the front door with the dogs as the trap reached the Manor. She walked over to meet them. Looking up at the trap, Her Ladyship had her hand to her eyes to shield them from the sun.

"Hello, Grace, lovely to see you again." She held out her hand and helped her guest down.

"Hello, Jane, thank you for sending Bartholomew; he's been most excellent company."

"Oh yes, he'll tell you a tale or two."

The butler smiled, doffed his cap, and clicked his tongue to encourage the horse forward.

"Come on in, I've some news for you. We can chat over tea before we go to the stables."

In the absence of Bartholomew, who was attending to the horse, a stout woman in her forties came from the kitchen.

"Would you want some tea, m'lady?"

"Ah, Dora, yes please. You remember Grace from Saturday."

"Aye, of course. How are you, dear?" asked Dora.

"I'm well, thank you, Dora," replied Grace.

The cook turned to Her Ladyship. "Will you be wanting an extra place for dinner?"

Lady Jane looked at Grace. "You will stay, won't you?"

"Yes, I would love to." She turned to the cook. "I enjoyed your cooking very much on Saturday."

"Thank you, you're very kind," acknowledged Dora.

"That's settled then, come through to the sitting room; Cook will bring us some refreshments… You must tell me what you've been doing? Have you progressed with your driving?"

"Aye, yes, I have, I had more instruction yesterday. I must say, it's hard work using the handle… to start the car," Grace clarified with suitable hand movements. "Mr Pease took me round town; it was most enjoyable."

"Well, that's progress indeed."

They walked into the sitting room which was bathed in

sunshine and Jane invited Grace to sit on the large settee. Her Ladyship was seated on an adjoining armchair, erect and business-like.

"Well, as I said, I do have some good news; I've spoken to Flora... Lieutenant Ashley-Smythe, the officer in charge," she clarified, "And told her what an excellent recruit you would make and she said she will be delighted to have you onboard. She says you can join as soon as you wish. I have suggested next Monday if that's not too soon?"

"No, no, that should be most acceptable. We have found someone to take over at the bakery. What will I need to take?"

"Well, the usual things, I expect, but I'll speak to Flora again tomorrow and get the details for you."

"Where will I need to go?"

"It's in Surrey, a place called Brookwood. It will mean taking the train and a cabbie, but don't worry, I will take care of the fare."

"Thank you, Jane, that's most kind."

Grace was in all manner of thoughts as Dora brought in a tray of tea and homemade fruit cake, neatly sliced in pieces and presented on a silver cake stand.

They continued chatting as best friends might do over their refreshments, then Jane got up.

"Right, let's go to the stables. I've asked the groom to prepare Sooty. She's a lovely mare and very placid; she will be just right for you on which to learn."

Grace followed her host through the beautiful gardens to the paddock where Peter the groom was attending a grey horse. He walked towards them holding onto the bridle, the horse nodding in time with the steps.

"Hello, Peter, you remember Grace from Saturday?"

"Aye, ma'am, hello," he said and doffed his cap.

"Peter is more than a groom; he's an excellent trainer, he's so good with horses. He used to be a steeplechase jockey. That's right, Peter?"

"Aye, ma'am, but too many years ago than I would like to remember."

Jane turned to Grace. "Do you have any riding boots?"

Grace looked down at her new booties. "No, I don't, only these."

"Oh, well, wait here a moment, I might have a spare pair."

Jane walked off into a small building next to the stables where Grace could see an array of tack hanging from hooks. A few minutes later, Jane appeared holding a pair of riding boots.

"I thought I had a spare pair; I don't think they've ever been used. My late husband bought them for me." She rubbed down the leather to remove a layer of dust. "I don't know if they fit, but we look around the same size."

Grace removed one of her booties and held onto Jane as she manoeuvred her foot into the riding boot.

"Well, that one seems to fit; try the other," said Jane.

The exercise was repeated and Grace looked down.

"Well they certainly do seem to fit; how do they feel?"

Grace walked a few paces. "Comfortable, Jane, thank you."

"You must take them with you, they're only gathering dust here. You might want to consider buying some riding breeches, too. Dresses I find are so cumbersome."

"Yes, I will."

"I think there's something tremendously liberating about wearing trousers. It means you can sit astride instead of side-saddle; it's so much more comfortable, I think."

"Yes, Jane, I can imagine… and I will certainly acquire some before I leave."

The groom was carrying a small wooden set of steps which he placed next to the horse.

"If you're ready, Peter will help you onto Sooty and will tell you what to do," said Jane.

It wasn't the most elegant of mounts but Grace managed to climb up onto the saddle. Instinctively she leant forward to maintain her balance.

"Sit upright, ma'am," instructed the groom, and Grace slowly complied and began to relax. Peter held the bridle and walked the horse slowly around the yard.

After an hour's instruction, Grace was able to ride without assistance and was trotting effortlessly around the paddock. Jane spoke to the groom.

"Peter's going to prepare Amber for me and we can ride out for a while; I'll just go and change."

Grace continued practising on her own and was beginning to feel quite at home. Sitting side-saddle had a certain elegance about it.

A few minutes later, the groom appeared with a brown horse, a beautiful looking Cleveland Bay. Jane returned from the tack shed wearing tight-fitting jodhpurs. She went to the horse and mounted effortlessly. She rode up to Grace and the pair headed out through the gate at the end of the yard into open countryside. The pair chatted as they trotted slowly along the bridle path; Grace's confidence was growing with every stride.

"What beautiful scenery," said Grace as the path opened and revealed verdant moorland, the purple heather in full bloom.

"Thank you. These are our grouse moors; the season hasn't really got going this year. Do you shoot at all?" asked Jane.

"Goodness no, I wouldn't know one end of a rifle from

the other."

While Grace was enjoying the company and tuition of Her Ladyship, back at the house, Mildred had an unexpected visitor. The family had just finished their evening meal and were in the kitchen. Agnes was describing her latest adventure at the theatre.

"Who could that be?" asked Mildred as the tinkle of the entrance bell echoed around the hall. Mildred went to investigate.

"Daisy, do come in; I wasn't expecting to see you this evening."

"Yes, I asked Oswald to bring me down; I shan't stop." Mildred could see the van parked outside.

"I just wanted to let you know, I've spoken to my brother and he would be delighted to take up your kind offer."

"Oh, that's wonderful news."

"I said I would call back and let him know what he should do."

"Yes, let me think a moment. Where does he live?"

"In town, Norton Avenue."

"I don't know where that is."

"Not far from the station."

"Very well, I'll travel into town and meet him at the bakery at eleven o'clock tomorrow. Will you be able to get a message to him?"

"Yes, I will get Oswald to take me directly."

Back at the manor, Grace and Jane returned to the paddock after their ride. Peter the groom was in the yard and fetched the steps for Grace to dismount.

"Thank you, Peter, let me see if I can manage without the steps," said Grace, having seen Jane complete the manoeuvre with the elegant aplomb of a seasoned rider.

It was a little undignified and Peter had to intervene with a helping hand. Grace stood upright and winced as her muscles complained at the exercise.

"Ha, ha, yes, you'll be stiff for a while; I recommend a nice hot bath... I know, why don't you have one here? I'll get Bartholomew to prepare the water. Then we can eat when you've finished."

"If you don't mind, thank you."

"Excellent, I've some salts that will relax your muscles."

They reached the house and the butler was duly dispatched to prepare the bath water for Grace. A few minutes later, Jane led the way up the wide staircase.

"Just here," said Jane when they had reached the bathroom.

Grace couldn't believe her eyes. It was as big as her bedroom back in the bakery. The bath was the centrepiece in the middle of the room, a white porcelain tub with a mahogany surround; steaming water was rising from it. There were large murals of hunting scenes all around the room and, to the right, a dressing table with an elegant mirror with an ornate frame flanked by two wall lights and a deep red velvet-padded stool in front. There was a mixture of creams and makeup on top of the table. The room even had an iron radiator for heating. A white towelling dressing gown was hung by a hook behind the door. Grace was trying to take it all in.

"There are some salts up there, help yourself. I'll just get you some towels," said Jane, pointing to a jar on one of the mahogany shelves next to the window.

Grace undressed and poured in a handful of crystals into the bathwater which gave off a wonderful aroma, then she gently lowered herself in as Jane arrived with the towels.

With three sisters regularly sharing a bath, Grace thought nothing of Jane's presence.

"I'll put the towel here," said Jane. Next to the radiator, there was a varnished wooden drying frame and Jane draped the white towel over it. "I'll leave you to it; I'll just check with Cook on the dinner."

Jane shut the door allowing Grace to luxuriate.

After a convivial evening, Grace arrived back at the hall around nine-thirty, having arranged a further visit on Friday. The return journey was quite dark and Grace was concerned about Bartholomew's well-being. He reassured Grace by lighting two hurricane lamps positioned on the front board. They would give no illumination of the road but at least he could be seen. 'I'm used to it, ma'am,' he had said as he headed away.

"Hello, dear, how was your riding lesson?" asked Mildred as Grace entered the sitting room.

Grace spent a few minutes describing her day, and especially the bathroom.

"When will you be leaving?" asked Mildred.

"Next Monday, Jane's arranging a railway ticket for me."

"My, that soon," Mildred sighed. "We must see that we have everything you'll need."

"Aye, I need some riding breeches; Jane said they are far more practical than a dress for riding."

"Yes, I can imagine they will be."

Mildred mentioned the possibility of the new baker. "I am meeting him at the bakery tomorrow, I would welcome your thoughts."

Agnes was laid in bed, thinking about her day. The rehearsals were going well and she had become a firm favourite among the cast. She had made more friends than she had in her entire life; there was great camaraderie. Wednesday was going to be the first dress rehearsal and she was wondering what had been arranged for her; all she had been told was that it was going to be glamourous.

Her mind suddenly drifted to Norman; she wondered what he was doing now and how he was coping with army life. She missed him so much. She still had the knitted doll that they had won on the garden party tombola just a few weeks ago; it was lay on her pillow next to her.

She switched on her beside light and took out a pencil and paper. '*Dear Norman…*' she started. She had the army postal details from Arthur's letter, although she did not know his army number. She would address it to Lieutenant Norman Hoskins; she was sure it would reach him.

The following morning around nine-thirty, Mildred left for her meeting with the prospective baker. As she went outside the front door, she was greeted by a pile of horse droppings and some patches of oil from the visitors' transport the previous afternoon. She quickly returned inside and instructed Daisy to ask Jed the gardener to clean it up.

She caught the ten o'clock trolleybus and, with rain threatening, decided to sit in the lower deck. With most passengers taking the same precaution, the bus soon became cramped and most unpleasant. They eventually arrived in town just after ten-forty and she walked through the park to the bakery.

As usual, trade was brisk with a small queue which was being swelled by new arrivals. Mildred entered the shop and let herself in behind the counter. It had just started to rain and she brushed herself down while she waited for Grace to finish serving.

Grace greeted her mother. "Hello, Mam, you've met

Betty, but not Ruth. Ruth, this is my mam," she said by way of introduction.

The new recruit shook hands with Mildred and offered a small curtsy.

"Please to meet you, ma'am, I'm sure," she said with a smile. Mildred acknowledged.

"I'm just going to see Ivy," said Mildred and walked along the short corridor to the baking shed.

Ivy was busy with her third mix and looked up from her labours, noticing Mildred's arrival.

"'Ow do, Mrs Marsden."

"Hello, Ivy, how are you feeling?"

"Aye, still a bit sick but 'appen pills have helped."

"Oh, I am pleased... I'm seeing someone shortly who may be able to take over from you."

"I'm alright, Mrs Marsden, at moment, honest."

"Nonsense, Ivy, you can't be lifting heavy bags of flour in your condition."

"But what will I do?"

"You can help in the shop next week. Grace is leaving on Saturday and won't be returning. There will be plenty of work to go round, I have no doubt. When things start to show, we can make other arrangements... Your mother will be calling later, she's going to take over the books."

"Aye, she said as much when I saw her."

"And what about Glynis?"

"Aye, she stayed last night; she were good company."

"Excellent, excellent. Well, you certainly look better."

"Aye, 'appen I slept well last night."

There was a call from the shop. "Mam, there's a Mr Ainsworth for you."

"That will be him, I'll bring him along shortly," said Mildred and walked back along the corridor.

She opened the wooden flap and called him through.

"Mr Ainsworth, Mildred Marsden, let's go up to the parlour and we can talk more easily."

Mildred led the man up the stairs and into the living room.

"Have a seat, Mr Ainsworth." He complied.

Mildred looked at the man. On the weighty side with a full set of whiskers, he had a smiley face with a red complexion, as if he had drunk many glasses of port.

"Your sister informs me you have experience as a baker."

"Aye, worked for Lockwood's for twenty year or more. I were head baker for last five."

"And you were affected by the fire, I understand."

"Aye, there were nothing left; it were just a shell by time fire were out."

"Yes, I saw the report in the newspaper, so sad. It was fortunate no-one was seriously hurt."

"Aye."

"What have you been doing since the fire?"

"Just a few odd jobs for folk mainly; it's not been easy."

"No, I am sure not, and you have a family, Mrs Jessop informs me."

"Aye, that I do, a wife and two daughters."

They continued the discussion for another fifteen minutes before Mildred made a suggestion.

"Let me take you down to the baking shed and introduce you to Ivy, who is presently undertaking the task."

"Aye, right you are," said the baker and Mildred led the way.

Ivy was just loading another batch of dough into the oven.

"Ivy, this is Mr Ainsworth."

"'Ow do," said Ivy as she closed the oven door.

The man looked around the shed. "It's much smaller than I'm used to."

"Yes, well, it's served us and the folk of Keighley well enough for a hundred years," countered Mildred.

"Aye, aye, I meant no offence, I was just saying."

The baker watched as Ivy started another mix. He intervened as he saw Ivy start to lift the hundredweight bag of flower.

"Nay, lass, tha mustn't be doing that, let me."

He picked up the bag with the minimum of effort and started filling the mixing vat.

"Can I see tha mix?" he asked Ivy as she began preparing the ingredients.

"It was how I was taught by Arthur," she explained.

"Aye, it's a good mix, sure enough."

Mildred watched the pair.

"I will leave you with Ivy, Mr Ainsworth. I'll be in the parlour when you've finished looking around. Feel free to ask any questions."

"Aye, right you are, Mrs Marsden, that I will."

Ivy was only too willing to show the baker her methods and Charles, as he wanted to be known, helped her complete the morning's breadmaking. He returned to the parlour around twelve-thirty, his hands and hair covered in flour.

"Ah, Mr Ainsworth, how did you find it?"

"Aye, as I say, it's different, but 'appen I'll get used to it."

"Excellent, excellent… When would you like to start?"

"Anytime tha wants."

"Well, you can start tomorrow. It's early, the miller is usually here for around five o'clock."

"That's of no mind; I were up afore that at Lockwood's."

"Very well, and I will pay you what you were getting at Lockwood's, weekly, in cash. Is that acceptable?"

"Aye, ma'am, very acceptable."

"Shall we say a month's trial and see how we get on? You

can spend the rest of the week with Ivy and then on Monday she can work in the shop."

"Aye, 'appen that suits fine."

Mildred escorted the baker to the front door and then went to see Ivy in the shed. The final batch had been completed and she was washing out the mixing vat.

"So, Ivy, what was your impression of Mr Ainsworth?"

"Aye, he knows his bread alright, 'appen he'll be just fine."

"Good, I've asked him to start tomorrow at five o'clock. Can you introduce him to Mr Buxton?"

"Aye, I'll do that."

"And don't go lifting any heavy sacks of flour. You need to look after yourself."

"Aye, Mrs Marsden, and thank you."

"No, it's me who should be thanking you. There would have been no bread if it weren't for you. I am very grateful, and don't worry about any rent money; you can stay free until we know what's to be done."

Later that afternoon, Violet Stonehouse made the short walk from the butcher's to the bakery to see Grace and take over the bookkeeping. It meant that come Monday and Grace's departure to join the FANYs, there would be no-one from the Marsden family working at the bakery for the first time in a hundred years. It was a point not lost on Mildred, but with the children now occupied elsewhere, there was little option; she had no desire to take any personal involvement. She had even considered selling the business but there would need to be a job for Arthur when he returned from the war.

Arthur had no idea what was going on; he was continuing

his training somewhere in the depths of the Yorkshire Dales. He had, however, received his first letter. It was from Ivy. When he saw the pencil-addressed envelope and the unfamiliar writing, he experienced a sense of anticipation as he opened it.

'Dear Arthur, It were good to receive your letter. I have read it so many times. I hope you are well. I think about you all the time. Things at the bakery are well enough, Mr Buxton is bringing the flour still. It seems Grace is leaving shortly and Ruth from the drapery is working in the shop. Your mam has been very kind and allowed Glynis to stay with me to keep me company. I hope you don't mind; it has been very lonely since you left. I have missed you more than I can say. I hope you will keep safe and return to me as soon as you can. With fondest love, Ivy'.

He read it again and considered the contents. He wondered about Grace leaving and the whereabouts of Agnes; he was unaware of her concert tour. He would write back and try to find out what was going on. First, though, there was the small matter of the shooting competition.

The previous afternoon, Thomas Able, a bookbinder from Skipton, had won the second round of the contest. He was a resident of hut fifteen and the rivalry between the two huts increased significantly. The bookmaker had slashed the odds on Arthur as rumour had got around about his skill, and he was now firm favourite in what was a two-horse race. There was some lively banter during the morning's drill session which continued into the mess hall.

Down at the range, there were about thirty or forty recruits lined up to watch the competition, including the commanding officer, who arrived on a white horse. Lieutenant Hoskins was supervising proceedings and acting as scorekeeper. As before, two lanes had been set up with cardboard targets attached to wooden posts around a hundred yards away. The target consisted of three black rings numbered two, five and ten, representing points for the degree of difficulty, with the highest score for the centre. There was a soldier positioned close to each target with two flags, green and red. They would check the scores after each round.

Arthur and the rest of hut forty-three marched down to the range with Corporal Dorkins; they were joined a few minutes later by their adversaries from hut fifteen. The lieutenant explained the rules; there would be ten rounds of five shots. The necessary bullets had been drawn from the stores. After five minutes, Arthur and Private Able had taken up their firing positions on their respective lanes. Able was a tall and quite gangly lad and seemed an unlikely sharpshooter, looking very much the part of his occupation. However, it transpired that Able's father was a gamekeeper on one of the local estates and Able had spent many hours on the moors with him in the grouse season.

The men at the far end were holding red flags while they positioned the targets on the posts. Then they moved ten yards away and raised green flags. The lieutenant handed the men their first five bullets.

"In your own time, gentlemen."

Arthur took a deep breath and loaded his rifle. The noise from the watching recruits grew in intensity; there was a lot riding on the afternoon and tension was rising. The bookmaker was in attendance and was still taking bets out of sight of the officers.

The noise of the first shot made Arthur's ears sing. The lieutenant was watching the targets with a pair of binoculars, but it was difficult to make out the scores with any certainty. At the end of the first five shots, the red flags were raised while the scores were checked and relayed back to the lieutenant.

The wait increased the tension; there was a great deal of prestige at stake, not counting the money involved. The scores were chalked up on the board; Round One – Marsden thirty-seven; Able twenty-four, with one bullet missing the target altogether. A good start for Arthur and a huge cheer went up from hut forty-three as the scores were announced.

An hour later, Arthur was declared the winner to more cheers from his comrades. He had scored three hundred and ten to Able's two hundred and forty-six. The men of hut forty-three went wild as the two competitors sportingly shook hands. Major Foster, who had been watching the proceedings on horseback, dismounted and presented Arthur with a trophy; the barrel of ale would be made available later, he explained to more approving cheers.

There was much back-slapping on the return journey to the hut, much to Arthur's embarrassment. Most of the residents had placed money on their champion and the bookmaker later paid out the equivalent to a day's wages and more in most circumstances. Even Harold Dace was complimentary, having pocketed five shillings on the back of Arthur's win. The beer would be delivered to the hut later.

Back in the officers' mess, Major Foster was discussing Arthur with the lieutenant.

"What do we know about Private Marsden, Lieutenant?"

"I happen to know the family, sir. He's a baker and has a good reputation."

"Hmm, has he indeed? We need to keep a close eye on him, his skills could be in demand when we get to Flanders... Has leadership qualities, I vouch."

"I would say so, sir."

"When are the field manoeuvres planned?"

"At the weekend, sir."

"Very well, arrange for him to lead a small platoon and see how he fares."

"Yes, sir."

The lieutenant had a question. "Have you heard anything, sir? When we might be called to active service, I mean?"

"Too early to say, Lieutenant. H.Q. are not in the habit of sending untrained recruits. A couple of months I would think, but we must make sure the men are ready."

"Yes, sir."

That afternoon at the theatre in Bradford, Agnes was being fitted with her costume which had been chosen for the performance on Monday. They were in an anti-room and the girls from the dancing chorus were also being clothed. Doris Armitage was the resident wardrobe mistress and she had been drafted in to oversee everything; she was aided by three assistants. The room was abuzz with chatter and giggles. Agnes looked on and was surprised at the revealing nature of their costumes; a military tunic, cap and little else, just knee-length black shorts, stockings and tap shoes.

"We're going to give those boys a treat," said Doris as she lined up the eight girls to check them over. She clapped her hands like a school ma'am. "Right, girls, can you just try a routine to see if you can dance in them? We don't want any buttons coming undone and things popping out," she said and laughed.

One of the girls, a willowy blonde and definitely the leader, counted down and the girls started a tap-dance routine. Satisfied that there would be no malfunctions, after one or two minor adjustments the girls changed and came over to Agnes, with one of the assistants carrying a large box.

"I've just returned from the dressmaker; Cameron has

had this especially made for you."

Agnes couldn't believe her eyes when the pair gently removed the dress from the box.

"Try it on, my dear, and we can make any alterations."

Agnes undressed and stood in her underclothes as the wardrobe mistress undid the hooks and eyes at the back of the garment. Between them they manoeuvred it in place. Agnes stood while Doris straightened the skirt and adjusted the bosom. There was a full-length mirror and Agnes just stared, hardly able to take it all in. The skirt was floor-length with several layers of stiff net underneath, giving it a billowy look. But it was the pattern that was striking; a giant Union Jack with red, white and blue sleeves. It was low-cut with a deep decolletage showing a considerable amount of cleavage.

"My, Miss Agnes, the boys are going to love you," said Doris as she stood back and admired her handiwork. "Oh, I have these too." There was another box from which she took a pair of red satin boots.

"They should be your size," she added as she handed them to Agnes.

Just then Cameron the promotor came in. "My, Agnes, you look truly magnificent."

Agnes turned from the mirror. "Well, thank you, Cameron."

"No, thank *you*, I think you will be an enormous success. Wait here, I'll get Captain Henderson to join us."

Agnes was walking up and down the room as Doris checked for any adjustments when the promoter returned with the officer.

"What do you think, Captain?"

"My, my, my, you look so pretty, my dear," he said, eyeing Agnes up and down. She suddenly felt uncomfortable with the scrutiny, but realised she was in a new world now.

"Thank you, sir," she said and made a dramatic curtsy. The men applauded.

"Oh, I nearly forgot, I have those tickets you asked for," said Cameron. He put his hands in the inside pocket of his jacket and took out the said items and handed them to her. "Best seats in the house, I have reserved one of the boxes for your family. It will be big enough to accommodate them."

"Thank you, Cameron, that's very generous of you."

"Nonsense, my dear, you deserve the best of everything."

Chapter Eight

Thursday morning at the bakery at five o'clock and Ivy was leaving the parlour to open the baking shed. The stairs were dark; sunrise was not due for nearly an hour. She reached the shop and looked out towards the park as the sky was gradually turning colour. It was cloudy but dry. The rhythmic thrump of the various mills and factories echoed around the town.

She could see the shape of a man stood on the shop doorstep and, seeing her, he rapped on the glass pane to attract Ivy's attention. At first she was startled, then she remembered the new baker; it had slipped her mind. She was still not feeling her usual self; it was as if every move was an effort. There was a loud 'clang' as she opened the door.

"'Ow do," said Ivy.

"Eh up, Ivy, not a bad morning."

"Aye, tha best come through; I'll show tha what needs to be done."

The pair walked along the corridor. The baking shed was in total darkness and Ivy turned on the gas lamp next to the entrance which bathed the area in a soft light. She walked to the shed doors to open them.

"Nay, lass, I'll do that for tha," said the man. He opened the double doors.

"Coal and wood for t'oven is over yonder by t'privy," said Ivy pointing to a concrete coal bunker at the end of the yard. "Bucket's there."

Charles Ainsworth picked up the bucket and ambled to the bunker to collect the coal and tinder. Within five minutes, the oven was lit.

"There's still a bag of flour left from yesterday," said Ivy.

"'Appen we can make a start afore miller gets here."

"Aye," said the baker and he retrieved the hundredweight sack from the corner of the shed, slung it over his shoulders as if it were a bag of feathers, and carried it the short distance to the mixing vat. Ivy watched; she would normally have to drag the heavy sacks.

Just then, the sound of Buxton's lorry interrupted their labours as it trundled into the yard. Edward Buxton got down from the cab and walked towards the shed.

"Eh up, Charles, good to see tha. What're tha doing here?"

"'Ow do, Edward, 'appen I work here now."

"Aye…? Well, that's grand," replied the miller.

"You two know each other then?" observed Ivy watching the bonhomie.

"Oh, aye, I used to see Charles when I visited Lockwood's, when was it…? Back in May, was it?" said the miller.

"Aye, more than three months now."

"Aye, bad do, bad do; all those men out of work."

"Aye, that's right enough."

"So what's tha been doing?" asked the miller.

"This and that, a few odd jobs when I can, tha knows how it is."

"Aye, Charles, that I do. There's many a folk in the same boat. I knows a few lads that's joined up just to put some money on table."

"Ha, too old for that, but 'appen I'd do t'same but for a few years. I'd welcome chance to do my bit."

"Well, I suppose tha'll be doing tha bit here. Folk'll need bread."

"Aye, right enough."

"Any road, best get on. What d'tha need?" The baker looked at Ivy.

"What can tha spare, Mr Buxton?" said Ivy.

"'Appen I can let tha have three."

"Aye, that'll have to do then."

Ivy showed the new baker where the money was kept. "Tha'll need to get coin from shop when it closes so tha can pay miller... One pound fourteen shillings a bag. Tha'll need enough for three and there's a bit spare in case miller puts up price again." She turned and looked towards the miller, who was standing by his lorry and didn't hear the remark.

"Aye, right," said the man, hoping he would remember.

"Don't worry, the girls'll remind tha."

With the transaction completed, Edward Buxton returned to his cab and reversed the lorry from the yard.

Grace arrived around seven forty-five. Betty and Ruth were already starting to prepare the shelves with the first batch of bread. She changed into her working uniform then went to see Ivy.

"'Ow do, Grace," said Ivy as she entered the shed.

"Hello, Ivy, Charles, how are you?"

"Aye, fine, Miss Grace," replied Ivy. "'Appen Charles has shown me how he makes it. Saves on flour, he reckons."

"Morning," said the new baker. "Aye, just a few changes in t'mix. 'Appen it'll save tha a bob or two."

"As long as customers don't complain," said Grace.

"Nay, they won't notice a thing once they've smeared it with jam and dripping," said the baker.

Satisfied all was well in the shed, Grace returned to the shop ready for opening.

In Blossom Cottage, Kitty was up early. She had a new commission for one of her regular clients and was in her atelier cutting cloth. She was finding it difficult to concentrate; it had been nearly three weeks since Freddie had signed up and she had no idea where he was or what he was doing. She missed him so much.

She finished her cutting and there was a knock on the door. She checked the time on the mantle clock; five-to-nine, it would be Molly. Kitty left her project and walked to the front door.

"Hello, Molly, come in… How are you?"

"Aye, well enough, thank you, Kitty."

Kitty stepped to one side to allow Molly to enter when she noticed someone at the gate. It was the postman. She waited for him to walk down the path and he handed her a letter. She looked at the scrawly handwriting.

"Oh, thank you, thank you," said Kitty, her face beaming with smiles.

"Is it from your son?" said the postie. Kitty had confronted him several times over the past two weeks in the hope of some news from Freddie.

"Yes, it is, thank you."

"Well, let's hope it's good news, eh?" The postman touched his cap and walked back up the path.

Kitty closed the door and Molly could see her clutching a letter.

"Is that from Freddie?"

"Yes, it is."

"What does he say?"

"I don't know, let me open it."

The pair went back to Kitty's studio and she took a pair of scissors, slit open the envelope and started to read. It wasn't easy to make out the words; the paper was poor quality and yellowing, and the pencil needed sharpening. Kitty squinted trying to make out the writing and dictated.

"Dearest Mam, I am sorry for not writing sooner but there is little time here. I am at a training camp which I cannot say where. We don't know how long we will be here..." Kitty tried to decipher the next line. "We are... looked after well... I hope you are well..."

Kitty started to cry; Molly put her arm around her to console her. Kitty paused for a moment, then continued. "How is the garden...? Have you... managed to find someone to look after it?" Kitty looked at Molly. "I must remember to tell him about Jed," she said aloud, then continued with the letter. "You can write to me here at the camp... the post office will find me. My fondest love, Freddie." He had written his army number next to his name.

"Oh, Molly, I'm so glad he's safe."

"Aye, I'll let me mam know you've heard from him... and Grace, I know she's fond of him."

"Yes, if you would, tell your mam, but say nothing to Grace for the moment."

From what was said, Kitty was unsure whether Molly was aware of Freddie's connection with the Marsden family but she had no intention of opening old wounds. She quickly changed the subject.

"Have you heard anything from Arthur?"

"Only the one letter. I think Mam has written back."

"Why don't you write to him? You can tell him about your work here; I'm sure he will be pleased to hear."

"Aye, 'appen I will."

Molly had been carrying a hessian bag which she opened.

"I finished this last night." She produced an embroidery of dazzling colour and skill.

Kitty put Freddie's letter down on the table, which she would read again later, and picked up Molly's creation.

"Oh, Molly, this is exquisite. What are you wanting to do with it?"

"'Appen I'd sell it, if tha think it's worth anything?"

"Oh, most certainly. Do you still have the others you have done?"

"Aye, they're in the bag."

Molly took out about twenty similar embroideries which Kitty examined closely.

"These really are beautiful and I know just the place for them. It will mean a trip into town but there's a shop where I buy fancy linen and lacework for the dresses. I'm sure they'll be interested. As it happens, I'm going there this afternoon to buy some more fabric. Why don't you come with me? We deserve a break from the studio. We can stay for a cup of tea."

"Aye, I'd welcome that."

At Colsterdale in hut forty-three, the empty barrel of beer – the reward for Arthur's success at the rifle range – was still in the corner where it had been drained the previous evening. With no beer glasses, the men had used their mess tins as drinking vessels. The room smelled of alcohol.

There had been another postal delivery after the morning drill. Arthur was reading his mother's letter which detailed the changes that had happened to the bakery. Wilfred, too, had received a letter from his mother, which contained an update of events at the butcher's and also the fact that she was taking over the books of the bakery. Wilfred and Arthur discussed the information.

"'Appen I'm not going to know the place by the time I get back," said Arthur.

"Do that knows this Ainsworth fellow?"

"Nay, can't say I do. Hope he knows what he's about."

"Aye," replied Wilfred just as the corporal entered the hut.

"Atten-shun!" he shouted as Lieutenant Hoskins followed

him.

The men leapt off their beds and stood to attention.

"At ease, men," said the lieutenant. "In accordance with Field Service Regulations, this Saturday you will be participating in manoeuvres as part of your field-craft training. You'll be given an objective and a time in which you must complete it. There will be a full briefing on Friday at sixteen-hundred hours… Dismissed."

The officer left the hut leaving the occupants to deliberate on the possible events.

"'Appen there'll be no leave this Saturday night then," said Henry.

"Aye, tha's not wrong there," said Arthur.

Lieutenant Hoskins arrived back at the officers' mess. There were three other new officers that had arrived to complete their training and would be helping in administering the weekend's activities.

"Letter for you, Lieutenant," said the mess orderly and handed Norman a letter.

Norman took the letter and sat down in the corner to open it.

'My dearest Norman, I hope that all is well with you. I am well and about to undertake a new concert tour for Mr Delaney to encourage men to join the fight. I feel that I am doing my bit for the war effort in a small way. We start next week and I am singing five songs. I even have an orchestra. I do think of you most fondly and our meetings in the park. How things have changed since those times. I hope this war will soon be over and you can return safely. Affectionately yours, Agnes'.

Norman was taken aback momentarily; he had been concentrating on his military career and trying desperately to expunge any romantic thoughts about Agnes from his mind. His marriage proposal being rejected had hurt beyond all measure. His mind flipped to romantic meetings in the park, the visit to the theatre, and accompanying Agnes to her first audition. He would swap anything just to relive those fleeting moments. His reminiscences were swiftly interrupted.

"Lieutenant!" bellowed the C.O.

Norman folded the letter and placed it in his breast pocket.

"Aye, sir," he said as he obeyed the command and walked swiftly to his office.

That afternoon, Grace had what was to be her final driving lesson. With no other appointments, Herbert Pease extended the lesson and gave Grace some mechanical instruction, describing how the car functioned and what to check if the car were to break down, which they frequently did. He also showed her how to change a wheel and how to use the starting handle, which required 'a knack', he said. As she drove back to the bakery in the Wolseley accompanied by the car salesman, she felt confident in her ability, and with a little practise she believed she would soon master how to drive an ambulance.

As she approached the shop, she was surprised to see Molly and Kitty standing in the doorway. Archie Slater was next to them, delivering his clarion call to attract more customers to buy his papers. Grace stopped the car at the cabbie stop and handed her instructor the keys.

"Thank you very much, Mr Pease. 'Appen you've taught me well enough; I think."

She paid the man for the instruction and left the car, then crossed James Street and attracted the attention of Molly.

"Hello, Molly, Kitty, what are you doing here?"

Kitty answered. "We've been in town to sell some of

Molly's embroideries. We were about to head home but we thought we would see if you were here."

"That's most kind of you; I've just been for a driving lesson."

"Yes, we saw you in the car, most exciting, and it seems you have mastered it well enough."

"Yes, they need me to be able to drive."

"Who?"

"The FANYs."

"Fannies?" queried Kitty.

"Yes, I'm joining them next week. Come on, we can take a cabbie. I'll explain everything... And Molly, were you able to sell your embroideries?"

"Aye, look." Molly opened her purse to show Grace a pound note.

"My, you have done so well."

"Molly shows a great deal of skill for someone of her age; the haberdasher was most complimentary," commented Kitty.

They crossed the road and waited for the next taxi to take them to Oakworth. James Street was busy as usual, bustling with buses, cars, bicycles, and even the occasional horse and cart. It was only a ten-minute wait and a small queue had formed. During the journey, Grace explained her new vocation to Kitty describing the work of the FANYs.

"My, that sounds dangerous, Grace," said Kitty as she listened to the remit.

"It's no more than what our Arthur is doing for his country... and Freddie." Kitty looked at Grace.

"Have you heard anything from Freddie?" Grace added.

Kitty was not sure how to reply, but with the secret now out, she answered truthfully.

"Yes, I had a letter this morning, as it happens."

"Really! What did he say? Is he safe?"

"Yes, he is, he's still at a training camp somewhere."

"Same as our Arthur, I warrant. I wonder if he's in the same camp," said Grace.

"Well, it's possible I suppose, but Freddie's never met Arthur as far as I know."

"No, he hasn't… Maybe I should write and tell him he has a brother."

"What's this about a brother?" said Molly having overheard.

"Oh, nothing," replied Grace. Molly didn't pursue it.

"No, I should leave things be, it might cause problems if they are in the same camp," said Kitty.

"Yes, you're right. Do you mind if I write to Freddie?"

"Do you think that's wise in the circumstances? Freddie has enough to consider; it might upset him."

"Hmm, yes, very well, I understand. But when you write back, please send him my fondest wishes."

"Of course," said Kitty just as the cabbie arrived at Blossom Cottage.

Kitty got out, leaving Molly and Grace to continue the journey to the house.

"What's this about a brother?" asked Molly again.

"It's of no concern, Molly, let it be."

When Grace and Molly arrived back at Springfield Hall, there were three cars parked in front of the house with their drivers chatting. There was also a pony and trap. Grace remembered her mother had another committee meeting this afternoon. Grace acknowledged the drivers, and as she walked past, she could sense their eyes following her.

Friday would be Grace's final day in the bakery after six years. The queues hadn't diminished to any degree, but with three assistants serving, they were managed speedily. On hearing of her pending departure, several customers wished her well.

In the shed, Charles had taken over the baking completely with Ivy helping and cleaning. On Monday, she would be serving in the shop with Ruth and Betty. The flour supplies had remained steady, but with Charles' new mix, it was lasting longer. As he had said, no-one seemed to have noticed any difference, or if they had, they had not said anything. In the last few weeks, all the bread had been sold by lunchtime but today there would be sufficient to enable the shop to be open later.

Grace finally said her goodbyes around two-thirty when the final loaf had been sold. She took one last look at the counter; Betty and Ruth had started cleaning down. There was the familiar 'clang' of the bell as she opened the door and then she was gone without a backward glance. She walked up James Street; there was a purchase she needed to make before heading back.

Along the High Street past Granger's grocery store there was Pendleton's, a place where you could buy all manner of products to do with the country. Frequented by farmers, landowners and the gentry, it was where they bought riding equipment, shotguns, cartridges, fishing tackle and such like. The window was adorned with outdoor clothing, saddlery and tack. Grace entered the emporium to be greeted by that wonderful smell of leather. It was not a large store and inside it was dark but cosy with stock everywhere. Grace navigated the short distance to the counter around a display of wellington boots, where a man of advanced years with white hair and a ruddy complexion was stood. He resembled a country squire.

"Can I help you, miss?" he enquired.

"Yes, sir. I need a pair of lady's riding breeches, please."

"Yes, I have a variety of jodhpurs in stock; is it for yourself, miss?"

"Oh, yes, jodhpurs," said Grace, remembering the more popular name for the garments.

The man walked into a backroom where Grace could see more stock stacked on shelves, and after a few moments, he returned with a number of items. Grace chose a pair that resembled those worn by Lady Jane.

"You might want to try them on, miss."

"Yes, thank you."

"You can use the stock room," he said. He showed her into the room from which he had just returned and closed the door. "You won't be disturbed, miss."

After ensuring a suitable fit, Grace returned to the shop and paid the proprietor.

"Was there anything else I can help you with, miss?" he enquired as he put Grace's purchase in a large carrier bag with string handles.

"No, thank you for your help," said Grace and left the store.

She returned to James Street and there was a cabbie parked in one of the bays opposite the bakery. Grace had already decided to take a taxi rather than the trolleybus; it would be quicker and she didn't want to be late for her meeting with Lady Jane.

Once home, Grace changed into her new breeches and riding boots. She walked into the kitchen where her mother and Freda were baking and modelled for them.

"They look very fetching, dear," said Mildred.

The sound of the pony and trap arriving prompted Grace to bid farewell.

"Afternoon, ma'am," said the butler as he came to a stop.

Grace approached and the man jumped down to assist her.

"Hello, Bartholomew," replied Grace as he helped her on board.

"I see tha's come prepared, Miss Grace," he said as he clicked his tongue and tapped the horse on its hind quarters with his riding whip to encourage it forward.

They exchanged pleasantries on the journey. The weather was still clement, although cloudier, but pleasantly mild. Grace was not used to wearing trousers and was beginning to enjoy the freedom they gave, so different to her usual skirts.

Lady Jane was at the front of the house holding a wicker trug and deadheading a rose bush, accompanied by her two dogs. As the carriage arrived, she turned and waved to Grace.

"Hello, Grace, lovely to see you," she said as she walked towards them.

Grace was able to jump down from the seat before Bartholomew could lend a hand.

"Hello, Jane," said Grace and they exchanged cheek-kisses.

"My, you do look fine in your jodhpurs."

"Thank you, I bought them earlier from Pendleton's."

"Ah, yes, Basil Pendleton, how is he? I haven't paid him a call for quite some time."

"Aye, he seemed well enough," said Grace as Jane led her into the house.

"I've asked Cook to make a special meal for us tonight as it will be our last time together. Come through into the drawing room." Jane led the way followed by the two dogs, who decided to head to the kitchen.

The drawing room was a smaller version to the one they had used on Grace's last visit but still exquisitely presented. There were two large windows with heavy drapes and pelmets; some hazy sunshine streamed through. The room was adorned with candelabra, tables, chairs, more paintings – this time of working dogs – a large fireplace and two long settees. A tray of refreshments had been set out on the low occasional table positioned between the sofas.

"Take a seat, you must tell me all your news," said Jane as she started to pour the tea.

Grace recounted her driving lesson and the instruction given by Mr Pease.

"It was so interesting and I can change a wheel, too."

"How fascinating, I'm sure that will be most useful..." She handed Grace a cup. "I expect you want to hear the news."

"Yes, please."

"Well, I've spoken again to my friend, Flora, the C.O., and she's more than happy for you to join the unit next Monday. She's looking forward to meeting you." Jane was holding two pieces of paper. "She sent me a pass which will enable you to use the railway." She held it up to show Grace.

"I asked Bartholomew to go to the station and find out the times of the trains. I have the information here..." She read the details from a note. "There's a train from Oakworth at five-past-ten which will take you into Bradford to catch the eleven-fifteen to St Pancras. I've written it down for you." She passed Grace the small note and the travel warrant. "You will need to take a taxicab to Waterloo Station and catch another train to Basingstoke which stops at Brookwood. You can take a taxicab from there to the camp."

Grace took the papers and put them in her pocket.

"Thank you, that's very kind. Did she say what I need to take?"

"Not specifically, but you'll need some warm clothes and your riding apparel. It seems the accommodation is very basic."

"Basic?"

"Yes, it will be tents, I'm afraid, but I'm sure you will make do."

"How long will I have to stay there?"

"It depends on how long before they need you at the front. I would think a few weeks, there will be quite a lot to learn. Who knows, it may be that the war will be over soon; some commentators in the newspapers have suggested as such, but I'm not so sure. I've been to Germany; they are a proud bunch and I am sure they will fight hard for their country."

"As will we for ours," countered Grace.

"Precisely my point."

They finished their refreshments and Jane escorted Grace through the kitchen and out into the back garden. The sun was beginning to make an appearance.

"It's a fine afternoon. Let's go to the moors again."

"Yes, that will be lovely."

In the paddock, Peter the groom was in one of the stalls preparing Sooty for Grace. He had replaced the side-saddle with the traditional version. On seeing Jane and Grace, he led the mare into the yard by the bridle. Grace went to the animal and started stroking its head.

"Thank you, Peter," said Jane.

"I've put the old saddle on like you said, ma'am. Would you like a hand up, miss?"

"Let me see if I can do it. I've a feeling it will be a lot easier in breeches."

With Peter holding the horse steady, Grace clutched the saddle horn, put her left leg in the stirrup, and pushed upwards at the same time as she cocked her leg over the horse. She fell forward slightly but regained her balance and sat up.

"Well done," said Jane. "How does it feel?"

"It's different, but I am sure I will get used to it," replied Grace.

After another trot around the yard, Jane appeared on her horse and the pair wandered off towards the open moors.

While Grace was being regally entertained by Lady Jane, at the army training camp, the residents of hut forty-three were being briefed on the field-craft manoeuvres that were going to take place the following day. There were four huts chosen for this particular exercise and Lieutenant Hoskins was in the mess hall conducting the briefing accompanied by two other officers. He had a blackboard and easel with a diagram drawn on it.

"You will be dropped off in your hut units at four separate points, the same distance from your objective here." He pointed to an 'X' on the board. "Your task is to reach that point. You will be given map references, a map and a compass. There will be a barrel of beer to the winning team; the one that successfully completes the task in the shortest time. But, beware..." He adopted a serious expression. "There will be enemy soldiers patrolling the routes and if you are spotted you will be eliminated. Sergeant Major Stafford here will show you how to use the maps and compasses after this briefing, so pay attention. Marsden, you can lead your hut." He nominated leaders from the other huts.

"Any questions?" The men just looked at each other blankly. "Good, carry on, Sergeant Major," said the officer and he left the mess hall accompanied by his colleagues.

There was a general hubbub around the room as the troops considered the brief.

"Why did they ask you?" asked Wilfred.

"I have no idea; I was trying to work that out meself."

After an hour's instruction on map reading from the sergeant major, which went over the heads of most of the men, they returned to their respective huts.

"So, what's the plan?" asked Henry as they reclined on their beds. One or two had started to read or write letters.

"Don't know, but 'appen we've got a long walk tomorrow," replied Arthur.

Responsibility had never sat comfortably on Arthur's shoulders, having always been sheltered by his late father and, latterly, his mother. Decision-making had been mostly out of his hands. His prowess on the rifle range had, however, earned him a great deal of respect from his colleagues and no-one seemed to question his appointment.

Having been placed in this situation, Arthur decided he would make the best of it. His success in the shooting contest had given him a competitive edge, something he had never experienced before, and if he was going to be team leader then he wanted to win. The barrel of beer was an added bonus.

He got off his bed and spoke to the other fourteen.

"Eh up, lads." There was little reaction. He raised his voice to attract attention. "'Appen tha wants to win tomorrow; what do tha say?"

"Aye," came the response from half the lads; the rest seemed uninterested, preoccupied with other tasks.

He looked around and addressed those. "Well, as I sees it, we'll need to be pulling together."

"So, what do tha want us to do?" asked Henry.

"Well, we need to understand how use this for a start," he said, holding up the compass.

"Aye, I knows how to use one of them," said Eric Shipton. Arthur had had little interaction with Eric, who was at the far end of the hut.

"'Ow come?" asked Arthur.

"Me dad's a hill farmer wi' three hundred sheep, 'appen he spends his life on t'hills. When mist comes down and we can't see us way, it gets us home."

"So tha can be in charge of compass then, Eric?"

"Aye, I can do that for tha."

"Do you know these hills then?"

"Nay, not here, 'appen we be about fifty mile away, but hills round here are all t'same. T'map'll tell us."

"Can tha read maps an'all?"

"Aye, 'appen I can, let's have a look."

The other hut members crowded round as Eric studied the map.

In the sweeping countryside surrounding Laycock, after an hour's riding Grace felt quite at home on horseback and even managed a brisk canter under Jane's watchful eye. The scenery was spectacular – the purple of the heather, the cragginess of the landscape, unforgiving at certain times of the year but today placid and calm.

As they trotted back to the manor, Grace thought about Freddie. Most nights she would remember the walk by the river and how she felt when he held her: the kissing, the intimacy. How cruel that life had snatched that away from her. She considered Kitty's counsel but deep down she wanted to write to Freddie, just to… She couldn't think of a reason; deep down she just wanted to carry on as if nothing had happened, to rekindle those romantic thoughts.

"What do you think of the moors?" Jane's voice interrupted her reminiscences.

"Oh, they're beautiful, thanks, Jane, so peaceful."

"Well, you certainly have taken to horse riding, I can see that."

"Yes, it's wonderful."

"If we had had more time, I could have introduced you to some of the other horses a little more lively than Sooty."

"Sooty's well enough, Jane."

Arriving at the Manor, the groom was waiting in the yard for Jane and Grace and welcomed their return. Grace managed to dismount without assistance to playful applause from Her Ladyship.

Later, they enjoyed a convivial evening and Cook was true to her word in making the most wonderful game pie with all the trimmings. They were sat in the drawing room after their meal discussing Grace's training and what she might expect. She felt a pang of excitement. The magnificent grandfather clock in its beautiful marquetry walnut case struck the hour. Nine o'clock.

"I should be leaving," said Grace.

"Oh, that's such a shame, I wish we could continue. Wait a moment, I have something for you before you leave."

Grace was sat on one of the settees and started studying the pictures around the room in their fine frames.

"Here, I want you to have this," said Jane as she returned to the room and handed Grace a long, thin cardboard box.

"What's this?" asked Grace.

"Open it and see, it's just a small gift to say thank you. I'm going to miss your company."

Grace opened the box as a child would do on Christmas Day.

"Oh, my… but it's beautiful." Grace took out the contents; a beautiful leather riding crop.

"I've had them put your name on it."

Grace examined it and, sure enough, 'Grace Marsden' was written in gold script along the side.

Grace got up and hugged Jane. "Thank you so much…

for everything."

"It's been my pleasure; it's a brave thing you're about to do. I've asked Bartholomew to bring the trap round, he won't be a moment. I think it's raining. I will find you a shawl."

"There's no bother, Jane; a drop of rain's of no consequence."

"As long as you're sure... You will write, won't you?"

"Of course," replied Grace and Jane led her to the door.

"Goodbye, Grace, look after yourself, won't you?"

"Aye, I will," said Grace. She left the house and ascended the awaiting trap carrying her cardboard box.

As Jane had said, the weather had changed and there was steady drizzle as they headed up the lane towards Oakworth. They were not far from the cricket ground when suddenly a car appeared around a particularly treacherous bend. It was driving much too fast for the conditions. The movement spooked the horse and it instinctively reared onto its hind legs to avoid the oncoming vehicle. The momentum caused the trap to overturn, throwing Grace and the butler out of their seats.

Chapter Nine

Grace felt herself flying through the air. With good fortune, the bank was high and grassy and protected her from any serious injury. The butler, however, appeared to be unconscious as Grace got to her feet and examined the scene. The driver of the car had managed to stop before actually hitting the horse, which was now lying on its side restrained by the cart poles, kicking its legs and baying frantically, trying to escape its tethers. Grace immediately went to it and started to stroke its head.

"Shh, shh, my beauty."

The man in the car approached. "I didn't see tha, I didn't see tha," he cried.

"Help me free the horse," shouted Grace.

Between them, they managed to unbuckle the wooden struts which tethered the horse to the carriage. Grace grabbed the bridle, recognising the horse's first instinct when it had been freed would be to bolt. She gradually got the horse to its feet. It was nodding its head trying to escape Grace's grip, but within a few moments, the horse was calm.

"We need to get some help here," said Grace.

"Aye, 'appen there's folk about at cricket club, they'll shift cart alright."

The man returned to his vehicle and Grace watched as it reversed back around the bend. She could see the butler was now stirring and breathed a sigh of relief.

"Bartholomew, thank God you're alright."

He was holding his head. "What happened?" he moaned.

"Trap's tipped over. Can you give us a hand with the horse? She's very shaken."

The butler slowly got to his feet, staggered as he cleared

his head, then walked towards Grace. As he got closer, she could see blood trickling down the side of his face.

"You're bleeding. Here, hold the horse, let me see to it."

He was still very unsteady on his feet but managed to take the bridle from Grace; the horse nodded its head again, still agitated.

"Shh, shh," said Grace, trying to keep it calm. She turned to Bartholomew and examined his scalp. "There's a nasty gash there; here, let me. Try to keep still."

It was taking his strength to hold the horse steady. It seemed to respond to his voice, being familiar with the butler's commands.

Grace undid the buttons on her blouse and removed it, then ripped off the sleeve; it was no time for modesty. She started using it as a swab.

"You might need to see a doctor, but it's clean enough for now. Can you hold it there, try and stop the bleeding?"

The butler pressed the make-do swab to the side of his head just forward of his ear.

"Reckon you hit a rock," said Grace.

"I don't know, I can't remember a thing."

"The trap tipped over; the horse got startled by the car."

"Ah, yes, I remember that."

"The driver's gone back to the cricket club to get some help."

A few minutes later the car returned, more slowly this time, the dim headlights providing only a modicum of illumination. The horse became agitated again but Bartholomew held the bridle tight. They were quickly surrounded by five men; the driver approached Grace, who was stood in her underclothes and breeches.

"I've managed to get some help. What do you need us to do?" said the driver.

"Well, the horse seems calm enough; if we could right the pony cart, we can hitch her up. We need to turn it and point it the way we came. We'll return to the Manor."

The man gave orders to the four burly cricketers, still dressed in their white kits. They heaved on the heavy trap and managed to get it upright. The wheels were sturdy and hadn't buckled. Slowly, the butler walked the horse to the front and the cricketers re-attached the poles and harness that connected the trap, checking everything was secure. Grace was faced with a dilemma; she didn't feel that Bartholomew should be on his own. She thought quickly and approached the motorist.

"Look, I'm going to have to return with this man to Laycock; he's injured and needs to see a doctor. Could you deliver a message for me? My mother will be worried."

"Aye, miss, it's the least I can do. I need to drop these lads back, anyhow."

"Do you know Springfield Hall?"

"Aye, of course."

"I'm Grace Marsden, I live there. Can you tell my mother what's happened? Tell her I'll return in the morning and not to worry."

"Aye, I can do that."

"Thank you, Mr...?"

"James... Daniel James, Providence Mill."

She thanked the men, and Mr James held the harness while Grace boarded the trap. Then one of the cricketers came up to her.

"Is this yours, miss?" It was her riding crop still in its box.

"Oh, thank you, sir, yes, it is. A most treasured possession."

The butler was still not feeling well and it took two of the cricketers to help him on board.

"You'll be needing this, miss," said another of the men holding the riding whip.

Grace thanked the man and took the reins. She had never driven a pony and trap before but having watched the butler on her recent trips to Laycock, she felt she could manage.

"Come on girl, walk on," she said and flicked the leather reins. Slowly the horse moved forward.

Bartholomew sat next to Grace, holding the makeshift swab to his head, and was moaning to himself in a delirium. Grace was very careful, the horse moving at no more than a brisk walk. The lane was in total darkness now but the mare seemed to know the way.

Twenty minutes later, the trap arrived in front of the manor house. Grace jumped down from the cart and knocked on the door urgently. Jane answered in a gaily coloured silk dressing gown.

"Grace, what are you doing back… and in your underclothes?"

"Quick, there's been an accident. It's Bartholomew; he's hit his head."

The pair walked up to the trap. The butler was still incoherent but slowly they managed to get him down from the cart. He was holding the makeshift swab to his head, which was now quite red.

"What happened?"

"The trap tipped over; a car startled the horse."

They half-carried, half-walked Bartholomew into the Manor, leaving the horse and trap outside.

"What about the horse?" said Grace as they reached the entrance.

"Let's see to Bartholomew, we can attend to the horse in a minute."

They went through into the kitchen where the light

enabled them to see the extent of his injuries.

"I think he may have a concussion," said Grace, as she described the incident.

"Are you hurt at all, Grace?"

She looked down at her mud-stained jodhpurs. Her ruined blouse was still on the trap.

"No, although I might have a bruise or two in the morning."

"And your blouse?"

"Used it as a swab."

"Well, that was quick thinking. Don't worry, I will find you a replacement."

"Thank you, but there's no need."

"Nonsense, I have spare." Jane looked down and checked the butler's head, then at Grace. "It's stopped bleeding but it's a nasty gash. I can clean that for him but I think I need to call Doctor Rogers."

"Doctor Rogers?"

"Yes, he's my personal physician. He's in town but he will come out."

"I'm sorry, ma'am, for all this," said Bartholomew.

"Don't worry, Bartholomew, it's not your fault."

Jane went to the sitting room. She picked up the receiver of the candlestick telephone and lifted the earpiece from the cradle which would alert the operator. Given the hour, it was not unusual for there to be a delay. Jane jiggled the cradle up and down several times. Then a voice.

"Doctor Rogers, please. Keighley, two hundred and thirty-seven." The line connected.

"Doctor Rogers' residence," came the voice from the other end.

"Oh, hello, it's Jane Garner from the Manor, my butler has had an accident; he's hit his head. Could Doctor Rogers attend please?" There was another delay.

"Doctor Rogers here, Your Ladyship, what appears to be the problem?"

"Hello, Doctor, I'm sorry to bother you at this hour but it's my butler; there's been an accident. He's hit his head and I think he needs medical attention."

"Very well, I'll come out directly."

Jane returned to the kitchen where Bartholomew was still being cared for by Grace.

"Doctor's on his way. How is he?" she asked.

"I'm not sure, he keeps mythering about the horse."

"Don't worry about the horse, I'll attend to it."

"Do you need a hand?" asked Grace.

"No, thank you, I can manage, but if you can look after Bartholomew. I'll just go and find a blouse for you before the doctor arrives."

Jane left the kitchen and returned a few minutes later with a beautiful high-neck blouse in white lace.

"Here, Grace, you must take this," said Jane, handing the garment to her.

"Oh, but Jane, this is magnificent, I cannot possibly wear this."

"Of course you can, I insist. Here, let me help you with it." Jane supervised Grace's wardrobe. "There, it suits you."

"Not sure about the breeches," said Grace with a smile.

"Ha, yes. I can get them washed for you if you wish."

"No, no, I can see to that when I get home."

"Do you want to stay here the night? It's getting quite late. I have plenty of room, or I could ask Doctor Rogers to call by your house on his return to town."

"That's most kind. I think I would like to stay if it's not an inconvenience."

"Not at all. I will go and attend to the horse and then I'll show you to your room."

Jane left Grace in the kitchen to go and take the horse to the stables and bed her down. The mare was calm now after her experience and was just waiting in front of the house, looking quite forlorn. Jane got onboard the trap and gently encouraged it to walk to the stables. Then it was merely a case of unbuckling the cart poles and leading the horse into the stall. Jane checked she had fresh straw and water. Peter the groom would check on her in the morning.

It was almost midnight before the doctor arrived carrying a Gladstone bag containing his medical necessities. Jane and Grace had helped the butler to his room and he was now in bed. Jane welcomed the medic and escorted him to the butler's quarters; Grace was still with him.

"Hello, I'm Grace," she said as the doctor entered the bedroom.

"Hector Rogers at your service. Can you tell me what happened?"

Grace described the accident. "Hit his head on the road, it would seem."

The medic looked at Bartholomew and examined his wound, then did some checks looking into the butler's eyes.

"Yes, he's definitely got a concussion, may have fractured his skull, too. The wound is congealing nicely and will heal. I'll give you some plasters to keep it clean. You will need to cut his hair a fraction." He demonstrated to Jane what was required.

"Oh dear," said Jane. "Will he be alright?"

"Yes, with rest. I can give him some medicine which might help, but it's really a case of letting nature take its course. I will leave you with something to help him sleep." He opened his Gladstone bag and handed Jane a bottle. "Just a teaspoonful when required but no more than four times a day. Laudanum can be addictive."

Saturday, August 29th, 1914, five-thirty a.m., and it was reveille, at Colsterdale Camp. There were groans of complaint from the hut.

"I've only just got to sleep," said Wilfred.

Arthur was laid flat on his bed staring at the ceiling. "Aye, 'appen we've got a long day, an' all."

Gradually, the men crawled out of bed and made their way to the washroom.

After the first parade, the members of the four huts who were participating in today's exercise were kept back as the remainder of the camp went about their duties. Lieutenant Hoskins and the three other recently arrived officers came out of the main office and the Sergeant Major called them to attention.

"Thank you, Sergeant Major," said Hoskins.

"At ease," ordered the officer. There was a smart click of heels as the order was obeyed.

The lieutenant outlined what was going to happen. As appointed hut leader, Arthur was listening attentively. Four officers would be acting observers, one for each hut; they were introduced in turn to the troops. Hut forty-three had been allocated Lieutenant Shaw, who had recently arrived at the camp just three days earlier. His uniform looked pristine, like it had only just been removed from its packaging. He appeared remarkably young.

Once the briefing had been completed, the men were given squad identification colours; hut forty-three was 'orange squad'. Then they were dismissed and ordered to the stores to collect their rations and weapons – just rifles, there would be no ammunition. They would be in full kit today.

There were four trucks parked up next to the parade

ground which had been allocated as transport. The lads clambered onto the open back and sat on the two rows of benches facing each other. The officers climbed on board the trucks next to the drivers. Arthur was sat next to Wilfred and opposite Eric the sheep farmer.

"Tha got map and compass?" asked Arthur.

"Aye, it's safe enough," replied Eric tapping the breast pocket of his tunic.

"So where do we start from?" asked Wilfred.

"Not been told, 'appen we've got to work that out," said Arthur.

After nearly an hour, the truck stopped. The others had turned off at various points of the journey to their respective starting points. Lieutenant Shaw went to the back of the vehicle.

"Right, men, we've arrived at the start point; you may begin your exercise. I will just be observing but can make no comment on your decisions," he explained.

Shaw's brief was in line with his officer training remit; observing his men, watching for strengths and weaknesses that might need further training. He would be required to provide a full briefing once the exercise was over. The lads disembarked.

"Let's get some idea of where we are," said Arthur and he walked to the front of the truck. "Open up map, Eric."

Eric spread the map over the truck's bonnet; the men crowded around.

"Give us a bit of room," said Arthur.

Eric examined the map closely and then the unforgiving countryside.

The truck had stopped in a gravel area on the top of a sweeping bank which stretched two or three hundred feet down to the left. At the bottom there was a stream. To the right, a rocky outcrop stretched up for about sixty feet and it was impossible to see beyond it. The road had finished and there were no vehicle tracks beyond, just a narrow footpath. Eric lifted up the map and looked at the scenery with an expert eye.

"Eh up, Arthur, I reckon we're here." He pointed a chubby, gnarled index finger at a point on the map. Arthur looked at it closely. "See t'stream, and there's track, look, stops just there, and tha can see incline there."

"Aye, Eric, that's good. So where's t'hill we need to be?"

Eric picked up the map. He had marked the objective with a cross and examined the area tracing his fingers at a possible route.

"I reckon it be fifteen-twenty mile, give or take, but there's no path direct as I can see. If we walk along here for a mile or so, we should be able to see better."

Eric's assurance had given the lads a degree of confidence and they collected their gear and kitted up. Arthur led the way with Eric beside him checking the map for reference points.

"Eyes sharp, lads," said Arthur. "Watch out for enemy."

"'Ow do we know what they look like?" asked Harold Dace.

"I've no idea, Harold, but 'appen if they ain't us they must be t'enemy," replied Arthur.

After an hour's march, they appeared to be no closer to their objective, such was the terrain. They had arrived at a small copse of trees and Eric pointed out a wooden stile on the right-hand side.

"'Appen we need to go through there," said Eric pointing to the trees.

"Aye, we'll take a break." Arthur gathered the men around. "Right, lads, five minutes."

The squad started rummaging around their kitbags to retrieve some food. They were carrying hip flasks for water. The officer was behind the men on his own, watching proceedings; he, too, took on some refreshment.

Although he would not recognise it, the army had changed Arthur considerably. The anxious lad whose life had been dominated by his abusive father and his protective mother had matured into a confident young man in a few short weeks. He was still principled in his political and social beliefs and outspoken in his defence of those less fortunate. It had earned him a great deal of respect from his hut pals, who were happy to listen to his views on the world gleaned from hours of reading newspapers and supping pints at the Malt Shovel. He called time and the group lined up in the same order with the officer following a few yards behind.

After three hours of slow progress, they were within sight of their objective, just three miles or so in the distance. The group were starting to climb; the landscape changed to crags and rocks with streams cutting down small gullies. Suddenly, Arthur spotted movement ahead.

"Down!" he shout-whispered and gestured by lowering his arm. The group dropped low.

"What is it?" asked Wilfred, who had joined Arthur.

"I don't know; there're three lads in uniform yonder, 'appen it's enemy. Go and tell the others. We'll wait here till they've gone."

Wilfred whispered to the group and they passed the message down the line. Everyone was on their haunches or laid flat, including the lieutenant. After about ten minutes, the three soldiers had disappeared from sight.

"Right, we're off again," said Arthur in no more than a whisper. Eric was beside him.

"If we skirt round here, we'll be away from them soldiers

and only about a mile or thereabouts from us hill," said Eric.

"Aye, we'll do that," said Arthur.

Just then there was a loud scream at the back of the line. It was the officer and he appeared to be in trouble. Arthur halted the squad and went to investigate. The lieutenant was stood with his right leg stuck down a hole.

"What's up, sir?" asked Arthur.

"My leg… the ground gave way."

"Stay still, sir, looks like a rabbit burrow; we'll soon have tha out." Arthur looked up the line. "Harold, give us a hand here."

Harold, the former hut bully, moved to join Arthur. As the biggest and fittest man in the squad, he put his arm around the officer's waist then lifted. The officer winced in pain as his leg was freed.

"Lie him down, let's have a look," said Arthur. His right ankle was already starting to swell. "'Appen tha's broken yer ankle," he said. The lads had gathered around.

"We need to bind it tight. Best leave boot on, it'll stop swelling too much. Who's got medical kit?"

Each squad was given a small medical box with a few essentials, including an emergency bandage.

"I've got it, Arthur," said Henry.

"Give us a hand bind his ankle." Henry removed the bandage and wrapping and they bound the officer's ankle as tight as they could. The lieutenant was in a great deal of pain.

"Can tha stand up, sir?" asked Arthur. Slowly the officer stood up but winced as soon as he tried to bear any weight on his leg. "Harold, can tha support the officer? 'Appen we're not far from t'hill. There should be some help there, I reckon."

They continued their trek. With their objective less than

half a mile away, the squad reached a long, steep incline stretching up for about two hundred yards covered with rocks and boulders. Eric looked at Arthur.

"It's either that or three mile round."

"Aye, 'appen we'll make the climb."

At the back of the group, Dace and one of the other squad were supporting Lieutenant Shaw.

"Can tha make it up there, sir?" asked Arthur. "It's that or three mile round."

"No, you carry on, Private, I'll make it."

It took over twenty minutes and a great deal of effort to reach the top, with Harold Dace the coal merchant from Skipton carrying Lieutenant Shaw the last twenty feet. Eric was with Arthur and checked his map.

"'Appen it should be over there, t'other side of bluff," said Eric pointing to a large outcrop about a hundred yards away.

The group lined up and Arthur led them to the rendezvous point, with Harold and Henry bringing up the rear supporting the lieutenant. They rounded the bluff and there was a small flat area with amazing views across the surrounding valleys. In front of them was a small stone obelisk and several men in uniform were stood together next to it; one or two were smoking. They looked around seeing the new arrivals.

Arthur recognised Lieutenant Hoskins; he walked towards them.

"Marsden, well done, your team's the first to arrive," said the lieutenant.

Arthur saluted. "'Appen we have a problem, sir. Lieutenant Shaw's injured; I think he's broke his ankle."

Harold and Henry supporting Lieutenant Shaw reached the welcoming committee. There were concerned looks.

"He needs to go to a hospital," said Arthur.

"I'm well enough if I can get back to camp, I'm sure the doctor will fix me up," said Shaw.

"Well, the transport's about half a mile away. Can you make it, Lieutenant, or do you need a stretcher?" asked Hoskins.

"I'll make it," he said and winced in pain.

It later transpired that Arthur's squad were the only team to reach the objective. Two others were 'captured by the enemy' and disqualified; the fourth group got so lost a search party was launched and they were discovered walking down a road ten miles from the objective trying to reach camp.

Another barrel of beer was delivered to hut forty-three with much celebration.

Earlier in Coltswood Manor, Jane and Grace were enjoying breakfast. Bartholomew had awoken around six o'clock complaining of a headache and dizziness. The cook had taken over his care and he was now sleeping as a result of the medicine.

"I'm glad you stayed last night," said Jane.

"Yes, me too, and thank you for this lovely blouse, I'm going to take it with me on Monday."

"Think nothing of it; it was my pleasure." Jane took a sip of her tea. She was dressed in her silk dressing gown. She looked at Grace. "I really enjoy your company… I'm going to miss you, you know. You will write, won't you?"

"Yes, of course I will."

"Actually, we need to think about getting you back; I'm sure you'll have a hundred things to do. I could drive the trap but I think Rosa could do with a rest today… the mare," clarified Jane, seeing Grace's disconnect.

"I can walk, it's a nice morning."

"No, nothing of the sort. I'll phone Mr Jessop and see if

he'll collect you."

"I didn't know he had a phone."

"I don't think he announces it; he's worried people will think he has money and stop shopping with him." Jane laughed.

"Very well if he's in agreement. If not, I will walk."

"Let me call and ask him."

Having secured Grace a ride back to the hall, Jane and Grace retired to the sitting room to wait.

"I do hope Bartholomew will be well soon," said Grace.

"Well, he's in good hands. Cook is very knowledgeable in medical matters and will look after him. If I know those two, he'll be trying to get himself out of bed just to be rid of her," Jane laughed. "They have that love/hate relationship, but I think deep down they are both fond of each other."

There was a sound of a van crunching on the gravel and then a hoot of a horn.

"That'll be Mr Jessop. Do you have everything?"

Grace was dressed in her jodhpurs, riding boots and her new blouse.

"Aye, and thanks again for this." She held her box containing the riding crop. "I'm so glad it wasn't lost in the accident; one of the cricketers found it."

They reached the door and Jane gave Grace a hug and a cheek-kiss.

"You will keep safe, Grace, won't you?"

"Yes, of course. I promise to write as soon as I can."

The storekeeper was out of his cab and waiting with the passenger door open. Jane walked with Grace and watched her board the van.

"Thank you, Mr Jessop, here's something for your trouble." Jane handed him a shilling; twice the cab fare.

"Thank you, m'lady," said Jessop and doffed his cap.

Back at the hall, Grace's arrival was greeted with a great deal of concern.

"Oh my, thank goodness," said Mildred as she entered the hallway. "How are you, my dear? Come into the kitchen and tell me all about it. Mr James said there had been an accident." The questions were fired without a breath as any concerned parent might do.

It was a Saturday morning; Freda and Molly were in the kitchen and also made a fuss of their sister as she came in.

"Aye," said Grace, and described the incident in detail. "So I thought it best to stay with Jane than to risk another collision."

"Yes, yes, most sensible… I like your blouse, is it new?"

"Aye, Jane gave it to me to replace the one I had to use as a bandage."

"That's most generous of her."

"Where's Agnes?" asked Grace.

"Bradford, they're having a full rehearsal today, she was saying," replied Mildred.

"Your breeches are all muddy," said Molly looking at her jodhpurs.

"Aye, I'll change them shortly; I need to wash them."

"I'll see to them," said Mildred. "Let me make you some tea."

Saturday August 29th 1914 was an important date in the history of Keighley. That evening, Ivy and her sister Glynis were in bed together. It had been a busy time in the bakery and both were in need of rest. In the early hours, they were aroused by a noise coming from the street.

"Ivy, are you awake?"

Ivy stirred. "What is it?"

"Summat's going on. Can tha hear that?"

"Aye, what is it?"

They got out of bed and ran to the parlour window to discover the source of the commotion. They couldn't believe their eyes. There were hordes of men and youths engaged in a pitched battle with the police. In scenes reminiscent of previous encounters in recent weeks, the constabulary were flaying their batons, indiscriminately hitting anyone in reach. Bricks were being thrown in retaliation, causing significant injury. One eyewitness later described the scene as a 'pig market' with the amount of blood being spilled.

Ivy and Glynis looked on in horror as the scenes played out. They noticed a group of youths directly below them walking up James Street, hurling abuse at the approaching police line. Then the sound of breaking glass; it seemed close.

"What shall us do, Ivy?"

"'Appen we'll stay put; we could come to harm if we venture out."

The clashes continued for several hours.

It was seven o'clock on Sunday morning. There was an eerie silence in the street outside and Ivy decided to venture down to the shop to see what was going on. She dressed, went into the parlour, and peered out of the window. She couldn't believe her eyes; it looked like a war zone. There was debris everywhere evidencing the ferocity of the clashes. Bricks, bottles, tree branches, discarded clothing and broken glass littered the entire street. She could see more devastation in the park.

She opened the parlour door and slowly went down the stairs to the shop. As she reached the bakery, she looked in horror. The front window had been completely smashed; glass littered the customer space. There was a gap where the NCR cash register would be. Ivy put her hand to her mouth in shock.

As she returned to the parlour, she felt the need to be sick; she rushed to the sink and retched.

"Ivy, are you alright?" asked Glynis as she joined her sister.

"Aye, but 'appen shops been looted."

"Nay!" exclaimed Glynis.

"Aye, shop window's been broke and till's gone."

"What shall us do?"

"'Appen I need to go to Oakworth and see Mrs Marsden."

"I'll come with tha," said Glynis. "How're we going to get there?"

"Mrs Marsden left some money for flour. We can get a cabbie; there'll be no trolleys yet."

Ivy and Glynis were both wearing their work smocks and white bonnets. The front door was locked; the perpetrators had not bothered to use it with the gaping hole where the window should be.

"Oh, my goodness," said Glynis seeing the devastation for herself.

"Aye, we need to see what's to be done."

They crossed over James Street to the cabbie stop. The road was littered with rubbish, missiles and other items that had been used in the carnage. There were pools of blood among them. It was seven-thirty and there was not a soul in sight.

"'Appen we might have a wait," said Ivy as they reached the taxi rank.

As they waited, the occasional vehicle made its way up James Street, dodging some of the larger items strewn across the roadway, crunching smaller ones. There were just a few people about, gripped by curiosity. They had been waiting for over half an hour before a taxi arrived.

"'Ow do," said the cabbie. "Weren't expecting a fare today. Where to?"

"Oakworth, Springfield Hall."

"Aye, hop in," said the cabbie. Once inside, they made their way out of town.

The devastation was not confined to James Street; the High Street, too, looked like a battle zone.

"What caused all this?" asked Ivy. "Do tha know?"

"Aye, I heard there were some trouble with the German butchers. Folk're getting a bit concerned, you know, with war and all that."

"But why?"

"Don't know, 'appen we'll be able to read all about it on Monday."

The road gradually cleared as they left the town centre and started the climb towards Oakworth. They reached Springfield Hall in about half an hour.

"Wait here," said Ivy as they left the cab.

Ivy pulled the bell chain to attract attention. It was Mildred who opened the door.

"Ivy, Glynis… what are you doing here?"

Chapter Ten

"There's been some trouble in town. Shop window's been broke and they've taken till."

"Who has?" said Mildred, seeing Ivy clearly distressed.

"'Appen it's them rioters."

"What rioters?"

"There's been riots in town last night. Cabbie says it were summat to do with the Germans."

"You better come in; I'll call Grace." Mildred walked to the cabbie. "Wait here, please, we're going to need you shortly. Would you like some tea while you're waiting?"

"Aye, that's very kind of you."

"Very well, someone will bring you a cup."

Sunday morning and the family were preparing for church, except Agnes, who had already left for her lift to Bradford for final rehearsals. Ivy and Glynis were ushered into the kitchen. They could hardly believe their eyes.

"My, what a wonderful house, Mrs Marsden," said Ivy.

Grace, Molly and Freda were in the kitchen finishing their breakfast.

"Molly, can you take the cabbie a cup of tea while we see what has to be done?"

"What's happened?" asked Grace.

Ivy interjected before Mildred could respond. "'Appen there's been problems in town last night. It were terrible; me and Glynis were watching from t'window. Riots and everything, police were charging with batons. Blood everywhere. They've smashed in shop window and taken till."

"I think we can forget church today, Grace. I think you and I should go into town and see what's happening," said

Mildred.

"I'll come too," said Molly. "I can help clean."

"Hmm, I'm not sure cabbie will have space. No, you stay here with your sister… We better change our clothes," said Mildred to Grace.

Molly made the tea and took out a cup to the taxi driver. Ivy and Glynis sat down at the table still taking in the splendour of Springfield Hall, while Mildred and Grace changed out of their Sunday best.

It was mid-morning by the time Mildred and Grace with the two Stonehouse sisters returned to the bakery. They couldn't believe the devastation.

"Aye, it's like this all over town," said the cabbie on hearing the exclamations.

"But why would anyone do this?" said Grace rhetorically as they arrived at the bakery, seeing the window smashed and the broken glass covering the pavement.

Mildred thought for a moment then addressed the cab driver. "Can you be at our disposal today…? Sorry, I don't know your name. I will reward you well."

"Aye, I can be. It's Walter Furness, ma'am."

"Do you know the whereabouts of a glazier?"

"Aye, there's Fraser's on Franklin Street. 'Appen they're going to be busy."

"Very well, can you take me there now? Grace, you and the girls go inside and see what needs to be done. We need to clear up all this glass."

The cabbie drove away with Mildred seeking a glazier as the girls went inside.

"I think I need to see how things are at the butcher's," said Ivy.

"Aye, we'll stay here and start clearing up," replied Grace.

As she left the shop, Ivy noticed the bank over the road; every window had been broken by stones. She turned and walked up James Street to the butcher's. There were more people around now and the shop proprietors were out in force clearing their frontages of debris. She spotted old Walter Nugent outside the greengrocer's.

"Eh up, Mr Nugent, 'ow be tha?" said Ivy as she approached.

"'Ow do, Ivy. 'Appen we was lucky, police caught up wi' mob afore they could do anything here."

"Aye… Bakery's been smashed up and they've taken till."

"Nay, that's grim, Ivy."

"Aye, Mrs Marsden's gone to find a glazier."

"Hmm, she'll be lucky, half the town's been smashed up according to what I've been hearing."

"So, what's it all about, Mr Nugent? Why would folk do all this?"

"'Appen feelings're running high. I heard it were started at Andrassy's."

"The butcher's?"

"Aye, he's German."

"Aye, but he's been here years. Our dad knew Mr Andrassy; he were a good man. He came to t'funeral, I recall."

"Aye, it's as may be, but 'appen he's a German."

"It don't seem right. He'll not have done owt wrong."

"'Appen folk don't see it that way."

Ivy turned and walked the few yards to the butcher's where her two brothers were clearing the footpath.

"Ow do, Ivy, 'ow be tha? Our Ronald's been down to see if tha were alright but there was no-one there. 'Appen there's a right mess at bakery, he was saying."

"Aye, we had to fetch Mrs Marsden from Oakworth. She's gone to get glazier."

"Aye, there'll be a few wanting their services today… What happened? Tha's not hurt or nothing?"

"Nay, we were in t'parlour. We heard all the noise and then someone smashed window and took till. Don't know why, there's nowt in it."

"There's no reasoning with some of 'em. Any road, glad tha's safe, I'll let Mam know; she's been mithering."

"Aye, ta, Ernest, best get back t'bakery. There's a lot to do. Let Mam know, will tha?"

"Aye, will do." Ernest went into the shop to pass on the news.

It was an hour before Mildred arrived back at the bakery. Glynis, Ivy and Grace had cleared all the glass and were starting to tidy the shop. As well as removing the till, the perpetrators had broken the shelving and smashed the glass display cabinets where shoppers could view the bread. Mildred asked the cabbie to wait for further orders.

Two lads, about sixteen or seventeen, accompanied Mildred and she led them into the shop. Grace looked up from behind the counter.

"Grace, this is Joseph and Frank from the glaziers. They're going to measure the window and come back later with some wood to board up the front. It seems it will take a day or two to get the glass."

"Aye, hello," said Grace. The lads doffed their caps. "We need something here, too; they've smashed the displays."

"Oh dear," said Mildred. She turned to one of the lads. "Can you see to that, please?"

"Aye, 'appen we can," he replied.

"Has anyone checked the baking shed?" asked Mildred.

"Aye," said Ivy. "They didn't go in t'shed."

"Oh, that's something."

Just then there was another arrival.

"'Ow do, Mrs Marsden." It was Charles Ainsworth, the new baker.

"Hello, Mr Ainsworth."

"Just heard about t'damage in town; thought I'd come and see tha were alright."

"Hmm, not entirely, as you can see."

"Is there owt I can do?"

"Well, these two lads are from the glaziers and they're measuring up for some new glass. There's some damage to the shelving, though."

"I can fix that for tha," said Ainsworth. "I'll get my toolbox." He looked around assessing the damage and what tools he would need. "I'll be back directly," he added as he left the shop.

By mid-afternoon, the glaziers had boarded up the shop window and the shelves had been repaired curtesy of Charles Ainsworth's carpentry skills. He had also completed a temporary fix to the display cabinets which would serve until the glass replacements had been fitted. Ruth and Betty had also arrived to lend a hand, having heard of the ransacking of the bakery whilst at church; it was all around the congregation, they said.

Mildred's next concern was the cash register; it was their most valuable single item and it would not be easily or cheaply replaced. It would mean a trip to Bradford.

"I can go and ask my uncle if tha can borrow one of his," said Betty.

"That would be most kind," said Mildred. "Let me come with you."

Mildred and Betty walked up James Street. The clearing up operation in the area was gathering momentum with council workers out clearing the roadway. There were others in the park; evidence of the carnage was everywhere.

They reached Granger's Store on the corner. The lights were on inside but the front door was closed. The façade looked as though it hadn't suffered any damage; the window was still intact, but there were pools of blood on the pavement outside.

Mildred knocked on the door and, after a few minutes, George Granger appeared and unlocked it.

"Mrs Marsden, 'ow be tha? 'Appen we was just talking about tha. How're things down bakery? Heard it were a right mess... 'Ow do, Betty," he added, seeing his niece.

"Yes, Mr Granger, it was. I'll get straight to the point. Betty mentioned you may be able to help with a cash register. Unfortunately, ours was stolen by those hooligans."

"Stolen? Why would they do that?"

"Who knows their minds? It was empty; there was no money to be had. It's a pity they weren't in the army fighting for their country like our Arthur."

"Aye, that's a fact... Hmm, let me think." He looked at the serving counter; it was nearly twice the size of the bakery. There were three tills, one at each end and one in the middle.

"Aye, I don't see why not. 'Appen we can manage for a day or two."

"Thank you, that's so kind, I'll make enquiries tomorrow about a replacement. I don't know where, my late husband dealt with such matters."

"Suttons in Bradford... they'll look after tha."

"Suttons...? I don't know them."

"They've always looked after us well enough, I can recommend them."

"Very well, Suttons it is, thank you for the recommendation.

I'll make arrangements to contact them directly."

"I'll get one of t'lads to bring down t'register on wheelbarrow; it's a bit heavy, like."

"That's most kind, Mr Granger, I'm much obliged."

After further discussion about the riots, Mildred and Betty returned to the bakery. Grace was waiting in the shop.

"I don't think there's more to be done, Mam. I need to get back; I have a lot to do."

"Of course, my dear, take a cabbie. I need to wait for Granger's lad, he's bringing a cash register his father is lending us."

Betty interjected. "If tha wants to go, 'appen me and t'girls can finish off."

"If you're sure."

"Aye, it'll be no bother. I knows how to use till; it's same as the one tha lost."

"Thank you, in which case, we'll take our leave. I'll just see Ivy... Where is she?"

"Aye, she's gone to parlour," said Glynis. "'Appen she's not feeling herself."

Mildred was concerned and ascended the stairs to the parlour. Ivy was laid on the settee and raised her head to see who had entered.

"Hello, Ivy, Grace and I are returning to Springfield, Betty says you're not feeling well."

"I'm alright, Mrs Marsden, I seem to lose energy this time of day."

"Hmm, well you make sure you look after yourself... I've been giving your situation a great deal of thought and I think you should come and stay at Springfield when you start to show. We have room enough."

"That's most kind, Mrs Marsden. I don't know what to say."

"Well, we need to look after Arthur's child."

"Aye, that's right enough."

Mildred was reflecting on the day as she and Grace rode the taxicab back to the house. Everything seemed to be in hand, and providing the miller arrived on time the following day, bread supplies would not be affected. She decided not to report the damage to the police; there was no point. She would though need to find a way to get to Bradford to buy a replacement cash register. She had an idea.

"What time is your train tomorrow?"

"Five-past-ten," replied Grace.

"I think I'll come with you as far as Bradford; I need to visit Suttons to purchase a new cash register for the bakery."

"Aye, I would be glad of that, Mam."

Meanwhile, In Colsterdale camp after Sunday morning church parade, the men were in their huts taking a short break before dispersing for their respective duties. Corporal Dorkins entered the hut.

"Marsden, the C.O. wants to see you in his office."

There were murmurs around the hut.

"What's tha done, Arthur?" said Wilfred.

"I have no idea," replied Arthur as he got off his bed and did up his tunic.

He followed the corporal out of the hut and walked up the narrow roadway to the officers' mess. Inside, it was a hive of activity. There was a map of Northern France and the Low Countries on the wall with coloured pins depicting troop movements. Two of the recently arrived officers were looking at what appeared to be telegrams and moving the pins, updating positions. There was also an open copy of The Times on the table. Lieutenant Hoskins was looking on and turned, seeing Arthur walk in.

Arthur stood to attention and saluted. "'Appen C.O. wants a word."

"Yes, he does… stand easy. I'll let him know you're here."

Arthur relaxed, wondering what the summons was all about. The lieutenant knocked on the door, then moments later called Arthur. Arthur marched smartly into the commanding officer's office, stood to attention and saluted. The C.O. returned the salute.

"Ah, Marsden, stand at ease…"

Arthur complied, feet the regulatory eighteen inches apart, hands behind his back.

"I wanted to congratulate you on your successful exercise yesterday; Lieutenant Shaw asked me to thank you. But for your quick thinking, he could well have lost his foot, according to Doctor Mackay."

"Aye, thank you, sir. How is the officer?" asked Arthur.

"He'll be well enough once his ankle has healed. He's in the infirmary in Harrogate. It seems you displayed a great deal of initiative, according to Lieutenant Hoskins, and, of course, you led the only team to compete the exercise."

"Thank you, sir, 'appen I had a good map-reader."

"Yes, but the essence of good leadership is to use your resources to the maximum effect to achieve your objectives, and yesterday you did that."

"Thank you, sir," repeated Arthur, having no idea what else to say.

"In the light of your actions yesterday, I am promoting you to Lance Corporal. We're going to need good squad leaders when we get to France and you've proved yourself to be such a person. Keep it up; I'm predicting good things for you, Marsden. Oh, I nearly forgot, it will mean a slight adjustment to your pay, an extra threepence a day, one shilling and sixpence."

"Thank you, sir," said Arthur.

"Dismissed, Marsden. Oh, you can pick up your stripes at the stores, although you'll probably have to stitch them on yourself." He chuckled.

Arthur stood to attention, saluted, did an about turn and left the office. Lieutenant Hoskins saw him leaving and approached him.

"Congratulations, Marsden, it was a bloody good show yesterday; you impressed a few people, including me."

"Thank you, sir," responded Arthur.

He walked back to the hut with the C.O.'s words echoing in his head; he'd never had such praise in his life before. Arthur was a little bemused. In his eyes, he had not done anything special; 'just doing his job' would be his stock reply, but without recognising it, Arthur had changed. He had also put on weight and was fitter now than he had ever been. His mother would barely recognise him.

Monday morning, August 31st, 1914. At Springfield Hall, there were mixed emotions. The family were sat around the kitchen table having breakfast, all locked in their own thoughts. For two of the girls, life was about to change forever. Mildred was fussing with Grace, making sure she had packed everything she would need to take to the camp. Agnes was nervously going over her songs for the umpteenth time, imagining her choreography. The final dress rehearsal the previous day seemed to go well enough; the promoter was pleased. It had included a small squad from the local regiment who had been detached to support the tour. The six men selected couldn't believe their luck! The costumes and lighting had been checked and checked again. Everything was ready, but Agnes was consumed with anxiety that she would let the company down. She didn't say anything to her mother, or sisters.

Mildred had ordered a taxi for nine-thirty, and she and Grace were waiting anxiously at the front door when the sound of crunching gravel coming down the drive alerted them to its arrival. The three sisters hugged Grace, then the cabbie took the suitcase and helped Mildred and Grace inside the taxi.

It was less than ten minutes by car to the station; a normally walkable journey, but with the heavy suitcase, that was not a viable option. As they reached the station forecourt, Mildred paid the driver. He chivalrously carried Grace's suitcase to the platform.

The station was remarkably impressive for a relatively small community. From the outside, it resembled three buildings joined together, constructed in Yorkshire stone darkened by years of smoke. It had a heavy slate roof with two large chimneys protruding from it. There was a waiting room with its own fireplace, a station master's quarters and a ticket office, but with Grace's fare already secured, she would not be using its service. As they waited on the platform for the train that would take them to Bradford, other passengers arrived.

Grace felt a range of emotions; sadness at leaving her family but also excitement for what lay ahead. She stared down the line as the sound of a train echoed in the distance, a plume of smoke visible behind the trees, then a whistle as it approached. To her left on the other side of the double tracks opposite the small engine shed she could see the signal box looking quite forlorn, isolated and alone. The train pulled in and Mildred and Grace climbed on board, a helpful youth having carried Grace's suitcase into the carriage. The journey to Bradford would take little over half an hour with several stops on the way.

The station in Bradford was a grand affair with an enormous glass canopy; it was very busy with people everywhere, including many men in uniform. Grace and Mildred managed to remove the suitcase from the carriage and summoned a porter who obligingly put it on a pushcart.

"Can you direct us to the London train, please?" enquired Mildred.

The porter led Grace and Mildred to the express which was in steam on an adjacent platform. There was a tearful farewell as Grace said goodbye to her mother with no idea when, or even if, she would see her again. With Grace safely on board, Mildred found the exit and went in search of a taxi that would take her to the emporium to purchase a new cash register.

On the train, Grace made herself comfortable for her long journey. A few minutes later, the engine's whistle blew; there was a lurch, a cloud of steam, followed by the familiar puffing sound as the engine took the strain and and slowly eased out of the station. There were five others in the compartment including two officers in uniform; quite dashing, thought Grace. One of them had manoeuvred her suitcase onto the overhead luggage rack; she acknowledged the courtesy.

As the train steamed across the Yorkshire countryside on its way to her destination, she thought again about Freddie and wondered what he was doing. She was carrying her handbag on her lap and suddenly remembered a letter that Jane had given her with instructions not to open it until she was on the train. She opened her bag and retrieved it. She looked at Jane's wonderful handwriting; like everything about her, so elegant. She slit the envelope with her finger and started reading.

'My dear Grace, I cannot tell you how much I have enjoyed your company over recent weeks. Your dedication and verve are something I admire greatly. I wanted to provide you with some money which will help cover your expenses while you are in training. I will miss you, Grace. Please write and tell me your news. May God keep and protect you. With fondest love, Jane'.

In the envelope there was a cheque drawn on Messrs Coutts & Co, bankers to royalty and the gentry, for fifty pounds; a year's wage for someone at the mill. She looked around the compartment to make sure no-one had seen it and put it back in her handbag.

Arriving at the terminus in London was an overwhelming experience for Grace. Like the rest of the family, Bradford constituted a large city, but London was on a different scale again. Her immediate reaction was to look up at the magnificent architecture of the station under a glass archway even larger than the canopy at Bradford. Then there was the noise; a thousand voices intermingled with the hissing of steam, the urgent puffing of train engines as they billowed their smoke, and the clatter of carriages. Newspaper vendors, flower sellers, tea shops, the smell of oil and smoke, made it a thrilling experience for Grace.

During the journey, she had struck up a conversation with the two officers, who proved to be excellent company, and the time just seemed to whizz by. She chuckled to herself as they seemed to compete to retrieve her suitcase from the luggage rack. The successful officer, a captain, carried it to the platform and called a porter.

"Where are you going?" he asked.

"To Brookwood. I need to go to Waterloo, I understand." Grace showed the captain her letter with instructions. "I'm going to join the FANYs."

"Brookwood…? Well, you're in luck; I'm reporting to Aldershot barracks, so I'm also going to Waterloo. Would you like to share a taxi… at my expense?" he added.

The other officer bade farewell to his travelling companions; he was transferring to Victoria and meeting his fiancée.

"You're very kind, sir," said Grace.

"It's Matthew, Matthew Keating."

"I'm Grace… Marsden."

"Please to meet you, Grace."

"And you, too, sir."

"So, you're going to join the Fannies? They do a marvellous job, you know. Quite dangerous, I might say."

"Yes, I had heard as such, but I want to serve my country."

"That's very noble of you."

The captain was tall, dark-haired, with one of those 'typical' officer moustaches which seemed all the rage. He was carrying a kitbag thrown over his shoulder and walked alongside Grace. The porter was in front pushing the cart with the luggage.

"Are you from Yorkshire, too, Captain?" asked Grace as they got to the exit.

"Yes, from Honley, not far from Huddersfield."

"Have you recently joined up or have you been in the army for some time?"

"I took a commission a year ago, just after I left university."

"University, my," said Grace. "You must be very clever."

"I don't know about that. My father wanted me to take over the family business, but I wanted to see some of the world before considering a career."

"What business is that?"

"He owns two woollen mills in Calderdale."

They reached the exit and joined the queue waiting for a taxi. The officer retrieved Grace's suitcase and tipped the porter a penny. It was a pleasantly mild day and the whole place seemed alive; the buses, bicycles, the occasional horse and cart, indicating a thriving metropolis. They continued chatting while they waited for their ride.

"Have you been to London before?" asked the captain.

"No, sir, this is my first time."

"Please call me Matthew."

She looked at him; she had never seen anyone looking so smart.

"Your family has a bakery, you were saying."

"Yes, my brother is the baker… or was. He's been called up."

"Has he indeed? Where's he stationed; do you know?"

"He's at a training camp somewhere, that's all we know."

"Yes, they've recruited seventy thousand already this month; that's a lot of training."

"Is that what you'll be doing?"

"Among other things, yes."

Cabbies seemed to be coming and going every few seconds and it was soon their turn. The captain helped stow Grace's luggage on the back of the taxi and said something to the driver, then got in and sat next to Grace.

"You're not in any hurry, are you?"

"No, the trains to Basingstoke are quite frequent, I understand."

"Good, because I've asked the cabbie to take you on a tour."

"Oh really? That's most kind."

Sure enough, the taxi drive to Waterloo took in Westminster Abbey, the Tower of London, Buckingham Palace, and the Houses of Parliament. Grace was in awe;

she'd only read about such places in magazines. The officer was only too delighted to provide a running commentary.

Eventually, they entered the station; it was still in the throes of reconstruction and parts resembled a building site. There were plans for a grand entrance with ornate statues and stonework, explained the officer. He had used the station quite frequently and appeared knowledgeable in such matters. They left the taxi; the captain paid the cabbie and retrieved Grace's suitcase.

"We can check the times with the boards; they chalk up the times and platforms... I'll show you."

The station was even busier than St Pancras, which Grace thought would be impossible, but with all the building work going on it was less grand. It covered a vast area with iron girders criss-crossing the glass canopy and had over twenty platforms. Again, there were hundreds of men in uniform waiting for their trains to take them to the many barracks that were served by the station.

They walked down the platforms, with Captain Keating still carrying Grace's suitcase, and after asking a porter found the correct one. It happened she had just missed a train and Grace was faced with an hour before the next.

"Would you like to go for a drink while we wait?" asked the captain. "We can use the Windsor Bar... It's one of the perks of being an officer." He laughed.

"What about your journey?"

"Don't worry, I can arrive any time. I would like to keep you company."

"Yes, very well, I would like that."

The officer was still carrying Grace's suitcase in one hand with his kitbag over his shoulder. He led the way to the back of the station and the famous Windsor Bar, with its beautiful glass frontage flanked by two domed glass booths. The one on the right was decked with an enormous arrangement of flowers, the other with a cash desk. Captain Keating walked up to the attendant and paid the entrance fee.

Inside, it was as grand as one might imagine. Grace was speechless as she looked at the amazing opulence. Shining chrome and glass everywhere. It was also busy with customers, many smoking, resulting in a blue haze. They found a vacant table and the captain placed the suitcase and his kitbag underneath.

"Wait here, I'll get a drink. What would you like?"

"I don't know. I've only ever had a beer. What do you suggest?"

"I'll get a gin and tonic."

After a few minutes, the captain returned with two glasses and put them down on the table.

"I hope you like it." He lifted his glass. "Here's to new acquaintances," he said, and Grace picked up hers and acknowledged the toast.

"New acquaintances," repeated Grace and clinked glasses. She sipped the drink. "What an unusual flavour, quite bitter."

"Yes, but very refreshing." He looked at her with his dark, brooding eyes; it almost took her breath away. "I'm so glad to have met you, Grace. It is such a shame that it has been under such circumstances. I would like to meet you again."

"Yes, I would like that," said Grace. She felt a strange sensation and shivered.

"Well, you could write to me. I can write down my regiment and my number. It will find me." He took out a silver pencil from his tunic.

"I have some paper," said Grace seeing the officer searching his pockets. She pulled out the envelope from Jane and handed it to him. He wrote his details and handed it back. Grace checked his handwriting.

"First Guards Brigade," she said to clarify.

"Yes…" The officer looked around. "Between you and me, we could be seeing some action pretty soon… You will write?"

"Yes, of course I will."

"And I can write to you?"

"Yes, although I don't know the address."

"I can send it to the camp at Brookwood; it will find you."

All too soon, they had finished their drinks and headed back to the concourse. It was still heaving with people. The captain escorted Grace to the appropriate platform where the train was waiting to depart. The compartments were grubby with just two rows of five seats and slam-shut doors. They found an empty one and Grace got in. The captain pushed in the suitcase and slid it along the floor. Grace shut the door but released the leather strap that dropped down the window. She stood for a moment.

"Thank you for your kindness today… Matthew," said Grace, not really knowing what to say. There were so many things that, later, she had wished she had said.

"My pleasure, I have enjoyed your company immensely."

"Me too," said Grace.

There was a distant whistle and slowly the train started moving. For a moment, the captain kept pace, but then he waved, picked up his kitbag and turned back down the platform. Grace was left with all manner of emotions; all of them good.

She watched the London skyline as the train crossed the River Thames. It was a forty-minute journey and late afternoon as the train pulled into the station at Brookwood. There were two other people in the compartment and one of them helped Grace with the suitcase.

After the grandeur of Waterloo, Brookwood was a disappointment. The station wasn't even as large as Oakworth and the chances of a porter would be negligeable. Luckily, there was a cabbie; he saw Grace struggling with her suitcase and went to assist.

"Would you be wanting a cabbie, miss?" It was not an accent she was familiar with and after a second's interpretation she responded in the affirmative.

"Thank you. Brookwood camp, please."

"Yes, miss," replied the cabbie, and with the baggage secured he set off.

It was about fifteen minutes when Grace saw the camp in a field some distance from the road. She could see khaki figures working busily. The taxi turned left onto no more than a rutted track in the grass made by numerous vehicles. They approached a group of tents and stopped. The cabbie removed Grace's suitcase and she paid. Then he was gone.

Grace suddenly felt alone, stood in a field staring at a line of canvas. At the bottom of the field, she could see about twenty horses tethered to a long post. The tent to the right was larger, about the size of a marquee, and Grace walked towards it. Several girls were walking between the tents and one of them saw Grace and approached.

"Hello, just arrived?"

"Yes," said Grace, a little anxiously.

"I'm Hetty, welcome to Brookwood. I'll let the C.O. know you've arrived."

"I'm Grace… Marsden."

She walked towards the large mess tent with Grace dragging her suitcase behind, churning up a great deal of mud.

"Wait here," said Hetty.

A few moments later, an older woman appeared, probably

in her late thirties and clearly enshrined in military service. It was obvious by the way she walked and carried herself.

"Ah, so you're Grace Marsden."

"Yes, ma'am," said Grace.

"Welcome to Brookwood, Lady Garner has told me all about you; she was singing your praises. We need people with that resolve," she added. "I'll let Hetty take you to your quarters and then you can report back here."

Hetty joined Grace. "Here, let me give you a hand," she said and took the other end of Grace's suitcase.

They walked down the line of bell-tents and stopped at the last but one.

"This one is yours; you're on your own at the moment but these hold four and I'm sure you will be having company quite soon." Hetty opened the flap and on the floor were four paillasses with an army blanket on top of each.

"Choose any one you like," said Hetty. "They're remarkably comfortable once you get used to them."

Grace went in and placed her suitcase next to the straw mattress the farthest away from the flap, believing it might be warmer. She realised this would be her new home for the foreseeable future.

Chapter Eleven

Excitement was building with Agnes's first night of her tour only a few hours away. Mildred had returned from Bradford with several carrier bags and news that the replacement cash register would be delivered the following day. With Grace having left for her camp, Mildred called in to see if Kitty would like to have the spare ticket. She accepted immediately.

While the girls were getting ready, Mildred was reading a copy of The News which Daisy had left for her. It had more information about the riots. *'A certain section of Keighley's inhabitants seem to be bent on gaining for the town an unenviable notoriety for hooliganism'*, said the scathing editorial. It went on to remind the townspeople of their duty to be sensible in these trying times. It ridiculed the suggestion that the protests were 'war' riots, or even anti-German, but a continuation of the industrial unrest that had blighted the community for several months.

The editorial ended with a blast on the protesters in a blistering tirade: *'We shall win in this war and destroy forever Germany's military menace in Europe by the action of truly brave men meeting the enemy in the field and fighting him there, not by the outbursts of tap-room patriots and window-smashing warriors, whose courage cannot rise beyond the height of an attack in overwhelming numbers on helpless foreigners, and who can conceive of no nobler duty in this time of stress of the looting of the shops of their fellow townspeople.'*

Mildred felt a sense of satisfaction that her feelings had so eloquently been portrayed by the newspaper editor. In what was described as 'better news', the troop recruitment was ahead of schedule, with numbers in the town approaching one thousand against the original target of five hundred. She wondered with sadness how many mothers would be mourning loved ones once the conflict was over.

With Agnes already at the Alhambra Theatre, it was just Molly and Freda accompanying Mildred and Kitty in the taxi. They had left Oakworth by six o'clock to ensure they were in good time for the seven-thirty curtain-up. The two girls chatted away animatedly, looking forward to their sister's big moment.

They arrived in under an hour and outside the theatre there was a queue of people waiting to enter. Mildred paid the cabbie and requested a return after the show.

"Mam, look at that," said Molly as the four left the cab.

"Oh my," said Mildred.

On the side of the theatre there was an enormous poster with the headline, 'Recruitment Concert Party – starring the new singing sensation, Agnes Marsden.' Around the entrance, there were smaller 'flyer' posters including a very glamorous picture of Agnes created by a local artist, according to the small print. She had said nothing to the family about the publicity; she was too embarrassed. Mildred felt a sense of occasion, but that masked an underlying nervousness, knowing that Agnes would be feeling anxious.

With tickets already in hand, there was no queuing for the box office and the party walked inside. As a recently completed building, everything seemed shiny and new, and more than a little opulent.

"You must be very proud of Agnes," said Kitty as they walked into the foyer, where there were even more posters and an easel with the list of the acts in order of performance. The master of ceremonies was the 'incomparable' Cameron Delaney; 'friend of the stars', it said.

In the large foyer, there were several refreshment stalls selling sweets and chocolates. Kitty insisted on buying a selection for consumption during the performance. There was an usher in a smart uniform helping people find their way to their seats. Mildred approached him and showed him the tickets. The man doffed his cap when he saw they were for one of the boxes. There was a wide staircase with luxurious carpet which led to the entrance to the boxes; another attendant was on hand to point them to the correct door.

As they entered, the scene was breath-taking. The box faced directly over the stage, less than twenty feet away. It was luxuriously decorated, with four velvet-covered chairs in place; opera glasses were in special receptacles in front of them. The beautiful auditorium was bathed in bright lights; the huge curtain, with its elaborate pattern, was down. Below them, there was a hubbub of expectation among the audience as they took their seats. Mildred could clearly see the orchestra taking their places, all dressed in their dinner jackets and bow ties, adding to the sense of occasion. Then the sound of instruments being tuned. The countdown began and the excitement was building.

Backstage, Agnes was trying to stay calm. She had made friends with all the cast and the dressing rooms were buzzing with nervous energy. The chorus girls were in the corridor going through their warm-up routines, stretching their legs in splits that would defy medical science.

Gloria Davidson, who had become Agnes's closest friend, joined Agnes in her dressing room.

"How're you feeling, kiddo?" She had taken to addressing Agnes in this way.

"Hello, Gloria. I'm right enough, although I keep needing the privvy."

"Don't worry, Agnes, we all get like that. I wear extra padding in case of accidents, with my costume it would be embarrassing."

Gloria chuckled; she was wearing a gold lame body suit with black tights and holding three shiny gold-coloured juggling clubs. She flicked up the clubs with impressive skill. Then came the shout.

"This is your five-minute call. Beginners to stage, please."

The chorus girls lined up in the corridor and went on stage, ready to start.

Mildred, Kitty and the two girls were taking everything in; two months ago, this would have been a dream beyond measure. The theatre was full; there were no empty seats that Mildred could see. Mildred remembered the audience from her night at the Hippodrome, and as she scanned the stalls and circle, there were many young men – certainly not of gentry stock, judging by their appearance. Then the orchestra struck up the overture, with George Tooley as musical director conducting. The houselights dimmed and then the curtain rose.

The light was dazzling, the chorus girls starting their high kicking routine. Then a group of soldiers marched smartly from the back of the stage, across the front of the dancers, turned to the audience and saluted. The audience went wild, whistling, hooting and applauding; some had stood up. Then they marched off and the girls were centre stage, finishing their routine to even more whistles.

The spotlight shone in the centre of the stage and on walked Cameron Delaney in an even more flamboyant suit than usual. The audience applauded warmly as he started the proceedings with a few jokes, mostly aimed at the Kaiser, the German army, and… sausages. There were howls of laughter and applause.

Then he introduced the sponsor, Captain Henderson, who walked on in his immaculate officer's uniform. He addressed the audience and explained they were looking for fit and healthy young men to serve their King and country. There would be a special stand in the foyer where they could sign up after the show. He left the stage to more applause and Delaney announced the next act.

In the box, Mildred, Kitty and the two girls were enthralled; the whole experience was breath-taking. All four had retrieved their mini binoculars, giving them close-ups of the performances. In no time, it was the interval and a waiter entered the box seeking drink orders. Mildred was tempted to order something extravagant, but in the end settled for a fruit cordial; Kitty and the girls ordered the same.

In the dressing rooms, there was a huge buzz of excitement. The first half had gone like clockwork and the performers were ecstatic about the audience reception. Agnes was with Gloria in her dressing room, trying to go through her songs for the umpteenth time, but wanted to be sick.

"I can give you something to help your nerves if you'd like. I have a doctor friend who gets me stuff from time to time. I have some in my dressing room."

"I'll manage, Gloria, but thank you," said Agnes, who took another sip of water and repeated the words to her opening song.

The five-minute call was announced and the dancers lined up again in a change of costume, ready for their second performance.

"Well, if you're sure… Anyway, I'd better go; I'm on after the hoofers."

In the box, the excitement was growing as the time for Agnes's appearance drew closer. The curtain opened and the chorus girls appeared, their outfits leaving very little to the imagination. They were greeted with raucous whistles and shouting from the male members of the audience. Cameron Delaney entertained the audience again before introducing Gloria Davidson, described as the 'juggler extraordinaire' by the master of ceremonies. Then, after three more acts, it was time. Delaney came on stage. The curtain descended behind him.

"And now, ladies and gentlemen, for the star of our show," he announced. "A young lady with the voice of an angel... and the looks of a goddess. I give you... Agnes Marsden."

There was rapturous applause. Mildred, Kitty and the girls were on their feet clapping as hard as they could. The curtain opened, the lights dimmed, and then a single follow spotlight. Agnes was silhouetted. The orchestra played the opening refrain. Agnes took one look at the audience and opened her mouth; it was slow and breathy. You could hear a pin drop as her voice filled the theatre. Mildred had goosebumps.

The song gathered pace: 'Kitchener's Boys'. Not the most romantic song, but given Agnes's treatment, it grew into a rousing chorus. More lights bathed the stage, with Agnes at the centre. Whatever nerves she had had just vanished. She worked the audience, played with them.

After she had finished her second number, a wag from the middle of the stalls shouted out, "Show us tha tits, Aggie."

"Tha couldn't handle 'em, duckie," she reposted. A phrase she had learned from Gloria in rehearsals; it was one of Marie Lloyd's favourite lines, she said. The audience went wild and the perpetrator of the heckle sank in his seat and was not heard of again.

The remaining songs followed, each received with

ecstatic applause. She sang the finale and then was joined on stage by the soldiers, marching on the spot as she sang 'Land of Hope and Glory'. Everyone was out of their seats; some were in tears – not just women but grown men were seen with streaks down their cheeks.

Cameron Delaney came on stage carrying a large bouquet of flowers, accompanied by the captain, and presented them to Agnes to roars of approval from the audience. The captain spoke and reminded everyone of the recruitment stand in the foyer before inviting them to stand for the National Anthem. All the performers were on stage including the soldiers; the officer saluted. Then the curtain came down. There were calls for more; the curtain was raised and the performers took a bow, then one final time with just Agnes carrying her bouquet of flowers. She curtsied for the audience, then the curtain fell for the last time and the houselights came on. In the box, Mildred was speechless.

"Wasn't our Agnes good?" said Molly.

"Aye," said Mildred wiping away a tear.

In the dressing rooms, the promoter was doing his rounds congratulating his acts. When he got to Agnes's room, she was sat staring at the mirror with her flowers next to her trying to take in what had happened. He knocked on the door and she turned around.

"Agnes, I just wanted to say, in all my years as a promoter, I have never witnessed what I saw tonight. You were outstanding, my dear… And Captain Henderson was also full of praise. When I last looked, the queue to sign up was out of the door and along the street."

Gloria joined them and was just as effusive.

"Your mam will be so proud of you," she said.

Mildred, Kitty and the girls left the box and stood for a moment watching the crowd shuffling towards the exit.

"I'm going to find Agnes," said Mildred.

"I want to come, Mam," said Molly.

"We'll all go," said Mildred and spotted an attendant. "I'm Mildred Marsden, Agnes Marsden's mother, is it possible to see her?"

"Aye, it should be. I'll take you down," said the lad. They reached the stage door. "Wait here, ma'am; I'll just go and check."

A few moments later, the attendant reappeared with Cameron Delaney behind him.

"Mrs Marsden? I'm Cameron Delaney, come through."

"Thank you, Mr Delaney, that's most kind." She turned and gave the lad a penny.

"I cannot say enough about Agnes's performance," said the promoter over his shoulder as he led them down a long corridor.

"Thank you, we enjoyed the show very much," replied Mildred.

"Here we are," said Delaney as they reached the dressing rooms. He knocked on the third door.

"Are you decent?" he shouted.

"Aye, come in," said Agnes.

Delaney went inside followed by Mildred, Kitty and the two girls. "I have visitors for you."

"Mam!" shouted Agnes.

She was still in her costume seated in front of her mirror. She got up and embraced her mother then her sisters in turn.

"You were very good," echoed Kitty.

Just then they were joined by Gloria, puffing away on a cigarette and holding a hip flask.

"Hi, kiddo, hope I'm not interrupting, just thought you might like to celebrate." She offered Agnes her hipflask.

"Oh, I best not," said Agnes. "Me mam's here." They

laughed and Agnes made the introductions. The dressing room was starting to get really busy as other performers joined them to offer congratulations.

After twenty minutes, Agnes called time; she needed to get changed. The dressing room emptied just leaving the family.

"How are you getting home?" asked Mildred.

"Cameron said he would arrange transport."

"Very well, we'll head home but I'll wait up for you," said Mildred, and the four visitors left the dressing room and made their way to the exit. There was a queue of young men stretching out of the theatre.

The cabbie was waiting outside the entrance.

"That was the best night ever," said Molly as the taxi pulled away. Mildred thought the same.

Tuesday, September 1st, 1914. Grace had found sleeping difficult; lying on a straw mattress with just a blanket for covering was something she was not used to. Then there was the noise. The wind caused the canvas to flap, then the horses would make their snickering sounds, all serving to disrupt Grace's night. She was also wrestling with her thoughts, mostly about the dashing captain. She would write to him today, she had decided. Freddie was less prominent in her mind for the first time in a while.

Hetty had proved to be an excellent mentor, and following a further meeting with the C.O., she had taken Grace around the camp and introduced her to various people. She would try and remember their names this morning.

Hetty gave Grace some personal background. Her father had been a vicar before his untimely death and her mother, a nurse before marrying. Caring for others had therefore come naturally to Hetty. She eventually joined the FANYs the previous March, having read an article in a newspaper; they were seeking volunteers and she applied.

Before the start of the war, preparations had been put in place for the unit to be sent to Ireland in the light of the present tensions there. Lieutenant Ashley-Smyth had even spent a fortnight in Belfast to arrange stables and housing, but all that had been put on hold since the start of hostilities.

"I think we'll be stuck here until they know what to do with us," Hetty had exclaimed in frustration.

Grace dressed and folded her blanket as she had been instructed. She was to report to the mess tent for duty at seven-thirty. Hetty was waiting as Grace walked up the line of tents and arrived at the large marquee which served as the mess tent.

"Good morning, Grace, have you had breakfast yet?"

"Good morning, Hetty. No, not yet."

"No, me neither. Come on, I'll show you."

There was another large tent adjoined at the back of the mess where tables and chairs were set out. Like the rest of the marquee, a tarpaulin floor had been laid so underfoot was reasonably dry. The field kitchen was in an adjacent tent. Several girls were eating slices of bread and drinking tea from large urns.

"We help ourselves," she explained. "If you want a shower, the soldiers have constructed one for us. It's not very good or very warm, but it does the job. There are towels there."

"Thank you, I will do that directly."

"Oh, you'll need a uniform, too. I'll take you to the stores after you've had your shower and get you kitted out."

By ten o'clock, Hetty and Grace, suitably clothed, were at the horse lines helping groom the mounts with four other 'Fannies'. For the moment, Grace's duties each morning would involve working with the horses, including exercising them; something she was thrilled to do. The afternoons would be learning about the medical side of the role, which included lectures by officers from the Royal Army Medical Corp on field treatment, dealing with wounds, head trauma and the like. They would also be practising stretcher duties, carrying 'patients' over a cross-country course. Unfortunately, the only ambulance they possessed was horse-drawn, much to Grace's disappointment.

That evening before it got too dark to see, she wrote two letters; one to her mother, the second to a certain dashing captain who had been in her thoughts. It had been a warm and pleasant day, but around nine o'clock, there was a change in the wind direction. The atmosphere was heavy, then suddenly, the first clap of thunder. The storm was nowhere near as destructive as the one in July which had so devasted Keighley, but bad enough. She could hear the horses, agitated at their posts. Water dripped through the flimsy canvass. She opened the tent flap and looked out. It was pouring down.

She left the tent and spotted several others running towards the horses. She joined them and reached one of the mares. She grabbed the bridle, as she had done after the accident on the lane, and stroked its head trying to calm it. Luckily, the thunder was isolated; it was just torrential rain and they soon had the horses under control.

Hetty had also been involved and walked towards Grace holding one of the horses by the bridle.

"Goodness," said Grace. "That was unexpected."

"Yes, but I think they're all calm now; they've been trained under gunfire so they'll soon settle."

With all the horses checked, Grace walked back to her tent with Hetty.

"Goodness, I'm soaked," said Grace. "And the tent's leaking."

"Yes, they all will be. They're not designed for rain. I think they were intended for desert use... Have you got a change of clothing?" added Hetty.

"Yes, but I think my blanket will be wet."

"I can find you a spare," said Hetty.

They walked back to Hetty's tent where a spare blanket was found. Grace thanked her and returned to her tent. Inside, the water was dripping through in several places. It was going to be a wet night.

Tuesday morning, Keighley still showed evidence of the riots. The bakery bore the scars with its boarded window. The disturbances had had little impact on trade, however, and the usual queues had formed well before opening. Charles the new baker was now very much at home in his new surroundings and no-one seemed to notice his different mix; or if they had, no-one was saying anything. Ivy, Betty and Ruth were serving the customers while Glynis was upstairs in the parlour tidying up.

Around eleven, a man wearing overalls and a flat cap entered the shop. He approached the counter.

"Suttons of Bradford, there's a new till for tha; where do tha want it?"

Ivy took control. "Here, please," she said, indicating the space where the replacement was situated.

It took a few minutes, but eventually the man and a young lad assistant had carried in the new cash register and removed the borrowed one, which they placed in the corridor.

"I'll let my uncle know," said Betty. "'Appen he'll send lads down to collect it."

There was a slight disruption as the cash registers were

switched and a brief instruction on operating the new one.

"It's the latest model," the man announced proudly.

It was gone one a.m. when Agnes eventually returned from the theatre. Mildred had fallen asleep in the chair in the sitting room but awoke as soon as she heard a vehicle crunching the drive.

"Hello, dear," said Mildred as she went to greet her daughter.

Agnes had changed but she was still wearing the garish stage makeup and hairstyle from the performance. Her costume would remain at the theatre ready for Tuesday's performance. Mildred made them both a drink and chatted for over half an hour before the adrenaline rush had subsided and Agnes was overcome by overwhelming fatigue. She would lie in.

Later that afternoon, Mildred was in the sitting room; Agnes had already left for the theatre in the car sent by the promoter. Mildred had taken a stroll to the village store to buy The Telegraph and Argus, the Bradford newspaper. All day the talk was of the theatre production and Agnes's performance. Mildred had already bored Jed the gardener, who eventually had to call time on their chat as he had 'things to do' in the meadow.

Daisy Jessop was in the kitchen preparing food when she heard shouts coming from the sitting room.

"Whatever's up?" she said as she went to see the reason for the commotion.

"Look, Daisy, see what it says."

Daisy picked up the newspaper and started reading. 'A star is born' was the banner headline on the entertainment page. *'It seems like we have a new star in our midst; Agnes Marsden, a baker's daughter from Keighley, drew rapturous*

*applause from the first night audience in Cameron Delaney's
new concert tour in support of the army recruitment
campaign.'* The review continued to extol Agnes's
performance, commenting on her maturity and vocal ability,
even suggesting she could be the next Marie Lloyd.

"My, that is just wonderful, Mildred."

"It most certainly is. I will save it for Agnes."

News of the war was filtering through to Colsterdale
Camp. It was clear that the Franco-British armies were
experiencing difficulties against better prepared German
forces. The retreat from Mons and the subsequent Battle of
the Frontiers had left the Germans on the outskirts of Paris.
However, a major counter-offensive was about to take place.

Arthur's promotion had been surprisingly well received
by his pals. One of the lads, a tailor from Silsden, had even
sewed on his stripes, one on each shoulder. Arthur had
mixed feelings; he had led a solitary existence for most of
his life. For him, telling people what to do was just common
sense; he'd done it without thinking. He had yet to hear what
his new position required, but it was clear he was now 'in
charge' of hut forty-three.

With matters on the continent starting to cause concern,
training was going to be stepped up and the C.O. had called
the officers and squad leaders together. Arthur was included
in this briefing. It was after lunch and Arthur was in the mess
hut, unsure why he was there. A number of chairs had been
set out facing a notice board with a map attached. There
were about twenty men present when Major Foster entered
the room accompanied by Lieutenant Hoskins, the senior of
the four officers. The assembled stood up.

"Be seated, gentlemen," said the C.O. He stood
authoritatively in an 'at ease' posture but looked far from it.

He started confidently. "I wanted to brief you today on the progress of the war. I know some of you have been following events closely in The Times."

Arthur chuckled to himself.

"I might say that it does not paint a very positive picture, but I am confident our boys will soon prevail. Now, I know you're all anxious to get over there and play your part, but it's important the men are fully trained before facing a formidable foe. For that reason, training is being stepped up. We have this morning taken delivery of a Vickers machine gun which I have asked Sergeant Major Stafford to demonstrate this afternoon. A selected group will be trained on how to fire it. There will also be additional bayonet practice as part of the morning drill. At this moment, I can't give you a date when we will be called, but every hour you are here you must continue to perform your tasks diligently."

Major Foster continued his briefing, using the map to illustrate troop movements.

Arthur left, mulling over the content. He decided to take a short detour and called into the post office on his way back to the hut. There was another letter waiting for him; the postmark was dated yesterday. He raised his eyebrows, impressed at the speed of the delivery. He recognised the handwriting straightaway and felt his mood change. He put it in his tunic pocket to read later.

On his return, he related the news to the hut to looks of resignation and shrugs of shoulders. He had noticed morale had deteriorated in recent days after the high from the exercise at the weekend. But it was Wilfred, his best pal, who was causing him real concern. He seemed morose and uncommunicative. He was also struggling with the physical demands of the training. Arthur decided to confront him.

"Eh up, Wilfred, what's up? Tha seems not thaself."

Wilfred was just sat on his bed, staring at the wall opposite.

"Nowt, Arthur, 'appen I'm thinking on t'shop."

"Have tha not heard owt from tha mam?"

"Aye, she says they're managing well enough, but our Phyllis is no butcher. She's a lass, and our Ernest is nowt but a lad."

"Aye, well, there's not much tha can do about it, Wilfred. If tha want my advice, tha should stop mithering; it serves no purpose, tha'll just get mardy."

"Aye, but easier said than done."

"Tell tha what, I've just had another letter from Ivy; I've not read it yet. Would tha like me to share it with tha? 'Appen it might lift tha spirits."

"Aye, go on, why not. Can't do any harm."

Arthur took out the envelope from his pocket and opened it. It was headed, 'Sunday night'. He squinted at the pencilled script and started reading. *'Dear Arthur, hope tha's well. I am thinking about tha all the time and wish that tha were safely back where you belong.'* Arthur decided not to read that part out loud and mumbled incoherently. He raised his voice. *'There was a big riot on Saturday night and someone broke the shop window and took the till. Me and Glynis were upstairs. It were really frightening. This morning, your mam came down and saw to everything. They have put wood at the window until we can get glass. I hope tha's safe. Sending tha much love, Ivy'.* He read the words slowly but omitted the salutation.

Wilfred sat upright. "What's that all about? Did she say owt about butcher's?"

"Nay, Wilfred, just what I read. I don't know what's happening. Can they still make bread or owt? She's not said." Now Arthur was worried. His attempt to bring some cheer to Wilfred had backfired. He tried again. "'Appen tha Glynis's moved in with Ivy. That's good; it'll be company for her." But Wilfred was back in his depression.

Arthur needed to find out what was going on back home. He would write following the afternoon's training.

After the break, Arthur led the group to the rifle range for the machine gun demonstration. With only a small amount of ammunition, it was a very short session, but with the way it scythed down the target posts they had used for rifle shooting, they were left in no doubt as to its destructive capability.

"I wouldn't want to be on the other end of that," said Henry as they watched the Sergeant Major sweep right and left, destroying everything in its path.

"Aye, well, 'appen Fritz's got 'em, an' all," replied Arthur. The group around him went quiet.

The atmosphere at the Alhambra Theatre concert party was euphoric following the reviews from the previous night's performance. Agnes was in her dressing room being attend to by the costumier, struggling to get her dress in place without her top giving way and exposing more than was acceptable. Safety pins solved the problem. There was knock on the door.

"Come in," shouted Agnes. It was Cameron Delaney.

"Agnes, my dear, how are you this evening?"

"Aye, well, thank you, Cameron."

"You've seen the reviews, I take it?"

"Aye, I have."

"Many congratulations, my dear, and well deserved if I may say. I wanted to tell you about arrangements for the rest of the week. As you know, we're in Bolton Thursday and Friday, with a gala performance at the Palace Theatre

Manchester on Saturday. There'll be over three thousand people at that one. I've been informed that tickets are selling well; I spoke to the box office this morning. It seems your reputation has gone ahead of you."

"Thank you," said Agnes. She could feel the weight of expectation rising.

"I've arranged for lodgings for you in Bolton and Manchester. I thought you could share with Gloria; I know you two are friends."

"Aye, that will be most acceptable."

At the promoter's request, the costumier had left the room; it was just Delaney and Agnes.

"I wanted to raise another issue with you, Agnes. Have you thought at all about an agent?"

"No, Cameron, I can't say I've put a mind to such a thing."

"Well, if I may be so bold, I would like to offer my services as your manager. I have no doubt I can get you onto the London stage when we have finished this tour. I will also introduce you to Miss Lloyd."

"Miss Lloyd…? Why, that would be a dream come true, it really would, Cameron, and I will be happy to be guided by you."

"I am delighted, Agnes. I have no doubt you have an excellent career ahead of you." The promoter left the dressing room with a smile as broad as would split his face in two.

That night, Agnes was again the star of the show and, importantly, the recruitment of new soldiers had exceeded expectations. The fame of Agnes Marsden was beginning to achieve some momentum.

Chapter Twelve

Tuesday, October 20th, 1914.

Grace had been at the camp for over six weeks and during that time her training had been intense. It was a combination of physical activities – route marches, grooming and exercising the horses, cross-country stretcher-bearing, which she disliked intensely as she would always end up covered in mud, and medical training. She had spent some time at the nearby R.A.M.C. hospital in Pirbright where wounded soldiers had been sent from the front in Belgium. There she witnessed the most horrific sights imaginable as they tried to put back the broken pieces of young men's lives.

She had got used to the rather spartan conditions, the leaky tent and beetle-ridden mattresses, and had built up an enduring friendship with Hetty, but her real joy was the regular letters she was receiving from a certain dashing captain. The contents of these letters had become more and more amorous to the extent that thoughts of Freddie had virtually disappeared.

She was in the mess tent finishing her lunch when Hetty walked in.

"Ah, there you are, Grace, I've been looking for you. There's a letter for you." She handed over the envelope. "It's from your captain by the look of it. He must be very keen on you; that's three in the last week."

"Yes, and I have feelings for him, too, I don't mind saying."

"Oh, how romantic. I wish I had a beau writing to me. I just get my stupid brother and his boarding school capers." She laughed. "I'll leave you to it, I'm going to tend the horses."

"I'll be with you shortly."

Grace opened the letter. *'My dearest Grace, How fondly you write, it makes my head spin and my heart whirl. I have some good news; I have been able to take my leave this weekend and I'm looking forward so much to meeting you again. As you said you would be free all weekend, I have taken the liberty of arranging a hotel for Saturday night. It's in The Strand and close to the theatres. I thought we could go to one of the shows. 'The Glad Eye' is playing at the Strand Theatre, which I am sure will meet with your approval. My train will arrive at ten o'clock on Saturday morning and I will wait for you in the Windsor Bar. Please write back and let me know. Yours in hope, Matthew'.*

Grace's heart skipped a beat. She walked back to her tent and scribbled a hasty reply. *'My dearest Matthew, I need to be quick, Hetty is waiting for me at the horses. Yes, I would love to go to the theatre and the production sounds most interesting. There is a train from Brookwood arriving in Waterloo about ten-twenty. I will meet you as arranged. Yours in anticipation, Grace'.* She addressed the envelope and returned to the mess hut where there was a postal delivery service. She skipped down to the horse posts unable to hide her joy.

There were strict rules on 'entertaining' men friends. FANY's were not allowed to dine alone with a man and would be required to be accompanied with another FANY in male company. Hetty would be sworn to secrecy.

At the outbreak of war, the FANY's commanding officer had immediately offered to support the British army with their services. Surprisingly, this offer was declined, believing the front was no place for a woman. However, a chance meeting with a Belgium official led to Lieutenant Ashley-Smyth being invited to Belgium to discuss deployment under their command, subject to the agreement of the British authorities. The permission was granted and the C.O. sailed over to Belgium in mid-September to make arrangements.

After experiencing some of the horrors of war first-hand, she eventually returned to Calais where she was based at Lamarck Military Hospital. It was formerly a Convent school, in desperate need of repair, and had been converted into a casualty clearing hospital for wounded Belgian soldiers. With the allied fighting in Northern France and Flanders intensifying, it was also being used to care for British troops before being sent back to hospitals in England. She had returned to Brookwood the previous Thursday.

Having completed their duties, Hetty and Grace returned to the mess hut for lunch to be greeted by a summons by the C.O. They made their way to her 'office' next to the mess tent.

"Ah, Mallender, Marsden, come in," she said seeing them arrive outside. The girls stood to attention. "At ease… I wanted to let you know I'm returning to Calais next week. I've managed to acquire a motor ambulance which is being delivered on Friday and I'll be taking it with me. The reason I have asked you here is I'm looking for six volunteers to join me."

Hetty looked at Grace. "Well, you can count me in," she said.

"Yes, me too," added Grace.

"Very well, thank you. We'll be leaving next Tuesday for Calais and there will be some preparation over the next few days."

Grace thought in horror. "Oh, Lieutenant, I have leave arranged for this weekend."

"Hmm, yes, of course… it's not ideal, but there should be enough time to complete the preparation as long as you're back on Sunday evening."

"Yes, Lieutenant."

"What about you, Mallinder?"

"No, I can cover for Grace, I've no plans."

"Thank you, there will be four others. When I've spoken to them, we'll meet again here at eighteen-hundred hours for an initial briefing. Dismissed."

Grace breathed a sigh of relief as she left the C.O.'s tent.

"Thanks, Hetty, for covering for me."

"Ha, ha, that's one favour you can return for me one day."

The mood in Colsterdale Camp was deteriorating; whilst training had been ramped up, there was still no news of deployment. The danger of 'over-cooking', the condition where the soldiers had passed the peak of readiness, was all too apparent. The men were tired and restless; conflicts were breaking out which had resulted in fights and punishment. Exercises were being undertaken with less enthusiasm. To try to alleviate the boredom, there had been two more Saturday night visits to Masham, but again, they were relatively low-key events; even getting drunk had lost its appeal for the majority.

In hut forty-three, Arthur could feel the lethargy among his squad; it was becoming more difficult to get them to obey orders, but it was his best pal Wilfred who was causing him the greatest concern. The physical demands were still a real issue, he was never the fittest of people, and his eyesight was so bad he could hardly see the target on the rifle range, never mind hit it. Off duty, he appeared to be in a deep depression. The occasional letter he received from his mother had lifted his mood to some extent, but they only served to remind him of home. At least his siblings seemed to be coping in the shop.

The war in Europe had reached a stalemate. After initial territorial gains which had brought them close to Paris, the German army was being driven back by the combined British and French troops following success at the First Battle of the Marne. The German retreat between 9th and 13th September marked the end of their attempt to defeat France by crushing the French armies with an invasion from the north through Belgium and in the south over the common border. The rival forces began reciprocal operations to envelop the northern flank of their opponent in what became known as the Race to the Sea, which culminated in the First Battle of Ypres. Both armies ground to a halt and had dug in; it was the start of the trench warfare which was going to define the war.

While Grace was considering her forthcoming meeting with Captain Keating, Arthur was laid on his bed. He had just received another letter from Ivy, who had been keeping him updated on things at the bakery. The shop window had been repaired and flour supplies were holding up. Charles the new baker seemed to be in control of everything. The main protagonists of the riots had been gaoled, according to the Keighley News. Ivy's sister Glynis had moved in and was keeping her company, and so on. Fairly mundane things, but it kept Arthur in touch with events at home.

Mildred had also been writing, although her letters were not so frequent and were dominated by news of Agnes's triumphant concert tour. He had yet to write to Agnes.

Arthur started reading Ivy's latest. *'My dear Arthur, I have some news which I have been loath to tell you for fear you might lose affection for me, but the thing is, I am with child. I know it will come as a shock to you as it was for me. I have told your mam and she has said I can stay with her to save any talk. I have not said owt to my mam yet. Your mam said she will tell her. I hope you're safe. I think about you and pray you'll return to me and your child safe and sound. With fondest love, Ivy'.*

Arthur read it again. The colour drained from his cheeks. Wilfred was on the next bed and noticed Arthur's reaction to the letter.

"Eh up, Arthur, are tha alright? Tha looks like tha's seen a ghost. Nowt wrong is tha?"

"What…? Nay, nay. Everything's well enough."

But Arthur wasn't alright; he was trying to process the information and the repercussions. He had no idea how he felt. He would write back to Ivy but had no thought on what he was going to say.

At Springfield Hall, Mildred's charity drive was gaining momentum. At the end of September, a group of refugees from Belgium had arrived in the area and there was a great deal of sympathy for their plight. The News ran an article describing their journey and Mildred and her committee rallied to the cause to provide them with food and clothing.

Saturday, October 24th, 1914. There had been a great deal of excitement when the new ambulance arrived at the camp the previous day and it was quickly surrounded by several of the girls wanting to take a closer look, including Hetty and Grace.

It was a strange-looking vehicle and not the most comfortable form of transport. It was built by Wolseley, the same manufacturer who had designed the car in which Grace had learned to drive. The driver and passenger sat behind a long bonnet in an open cab with a pull-down concertina canopy, a larger version to that used on baby's prams. Behind the driving compartment was a box-like container where the patient and medical equipment were housed. It was covered in a khaki canvas with a red cross painted on the side; it appeared quite flimsy. Nevertheless, it was a huge improvement on the horse-drawn ambulances that were the norm at this time.

Grace was at Brookwood station; the C.O. had driven her in the new ambulance as she wanted to get used to driving it. She shivered as she stood waiting on the platform for the train, though not because it was particularly cold. It was a windy morning with the threat of rain but still quite mild for late October. Grace had dressed in her best outfit, the one that Kitty had made, together with a fine hat and booties. She was carrying her handbag and a small valise she had borrowed from Hetty containing her overnight things. She didn't want to drag her big suitcase around.

The train arrived and it was crowded, the numbers swelled by men in uniform. She walked down the green carriages and found a compartment that had two vacant seats then got on. By the time the train reached Waterloo, Grace's carriage was crammed with passengers. All the seats were taken and they were even standing in the middle of the compartment, making it extremely claustrophobic. Grace felt a sense of relief as they pulled into the terminus. The large clock on the concourse said ten-twenty-five as she passed through the ticket barrier and made her way to the bar. She felt a mixture of nervousness and excitement. She appeared at the entrance and spoke to the attendant.

"Captain Keating is expecting me."

"Yes, miss, go through, he's seated on the right."

Grace entered the bar and could see the captain in the corner dressed in a smart suit; her stomach churned. He seemed to be scanning the entrance. He saw her and immediately rose from his seat. He was smiling as he took her valise and placed it under the table next to his own, then he turned to her.

"Grace, it's so wonderful to see you." He kissed her warmly on the cheek as you would a fond aunt.

"I've taken the liberty of ordering some coffee and scones; it will be here shortly."

Despite his heritage, there was no trace of a Yorkshire accent, his voice directly from the gentry set. Grace looked at him. He was as handsome as she had remembered, and embellished, in her many dreams.

"Thank you, kind sir," she said demurely.

He indicated to the seat in front of him and he waited as she made herself comfortable. A waiter appeared in a smart uniform carrying a large, fancy tray with two gold-coloured carrying handles containing a coffee pot, two bone-China cups, milk, sugar and a plate of scones, butter and jam. He placed it on the table. The captain thanked him.

"How do you like your coffee?"

"What do you suggest? I've not had coffee before."

"I like it with a splash of milk."

"Very well, as you recommend, Matthew."

He poured two cups, added the milk, and watched as she took her first sip.

"That tastes nice. We have always had tea at home."

"I'm pleased you approve," said the captain. "It's so wonderful to see you, Grace, you have been on my mind a great deal."

"Yes, and you, too." She looked at him under her eyelids.

The pair continued chatting as they ate their scones, their togetherness obvious to any passing observer. The captain ordered another pot of coffee as they continued swapping news, Grace updating him on tales from the camp, many of them amusing, and the arrival of the new ambulance.

"I can't bear the thought of you leaving, Grace." Her hand was resting on the table and he took it, squeezing it fondly. "It could be very dangerous."

"Then so be it, but I want to do my duty. Why should men take all the risks?" she said assertively.

"That's so admirable a sentiment, Grace."

"But surely you will be joining the fight soon enough?"

"Yes, that's true, and it could happen at any time."

"Have you heard anything?"

"Not officially, but things in Flanders are not going so well. We are facing a determined enemy."

"Yes, we have been following events avidly."

After another half an hour, the captain suggested they leave for the hotel. Grace collected her belongings and they headed for a taxi arm in arm. The captain was carrying his small leather suitcase.

At Colsterdale Camp, Lieutenant Hoskins had received another letter from Agnes, his first in a fortnight. Returning to his quarters, he took time out to read it.

'My dearest Norman, I hope my letter finds you safe and well. I am sorry for not writing sooner but the tour has kept me so occupied. I cannot believe we have been on the road (that's what they call it!) for six weeks. Tonight we are in Darlington at the New Hippodrome and Palace Theatre of Varieties. Marie Loftus performed there recently so we are in good company. We continue to play to enthusiastic audiences and every night there is not a seat to be had. Cameron has been most complimentary and has even mentioned a London show when this run has finished. I do miss you and I think about you fondly. It would be very lonely if it were not for my greatest friend Gloria who keeps me amused and entertained. I will write again soon. Affectionately yours, Agnes'.

Lieutenant Hoskins read the letter again. He was trying to look for signs of affection but couldn't see any; he wondered about writing back, and decided he would. He still hung on to a glimmer of hope that one day they would be together.

That evening, the recruitment concert tour had reached Leeds City Varieties. It was another prestigious venue attracting audiences from across Yorkshire. At least Agnes had been able to go home the previous day and spend some time with her family. Mildred and the girls had been thrilled to have Agnes back and she was asked repeatedly to recount her stories of life in the theatre. Freda had been collecting reviews and articles from the newspapers and pasted them into a scrapbook. Agnes had presented them with a number of publicity photographs which Cameron Delaney had organised. These also went into the scrapbook, except for one which Mildred would frame.

Saturday afternoon, Agnes's car arrived to take her to the theatre at two o'clock. She was beginning to enjoy the 'star' treatment; flowers every night in the dressing room, assistants at her beck and call. She said farewell to her mother and sisters and carried her makeup bag to the waiting vehicle. The chauffeur greeted Agnes, took her bag, and opened the door for her to get in. Mildred and the girls waved as it pulled away and disappeared up the drive. Mildred was experiencing a feeling of pride, but sadness also; she was losing her daughter's dependency.

It would take the best part of an hour to reach Leeds, but well in time for a run-through and something to eat before the seven-thirty curtain.

Agnes walked on the stage for the rehearsal. The interior was long and rectangular, with cast-iron columns and foliage capitals supporting two bow-fronted balconies. The upper tier had received minor modifications thirty years earlier. Plaster female busts, swags and medallions adorned the balconies, while a three-centred proscenium arch, surmounted by the royal coat of arms, covered the shallow stage. The velvet seats seemed luxurious as Agnes peered out into the auditorium; they would soon be filled.

With several performances completed, Agnes was on top of her game, adding stagecraft to her natural singing ability. She still felt anxious before every performance, but once on stage, the nerves seemed to disappear. The travelling, though, was tiring and staying away from home was difficult sometimes. Gloria had been her rock and had proved to be an ideal companion, sharing rooms in the guest houses.

"How are you, kiddo?" she said as she came bouncing into Agnes's dressing room twenty minutes before curtain-call in her figure-hugging outfit and carrying her gold juggling clubs. She gave a swift demonstration.

Agnes was applying the last of her makeup. The costumier had given her several lessons on how to apply it; there was an art, she had explained. The eyes and lips were the most important. Agnes's face bore no resemblance to her usual visage.

"Nervous," replied Agnes.

"Would you like a cigarette? They always work for me… Or I can give you some of my friend's special powder."

"That's very kind, but 'appen I can manage; it's the waiting that's the worst."

Just then, Cameron Delaney the promoter knocked and entered.

"Can you excuse us a moment, Gloria? I just want a word with Agnes."

Gloria smiled, raised her eyebrows to Agnes and left.

"How are you feeling this evening, my dear?"

"Right enough," replied Agnes.

"That's good... I have some news for you. I've just received a telegram from one of my associates and they are offering you the opportunity to audition for one of the London shows in Drury Lane. It seems one of the agents saw your performance in Preston."

"London? The West End? My..." Agnes looked at Cameron and tried to take in the message. "When will it be?"

"Sometime next month probably, after the tour has finished. I will let you know more when I have it. Are you happy for me to reply in the affirmative?"

"Most certainly, Cameron."

That evening, once again, Agnes stole the show. Many were coming to see her for the third and fourth time. The recruitment campaign was also proving to be a great success, the numbers far outstripping expectations. Captain Henderson was delighted.

In London, Grace and the captain were in the back of the cab holding hands. She couldn't believe the scenes as they made their way to the hotel; the hustle and bustle made her head spin. As the cab pulled up outside the Strand Palace Hotel, her heart skipped a beat. It was her first time in a hotel, and after sleeping in a tent for over six weeks, the thought of a proper bed would be luxurious indeed. Outside the hotel, there was a line of cabbies waiting for service; some were horse-drawn for a more leisurely ride.

The driver opened the door of the taxi and Grace got out. She stared up at the illuminated glass and metal canopy over the entrance.

"It's only been opened for five years, but my father's stayed here and recommended it," said the captain as he joined her on the pavement.

"I'm sure it will be just fine," replied Grace, still trying to take in everything.

He paid the cabbie and they went inside. The atrium was equally grand with porters in smart uniforms offering to help customers with their luggage. With just overnight luggage, the captain declined their offer and went to the check-in desk.

"I've got us adjoining rooms, I hope that is acceptable," he said as he finished paying his five shillings and sixpence bed and breakfast for each room.

"Yes, that will be most acceptable," replied Grace.

They walked up the wide staircase with its magnificent carpet to the first floor and found their rooms.

"This is your key. I expect you will want to freshen up. I thought we could go for a walk around Covent Garden after lunch," said the captain, handing Grace the key attached to a large wooden tab with the number '128' stencilled on it. He checked the time on his fob watch, then gave the little winding wheel a turn. "I will call for you in one hour and we can find somewhere to eat."

If truth be told, Grace didn't want to leave her captain for one second.

She entered the room and, for a moment, just stared as she took in the opulence. It reminded her of Lady Jane's mansion. The accommodation was dominated by a magnificent four-poster bed. There was a long dressing table with a mirror on top, a chaise-longue, and a separate bathroom with a large bath and one of Thomas Crapper's toilets. There was a hand-basin and Grace splashed some water on her face and started applying her makeup.

The day was everything that Grace had hoped for and more. Captain Keating had entertained her royally; lunch in the hotel dining room followed by a walk around the arcades and shops of the Strand and the nearby Covent Garden.

After their excursion, they returned to the hotel where Grace luxuriated in the bath until her fingers took on a prune-like appearance. She used the sweet-smelling essence that was provided by the hotel. She changed into fresh underwear, a shift, drawers, petticoat and black stockings to go under her dress. With limited room in her suitcase, she had only brought one formal garment with her. Not for one moment when she had left home had she imagined being entertained in a five-star hotel by a handsome army officer.

There was a 'tap, tap' on her door at five-thirty. Grace was ready and opened the door; Matthew was stood there, looking... dashing.

He took a step back for a moment, admiring her beauty.

"Grace, darling, if I may say, you are quite wonderful."

The epithet made her shiver; no-one had ever addressed her in such a manner before.

"You may, Matthew, you may," she said and laughed.

They left the hotel arm in arm and wandered up the Strand towards the theatre.

"I have taken the liberty of reserving a table for dinner at the restaurant next to the theatre."

The restaurant was like nothing Grace had experienced in her life. Her excursions for outside food had been limited to the tea shops of Keighley.

"I hope you will like it," said the captain as he opened the door.

Grace looked at the stone façade with its cherubic figures on its stone canopy.

"It's very popular with theatre performers and musicians, I believe," he added. "And the King, too, is a patron."

"Oh, well, if it's good enough for His Majesty, I'm sure it will be wonderful," replied Grace, not coming close to describing how she felt.

The Maître D approached, a small, dark, swarthy man with a large moustache. He spoke in the strangest manner, but the captain seemed to understand. It more than lived up to the officer's billing. The food was something she had never tasted before.

"It's Italian, very popular in London," he said as they scanned the menu.

They chatted during the meal about their families. Matthew had had a privileged upbringing; private schooling and university. He was being groomed to take over the family business from his father. The decision to serve a short commission had happened before any hint of war; the predominant threat came from Ireland. He had spent three weeks there earlier in the summer and had expected to return before the hostilities with Germany had intervened. The discussion turned to the play they were about to see.

"What is it about? It has a strange title, 'Glad Eye'," asked Grace.

"I don't know much about it, only what I read in the newspaper; it's a comedy. French, I think, originally. In Paris, it's called, '*Le Zebre*'."

"You've been to Paris?" asked Grace, not so much in surprise but in admiration.

"Yes, two years ago. It's a beautiful city. I would love to take you there one day."

"Oh, my, yes, that would be such a dream," said Grace.

The meal was finished and the table cleared. Matthew looked at Grace and held both her hands, his dark eyes fixed on hers.

"I have something for you." He took out a jewellery box and placed it next to Grace's hand. "Open it."

Grace couldn't believe her eyes. "But Matthew, it's wonderful."

"I hope it will be something to remember me by when you're in France."

She took the brooch from the box.

"Here, let me," he said and pinned it to her dress where the shoulder strap met the bodice.

The jewels sparkled in the light, diamonds with a sapphire centre and swirls of white gold. From a distance, it seemed to be the shape of a butterfly.

"Oh, Matthew, it is so beautiful."

"It pales into insignificance when compared to your beauty, Grace."

Matthew checked his watch; it was seven-fifteen. "We better leave, the performance starts shortly, the theatre's only two minutes away."

They left the restaurant with the proprietor bidding farewell and his thanks in his strange accent.

There were hordes of people around the theatre. There wasn't a queue, as such, just a disorderly procession of people trying to enter. The captain and Grace joined the throng and five minutes later were taking their seats in the circle. There was a hum of conversation as people searched for their places. Grace looked around. It seemed older than the Hippodrome back home and, as such, slightly drab, the décor stained by a million cigarettes. Grace noticed the empty pit; there would be no orchestra. There was a haze as men lit their pipes and cigars, waiting for the show to start.

Just on seven-thirty, the houselights dimmed and the curtain opened. The whole stage was bathed in bright lights. The performance lasted two hours with a short intermission for drinks. The captain queued at the bar and bought Grace her second gin and tonic. The play was a little risqué but hilarious and Grace laughed more than she could remember.

The lights went up and the pair made their way to the exit.

Grace was feeling on top of the world; she never wanted the day to end. They walked back the short distance to the hotel.

"Would you like a drink before we retire?" said the officer as they reached the hotel reception.

"Yes, that would be lovely," said Grace.

They walked into the hotel bar and a waiter attended them as soon as they were seated.

"Two gin and tonics," ordered the captain without asking Grace.

"Not for me," interrupted Grace. "I will surely fall asleep with another. Just a fruit cordial, please."

The captain apologised. "Of course, darling." He looked at the waiter and nodded.

"Have you enjoyed today?" asked the captain.

"Oh, yes, Matthew, it's been my best day ever… And I love my brooch, it's beautiful." She looked at it admiringly.

The room was filling up with other theatre goers and with them came the inevitable smoke, which filled the room with a blue haze. The pair continued chatting until their drinks were consumed, then Grace called time.

"I think I would like to retire, Matthew."

"Yes, of course."

He paid the bill and the pair ascended the wide staircase to the first floor. It was dark outside but there were wall lights along the corridor. They reached the rooms and the captain turned to Grace.

"It has been a wonderful day, Grace, and I think I have fallen slightly in love with you."

"Have you indeed?" said Grace.

She looked into his eyes and leaned forward. The kiss was gentle, tentative, and then more confident. It seemed to last for several minutes; Grace was starting to feel flushed. Her mind flashed back to those moments with Freddie down by the river; she was experiencing the same sensations, the same passion.

"I suppose I had better let you sleep," said the captain, whose face was also red.

"Aye," said Grace. But her eyes said otherwise. She opened the door. "Goodnight, Matthew," she said and went inside.

She put on the light, closed the door, and leant against it. She didn't feel tired in the slightest, but she was experiencing other needs. She heard the captain's door open and shut. She went into the bathroom, removed her dress, and hung it on the hook behind the door. She removed her petticoat, drawers and shift. She washed herself down and put on the nightdress, which was laid on the bed. She liberally applied some Eau de cologne to repel the smell of smoke.

She was about to get into bed but, instead, she picked up the room key from the dressing table. She went to the adjoining door, rattled the key, and placed it into the lock, then turned the key as loudly as she could and tried the handle, ensuring it was unlocked. She returned to the bed, pulled back the covers and got in, then waited. Her heart was pounding.

Five minutes later, she could hear the door open and could see the shape of a man approaching the bed. She pulled back the covers.

"Oh, Matthew," was all she said.

Chapter Thirteen

Waking up with someone next to her was not a new experience for Grace; she had slept with her sisters since she was born, but the warmth of a man, his arms wrapped around her, strong and tender at the same time, was something she had only imagined in dreams.

As she lay there in those moments where sleep drifts into consciousness, she replayed the events of only a few hours earlier. The urgent passion followed by the feeling of fulfilment and deep contentment. The captain had been a considerate lover – not that Grace had any comparison, only what she had read in books, but it had been everything she had ever imagined.

He stirred, sensing her awakening. He put his arm underneath her waist and pulled her towards him; the spoons position. She turned her head and he kissed her. She wanted to stay like this forever.

They made love again and then both drifted back to sleep.

It was the captain who woke first.

"Grace, darling, are you awake?"

"Mmm, yes, I think so... I may be in heaven."

"They serve breakfast in bed in heaven. Shall I order?"

"Oh, please do," she replied, leaning up on one elbow.

He leant over and kissed her.

"I will have a bath," she added.

"I won't be long; I'll see the concierge."

Captain Keating went back to his room via the inter-connecting door and dressed, then went down to the ground floor to order breakfast for two. Grace went to the bathroom and started running her bath.

Sunday morning at Colsterdale Camp. Having endured the morning ritual of being barked at by the drill sergeant, Arthur and his hut-mates were back in their quarters awaiting church parade. Henry had taken his boots off and was on the next bed looking at his feet. The skin on the soles and heels was hard and calloused; blisters had healed and re-opened, toenails black and fungus-ridden.

"Why do we do this? No-one's ever won a war bloody marching up and down all day," he said to anyone who would listen.

"Aye, tha's not wrong there," said Arthur, picking up the comment.

The mood in the camp was still downbeat. Boredom, lethargy, and general physical and mental fatigue hung over the camp like a shroud. What would be heralded in the newspapers as 'England's finest' were anything but. They were fit and trained in basic weaponry but nowhere near prepared for what lay ahead.

Corporal Dorkins entered the hut to little more than passing interest.

"Corporal Marsden, mess room, now!"

Arthur looked up at the corporal. "What's up, Corp, someone shot the Kaiser?"

"Don't know, but summat's up, all squad leaders have been called by the C.O."

"Aye, give us a minute."

Dorkins left the hut. Arthur put his boots on and buttoned up his tunic.

"What's up, Arthur?" said Wilfred.

"Don't know, Dorkins said summat's up. C.O. wants to see squad leaders."

Arthur left the hut. The camp was unrecognisable from when they first arrived at the beginning of August. He joined the narrow road to the parade ground; to the right, row upon row of tents stretched as far as one could see. Men in uniform were milling about. Campfires were burning, mostly used for brewing tea to save the trek up to the canteen. Arthur was glad he was in a hut; at least it was reasonably dry.

He reached the C.O.'s quarters; there was a staff car parked outside with a bored-looking driver sat behind the wheel. Several other squad leaders were filing into the officers' hut. The men were lined up in rows; the seats had been removed due to lack of space.

"Atten-shun" called Sergeant Major Stafford, the fearsome drill sergeant, as he marched into the room. The manoeuvre was crisp and coordinated.

The sergeant major was followed by five lieutenants, the C.O., Major Foster and a Colonel.

"At ease," said the C.O.

The officers stood at the front facing the men.

"Let me introduce you to Colonel Radcliffe from Regimental H.Q."

"Thank you, Major. Well, gentlemen, I wanted to address you personally today to deliver some good news. The Regiment is being called to the front." There were looks around the room. "You will depart for France at oh-six-hundred on Tuesday 3rd November. Special trains will take you to Southampton. From there you will be taken by boat to the infantry base depot at Rouen, via Dieppe. I know you will be as delighted as I was to hear we have got the chance, at last, to serve our country, and that you will all do your duty. You have been well-trained, and from Major Foster's reports, you are more than ready to give the enemy a taste of Yorkshire steel… You will continue training for the remainder of this week prior to deployment. You can brief your men, but you must tell them on no account are they to communicate these movements to anyone, including loved ones. All outgoing letters will be opened and any soldier contravening this order will be subject to a court martial. Is that clear?"

"Yes, Colonel," was the group response.

"Excellent. It just remains for me to wish you jolly good luck and may God protect you... Thank you, Major Foster, carry on."

The colonel left the mess and the major addressed the men.

"After you are dismissed, you are to brief your squads; remember to mention the communication embargo. There will be a special church service at oh-eleven-hundred hours. Further details about travel will be delivered during this week, but we will leave camp a week tomorrow. Any questions? No? Right, dismissed."

There was a buzz of conversation as the men filed out of the mess. Arthur felt a need for the latrine.

What the colonel hadn't told the men was the reason why they were being deployed. Up to the end of October, British casualties since the start of the war at the beginning of August was approaching ninety thousand men. French and Belgian casualties were also high; the need for replacements was urgent. The British populace would not be reading that over their toast and marmalade.

Grace and Matthew enjoyed their breakfast in Grace's room. The feeling of loss was beginning to overtake them; the thought that in just a couple of hours they would part, neither knowing if they would ever meet again. There was an attempt at conversation but, in truth, thoughts of departure were affecting the mood. They finished breakfast.

"I'll come with you to Waterloo, I need to be back with

my regiment by midday," said the captain.

"Yes, thank you. I, too, should be back this afternoon; there's much to do."

Suddenly they were locked in an embrace.

"I love you, Grace, with all my heart."

"I love you, Matthew; I will pray for you every day."

"And I you, Grace."

The captain went back to his room to collect his things. Grace packed her valise and checked around. She looked at the bed, the sheets giving evidence of more than sleep. She sighed and then opened the door. The captain was waiting and they walked arm in arm down the stairs to reception in silence.

There were several taxis waiting outside the hotel. The concierge called one and helped the couple on board. "Hope to see you again soon," he said as he closed the door. The taxi pulled away.

In Springfield Hall, Mildred was in the kitchen with Molly and Freda. Agnes was still in bed. Oswald Jessop had just delivered The Sunday Times and Mildred was catching up with the news. The paper continued to paint a positive reflection of events in Belgium and the war elsewhere; fighting seemed to have broken out in much of Europe. Mildred noticed a list of fourteen officers who had died in combat serving their country between 20th and 21st October. She scanned the names in case she saw anyone she recognised, then thought of Arthur. She hadn't heard from him in over a week and had no idea where he was or what he was doing. She had received a letter from Grace telling her of her pending deployment to France, which was a further source of concern.

She looked outside the kitchen window. The immaculate

lawn reached out to the hedgerow in the distance; beyond that, the meadow, which Jed and his helpers had spent numerous hours converting into a vegetable patch and which was now starting to bear the fruits of their labours. Most she would distribute to others.

The previous evening, Mildred had again waited for Agnes to return from the theatre but had fallen asleep and hadn't heard her come in at one-thirty; there had been a party, she had explained. Agnes was another worry. The smell of smoke on her clothes and alcohol on her breath suggested her lifestyle was changing. At least she was not working today, which would give her a chance to rest. Then there was Ivy; her condition was starting to become all too apparent and arrangements would soon need to be made for her to stay at Springfield. She was not sure how Ivy's mother would react; it was going to mean a trip into town.

Later after church, she called in at Blossom Cottage to see Kitty. With the weight of the world on her shoulders, she needed a friend.

"Hello Kitty," said Mildred as the door opened.

"Mildred, what a wonderful surprise, come in; I was just going to make some tea, what excellent timing."

"How are you?" enquired Mildred, as she entered the cottage and removed her hat.

"Well, Mildred, very well, thank you. I received a letter from Freddie yesterday, which has lifted my spirits."

"Oh, that's wonderful. Unfortunately, Arthur's not so considerate: just one since he arrived at that camp. I have no idea where he is… Has Freddie any news?"

Mildred followed Kitty into the kitchen so she could continue her gossip.

"Not a great deal, it's just so good to have word that he's safe, but he says he's still at the same place."

"Has he said where?"

"No, I'm sure they're not allowed to say. What about Arthur?"

"No, the same. I wonder if they're at the same camp?"

"Well, it is possible, I suppose. I mean, they were both recruited in Bradford."

"Yes, that's right... I don't know what Arthur's reaction might be if he were to discover he has a brother."

"Yes, I've often wondered that too."

Mildred sat down on one of the wooden kitchen chairs.

"There is something I want to share with you. You remember Ivy, at the bakery?"

"Yes, she took over the baking when Arthur left, you mentioned."

"Well, she's with child; it's Arthur's."

"Oh my word." Kitty had a look of concern.

"Yes, he's taken after his father; it would seem." Kitty didn't react to this remark.

"What are you going to do?" Kitty started to pour the tea.

"I've invited her to stay at Springfield, at least until it's born. I truly hope that by then Arthur will be back and we can decide what's to be done, but I think they'll get wed. That is my wish."

Arthur had delivered the news to the hut about the pending deployment and the embargo on sharing it. The sombre mood showed no sign of abating; the reaction was not one the senior officers were hoping for. Far from being joyous at being able to fight for their king and country, the feeling was one of resignation and apprehension.

"Well, look on the bright side, lads; at least we'll get to see a new country," said Henry. "I wonder what the French girls look like?"

"Same as English girls, I reckon," said Samuel.

Wilfred was withdrawn and a pale shadow of his former self. Arthur was not the only one to have noticed the change in his friend.

"Come on, Wilfred," said Henry. "Tha never know, there might be a pretty French filly just waiting to fall into the arms of a handsome English butcher."

"Aye, leave him be, Henry. Wilfred will be right enough once we get over there. We'll see tha's alright," said Arthur looking at his pal.

Wilfred was looking at the ceiling and turned to Arthur.

"'Appen I won't be coming back; I just have this feeling."

"Don't say such things, Wilfred. 'Appen we'll be chasing Fritz back to Germany in no time once us lads get over there." Arthur's encouraging words were having little effect.

Henry took out a cigarette and lit up, then handed one to Wilfred.

"Here, try one of these; they settled the nerves."

Wilfred took it blindly. Henry produced his cigarette lighter and lit it. Wilfred coughed after the first draw but then continued to smoke his first cigarette. It made him feel lightheaded.

"Do you want a smoke, Arthur? Reckon tha could do with one."

"Nah, ta, Henry, but I'd murder a pint, right enough."

Grace arrived back at Brookwood by mid-afternoon. Hetty saw the cabbie pull up at the camp gate and went to meet her friend. She was dressed in her khaki FANY uniform; not the most fashionable but functional with its long full skirt, which allowed astride horse riding, and matching tunic, not dissimilar to the men's. It was a far cry from the original red and blue uniforms.

"Grace, hello, let me take your bag."

"Hello, Hetty, it's not heavy, I can manage."

Hetty walked alongside her. "So, tell me all, was it as romantic as I had imagined?"

"Aye, and more besides," replied Grace, trying to avoid the mud and puddles on the worn track to the mess tent. "What have you been doing?"

"Oh, nothing very exciting; mucking horses, preparing the ambulance, the usual."

"How are the preparations going?"

"Well, between you and me, I don't know what more can be done. If we clean the ambulance any more times, the paint will surely be gone."

"Has the C.O. said when we will leave?"

"It will be tomorrow sometime. The ship leaves at six-thirty Tuesday morning, but the C.O. said we'll need to be there early to load the ambulance."

They reached the mess tent and the C.O. came out of her office to greet Grace.

"Marsden, when you've changed, report back here for a briefing."

"Yes, ma'am," said Grace. She looked at Hetty and smiled.

"Welcome back," said Hetty.

Grace walked back to the tent; her mind was nowhere near. She was still in Matthew's arms.

Monday, November 2nd, 1914. At Springfield Hall, Mildred received a letter around eleven o'clock. Daisy Jessop was in the kitchen baking. Molly was working at Kitty's and Freda had taken the early trolleybus to school; she was now in her final year, though Mildred was keen for her to continue her education at the grammar school.

"What's that?" asked Daisy as Mildred returned to the kitchen clutching the envelope.

"It's from Grace, looking at the handwriting."

"Oh, I do hope she is safe," said Daisy seeing the concern on Mildred's face.

Mildred opened the letter. *'Dear Mam, I have so much to tell you. These past two days have been such an adventure. We reached Dover on Monday afternoon; the lieutenant let me drive much of the way. Let me tell you, that ambulance is a beast, worse than handling a hundred horses. Hetty and the other four girls sat in the back and in truth were better served, although they continually complained about being shaken up; at least they were dry, for it rained for an hour and the lieutenant and I were soaked to the skin by the time we finally arrived in Dover.*

'We were given a mug of tea at the docks by some lovely people who had set up some refreshments for the departing Tommies. It would be about one o'clock in the morning and there were hundreds waiting to embark. We had to leave the ambulance and watch as it was lifted onto the ship. I thought it might be too heavy as it is a big old thing but it went on as light as a feather. We set sail at dawn and tried to find some place to sleep, but with so many Tommies on board, it was impossible.

'We had to wait for our ambulance to be unloaded when we reached Calais. It was wonderful seeing our brave boys marching away to a great send off from the local townspeople; it lifted our spirits no end. Driving in France is so different. The roads are cobbles; they call them 'pavé' and not very comfortable, too. Hetty and the girls were thrown everywhere in the back. They also drive on the right so you have to remember that if you meet a car coming towards you.

'*We made our way to the hospital where the lieutenant had arranged for us to work. It's called Lamarck and it was not what I was expecting. It used to be a convent school before the war and hastily made into a hospital judging from the state of the place. There are two buildings; one for the 'blessés', which is what they call the wounded, with about fifty beds, and another similar for typhoid patients. The beautiful cathedral of Notre Dame is close by: its east window faces our yard! They have arranged a restroom for us on the top floor of the hospital, which we share with the chauffeurs, where we can take a breather.*

'*We have been billeted in an old shop in town not far from the hospital. It's not very comfortable but at least it's dry. We are sharing our beds with the nurses who work on the ward at night. I think that is all the news for now. I will write again soon. Send my love to Agnes and the girls. Much love, Grace*'.

Mildred read it again out loud for Daisy to hear.

"My, but that's so exciting. You must be so proud of her."

"Yes, although I would say, I wished she were safe here."

Mildred reflected on the letter. She would write back today.

Grace had been in Calais for five days and her feet had not touched the ground. The hospital was so short of staff that three of the six girls, including Grace and Hetty, were quickly allocated wards under the supervision of a trained sister. Grace was not prepared for what she was witnessing. The soldiers were all Belgian, transported by their own ambulances direct from the trenches on the Yser or from the forward dressing station at Oostkerke, where the other three girls had been sent. The ambulance drivers were all men; it was considered too dangerous and not something a woman would do. The wounds were so appalling that many didn't survive the journey and were dead on arrival. For some, the staff just did what they could until a padre arrived to ease them on their way to their final destination.

Around midday, the Directrice, as the commanding officer was known locally, visited the ward and approached Grace, who was attending an officer.

"Marsden, I have a job for you."

"Yes, ma'am."

"There are three English officers that need to be taken to the Gare Maritime. I said that you could take the ambulance."

"Yes, of course."

"One of the orderlies will accompany you to show you where to go."

The men required surgery which was not available at Lamarck and would be taken by boat to Cherbourg where there was a hospital ship. From there they would be transferred to England.

Grace left the ward and made her way to the compound in front of the hospital where the ambulances would deliver the wounded. The trusty Wolseley that they had brought from England was next to the entrance, and Grace watched as the three officers were carefully loaded inside accompanied by one of the local nurses. The orderly was waiting in the passenger seat wearing a pair of goggles. Hetty joined Grace to see what was happening.

"Taking Betty out for a spin," said Grace to her enquiry. The team had nicknamed the ambulance 'Betty' for no other reason than it seemed appropriate.

"What's that orderly doing in those goggles?" commented Hetty.

"Thinks we're going flying, I wouldn't wonder," replied Grace.

Hetty laughed. "Well, I want a full report when you get back."

Grace went to the vehicle. Starting the ambulance was no easy matter and involved several procedures before she was able to drive away. She opened the bonnet to turn on the petrol tap, turned on the magneto, primed the engine using the starting handle, then gave it a sharp turn. It chugged into life. The orderly and one or two onlookers were bemused. There were lots of mutterings in Flemish. In her khaki uniform, they couldn't decide if it was a man or woman.

Grace waved to Hetty as they left the hospital. There was no conversation with the orderly, despite Grace's attempt. He shrugged his shoulders when she asked him a question; it transpired he didn't speak a word of English. Grace negotiated the ambulance along the narrow streets and reached the docks and the boat that was waiting to transport the wounded to Cherbourg. It was a converted passenger ship that would have in better times been ferrying travellers on holiday from England to France.

The nurse got out from the back and took charge, shouting to two sailors to help with the stretchers. Eventually, the three soldiers were taken on board; Grace followed to ensure they were comfortable. She stopped in disbelief as she reached the companion way. The floor of the saloon was packed with stretchers, so close it was impossible to walk between them. One of the nurses was throwing cigarettes to any who could move enough to smoke them.

Then there was the smell of death and the pitiful cries of the dying; many were calling for their mothers. Men with half their faces shot away but somehow still clinging to life, others with missing limbs, the stumps wrapped in bandages. One poor soldier had been hit in the groin by a piece of shrapnel, completely removing his penis and testicles.

It was two hours before Grace returned to the hospital. As she drove along the cobbled streets with her mute companion, she reflected on the sights and sounds she had experienced; things that would never leave her for as long as she lived. Later, the hospital matron, an imposing Belgian woman in her late forties that Grace had only met briefly, caught up with her on the ward. She spoke reasonable English.

"Mam'selle Marsden, Monsieur Pierre was most complimentary on how you drive today; he said you were, how can I say...? More, er, careful than zee gentleman drivers."

"Thank you, ma'am," replied Grace.

Hetty heard the remark and mouthed 'well done' to her friend. Grace couldn't wait to put her exploits to paper and share it with her dashing captain.

Tuesday, November 3rd, 1914. It was their last day in camp. In hut forty-three, the atmosphere was strange. There was boyish behaviour; throwing kit about, abusive comments, expletives. Some were on their third cigarette despite the early hour. Arthur was concentrating on getting his gear together and couldn't be bothered to exercise any discipline. By six o'clock, they were ready. It was still dark and the dim single electric light gave no more than adequate illumination. The hut looked empty with all the usual clutter packed into tunics or their rucksacks. There was a great deal of 'rubbish' piled in the corner. Arthur checked on his pal Wilfred, who still seemed to be in a mind of his own.

"Eh up, Wilfred, 'ow be tha?"

"Aye, right enough, ta," was his weak reply.

"Come on, Wilfred, just think of all those mademoiselles waiting to show their appreciation," said Henry who was alongside them. "Here, have a fag, that'll sort tha out."

Henry lit one and passed it to Wilfred, who took it without responding.

They had all been given rifles now which had been cleaned fastidiously over recent weeks. 'Your life may depend on it,' said the drill sergeant when they were distributed.

Corporal Dorkins entered the hut.

"Right, lads, the trucks are waiting; get your arses over to the parade ground."

Arthur lined up the pals and looked around what had been their home for the past three months. It was just the August recruits, around seventy men, who were being shipped. Many of those in the tents would be relocated to the vacant huts. In the parade ground, there was a great deal of activity. There were five trucks waiting to take the lads to the station at Masham. The sergeant major lined them up outside the mess hut.

"Atten-shun," he bellowed as the C.O. appeared. A crisp click of heels followed.

"At ease, men," he shouted. "I just wanted to wish you jolly good luck and bon voyage. I know you will all do your duty and make your families and the country proud. Carry on, Sergeant Major."

He saluted, which the C.O. returned, then addressed the men.

"Right lads, one hut to one truck… dismissed."

Arthur led the pals to the nearest wagon and they clambered aboard. Corporal Dorkins also got in.

"Eh up, Corporal. They're not letting you loose on the Hun an' all?" said Henry. "They've got no bloody chance." There were howls of laughter from the lads.

"Aye, well, someone's got to look after yas, now tha mams're not here." More laughter.

Arthur noticed another familiar face, Lieutenant Norman

Hoskins, carrying a rifle and side arm in a leather holster with a large kitbag on his shoulder. He walked past the rear of the truck and got in next to the driver.

Mid-morning at Springfield Hall. Mildred was in the sitting room reading the latest news in The Times when the sound of the doorbell echoed around the hall.

"I'll go," shouted the housekeeper from the kitchen.

A few moments later, Daisy went into the sitting room.

"Two letters, Mildred. One for you and one for Agnes." She handed them over.

"Agnes is still asleep. I'll give it to her when she's awake; she needs her rest."

Daisy returned to the kitchen. Mildred looked at the scribbled handwriting and recognised it straight away. She ripped open the envelope and started to read. *'Dear Mam, I am just writing to tell you I will be leaving camp soon. I am not able to say when or where we are going but I may not be able to write much for a while. Ivy tells me she's with child and that you are going to look after her. Tell her we can get wed when I get back. Tell her that I will write when I can. Say hello to girls for me. Your loving son, Arthur'.*

Mildred sighed; typical Arthur.

Upstairs, Agnes was still in bed but sleep was illusive. The adrenaline from the previous night's performance was still giving her a high; that and a helping of Gloria's magic powder. Agnes had succumbed a week earlier after a particular gruelling journey to Carlisle.

Half an hour before curtain call, Gloria as usual came into the dressing room and could see Agnes was struggling. The anxiety coupled with fatigue from travelling had left her drained. She barely had the energy to apply her makeup.

"Don't worry, kiddo, we'll soon have you back on your

feet. I'll be back in a second."

She returned with a small powder compact, but inside was not the kind of powder you would apply on your face. Gloria put a pinch on the back of her hand as you would some snuff.

"Just sniff it up, kiddo; you'll feel better in no time."

She complied, lacking the energy to resist or argue. Within a few minutes, Agnes's energy had returned. In fact, she felt as if she could conquer the world. That night was another triumph. As well as the now familiar accolades, a further thirty new recruits were signed up. The army top brass were heralding the concert tour as a major success, and others were being run across the country.

Agnes was on top of her game, and during her performance, the promoter was beaming with pride seeing his protégé receiving yet another standing ovation. It was difficult to believe she was still six months shy of her nineteenth birthday.

After the show, Agnes's dressing room was the centre of attention and several of the performers had joined her for an after-show drink. Agnes's tipple was brandy and she had acquired a taste for it after the show to help wind down. That night she would be in yet another guest house, sharing a room with her best pal. Delaney entered the dressing room and cleared the visitors temporarily.

"Agnes, my dear, I just wanted to say you were magnificent tonight."

"Thank you, Cameron."

"I have some news. I was speaking on the telephone earlier to my contact in London and they would like to see you in London on Thursday 12th November for the audition. Don't worry, I will see to all the travel arrangements."

Agnes was removing her makeup and looking at the

promoter in the dressing table mirror.

"My, that's wonderful news indeed… Do you think I am ready for such a performance?"

"Yes, my dear, more than ready. There are few performers in the West End that can match your charisma or vocal ability, and there will be plenty more work to come, I can assure you of that, and at a better pay, I warrant."

"Thank you, Cameron, for having faith in me."

"No, no, my dear, I should be thanking you for having faith in me."

Agnes stirred. Tonight was her final performance; the tour was returning to Bradford by popular demand. She felt lightheaded; it had been another late night following a performance at the Hippodrome Theatre in Huddersfield the previous evening. It was gone two a.m. when the car arrived outside the house. Mildred had gone to bed.

She put on a dressing gown and went downstairs to the kitchen where her mother and Daisy were preparing food.

"Oh, hello, Agnes dear, how are you feeling?" said her mother.

"I will be well enough," she replied, filling a tumbler of water from the tap and drinking it down in one go.

"There's a letter for you," said Mildred and handed over the envelope. Agnes recognised the writing.

"It's from Norman," said Agnes. She sat down on one of the chairs and started reading it.

"He says he's being posted abroad. He can't say where."

"Yes, I had one from Arthur saying the same thing. It would be a coincidence if they were going to the same place."

Agnes continued reading. It was full of dedications of love. The letter ended with the phrase, *'remember me in your prayers'*. Agnes was trying to gauge her feelings. She was still fond of Norman, but it wasn't with the same passion she had felt in those meetings in the park. She picked up the letter and left the kitchen.

"I'm just going to have a bath, Mam."

Chapter Fourteen

Tuesday, November 3rd, 1914.

It was still dark as the five trucks left Colsterdale Camp and made their way down to Masham station, where a train was waiting to take the August recruits to Harrogate. There they joined other battalions for the journey to Southampton. Luckily, the longer train had toilets installed which would avoid the indignity of having to go 'out of the window', which Arthur had endured on his previous train excursion to London. There followed jokes and reminiscences between Arthur, Henry and Samuel about that experience. Wilfred was still not in good humour.

There were ten in the compartment, the luggage rack piled with kitbags and rifles. It was crowded and conversation was not high on the agenda; most were trying to snatch some sleep. Arthur, Wilfred, Henry and Samuel, the original pals from Keighley, were seated together. Each man had been given a field pack consisting of bullied beef and four hardtack biscuits to sustain them on their journey.

It was a dismal day, with the smoke from the train adding to the general gloom. Arthur was in the window seat, his head resting on his 'civvy' trousers which he had rolled up into a pillow to absorb the vibrations of the moving train. As it started to get lighter, he stared out of the window watching the countryside pass by; the occasional drifts of smoke and steam from the engine obscured the landscape. He thought of Ivy and those few days in the summer when she had assumed the role of housekeeper, which had developed into more. Suddenly, thoughts of home enveloped him. He wanted to be back in his bakery and life as it was, the comfort of familiarity.

With six of the ten occupants smoking, after a couple of hours, the compartment was starting to build up a blue fug and Arthur dropped the window down a couple of notches to let in some air. There were one or two complaints as the cold air swept in but most didn't seem to care. The floor was covered in dogends.

"Eh up, anyone having snap?" asked Henry sometime later as he started rummaging in his pockets for his tin of bullied beef. This seemed to trigger the rest of the carriage into action.

Samuel, who was seated opposite Arthur, pulled out one his biscuits and tapped it on the window making a hard rap-tapping sound.

"What're we supposed do with these? 'Appen it'll stop a bloody bullet, this."

Others were examining their stashes and drawing the same conclusion.

Around two-thirty, the train pulled into Reading station to take on water. The station master walked up and down the train announcing a twenty-minute stop, which resulted in a mass exodus. The carriage doors flew open and a hundred soldiers piled out onto the platform looking for some refreshment and a decent toilet. Some trestle tables had been set up on the station platform and tin mugs of tea were being dispensed from large urns by a posse of friendly women dressed in white aprons and caps.

"Eh up, misses, this is reet grand. 'Ow come tha's here?" asked Henry when it was his turn.

The woman who was serving from behind the table eventually managed to interpret the question. "We heard a troop train was calling," she replied in what he would describe as a 'posh' voice.

"Eh up, Arthur, 'appen if tha dips biscuit in tea, tha can eat it right enough," said Henry, demonstrating the technique.

"What about tha, Wilfred?" said Arthur, trying to engage his pal, who was stood with a vacant look watching the khaki crush around the tea urn. He'd hardly said a word the whole journey.

"Tha must get something to drink."

"Aye," he replied. "I'll just take a piss."

Wilfred went off in search of the toilet while Arthur took matters in his own hands and started queueing. By the time Wilfred had returned, Arthur had managed to get served with two mugs and handed one to his pal.

"Get that down tha," he said and handed Wilfred the drink.

"Ta," said Wilfred.

The platform was getting rowdy as the men intermingled, introducing themselves to each other and trying to swap cigarettes for chocolate or any other treats that maybe available. After the stated twenty minutes, the engine emitted a piercing hoot. The station master came from his office with a flag and started shouting, 'All aboard, all aboard'. There was a stampede to return to the carriages, which took five minutes, but eventually all the doors were closed. The station master waved his flag and blew his whistle.

Several of the tea women were alongside the train waving handkerchiefs as it slowly pulled away. Arthur had dropped down the window and waved back.

"God speed, God speed," they shouted.

The men had no idea where they were going – just to catch a boat, they had been told – and geography was not a strong point. So when they pulled into Southampton Docks station at just after five o'clock, there were looks of realisation from the pals in the compartment.

"Looks like we're here," said Arthur, and everyone stood up and started to collect their gear.

As they filed out onto the platform, the sergeant major was rounding up the lads from Colsterdale and had them lined up. Lieutenant Hoskins joined him from a carriage at the front of the train where other officers were exiting.

"Atten-shun," bellowed the sergeant major and saluted to the lieutenant.

Hoskins responded. "S.S. Ennisfallen," he said to the sergeant major. "It's over there." He pointed to a former Cork cattle steamer that had been converted into a troop carrier.

The sergeant major called his men forward and they marched towards the vessel. The dockside was a sea of khaki as maybe a thousand men waited in turn to embark on the Ennisfallen and another steamer docked next to her, the S.S. Sarnia. The N.C.O.s from each battalion had the troops lined up in rows and they embarked in turn, most efficiently, to avoid a crush.

Eventually, the Colsterdale contingent were onboard and trying to find somewhere to sit, or better, lay. Conditions below decks were dire, and it occurred to Arthur that should there be any mishap on the way to wherever they were going, there was no doubt they would all be killed. This was more than a possibility. Most of the troop ships at this time were departing from Southampton to avoid the Calais crossing because of the threat of mines and German submarines, which were now active in the Channel.

Arthur checked his father's fob watch, safely stowed in his tunic breast pocket, as they felt the vibrations of the propellers and heard the engines come to life. Eight o'clock. Arthur looked at Wilfred as the boat began to slowly leave the dock and started swaying as it was released from its mooring. He seemed to be crying.

"Don't tha worry, Wilfred, tha'll be well, we'll look after tha."

While Arthur was heading towards France in the bowels of a former cattle steamer, back at the Alhambra Theatre in Bradford, it was Agnes's last night on the recruitment tour. There was the usual buzz backstage; it was another sold-out event and Cameron Delaney, promoter to the stars, was fussing over his artists like a mother hen. Captain Henderson was also doing the rounds thanking everybody for their contribution; another six soldiers had been selected to take part in tonight's performance. There had been a waiting list, he joked.

Having spent the day resting at home, Agnes was feeling much better and ready for the evening's performance, but also with a feeling of sadness. She had made friends with all the performers and was going to miss them enormously once the evening was over. As she was applying her makeup, she was reflecting on some of the shows and the warmth of the audience to her performances. Freda's scrapbook was full of newspaper cuttings extolling her talent, and beauty.

As usual, Gloria joined Agnes in her dressing room a few minutes to curtain-up to see how she was.

"I'm going to miss you, kiddo."

"Aye, I'll miss you, too. Have you decided what you are going to do?"

"Cameron says he's got something lined up for me; awaiting confirmation, he said."

"Whereabouts, did he say?"

"London, he thinks."

"Well, wouldn't that be excellent if I am working there, too?"

"Indeed, it will be. When is your audition?"

"A week on Thursday."

"You must tell me how you fair."

"Most certainly I will. I will write to you directly."

Gloria went over and kissed Agnes on the cheek and whispered, "Would you like some magic powder tonight?"

"I'll manage, Gloria, but I think a celebration would be welcome after the show, don't you?"

There was standing room only in the theatre, with people still queuing to get in when the curtain rose. Like all the other shows on the tour, approaching thirty now, the reception was rapturous. Men in the audience were calling out Agnes's name, several asking for her hand in marriage, or words to that effect.

At the end of the show, the soldiers walked on and the chorus of 'Land of Hope and Glory' was sung with such gusto there was hardly a dry eye in the house. Agnes was presented with her now customary bouquet of flowers. The queue to sign up, again, stretched out of the theatre.

Captain Henderson and Cameron Delaney were the first to congratulate Agnes as she returned to her dressing room, and it was soon crowded with other performers armed with a variety of drinks and glasses. Agnes was still in her stage clothes. About thirty minutes later, the party was in full swing, Agnes was leading a sing-song when a stage attendant knocked on her door.

"Message for you, Miss Agnes."

Agnes got up, took the small envelope and opened it. It was a business card in gold lettering. *'David, Earl of Harford, Harford Hall, Ripon'*.

"The gentleman said he would wait for you at the stage door, ma'am. What should I tell him?" said the attendant.

"Tell him I'll be there directly," said Agnes, intrigued by such a request.

Agnes cleared the room, and the occupants moved elsewhere to continue the party while she changed into her day clothes. She was still wearing her stage makeup as she walked along the corridor to the exit. There was an attendant on the door.

"Good evening, Miss Agnes, there's a gentleman waiting for you; been there for a while, I reckon."

The man opened the door and moved aside to let Agnes pass.

The cold air was a shock to Agnes and she pulled her shawl together at her neck as she stood in the doorway. There were dozens of people milling about the stage door hoping for a glimpse of the performers. On the tour this had been a regular occurrence and, seeing Agnes, there was a surge forward, many holding the promotional photographs of her which were on sale in the foyer. Then Agnes noticed a tall, distinguished-looking man carrying a small posy. He pushed aside the gathering, stood in front of her, and bowed his head.

"David Harford, Miss Marsden, at your service. I would like to make your acquaintance."

"Would you indeed? You best come in then."

Agnes waved to the crowd and turned; the man followed. The attendant closed the door and Agnes walked down the corridor. There were rowdy scenes as they passed the dressing rooms. Agnes reached hers and opened the door.

"I don't normally entertain gentlemen," said Agnes as she led him inside and closed the door. The room was thick with cigarette smoke and smelt of alcohol. She sat on the stool in front of her dressing table as if she were holding court.

"Thank you for your indulgence," he replied and handed Agnes the small bunch of flowers.

She took them and placed it next to the enormous bouquet

that lay on the table waiting to be put into water.

"Thank you, what can I do for you?"

She looked at him – early-thirties with blue eyes, thick, wavy hair and a light, rust-coloured officer's moustache; he was immaculately presented. He was wearing a charcoal three-piece suit with a gold chain looping from his pocket to a buttonhole on his waistcoat; a grey woollen overcoat was draped around his shoulders. Everything about him exuded class.

"I'm a great admirer, Miss Marsden, I have seen you perform several times… I have a proposition for you."

"Thank you… Have you spoken to my agent?"

"No, I was not aware of such a person."

"It's of no mind, sir. What is your proposition?"

"It's Mama's seventieth birthday this weekend approaching and I would like to ask if you would kindly perform at a gala party we are holding in her honour." He spoke in a voice that could only come from someone of 'breeding'. "We will, of course, make suitable recompense… I just hope it is not too short a notice."

"No, tonight is the last of the tour. I have no other arrangements for this weekend."

"In which case, I do hope you will honour us with your presence."

"Where will you want me to be?" asked Agnes. There was a glass of water on the dressing table and she took a deliberate sip.

"At home, Harford Hall… We are arranging the ballroom to accommodate the musicians."

"Musicians?"

"Yes, just a small orchestra for dancing."

"Dancing?"

"Yes, there will be about sixty or seventy guests, Mama

is still inviting people," he smiled.

"What songs will you want me to sing?"

"I thought you might choose something suitable, something that Mama would like."

"Well, I don't know her tastes, sir."

"It's David, please call me David."

"What songs does she like, David?"

"She is wide in her tastes... She does like Marie Lloyd; she has several of her recordings, which is why I thought of you. Although I have to say, I think you sing much better."

"Thank you, that's most kind... You mentioned an orchestra, will there be an accompanist?"

"Most certainly, I will ensure it."

"Hmm... Yes, very well, how will I reach you?"

"I can collect you in the car; it will be my pleasure... and, of course, we'll arrange accommodation at the house for you. I can return you home on Sunday morning."

Agnes thought for a moment. "Yes, very well, but I still don't know what you would like me to sing or for how long?"

"If it were me, you could sing all night, but let's say forty-five minutes."

"Hmm, that will be about six songs; a selection, perhaps?"

"That would suit very well, I am sure... Do you have a telephone?"

"I'm afraid not."

"In which case, please, you choose; I am sure it will be perfect."

"Well, I will discuss it with my musical director and get his opinion, if I may. I will write to you tomorrow with my selection so you can tell the accompanist."

"Yes, Miss Marsden, that's most gracious of you."

"You mentioned recompense?"

"Yes, I did. I thought ten pounds might be acceptable."

Agnes was trying to not appear too enthusiastic at such a large amount.

"Yes, David, that would be acceptable."

"Very well, I will call for you on Saturday. Where do you live?"

"Springfield Hall, Oakworth, not ten miles away. Will you find it?"

"Oakworth? I'm sure I will… Springfield Hall, yes, I won't forget. Shall we say two o'clock?"

"Yes, two o'clock will be convenient."

"Thank you," said His Lordship. He took Agnes's hand and kissed it. "I will see you Saturday." His blue eyes fixed on Agnes. The stare unnerved her.

Wednesday, November 4th, 1914. The war had been raging for exactly three months and the thought that it would be over before Christmas seemed now a forlorn hope. Casualties on both sides were appalling. It was clear the opposing factions were evenly matched in both men and equipment with no side gaining an upper hand. A stalemate had ensued.

On the S.S. Ennisfallen, Arthur and his pals were stowed away below deck in a room with at least a hundred others, enduring a miserable night. The swaying of the boat had caused many to be sick and the deck floor was covered in vomit. The smell one could only imagine.

It was approaching five a.m.; Arthur was drifting in and out of sleep and suddenly felt the boat slowing down. There was a sharp bump as it reached its docking point; they had no idea where. The sudden jolt caused those standing up to fall over, sprawling onto the rancid floor. A naval officer appeared at the door of the deck.

"Right, lads, we've reached Le Havre. You might want to get

some fresh air and some food before we set sail again at eleven-hundred hours; we need to wait for the tide," he announced.

It was still dark outside but gradually most of the soldiers onboard made their way down the gangplanks and onto the dock. This time of the morning the area was deserted. There was little order as a thousand soldiers filled the area, milling about aimlessly. Arthur spotted the sergeant major.

"Eh up, Sarge, is there anywhere to get some snap? 'Appen lads are starving."

"Lieutenant's gone to find out what's happening; there's a depot here somewhere."

An hour later, many of the troops had dispersed from the port area to find food; others were just sitting around smoking or wandering about, just to stretch their legs. Then the sound of horses' hooves was heard coming from the direction of the town. There were cheers as two wagons approached the dock and pulled up alongside the boats. Several men started to distribute bread from the back, creating a stampede towards them. What started as a disciplined distribution suddenly became a free for all with the soldiers on the back of the trucks hurling the loaves into the crowd as if they were feeding seagulls.

It took one of the officers to calm everyone down and maintain some sort of discipline. The bread was soon gone and the wagons left with the promise of a return with more. Shortly after that, another wagon arrived with water barrels which enabled the soldiers to fill up their canteens. This time the queue was more orderly.

Arthur and his three pals, having consumed their bread, decided to walk into town; their first foray on foreign soil.

"Eh up, Wilfred, tha keep tha eyes open for t'French girls, 'appen they'll be all over tha," said Henry, to much hilarity.

"Well, I don't think much of this place, they're all asleep," said Samuel, who was walking alongside.

At this time, Le Havre was a major base in its own right, with headquarters of many different facilities established, including the Army Service Corps, the Army Ordnance Corps, and the Veterinary Corps. Just outside the town, there were three large, tented camps housing several thousand men being prepared as troop reinforcements. The camps also served as convalescent and rest centres. The base had two field hospitals.

By seven a.m., one or two shops had started to open. The centre of the town was swamped with troops and queues formed at the butchers and cheese shops. Henry wanted to get some cigarettes and found a *tabac*. He and Arthur went inside and stared at the range of products.

"Don't think they sell Woodbines," said Henry.

The proprietor was dressed in a faded waistcoat, collarless shirt and wearing a beret. He sported an impressive white moustache. Henry decided to try his luck.

"Er, excusay, missuer, avey vous some Woodbines?" He made a smoking gesture.

The man shrugged his shoulders.

"Cigarettes... Woodbines?" Henry tried again but louder.

"Ah, oui, Woodbines. Non, monsieur, seulement ce que vous voyez ici."

"What's he say?" said Arthur.

"Something about going on a voyage," said Henry.

"Tha better get in quick, then," said Arthur.

He scoured the hundreds of different packets, then chose one at random. He pointed to a yellow packet.

"Ah, oui, Gauloises, c'est bon choix. Vingt cinq francs, monsieur."

The tobacconist put the packet on the counter and looked at Henry expectantly.

"How much?" asked Henry. The man repeated.

"What's he say?" asked Arthur.

"Not sure," said Henry.

Henry put his hands in his pocket and pulled out a threepenny bit, the cost of a packet back home. The man looked at the coin.

"Non, monsieur, c'est l'argent anglaise. Je veux vingt cinq francs... Française."

"I don't think he wants English money, Arthur," said Henry.

"We've come here to save your bloody country," shouted Henry at the man.

The man looked at him, shrugged his shoulders and then pointed at the coin.

"Un autre," he said and raised his index finger.

"He wants another, Henry," said Arthur.

"Sixpence... for a packet of fags!" he exclaimed. "That's robbery."

"Here, I've got one somewhere," said Arthur, trying to avoid an embarrassing confrontation.

He took out a threepenny bit from his pocket and put it next to Henry's. The man looked at the two coins and smiled.

"Oui, oui, c'est bien." He handed Henry the smokes and pocketed the coins.

With so many English people in town, there was a good trade in pounds, shillings and pence; he would soon exchange it for francs. Henry nodded at the man and took the packet of cigarettes.

"Au revoir, monsieur, bon chance," said the man and smiled.

"Mercy, missuer, you're a bloody robber," said Henry, and the pair turned and walked out of the shop.

"How did tha get on?" asked Samuel, who was waiting outside the entrance. Wilfred looked on.

"Bloody robber, sixpence for a packet of smokes." Henry

showed Samuel and Wilfred the packet. "Don't know what they're like, mind."

"I didn't know tha could speak French," said Arthur as they walked back towards the centre.

"Aye, a bit… 'Appen, they don't speak it like I learned at school, though," said Henry.

"Tha learned French at school?" asked Samuel.

"Aye," replied Henry. "Let's see if us can find some snap, I'm bloody starving."

Arthur and his three pals had managed to find a *patisserie*, a baker's and a butcher's, and had stocked up on food; their tunics were bulging with stuff. Enough, they hoped, to last them for the last leg of the journey.

On the way back to the boat, they spotted Lieutenant Hoskins. Arthur had a question and confronted the officer.

"Sir, do you know where we're going?"

"Yes, Corporal, we're heading for the camp in Rouen, it's about six hours. Did you managed to find some food?"

"Aye, sir."

"Well, better make it last, I don't know how long it will be before we get fed again."

"Aye, 'appen we're stocked up well enough."

By half past ten, there was a stream of khaki heading back to the boat, and a few minutes later, a loud horn sounded from the ship's funnel. The men started to file on board ready for the last leg of the journey.

Meanwhile back in Oakworth, Agnes was again having a lie-in. She was still basking in the glory of the successful tour. The praises from the promoter and Captain Henderson from the previous evening were still echoing in her head, but it was her new acquaintance who was at the forefront of her mind. She eventually got up and walked down to the kitchen in a silk dressing gown.

"Hello, dear, how was last night?" said Mildred, seated at the kitchen table with a cup of tea. Daisy, the housekeeper, was opposite.

"Aye, it was very nice."

"I've put the flowers in water; a posy, too, I noticed."

"Aye, it was from a gentleman who wants me to sing at a party on Saturday evening."

"My, a party? How interesting."

"Yes, the Earl of Harford, it's his mother's birthday."

Mildred looked at Daisy. "The Earl of Harford?"

"Yes, Mam. I need to go into town and choose some music."

"Well, that's convenient. I have some business there also. We can go in together."

An hour later, Agnes and Mildred were downstairs on the trolleybus. Even wrapped up warm in overcoats, it was too cold to sit on the top deck. Agnes related the events of the previous evening and her encounter with the Earl. As they alighted the trolleybus opposite the park, Mildred turned to Agnes.

"Meet me back at the bakery when you've completed your business, we can share a cabbie back to Springfield."

Agnes continued walking along the High Street. To her right, the park, almost deserted, held happy memories and she could see the lights shining in the solicitor's office where Norman used to work. She started thinking about him and wondered where he was at that moment. After another hundred yards she reached Colston Lane, then crossed the road. Most shops seemed to be illuminated on this gloomy, late-autumn morning and she could see George Tooley in his music shop at the piano.

There was a 'clang' as she opened the shop door, which

startled George; he had been concentrating on whatever he was playing. He turned around.

"Agnes, what a lovely surprise, it's so good to see you." He stood up and walked towards her. "Would you like a drink? I was about to make one."

"Do you have coffee? I seem to have acquired a taste for it since I've been on the road."

"Yes, it's my preference, too. Wait here and I'll make some."

Agnes went over to the piano and started moving up and down the keyboard with her index finger. A few minutes later, George returned carrying two cups of coffee. Steam drifted from the surface. He joined Agnes at the piano.

"I don't know how much longer we're going to be able to get coffee. I was reading there's going to be an embargo," said George, handing over a cup.

"Hmm, just as I've a taste for it," she said ironically and smiled. She took a drink. "I'm thinking of getting a piano, George. Will you teach me how to play?"

"But of course, Agnes, I would be delighted to help you. Is that why you're here?"

"No, not exactly." She took another sip of coffee. "I also need your advice." Agnes explained the forthcoming performance for the Earl of Harford's mother. "I don't know what I should sing. I can't sing the recruitment songs."

"No, of course not. When we've finished our drinks, we can look through the music I've got in stock and you can choose something appropriate. I'll help you."

For half an hour, Agnes and the music shop proprietor scanned through the racks of sheet music looking for suitable songs. She eventually chose six, all music-hall favourites, including two of Marie Lloyd's. George returned to the piano and played them through with Agnes to ensure she could remember the tunes.

"I have to say, you have a remarkable ear for music," he said having played them through.

"Thank you," replied Agnes.

They walked to the cash register and Agnes paid for the music.

"Cameron tells me you're auditioning for the West End?"

"Yes, on the 14th."

"How exciting, I'm so pleased for you. I think you'll pass with flying colours... If you need any help with music, please let me know."

"That's very kind, George, thank you. I'm waiting to hear from Cameron to see what I need to do."

"Well, I'm more than happy to teach you to play the piano. You mentioned you want to buy one?"

"Yes, then I can practise at home."

"What kind were you looking for?"

"I don't know, what do you recommend?"

"One like this one; it doesn't take up too much room and has a good tone." George vamped the keys and then played a couple of chords to demonstrate.

"My, but that sounds wonderful. Can you deliver it?"

"Yes, of course... I have a new one in stock; I can let you have it later this week. I will need to get it tuned."

Agnes and George agreed on a price. She would pay for it with the money she would earn at the weekend.

While Agnes was being entertained in the music shop, Mildred had some delicate business to attend to. She called at the bakery. There was the usual stream of customers. Ruth, Betty and Ivy were all serving. Ivy saw Mildred and let her into the behind-the-counter area.

"'Ow do, Mrs Marsden, good to see tha," greeted Ivy.

"Have you a minute?"

"Aye, 'appen I have." Ivy wiped her hands on her overalls.

"How is everything in the bakery?"

"Aye, it's well enough. Flour's being delivered and customers seem to like Mr Ainsworth's bread... We've not had no complaints, anyhow."

Mildred took Ivy into the corridor away from the girls.

"The reason why I'm here, I think it's time to speak to your mother about your situation. You are three months gone now and you're starting to show."

"Aye, 'appen tha's right. I don't know what she'll say, mind."

"Well, I thought we could go and see her together. We'll go directly."

"What... now?" replied Ivy with a look of surprise and concern.

"The sooner it's done, the better. Take off your apron. I'm sure it won't take long."

Moments later, Ivy and Mildred were walking up James Street to the butcher's. Like the bakery, it was doing a good trade, and Ivy opened the door to the service area. Her sister Phyllis saw the pair and waved.

"'Ow do, Phyllis, just going to see Mam," shouted Ivy.

Ivy led the way up the stairs to the parlour on the first floor. Violet Stonehouse was in the kitchen and came out on hearing visitors.

"Hello, Ivy... and Mrs Marsden, to what do we owe this pleasure?"

"Hello, Mrs Stonehouse. It seems we have a situation which we need to discuss."

"You best sit down then," replied Violet.

They made themselves comfortable. There was a slight tension as Mildred composed herself.

"Hmm, well... I'll get straight to the point. Ivy here is

with child and it's Arthur's."

Violet looked at Ivy in a state of shock. "Oh my… Is this true, Ivy?"

"Aye, Mam, I'm so sorry." Ivy started crying.

"I don't know what to say. How could you have been so stupid, Ivy? Did he take advantage of you?"

"Nay, Mam, nay, I wanted it to happen. He was going to war."

Mildred interjected. "Mrs Stonehouse, I don't think it's time for recriminations; we need to look at the practicalities. I've had word from Arthur; Ivy has told him of her condition. He says he will do the right thing by her and will wed Ivy on his return from the war."

Violet was trying to take in the news. "What's to be done? You're not going to be able to manage on your own. You'll have to come back and live here, although heaven knows where you're going to sleep."

"No, that won't be necessary, Mrs Stonehouse. I've told Ivy she can stay at Springfield. We have the room."

"That's very generous of you, Mrs Marsden."

"Not at all; it's my first grandchild and I want it to be well provided for. She can stay until Arthur comes home and then they can decide what to do."

Violet Stonehouse was beginning to get over the shock and was effusive in her gratitude for Mildred's compassion.

"Not every mother would do that," she said.

Ivy went to her mother and put her arms around her. "I'm so sorry, Mam."

"That's alright, child. It seems Mrs Marsden has everything under control, for which I will be eternally grateful." She looked at Mildred and gave her a kind of smile, an expression of acknowledgement and reservation.

"What'll happen about flat? Our Glynis will be on her

own," said Ivy.

"Well, I can send Phyllis down; I know she would welcome the room," said Violet. "That's if Mrs Marsden has a mind."

"Yes, of course, why not? Very well; this weekend, let's say. We'll make the arrangements and Ivy can come and stay with us," said Mildred.

By the time they had finished their business, Agnes was waiting in the bakery. As they left for the cabbie to take them back to Oakworth, Agnes turned to her mother.

"I have a surprise for you, Mother."

"That's nice, Agnes. I think I have one for you, too."

Chapter Fifteen

It was seven-thirty before the S.S. Ennisfallen slowly made its dock in Rouen. Although almost sixty miles inland, the River Seine was navigable for the distance and the port was busy. In November 1914, it was a major depot for supplies and troops. It had excellent rail connections with Paris and the battle areas to the north. It was also a reception centre for the wounded with more than ten different hospitals across the city.

The conditions below decks had deteriorated considerably, and with the soldiers having eaten at Le Havre, the demand for toilet facilities meant queues had formed to use them. Many hadn't made it, leading to a very unpleasant journey.

With sleep virtually impossible, Arthur and his pals managed to make their way on deck. It was bitterly cold with rain flurries but at least the air was fresher, and for the remainder of the journey they hunkered down in a corner next to one of the life rafts. It was dark by the time the lights of the city came into view, and as the boat slowed, Arthur got his three pals together.

"Eh up, lads, I think we're here."

They joined the crush to disembark and for a while there was a great deal of confusion as the troops milled around on the dock looking where to go. The N.C.O.s took charge and eventually had the men lined up in their respective battalions. Sergeant Major Stafford was shepherding the Colsterdale contingent.

On the dockside, a temporary H.Q. had been set up to manage the disembarkation. Lieutenant Hoskins entered the wooden hut and after about ten minutes returned to speak to the sergeant major. After a brief discussion, Sergeant Major

Stafford called the men to order.

"Atten-shun… Forward march."

The battalions were dispersed to different camps with a soldier allocated as guide. He walked alongside the sergeant major and Lieutenant Hoskins at the front of the column.

It was a seven-kilometre march to the St Aignon rest centre where the battalion was to be based. After almost two days with little sleep and fatigue caused by travel, by the time they reached the camp, the men were utterly exhausted.

As Arthur had feared, they were going to be under canvas, and the men waited in turn to be billeted in their respective tents. It was still cold, and having rained recently, the field where the tents had been set up was a quagmire. There were groans of complaint as they followed a corporal, who had been given the task of allocating the accommodation. It was the familiar bell tent design, the same as at Colsterdale. The ranks were again segregated; fifteen men to a tent; sergeants, seven per tent; warrant officers, five per tent; and officers, three per tent.

Arthur managed to round up the hut forty-three squad to share a tent, although the conditions were far less agreeable than they had been used to back in Yorkshire. Inside, there were fifteen blankets placed in a starburst formation from the side of the tent to the pole in the middle. A groundsheet provided some protection from the soil underneath, but with the recent rain, it felt very damp. Space was at a premium and much of the kit was left outside. Arthur just wanted to sleep.

Further north at Lamarck Hospital, Grace was attending to patients in one of the wards when Hetty called in.

"Oh there you are, old thing. The Directrice wants a

word."

They walked together to the room in one of the hastily constructed wooden huts adjacent to the main hospital, which the Directrice had commandeered into an office. Lieutenant Ashley-Smythe was behind her desk writing and stood up as the pair entered the room. There were no formalities of saluting.

"Ah, Marsden, I want you and Mallender to go to the trenches tonight and deliver some supplies, and bring back any wounded you can fit in. Two nurses will join you, Sisters Belpair and Maison; they have been before several times and can direct you."

Grace looked at Hetty and raised an eyebrow.

"But first you'll need to go to the Belgian Army H.Q. in town to collect your passes and be given today's password. You won't be able to enter the trenches until after dark, so I suggest you find the forward base at Ramscapelle and stay there until it's safe to proceed. They will give you a guide to take you forward. Any questions?"

Grace looked at Hetty. "No, ma'am."

"Right, the ambulance is being loaded; you might want to check everything before you leave, and make sure you have sufficient petrol for the journey…. Good luck." She looked at the pair and smiled.

Grace and Hetty left the hut and made their way to the compound where the ambulance was parked. There was a line of orderlies passing parcels of socks, shirts, scarves, first aid chests and packets of extra dressings from the back of a truck and placing them inside. One of the sisters was already supervising the loading. She turned and saw Grace and Hetty approaching.

"Hello, which one of you is driving?" She spoke good English with only a hint of an accent.

"I am," said Grace.

"I'm Lisbeth Belpair, Emile will soon be along."

The sister was dressed in her nurses uniform, consisting of a white apron with a red cross over a grey shirt and long skirt, with a most flamboyant white headwear which seemed totally impractical. Grace had not met her before.

"I'll check the petrol," said Grace.

There was a large supply of five-gallon petrol cans stored in the corner of the yard. Grace asked two of the orderlies to fetch four and oversaw the filling with the aid of a funnel. She then had them strap two additional cans to each side of the vehicle at the back of the running board. Satisfied the petrol tank was full, Grace joined Hetty and Sister Belpair watching the loading.

It was another hour before everything was ready and Grace commenced the laborious process of starting 'Betty'. She said a silent prayer as she gave the handle one almighty turn. The engine coughed into life and Grace breathed a sigh of relief. Sister Belpair joined Hetty and Grace in the front to provide direction. Sister Maison was in the back with the supplies.

They trundled out of the hospital, the ambulance rocking from side to side over the cobbled roads which seemed to be the norm in Calais. They reached the Belgian Army headquarters and Grace parked outside with the engine running while the nurse and Hetty went inside. Sister Belpair acted as translator.

Having received their passes and been provided with the appropriate password, Grace drove north to Dunkirk. The ambulance rumbled across the drawbridge that took them through the grey city walls and past its medieval towers. The roads were full of military vehicles and marching Belgian soldiers with their tasselled caps, making for a slow journey.

They soon left Dunkirk behind them and crossed the border into Belgium. As they approached the small town of Furnes, they spotted a Belgian officer who waved frantically to them. Grace slowed to a walking pace and the officer came alongside and spoke in Flemish. Sister Belpair translated.

"He says he needs to get to Ramscapelle urgently."

"Well, that's where we're going." Grace shouted to the officer. "Hop on."

She stopped long enough for the officer to climb in the back with Sister Maison, giving her a frightful start.

Grace drove through the town at little more than a brisk march; she couldn't believe her eyes. There was hardly a building left standing, just grey, empty shells of houses, and rubble everywhere. Shop frontages blown out, their signs giving a hint of better times – '*la boulangerie*', '*le charcutier*' – now desolated and totally abandoned, their contents long since looted. The craters and potholes in the road made the driving doubly difficult as Grace manoeuvred the ambulance around the obstacles.

"Oh my God, the poor people. What's happened to them?" said Hetty staring at the bleak scene unfolding before them.

"Gone," said Sister Belpair. "Everywhere it is like this."

On the other side of the town, the landscape was flat with poplar trees lining the road. They came to a stationary column of military vehicles, which again Grace had to negotiate with great care as the verges were just a sea of thick, clayey mud. One slip and the ambulance would be immobilised. The soldiers waved at them enthusiastically as they drove by.

Suddenly, they could hear the unmistakable sound of gunfire in the distance, at first like thunder but somehow more rhythmic, a thrump as the Allied shells were launched towards the German lines. Far from being frightened, Grace felt a mix of excitement and awe. She was now at war.

As they neared the town of Ramscapelle, the forward headquarters, it was clear they were getting closer to the action. Carcasses of horses and more ruined buildings littered the roadside. Every so often, they would come across small columns of refugees walking in the opposite direction, pushing carts or lugging suitcases. Grace spotted a gutted-out farmhouse, its red-tiled roof caved in, just off the road to the right. There was smoke coming from the interior and outside a French soldier was waving to them. Grace stopped the ambulance and Hetty and Sister Belpair got out. They were not prepared for what they were about to witness.

The soldier approached them and appeared to be sobbing. He just pointed, seemingly unable to speak. A few yards away, the evidence of an explosion, a large crater. Body parts were strewn everywhere – four or five men, it was difficult to tell. A severed head looked up at Grace, his eyes still open.

"Mes amis, mes amis," he kept saying through his sobs.

Grace didn't need an interpreter. She looked at Hetty, who was viewing the scene with an expression of horror. The Belgian hitchhiker got down from the back of the ambulance and joined them. He spoke to the soldier firmly, which seemed to calm him down. The officer then addressed Sister Belpair, who translated for Grace.

"He says can we take him to Ramscapelle? They will look after him there."

"Of course," said Grace.

They helped the soldier into the back of the ambulance and a few minutes later entered the town of Ramscapelle. It, too, bore the marks of fighting.

As Grace continued, she tried to put her feelings aside; she was determined to complete her mission. The steady 'boom-boom' in the distance seemed to be getting louder, the road muddier and muddier.

As they reached the centre of the town, Grace and Hetty looked at each other. Ramscapelle was in a similar state to the other places they had passed through, gutted buildings dominating the landscape. Few walls were left intact, just the odd gable-end standing proud, thumbing its nose at the devastating German artillery. Grace was looking left and right, taking in the surroundings; she could see broken furniture and personal effects strewn about amongst the rubble, a bath tipped on its side, someone's cooker, never again to provide food for its owner. Hetty was in tears.

"How could anyone do this?" she sobbed.

"Come on, Hetty, chin up, we have work to do," said Grace and pressed on.

In what was probably the high street, there was one building with green shutters which seemed to have escaped the devastation. Grace slowed down.

"It's here," said Sister Belpair, "The headquarters."

Grace stopped the ambulance and looked at the building. Although it still had its roof and walls, the outside was pock-marked with bullet holes. The street was a sea of mud, and Grace, her three companions and the two passengers squelched across the cobbles to the doorway where an orderly had appeared. He spoke to them in Flemish and Sister Belpair translated.

"He says they have been expecting us. The officer in charge wants to see us."

They were led through the house to a back room where a Belgian major was seated looking at a map with three other soldiers. There was something universal about officers. As Grace looked at the man, his grey uniform, different from that of his soldiers, made him stand out, but there was something else. He just seemed 'in charge'. He spoke to his colleagues and they left the office.

"I am Major Maes. You come… with medicines?" He spoke in a strong accent.

"Yes," said Grace, "And some clothing which we've been ordered to take to the trenches. We can bring back some wounded." She looked at Hetty and the nurses. "Four, maybe." Sister Belpair nodded.

The major hesitated while he translated the words. He spoke slowly.

"Yes, of course… I will get one of my men to take you to the, er… *croix rouge*; it is not so far. They will help with the supplies. You will not be able to go to the front until it is dark, it is too dangerous."

Grace looked at Hetty.

"When you have delivered your supplies, return here and wait; it is safe, I think… I will ask one of the doctors to go with you to the, er… trench, later. He will know who is going to survive the journey… Have you eaten?"

"Not since breakfast."

"Then you will be hungry. If you go to the church, there is food there. They will give you something to eat."

"Thank you, Major," said Grace.

He called one of the orderlies. "This man will take you to the *croix rouge* and then you can get some food. Return here when you have finished."

Outside, the hitchhiking officer and French soldier were smoking cigarettes.

"Merci, merci," said the soldier.

The officer saluted. *"Bon chance, mes amies,"* he said.

Grace and Hetty smiled. "Thank you," said Grace.

Instead of climbing onto the seat alongside Grace and Hetty, the orderly stood on the running board and grabbed hold of the passenger door. The two nurses climbed in the back among the supplies. They drove along at a snail's pace, the devastation all too apparent. Along the way, the orderly pointed at various points of interest and spoke in Flemish. Grace nodded.

Driving was extremely hazardous; many of the cobbles had been blown up and the resulting craters hastily filled in. The ambulance lurched from side to side as Grace negotiated the roadway. No amount of training could have prepared her for this day.

They reached the bandage station. It was another building that had survived much of the bombardment. A large awning with a red cross appended had been erected in front of the entrance. The orderly jumped down and went into the makeshift first-aid station. Here they would dispense medicine or patch up the walking wounded and send them back to the front. The nurses exited the back of the ambulance and joined Grace and Hetty.

A doctor emerged from the building followed by several soldiers and another nurse. Sisters Belpair and Maison chatted to the nurse animatedly; they were clearly good friends. The medical supplies were unloaded, just leaving the clothing which was to go to the trenches. The orderly saw a parcel containing a pair of socks. He picked it up.

"Missy… *pour moi*?" he said and looked at Grace expectantly.

"Of course, er… *bien sûr*," said Grace and gave him another pair.

The soldier took the woollen socks and his face resembled a child's at Christmas.

"Merci, merci, missy," he beamed.

Grace noticed that 'missy' seemed to be the given form of address by the local soldiers.

With the supplies unloaded, the next priority was

something to eat. The doctor was still chatting to the nurses.

"Where can we get some food?" interrupted Grace.

"*Mais oui*, of course, er, *l'église*, zee church." He pointed to the right. Grace could see the spire the other side of a row of dilapidated houses, their innards eviscerated by German shelling.

They climbed back onboard the ambulance. The orderly again took up position on the running board, his new socks safely stowed inside his tunic, and Grace headed in the direction of the spire. After a few more minutes of avoiding craters and building debris, they pulled up outside the church. It, too, had not been spared the ravages of the German artillery. The spire was holed in several places and scars from shrapnel peppered the exterior.

The orderly accompanied them inside where more damage was visible; holes in the walls and ceiling let in shafts of light. There were several French and Belgian soldiers taking a break, smoking and chatting away. One or two were trying to catch some sleep, lying prostrate on the long pews.

The conversation stopped as the men saw the women appear. They were trying to make sense of Grace and Hetty's uniform. One of them spoke to Sister Belpair and she laughed.

"He wanted to know if you were a man or a woman," she said.

Grace thought it a compliment and took no offense. The *curé* approached them and spoke French. Again, Sister Belpair translated.

"He says you are most welcome and the sisters will find you some food."

There were several nuns engaged in cleaning and serving food. One was attending a large urn and started to ladle out what looked like a meat stew into tin bowls. It was accompanied by chunks of bread which were in trays in front of them. Grace and Hetty lost no time in satisfying their appetite. They both agreed it was one of the best meals they had had since arriving in France.

It was starting to get dark by the time they had finished; they thanked their hosts and headed back to the army headquarters. Major Maes was in his office and welcomed the women with a bottle of cognac which he waved in front of them.

"This will keep the cold out, I think," he said and laughed. He poured liberal helpings into tin mugs and gave a toast. *"Vive la Belgique,"* he said.

The women responded. Grace took a large gulp and coughed. He then outlined what would happen. The sound of gunfire, which had continued since they had arrived in the town, had stopped; it was eerily quiet.

"The guns, now, they have stopped. Unless the Boche fire, no more boom-boom tonight."

He explained he had allocated three more orderlies to go with them and help carry the supplies. The doctor would join them around six-thirty.

It was the same doctor from the bandage station who entered the house at the appointed hour, ready for the two-mile trek to the trenches. He was dressed in a long overcoat over his white uniform. There were more introductions, and more cognac, before the major escorted them to the ambulance.

The journey would be on foot; the ambulance would make an easy target for German gunners, so they piled the clothing from the back of the vehicle onto four stretchers before setting off. Grace, Hetty, the two nurses, the doctor and the orderlies carried the supplies in pairs. They made their way out of the town.

Conditions underfoot were treacherous; predominantly mud with the occasional boulder from a fallen building. They were instructed to keep low as they reached the narrow road leading to the frontline. It was crowded with soldiers filing forward to the trenches, carrying sacks of straw on their backs to use as bedding or a dry place to sit. Mysterious 'star-lights' lit the night sky over the German trenches for a few seconds before fading away, leaving a dreary darkness. Their eyes had adapted to the luminosity, and visibility was reasonable. Occasionally they were stopped by a sentry, which required giving the password, but after what seemed an eternity, they reached a long, thin, dark line that stretched right and left for as far as the eye could see.

Grace and Hetty followed the doctor down into the trench along a very slippery plank. It was hard work manoeuvring the stretchers and their cargo without sliding over. Once in the trench, the bottom was a mixture of thick mud and planks of wood and was littered with straw. At last, they could stand up; stoop-walking was energy-sapping and hard on the back.

Still keeping their heads down, they continued following the doctor for several hundred yards, passing more soldiers who would call the trench home. Some had lit braziers to keep themselves warm. The ambulance party were still carrying their precious merchandise, which was now getting quite heavy.

Eventually, they reached a wider area where Grace could see men resting in the light of candles set into the sides of the trench. Most were smoking. An officer approached them and spoke in French.

"He says he is very pleased to see us," said Sister Belpair.

Grace's heart was pounding; the sense of danger was palpable. She wondered how on earth anyone could live in such conditions. There followed a swift exchange, with the parcels of clothing unloaded from the stretchers and placed on three large pallets, raised above the floor to keep them dry ready for distribution in the morning.

There was a line of twenty or thirty wounded soldiers lying on planks of wood waiting to be moved back for treatment. The doctor examined each one by candlelight and chose four that he thought had the best chance of survival; one had lost a leg above the knee, his bandaged stump red with blood. Several soldiers helped to load those chosen onto the stretchers and carried them out of the trench before handing them over to the women. Grace and Hetty were carrying a lad about Arthur's age. He was crying in pain from his left hand which had been taken off by a piece of shrapnel, such is the randomness of flying metal. The injury had been crudely bandaged and he had lost a lot of blood.

It was gruelling work, stoop-walking down the track back to Ramscapelle as Grace and Hetty struggled with the stretcher. The training they had received at the camp had prepared them physically for the task but not emotionally. Soldiers continued to file past walking in the opposite direction towards the trenches. The red glow of cigarettes illuminated faces, but no-one was talking.

Grace couldn't help but feel relieved as they reached the Belgian Army H.Q., not just from the sheer effort but from the fear of being shelled. The ambulance was still parked in front of the building. They loaded the patients into the back of it and said goodbye to the orderlies and the doctor that had helped them. The two nurses were now attending the four soldiers in the back, cleaning their wounds as best they could. Grace went through the starting process again, said a prayer, and 'Betty' sprang into life, much to her relief.

The fifty-mile return journey to Calais was uneventful but extremely exhausting for Grace as she tried to keep the ambulance on the narrow road and avoid the many hazards. Without the benefit of headlights, it took all of Grace's powers of concentration. It was a day she would never forget for as long as she lived.

It was one-thirty a.m. as they arrived back at Lamarck Hospital, and there was relief all round. After the patients had been transferred from the ambulance into the hospital, Grace and Hetty retired to their billet.

Saturday, November 7th, 1914. Back in Oakworth, it had been a busy week for Agnes. Her new piano had been installed. George Tooley had made the delivery personally with one of his assistants and helped set it up, then showed Agnes some basic exercises to get her going. Mildred had insisted it would be positioned in the drawing room as there was more space.

They also ran through the six numbers she had chosen to sing for Earl Harford's mother, and by Saturday, she was ready. She had packed an overnight bag and a suitcase containing her new stage costume, which she had bought for the occasion on her last visit into town. She had another on order from Kitty for her audition.

His Lordship was early. Agnes was finishing her makeup as the sound of crunching gravel alerted them to an arrival. Mildred went to answer it. The thought of an earl visiting a Marsden household would have been unthinkable less than six months earlier, but now Mildred took it all in her stride.

She stood in the doorway and watched as the earl's chauffeur went to the rear of the Rolls Royce and opened the door for His Lordship to exit. He got out and walked towards the entrance.

"Lord Harford...? Mildred Marsden, Agnes's mother. Welcome to Springfield Hall," she announced regally.

"Would you and your chauffeur like some refreshment? You have had a long journey, I think."

"Yes, that would be most welcome. We are a little early, we made better time than expected, and the proprietor of your village store was most precise in his directions."

Mildred offered her hand to shake. Instead, he lifted it to his lips and kissed it.

"Please do come in."

His Lordship followed Mildred into the hall. The chauffeur stood hesitantly in the entrance.

"Come in, come in, you'll catch your death out there."

The driver took off his cap and followed them into the sitting room.

"Please be seated, I'm sure Agnes will be along directly… What would you like to drink? I have tea… oh, and some coffee, which my daughter appears to have taken a fondness to."

"Tea would be fine, Mrs Marsden."

The chauffeur, who appeared less than relaxed, nodded.

"Thank you, ma'am," he replied in not much more than a whisper.

Mildred went to the kitchen just as Agnes came downstairs carrying her two bags. She left them by the front door and went to see her guest. As she entered the sitting room, the two men stood up.

"Good afternoon, David," she said and extended her hand, which His Lordship kissed. She nodded to the chauffeur. "It's so good of you to come all this way. Would you like a drink?"

"Your mother has kindly offered already… Can I say how wonderful you look?"

"Thank you, please sit down."

Agnes was in one of her new day dresses and had

applied more makeup than she would normally wear. She was seated opposite His Lordship on one of the armchairs. The chauffeur was on an occasional chair by the window, nervously playing with his cap.

Mildred called Agnes from the kitchen.

"I'll just help my mother," said Agnes, and she left the men and walked into the kitchen.

Daisy the housekeeper had made some cakes the previous day and Mildred was serving them on plates on a tray.

"Take those in, dear. I'll bring the teas."

The refreshments were duly dispensed and enjoyed with polite conversation. Mildred listened to His Lordship; his voice had a resonance like velvet, with a refinement only gained from generations of breeding. After twenty minutes or so, the food and drinks had been consumed and His Lordship looked at the clock on the mantlepiece.

"I think we must take our leave, Mrs Marsden. We have a distance and I would like to arrive back before dark."

Everyone stood up and the chauffeur went into the hall to collect Agnes's luggage.

His Lordship kissed Mildred's hand in farewell.

"Thank you so much for your kind hospitality. You have a very beautiful and talented daughter, if I may say, Mrs Marsden."

Agnes heard the compliment and looked down in embarrassment.

"You are very kind, Your Lordship. I hope you will join us again."

"I hope for that too, very much," he replied.

Agnes kissed her mother and left the house. His Lordship was waiting at the car door and held her hand for her to get in. The chauffeur gave Agnes a blanket before setting off; Agnes waved to her mother as they turned in the drive.

The conversation was polite, much about Agnes's singing career. It was a cold day but Agnes was wrapped up well and, with the blanket, was warm enough.

After an hour, Agnes broached a question she had been wanting to ask for some time.

"Do you mind if I ask you a question, David?"

"Why, of course not," said His Lordship.

"Did my singing not inspire you?"

"But of course, it was very inspirational indeed."

"Then why, may I ask, have you not yet signed up to do your duty?"

"That's quite simple; my mother insists I stay and look after the estate. Since my father died last year, she has been grief-stricken and finds it very hard to cope. I am hoping the party we are having this evening will give her a much-welcomed boost. I have to say, her mood has greatly improved since we announced it, although it has taken much arranging, as you can imagine."

"But surely, should we not be doing all we can to serve our country at this moment?"

"But I am, we provide employment for thirty people."

Agnes was feeling angry but was controlling her emotions.

"And you feel that is the best use of your talents? You will get an officer's commission, you know that. Captain Henderson said we are so short of officers."

"Well, they say it will all be over by Christmas. For the moment, I am best served here."

Agnes was not giving up. "My brother and a close friend are already in France. It seems they are risking their lives so you can indulge your mother. I'm sorry to speak so bluntly."

His Lordship was feeling suitably chastened and realised that any hope of courting Agnes was probably lost. "You are a woman of opinions, I see."

"Aye, when I have a mind, I'll say what needs to be said."

It was an argument that he was not going to win and the remainder of the journey was spent in silence.

The scenery was increasingly wintry; most of the deciduous trees had lost their leaves, which widened the vista. The journey time was just under two hours as they reached Harford Hall. Agnes stared out of the window at the magnificent building as it came into view along the long drive. It was a stately home in every sense of the word; there were even peacocks on the lawns, which stretched to a lake in the distance. Four Gothic columns in grey stone formed a guard of honour up a flight of stone steps to the entrance.

The Rolls Royce came to a stop; immediately the front door opened and a footman hurried down the steps to open the door for the passengers. Agnes exited first followed by His Lordship. She stopped for a moment and looked at the magnificent structure. She turned to him.

"It's beautiful, David, and it's just you and your mother?"

"And the staff," added His Lordship.

"Of course," said Agnes. She still remembered sleeping four to a bed above the bakery not so long ago.

They had made their deadline; it wasn't quite dark as the footman led the way carrying Agnes's bags. The chauffeur had driven away. He opened the door for them into the Great Hall; it was aptly named. A woman came down the sweeping staircase to the right and walked towards them.

"Miss Marsden, welcome to Harford Hall. Lady Margaret Harford, pleased to meet you. My son speaks highly of you." She held out her hand in greeting.

Chapter Sixteen

Agnes looked at the woman, the epitome of the English aristocracy, immaculately presented in a green silk dress with gold-patterned swirls in an oriental style, which may have come direct from Paris. The footman had left Agnes's luggage and return to door duties awaiting the visitors; His Lordship was alongside.

"You're a showgirl, David was telling me."

"I work in the theatre, yes."

"How wonderful, we can't wait to hear you sing. David has been telling me all about you. I'll get someone to take you to your room. I expect you will want to freshen up after your journey."

"Yes, ma'am, thank you."

The greeting had been cordial enough but brief. Agnes felt she was being scrutinised, Her Ladyship's eyes scanning her from head to toe.

Another man was duly summoned. Again, like the footman, he was dressed in uniform.

"Ah, Benson, there you are." Her Ladyship turned to Agnes. "This is Benson, my head butler. He will escort you to your room and then you can join us in the drawing room."

Agnes followed the butler up the wide staircase to the second floor and along a corridor. She had lost count of the number of bedrooms. Eventually, they reached one at the end of the building and Benson opened the door. Agnes entered and tried to take in the opulence; something beyond her wildest imagination. The four-poster bed was a credit to the woodcarver's art, with ornate engravings and patterns. She looked out of the window. The light was fading fast but the front lawns and the lake in the distance were just visible.

There was a separate adjoining room with its own bath and water closet. She thanked the butler, who returned to his duties.

Twenty minutes later, she returned to the hall. Sanders the footman was on duty at the front the door, waiting to greet guests, and saw Agnes coming down the stairs.

"I understand Her Ladyship has requested you join her in the drawing room, ma'am."

He led the way along another corridor and opened a door to a room on the front of the house. Both mother and son were seated on a large decorative sofa drinking from bone-China teacups.

"Ah, there you are, Agnes, please join us. Would you like some refreshment?"

"Do you have coffee?"

"Er, yes, I think so, although it's not something we would normally drink at this time. I'll get cook to check… Sanders, would you make enquiries for our guest?" She looked at Agnes. "Do sit down, dear."

Agnes made herself comfortable on an adjoining armchair. The footman left and a few minutes later Benson entered the room carrying a tray with Agnes's drink.

"So, before you worked on the stage, what did you do? David tells me you were a shop girl," asked Her Ladyship. David looked on.

"I worked in my father's bakery."

"How interesting." Her Ladyship looked at her son with a raised eyebrow. "And you live in Springfield Hall, now." It was a statement, not a question.

"Yes, do you know it?" Agnes took her first sip of coffee.

"No, no, but David tells me it's a fine residence."

"Yes, it is."

"And how long have you lived there?"

"Not long, since August." Agnes was tiring of the inane questioning and quickly finished her coffee. "Do you mind if I could see where I'll be singing this evening? I like to acquaint myself with my surroundings before I perform."

"Why, of course, my dear. David will show you, won't you, David?" This was a cue for David to get up.

"Yes, Mama." He pronounced it 'mummar', as all in gentry circles might do.

Agnes smiled at Her Ladyship as she rose from the armchair and followed David.

At the end of the corridor they came to an enormous room with a high ceiling, gaily painted in the style of Michelangelo. Gold and white corniches decorated the room. At the far end there were a number of men holding musical instruments. A grand piano was in the corner with another man in a dress-suit practising a piece of classical music that Agnes didn't recognise.

"This is the ballroom; it's only used on special occasions. My grandfather entertained Queen Victoria here many times. They were really grand affairs."

"Yes, I can imagine."

Several staff were placing chairs in rows of ten facing the musicians. Agnes's shoes made a clop-clopping sound on the highly polished wooden floor as they approached the piano. The man stopped playing and looked up at the arrivals.

"Monsieur Descartes, may I introduce you to Agnes Marsden." His Lordship turned to Agnes. "Monsieur Descartes is from the Conservatoire De Musique in Brussels. He's just escaped from there with his family."

"Pleased to meet you, Monsieur Descartes," said Agnes and offered her hand, which the Belgian shook. "Can I just say how brave I think you all are; it must have been so hard for you leaving your home like that."

"*Enchanté, mam'selle. Merci,* yes… It has been very difficult." He looked down momentarily. "It is a pleasure to meet you and an honour to be playing for you tonight. You have the music?"

"Yes, in my room, I will bring it for you shortly."

"I will leave you, Agnes, there are guests arriving I should greet," said His Lordship.

The earl left the ballroom. Agnes chatted to the pianist and was introduced to the other musicians, three of whom were also Belgians refugees and had escaped with Descartes.

By seven-thirty, most of the guests had arrived and had been given plates of food in the grand hall. The orchestra could be heard playing in the background. Agnes had been asked to perform at nine o'clock. She had provided Monsieur Descartes with the music and had had a quick rehearsal. She was used to a piano accompanist; George Tooley was her regular partner, but the Belgian was in a different class entirely and seemed to make the instrument sing. After her run through, she sat and watched the musicians for a few minutes before it was time to change.

She returned to her room and put on the stage costume she had chosen for the occasion, then made her way to the ballroom shortly before the allotted time. She stood at the back and listened as the orchestra played an extract from Beethoven's Moonlight Sonata to great applause. His Lordship had been watching for Agnes to appear; he saw her standing at the back of the room and waved. Agnes acknowledged.

After the musicians had finished, he went to the front and addressed the audience. He was dressed in a dinner jacket and bow tie, as were all of the male members of the guests.

"I'm not going to make a big speech," he announced.

"Thank goodness," shouted a young man, clearly a friend

of His Lordship, which was greeted with much hilarity.

The earl thanked everyone for coming. He looked at his mother, who was seated in the middle of the front row, and paid a warm tribute to her. He continued.

"Now, it's my great pleasure to introduce to you our special guest, ladies and gentlemen… Agnes Marsden."

There was a ripple of applause. Despite her successful tour, she was not yet a household name and most of the guests were unaware of her. She reached the front and curtsied, then nodded to the pianist. She launched into her first song and watched as the audience were captivated by her voice. She received rapturous applause. The second number was one of Marie Lloyd's, and as well as humorous, was slightly risqué. Again, the audience lapped it up.

By the time she had finished her final number, the guests stood and cheered; there were cries for more. Agnes was hoping for this opportunity. She handed the pianist another piece of music. He looked at the title and smiled.

"My lords, ladies and gentlemen, thank you for that wonderful reception. Some of you may know that I have recently finished a concert tour encouraging our young men to do their duty and sign up to defend our country. I hope my last song will encourage those of you who have not yet done so."

The pianist played the opening bars, then the refrain. 'Now You've Got Your Khaki On' was a popular song from the tour and unashamedly aimed at increasing recruitment, the singer promising 'extra cuddles' once her beau was in uniform. There were a few embarrassing looks. Many of the audience, like His Lordship, were of serving age. Agnes had made her point and the applause at the end of the song was generous.

Agnes waved to the crowd and bowed her head to Her

Ladyship, then walked to the back of the ballroom and out of the door. His Lordship announced a break in the entertainment before the dancing would begin, then went to see where Agnes had gone. She had returned to her bedroom to change out of her costume. His Lordship followed her up the staircase and knocked on her door.

"Come in," shouted Agnes. She was seated in front of her dressing table repairing her makeup; she had changed into her day dress. His Lordship entered.

"I wanted to say I thought you were wonderful, Agnes."

She looked at him. In his home surroundings, he seemed different; not the cocksure individual she had met in Bradford and shared the Rolls Royce with.

"Thank you, David."

"Are you joining us for the dancing? I'm sure Mama would like to thank you personally for your performance."

"I will join you shortly, David."

"Yes, of course. I will see you in the ballroom." His Lordship left.

A few minutes later, she made her entrance to the ballroom; she could feel that scrutiny again as the eyes of the guests centred on her. There was a general hubbub of conversation. Many guests were smoking, most were drinking.

"Wonderful performance, my dear," said one.

"Such a fine voice," said another as she walked through the crowd towards the front where David was holding a goblet of drink, talking to his mother.

Agnes acknowledged the compliments, nodding and smiling. David broke off his conversation and went to escort Agnes.

"You have a wonderful voice, my dear," said Lady Harford as she approached the host.

"Thank you, ma'am."

"And you think sending all our men to war is a noble pursuit, do you?" This was clearly an emotive subject for Her Ladyship.

"Most certainly, ma'am, I do. Our country needs all who can fight to defend our Empire and our way of life."

"Hmm, it seems David has been seduced by your words." She looked at her son. "He wants to apply for a commission."

Agnes looked at David. "Then he's the man I thought he was, ma'am."

Agnes left the dance before midnight and did give the earl 'the honour' of three dances. She was in great demand with many guests wanting to make her acquaintance. His Lordship was in close proximity, mainly to ward off other prowling male friends eager to court favour.

The following morning, Agnes shared a hearty breakfast with His Lordship, unsurprisingly, in the breakfast room. Then later, she walked down the grand staircase for the last time. Her bags had been collected and placed by the front door by the footman. The earl and his mother were chatting in the hall. She stopped and curtsied politely to Her Ladyship as she approached.

"Thank you again, my dear, for your performance last night. You have a wonderful voice if I might say… Before you go, I have a little something for you." Her Ladyship presented Agnes with a small box.

"Thank you, Your Ladyship, it has been my pleasure."

"No, I should thank you, Agnes. You will always be welcome at Harford Hall."

The earl handed her an envelope. "As we agreed," he said. "I hope we can meet again." He bowed his head, took her hand, and kissed it.

"Thank you, David. I hope so too."

The chauffeur was attending the rear door of the Rolls

Royce for her to enter. She would be unaccompanied; His Lordship had appointments, he explained. There were exchanged waves as the car pulled away and set off for the journey back to Oakworth. Agnes settled back into her seat and considered the experience. As they drove off, she opened the present from Her Ladyship and gasped as she saw a beautiful gold bracelet.

Saturday, November 28th, 1914. Arthur and his pals had been under canvas at the British Infantry Base Depot at Mon St Aignon for over three weeks; it had been a miserable existence. The weather had been described euphemistically as 'mixed', which meant there had been a great deal of rain, making sleeping conditions dreadful. The camp was enormous and by this time covered an area of almost six miles, not with just men and supplies but also horses, which required significant space and attention. Fortunately, this fell to the cavalry regiments and Arthur's battalion was not involved. Instead, much of their time was spent route-marching. As far as the pals were concerned, it was a pointless exercise, causing more physical ailments and achieved little in battle readiness. Not that anything could prepare Arthur and his pals for what lay ahead.

There were some small compensations. There was a YMCA hut on camp that would put on entertainment in the evening: a film show, even the occasional concert. Most evenings were spent there, writing or playing cards. It was a welcome break from the misery of life under canvass.

Troops could also apply for passes to visit Rouen, which Arthur had done on three occasions. The break from army routines was a significant boost to morale. They were able to make use of the extensive tram system which gave easy access to many parts of the city. On the last excursion, Henry suggested that the lads visited a brothel; several had sprung up in the city and were widely used. Unfortunately, there were rumours of men returning with more than they had bargained for; the medical tent was a frequent destination following a session in a brothel. Arthur suggested they sampled the local ale instead.

Wilfred's mental state had begun to improve in the three weeks since they had arrived. He'd received regular letters from his mam, which seemed to lift his spirits and he was engaging more with his pals. According to Mrs Stonehouse's correspondence, Phylis and Ernest were coping well with the demands of the shop, which had eased some of his concerns. The trips into Rouen had also taken his mind off the war and the pals had spent time together admiring the architecture of the old city, including the famous cathedral, where prayers were said asking for divine protection.

"By 'eck, Arthur, not seen owt like this, not even in Bradford," observed Henry on their first visit.

Today at eleven-hundred hours, squad leaders were called to the local battalion headquarters, a large tent close to the entrance to the site. There had been no fraternisation between officers and the men and Arthur had not seen much of Lieutenant Hoskins since their arrival in France. The drill had been taken by the sergeant major.

The men were lined up outside and addressed by Major Foster, the battalion commander. Lieutenant Hoskins was alongside and nodded to Arthur.

"I have some good news for you. At last, we have been ordered forward to the frontline. We will leave by train from Rouen tomorrow; your squads will need to be ready to depart for the station at oh-six-hundred hours. There will be no duties for the remainder of the day... Carry on, Sergeant Major." The major and lieutenant turned and went back into the tent.

Arthur looked at the man next to him. "Looks like this is it, then?"

"Aye, let's hope they knows what they're about," was the response.

The squad leaders were dismissed and Arthur returned to the tent to brief his team.

Arthur had spent most of the intervening time writing to his mother and Ivy, although how long it would take for them to receive the letters was anyone's guess. Many of his pals were writing similar letters to their loved ones who would be waiting anxiously at home for news.

The following morning, after a gruelling six-mile march in full kit from the camp, the lads of hut forty-three arrived at the station in Rouen for the train that would take them north to Calais where another train would take them to the forward base. The station was going through a significant rebuild and parts of it looked like a building site, but there was a canteen of sorts where they were able to buy some food to top up the meagre rations they had been issued with for the journey.

"Eh up, Arthur, looks like we'll be peeing out the window again," said Henry as they walked down the train looking for a vacant compartment.

French carriages were 'slam-doors', similar to their British counterparts, but then a man dressed in the livery of the railway company arrived with a luggage trolley loaded with wooden buckets. Arthur looked at Henry and shrugged his shoulders; he managed to grab one before they were all gone.

There were over a hundred from the original camp in Yorkshire waiting to board the train. Arthur knew most of them now and gave the 'thumbs up' sign to one or two that made eye-contact. The numbers heading north were swelled considerably by other regiments. The journey to Calais had taken almost twelve hours, including stops for the engine to take on water and giving the troops a chance to buy food.

It was dark when they arrived at the *Gare Maritime* in Calais. A lieutenant walked up and down the carriages ordering everyone off and onto an adjoining train which would take them to the final destination. The journey had been arduous, and as the battalions switched platforms, there was a subdued atmosphere.

Poperinghe, known affectionately as 'Pops' by the Allied soldiers, was the gateway to the Western Front operations and contained various unit headquarters, as well as a casualty clearing hospital and billets for the troops. The sixty-mile journey had taken over two hours before the train came to a halt in a marshalling yard well outside the main station. The men were ordered off the train and told to fall in.

Sergeant Major Stafford soon had the Colsterdale contingent lined up in full kit and followed the column into the town square. Although it was dark, there was sufficient visibility to make out the impressive church of Saint Bertinuskerk that dominated the square. The men were dismissed but told to stay close while billeting arrangements were established. Most men lit up cigarettes, some chatted, others were eating the last of their rations.

It was almost an hour before the sergeant major was able to announce the accommodation. Hut forty-three were told to report to a house on Peperstraat about a quarter of a mile away. Many of the properties in the town had been requisitioned to be used as billets.

As they marched the short distance led by an adjutant from the local headquarters, Arthur was feeling philosophical; at least they would have a roof over their head after nearly a month under canvas.

Saturday, November 28th 1914. Life continued as normal for Mildred in Oakworth, but it was a new normal.

Grace and Arthur were in France and Agnes was now in London having successfully passed her audition. She was rehearsing for one of the West End productions due to start in early December. Mildred's connection with them was by letter. Grace and Agnes wrote frequently, but Arthur less so. Mildred treasured the correspondence from her children and had a special box in which she kept them.

As arranged, Ivy had now moved in and had taken the spare bedroom, which was originally going to be Arthur's. She had been kept occupied by helping Daisy with household chores and also with Mildred's charitable foundation. With the need to contact people regularly, Mildred had taken the decision to have a telephone installed. It made sense with most of her new acquaintances being connected. It also meant she could call for a taxicab rather than make the journeys into town on the trolleybus.

She was in the sitting room reading The Times, scanning the newspaper for any snippets of information of activity on the Western Front. She knew from her letters that Grace was still in Calais and Arthur in Rouen. Arthur was not the most articulate of correspondents but his description of the town painted a most favourable impression.

"Oh dear," said Mildred as she read an article headed, *'Fighting on the Yser'*.

Ivy was seated on the settee opposite knitting a scarf she wanted to send to Arthur.

"It says here the Germans have been firing on civilians… in Béthune and Armientiéres," she paraphrased from the account.

"Where's that?" asked Ivy.

"I don't know, France, I think. I do hope Arthur is nowhere near there. He did say he was expecting to be moved to the front in his last letter."

"Aye, he told me that, an' all."

"I think I'll go and make a cup of tea."

"I'll do it," said Ivy. "You read your paper, see if you can find any more news... I'll see if Molly and Freda would like one."

Saturday, November 29th, 1914. At the hospital in Calais, Grace couldn't hide her excitement; nearly a month since she arrived in France and she had been given a weekend pass. The even better news was that Captain Keating had also managed to get a pass. Grace had no idea where he was; he wasn't allowed to say, just 'somewhere in France'. The letters were regular – twice, sometimes three times a week – and always full of longing.

Paris, a place of romance and, for Grace, beyond her wildest dreams, but here she was waiting for her lift to the station. It was early and a chilly morning, but the temperature did not register. She checked her luggage, just an overnight suitcase. Hetty had been almost as excited. 'I want a full report when you get back; I want to know everything,' she had said the previous evening.

Grace laughed to herself as she remembered the remarks. Just then, the orderly pulled up in a car he had managed to commandeer. There was a great deal of goodwill towards the women of the First Aid Nursing Yeomanry and people were willing to help in any way they could. They reached the *Gare Maritime* around six-thirty; plenty of time for the seven o'clock departure. There was a regular service to Paris, but with troop trains continually using the station, the timetable was not always reliable.

Grace had made the journey in the ambulance many times carrying wounded from the hospital and would never tire of looking at the magnificent building. The station was a grand affair with its large, domed frontage combining the station with a hotel. As she reached the station concourse, there was some good news; the train was on time. Before boarding, Grace stocked up on some pastries to last the journey.

The train was an express with only two stops, but nevertheless, the hundred and fifty mile journey would take over four and a half hours. She found a compartment and made herself comfortable; a French officer in his immaculate blue tunic and red breeches placed her suitcase in the luggage rack and sat opposite her. Once settled, she re-read Captain Keating's letter; '*Gare du Nord, twelve-thirty*', it said. The train was due to arrive around eleven forty-five. As the train pulled away, the excitement mounted.

The train was only fifteen minutes late as it pulled into Paris's busiest station. Like Waterloo, it was full of soldiers in uniform, mostly French but also Belgian. The officer gallantly took Grace's suitcase from the luggage rack then carried it onto the platform. He turned and bowed his head.

"*Merci, monsieur,*" said Grace with as good as a pronunciation as she could manage. With her work at the hospital, she was beginning to be quite adept at the language.

She looked along the platform towards the exit; finding the captain among the thousands mingling on the station was going to be the next challenge. Before her was a sea of straw boaters and military caps.

The letter said he would meet her in one of the cafes but not which one. She reached the main concourse and scanned the station looking for such establishments. There were plenty of shops lining the exterior but she couldn't see any places of refreshment. She was starting to feel anxious and beginning to lose heart, but then in the corner, close to the exit, she noticed what appeared to be a bar with people outside at tables, chatting away over glasses of wine.

She battled through the throng of people, holding onto her suitcase, jostling, barging her way until she was stood at the entrance. She looked at the customers at the outside tables; there was no sign of him. She tentatively walked inside. It was dark and dreary, and quite spartan, with bare wooden floorboards and rustic-style tables and chairs. There were probably twenty people taking refreshment. The air was blue with cigarette smoke. Again, she stood and checked around but couldn't see him. Then, suddenly, there was a voice in her ear.

"Hello, Grace darling."

She turned and there he was.

"Matthew," was all she said, and flung her arms around him, a mixture of relief and joy.

"I'm sorry I'm late, my train has just arrived, and I had no idea where you might be... You look wonderful, my darling."

She looked at him as if to check he was real. He was wearing a smart suit and tie.

"It doesn't matter; you're here now. I've missed you so much."

"And I, you... Let's get out of here." The captain was also carrying a small item of luggage. "Let me take your case," he said and picked up Grace's valise.

She hooked her arm in his and they left the station. The scene almost took Grace's breath away. It seemed that the horse was still the main mode of transport. Immediately outside the station there were dozens of horse-drawn taxis waiting for passengers. She looked behind her at the distinctive façade with its huge canopy and arched window. Stone statues of women adorned the top of the canopy and the top of the building, the architecture typical of *La Belle Époque* era. They walked down the *Place Napoleon 111*; to the left there was a large hotel, the *Terminus Nord Hotel*. The captain pointed to the impressive building.

"We need to find somewhere to stay. There looks as good as anywhere."

They walked across the road and into the building. With its proximity to the station, the reception area was full of people, many in uniform, also taking some leave. They approached the clerk behind the desk. The captain looked at Grace.

"I think your French will be better than mine."

She smiled and spoke to the clerk, requesting a double room.

Formalities completed; a porter was called to escort them to their room. With just two small suitcases it seemed superfluous, but he would need the tip, and the pair followed him up the wide staircase to the left of the reception. The room was on the third floor and overlooked the station frontage and the wide street below. Matthew handed the porter a few francs, which he acknowledged with a theatrical bow of his head.

The room was small and dominated by the double bed and there was an adjoining bathroom which contained the basics; it was different to the room they had shared in London.

"Is the room satisfactory? I can change it if you prefer?" said the captain.

"It's perfect, Matthew." She went to him and draped her arms around his neck. The kiss was long, slow and tender, the kiss of two lovers meeting after too long apart. They broke away to draw breath.

"I love you, Grace."

"I love you, Matthew."

They hugged. It was Matthew who broke the silence.

"Are you hungry?"

"Yes, I am," replied Grace.

"Let's explore and find somewhere to eat."

"Yes, that's an excellent idea."

Late November and it was a cool day, but despite the grey skies, nothing could diminish the warmth that Grace felt as she was escorted by her captain along the Paris streets, taking in the wonder of the city. She was wrapped warm in a shawl over her shoulders. The brooch that Matthew had given her on their meeting in London was proudly pinned to her dress.

Since leaving home, Grace had experienced a sense of freedom that was almost unthinkable just a few months earlier. Meetings with potential beaus would have been clandestine affairs, like her liaisons with Freddie. She had thought about him from time to time, but only in a caring way, hoping he was safe. Any romantic thoughts had been replaced by her love for Matthew Keating.

They lunched at a small bistro on the *Rue La Fayette*; Grace was familiar with French cuisine from her occasional trips into Calais with Hetty and had acquired a taste for it.

While they ate, Matthew was able to put Grace's mind at rest on one important issue. He explained he was in military intelligence and based in a regional headquarters on the coast, not on the frontline. It was a great relief, and she shared her experience of her visit to the trenches and the effect it had had on her.

He held her hand. "Grace, I have something I want to ask you."

She looked up from her food. He reached in his pocket

and pulled out a small box.

"Will you marry me?" He opened the box to reveal a ring.

Grace put down her fork and reached for Matthew's hand.

"Oh yes, Matthew, I most certainly will."

"Then you have made me the happiest man in the world."

He took the ring from its box and placed it on her finger.

"Oh, my, it is so beautiful." She looked at it admiringly, moving her hand in different positions as the light reflected in the diamonds.

"I'll let you into a secret; it was the reason I was late. I was choosing a ring."

"Well, Matthew, you are forgiven for your tardiness." She gave him a long, wistful look. "But how will we get married, Matthew?"

"I don't know. We may have to wait until the war is over."

"Then let's hope it will be soon."

The excitement she felt was overwhelming; she couldn't wait to tell her mother. She eventually managed to finish her meal and Matthew paid the bill.

"Where would you like to go?" asked Matthew as they walked to the door.

"I think I would like to return to the hotel and rest for a while."

"Yes, that sounds a most excellent idea. I have a surprise for you tonight."

"Another surprise…? Why, Matthew, I don't think I can take such excitement." She smiled and held his hand. She could feel the ring on her finger and couldn't stop herself taking the occasional glance.

Outside the café, the wide boulevard was heaving with people. Horse-drawn, open-topped, double-decker buses packed with visitors seemed to be everywhere displaying signs indicating favourite places; Notre Dame, Eiffel Tower,

Arc de Triomphe. Names that Grace had only read about; she was trying to take it all in.

They arrived back at the hotel. Matthew removed his coat and Grace her shawl, then again, they were locked in a passionate kiss.

"I feel I should like to sleep, Matthew."

"Yes, of course." Matthew retired to the bathroom and could hear the rustling of clothes being removed from the bedroom.

"Matthew," called Grace, and he opened the bathroom door. He could see her head peering over the bed clothes. "Would you like to join me?" she said and smiled.

It was another special moment in their relationship. They made love and then slept for over an hour.

Matthew woke first; he could see Grace stirring.

"Would you like some refreshment? I will order some to be sent up."

"A cup of tea would be nice."

Chapter Seventeen

Later, the couple headed out of the hotel to Matthew's secret location. He hailed one of the cabbies and spoke to the driver; just two words, '*Folies Bergère*'. Grace was amazed as they travelled along the streets, trying to take in the sights and sounds; she pointed items of interest out to Matthew like an excited schoolgirl. The smell of horses made her think of home.

It wasn't a long journey and as they approached she noticed a queue of horse-drawn carriages waiting to park outside the building. Grace looked at the magnificent frontage and saw the name. She had heard of the theatre, of course; it was one of the most famous in the world. Traditional Paris architecture, with five large widows on the second floor, separated by Gothic columns. On the top of the building, a concrete lintel with the name '*Folies Bergère*' set in stone in the centre, above it, a giant dome. At street level, the entrance was quite non-descript and the rest of the building was festooned with posters, some many years old. Grace just looked in awe.

After a few minutes, the carriage drew up in front of the building and the captain helped Grace onto the pavement and paid the driver.

"This is magnificent," said Grace.

"Yes, it's somewhere I've always wanted to visit."

They joined the queue at the box office and eventually made their way inside. Grace's jaw nearly hit the floor as they entered the Great Hall, the magnificent ceiling with its wrought-iron drop chandeliers lit up in all their splendour. There were tables around the perimeter, all of which appeared taken, men in top hats and women in their finery with ornate headwear; most seemed to contain feathers, as was the fashion.

Matthew summoned one of the many waiters and ordered drinks.

"Oh, Matthew, this is the happiest day of my life," she said, and squeezed his arm affectionately.

They managed to finish their drinks just as the call came for the audience to take their seats. At the far end of the magnificent hall there was a double circular staircase which met together on the next floor. Grace and her captain made their way up the stairs and found their seats in the auditorium. Grace was trying to compare it to the Hippodrome, but there was no comparison. Steeped in history, the whole ambience was the height of chic.

The programme lasted for two hours, a mixture of singing, burlesque and dancers. There was a compere who spoke in French, which Grace attempted to translate for Matthew. All too soon, the show was over. The pair left the building and waited for a taxi to take them back to the hotel. The pavements were alive with people walking along the streets, hovering around the café bars. It was difficult to believe there was a war on.

The following morning, the mood had understandably changed; almost the antithesis of the previous day's highs. There was not a great deal of talking; words seemed superfluous.

Over breakfast in the large restaurant, the conversation was polite.

"It's busy today," said Grace looking at all the number of diners. She looked at her engagement ring which seemed to sparkle in the artificial light from the numerous chandeliers. "When will we see each other again, Matthew?"

The captain picked up her hand and held it in his. "We

don't know what God, in his wisdom, holds for us, but we need to be strong. I love you with all my heart and that love will sustain us for what lies ahead. You will never be away from me, not for one second."

Grace felt an overwhelming feeling of sadness. A tear fell down her cheek which she quickly brushed aside; she didn't want Matthew to see her pain.

After breakfast, the pair returned to the room and collected their belongings. The station was just a short walk. Outside the hotel, Grace looked up. The grey skies lacked any apricity which seemed to match her gloom; it was as though every cloud was mocking her for experiencing so much joy.

Matthew was again on suitcase-carrying duties, and the pair negotiated the hundreds of people mingling around the station entrance. They checked the times of the trains; she noticed his destination, Le Havre. He saw her realisation.

"Yes, it's where I'm based at the moment, but I am sure that will change." There was half an hour before his departure.

They found the platform for the next Calais train. The captain checked the time on his fob watch.

"Twenty minutes, we'd better get you on board."

They walked down the carriages and found an empty compartment. It was much less busy than the previous day's journey. There was one last lingering kiss; not the done thing, but they didn't care – they were in Paris.

"I love you so much, Matthew."

"I love you, too, Grace. Please take care of yourself and don't volunteer for anything dangerous."

He helped her with the suitcase and watched through the window as she found her seat. She was at the window and drew a love heart with her finger in the condensation, then blew a kiss. A few minutes later, there were whistles, the hiss of steam, the slamming of doors, and then the slow inexorable move of the carriage. Grace blew more kisses, then waved as Matthew gave up the challenge of keeping up with the train. Then Grace was on her own again, swept by a feeling of despair.

Sunday, November 29th, 1914. While Grace was saying a sad farewell to her gallant captain, Agnes was recovering from a night of excess in her Bloomsbury House. Her head was fuzzy as she awoke from the heavy sleep, brought on by several brandy hits. It was just a week since her move to the capital, arranged by Cameron Delaney, owner of the property she was now calling home. An elegant Georgian townhouse in a smart terrace, it was in the epicentre of the cultural life in London, frequented by middle-class literary people, artists and academics referred to as 'The Bloomsbury Set'. There was also several members of the acting profession in close proximity and Agnes had already made some new acquaintances through her manager's connections.

She staggered from her bed to the bathroom, which had been suitably furnished with a new water closet and bath, then into the sitting room, wearing a dressing gown. She gasped as she saw the mess, then noticed two men lay together on the settee that she did not recognise. One had his arms around his companion.

"Hello, who are you?" she said as she saw one of them stir.

The man was on the edge of the settee and fell onto the floor; he tried to stand.

"Marmaduke Hersey, at your service, Miss Agnes."

"I will let you put your breeches on. I'm making coffee… Who is your friend?"

"Viscount Stillwell, ma'am."

"You better wake him."

Agnes went into the kitchenette and could hear urgent whispers from the sitting room as she boiled a kettle on the gas stove. She made three cups and returned to the sitting room where the two gentlemen were now seated. She could see that the viscount was a much older gentleman.

"I don't know if we have been acquainted," said Agnes as she put the tray down on the floor.

"No, I think you had retired when we arrived," said Hersey.

The elder man looked haggard and worse for wear. "I do apologise for my appearance, most profusely, most profusely," he repeated.

"Pay no heed, I've seen a lot worse," she said.

"And for prevailing upon your hospitality. It was quite late to get a cabbie. I hope you will forgive me."

"Well, you can pay your keep by helping me clean up."

"Yes, yes, of course," said Hersey. "It's the least we can do."

"So, why, may I ask, are you not in uniform, Master Marmaduke?"

"It's my eyesight, Miss Agnes, I failed the test. I had every intention of doing my duty."

"What about you, sir?" asked Agnes, looking at the other man.

"You do me a great service, ma'am, if you think I am of fighting age. I served in South Africa in 1902."

"With distinction, Miss Agnes," interrupted Marmaduke.

"I see, but what do you do?"

"I design sets at the Trouville Theatre."

"Really...? But that's where I am to perform shortly."

"I am well aware, Miss Agnes. I have heard you sing

many times in rehearsal. We were told there was to be a gathering here last night."

"Yes, it does seem the invitations had got out of hand."

"I hope our presence has not offended you."

"No, but a formal invitation would have been more appropriate."

"Yes, of course, please forgive the ill manners."

"Say no more about it… What about you, sir?" Agnes looked at the aristocrat; even in his dishevelled state, he had a certain bearing that Agnes was beginning to recognise.

"The theatre is my passion, my dear."

"He's being too modest, Miss Agnes… James is the owner."

Agnes nearly spilt her coffee. "Really, I had no idea. I thought it was one of Cameron's establishments."

"No, ma'am, he rents it from me but I have a keen interest in his productions; I have financed many of them… You are a friend of Lord Harford, I understand."

"Why, yes, do you know him?"

"Indeed I do, although I know his mother much better." He looked down. "David is a member of my club. I see him when he's in town, a delightful young man. It was he who alerted me to your talent."

"Well, thank you," replied Agnes humbly.

"I think the production is going to be a huge success. I will be there tomorrow to see Cameron and gauge progress… I understand Miss Lloyd is keen to meet you."

Agnes was trying to take in the revelations. "And I her," replied Agnes with suitable restraint.

Given the standing of the uninvited guests, she was starting to feel embarrassed she had asked them to help clean up, but in the event, they were more than happy, and after an hour, all traces of the previous night's excesses had gone. Marmaduke and the viscount thanked Agnes for her hospitality and left the house to be met by the chill of London's wintry air.

A little later, having bathed and breakfasted, Agnes sat down at her desk and started writing a letter.

'23 Madison Close, Bloomsbury, London. Sunday 29th November. My dearest Norman, I have not heard from you in some while and I can only hope and pray that you are safe. I am writing to let you know that I have moved to London for the duration of the production and have acquired temporary accommodation. If you wish to return a letter, it will arrive sooner by using this address. I have only been in London for a week and I find it so different to how it is at home, so much more liberated. I think I will like it here. I do think about you and all our boys fighting for our freedom and it makes me so proud to know you are doing your duty. Here in London there are little signs of war, but the recruitment continues apace. I do hope by dint of numbers the Boche will soon be defeated and you can return home. I hope this letter finds you well and I look forward to receiving your reply. With fondest love, Agnes'.

Meanwhile, Mildred was entertaining after church. She had invited Kitty for lunch; she had a proposition for her. Molly and Freda were in their rooms changing. Ivy had not gone to church now her condition was becoming more visible and had baked some cakes. She was waiting for the kettle to boil when the family returned. Mildred and Kitty walked into the kitchen.

"Hello, Ivy, how are you?" asked Kitty.

"I am keeping well, Kitty, thank you."

"I think I may have to make something a little larger for you," said the seamstress viewing Ivy.

"Why, thank you, but I can let out one or two of my dresses and Mrs Marsden has kindly bought me a suitable garment."

Kitty looked at Mildred. "Well, the offer is there, if you want another dress."

"That's most generous, Kitty," interrupted Mildred. "But I do have a proposal for you which may be quite time consuming, if you are willing to help."

Ivy put the plate of cakes on the table in front of them and handed them the cups of tea.

"Thank you, Ivy," said Kitty.

"Well, I'll get straight to the point. You are familiar with the charitable foundation I have established with the Honourable Lucy Hamilton?" said Mildred.

"Indeed I am, it's the talk of the village," replied Kitty.

"Thank you... Well, I want to start sending clothing to the troops – scarves, socks, and the like. It must be so dreadfully cold over there... and I wondered if you would be able to help in some way."

"Why, of course, in any way I can."

"That's most kind. Let me get to the point. I believe there's nothing like a parcel from home to boost our boys' morale, that's what I think."

"Yes, you're right, Mildred."

"Well, we're trying to get everyone in the village to make a scarf or a pair of socks. I know from Arthur's letters that is what they value most. I have someone from the Keighley News visiting tomorrow in the hope we can extend the idea to the town. The more we can do, the more boys we can keep warm this winter."

"Well, I have several patterns for scarves and socks. I'm sure I can supply some to your committee and then they can be copied. The main difficulty will be the material," said

Kitty.

"Ah, now that's where I can help. As you no doubt know, most of the mills are busy making uniforms for the army but I've been in contact with three of the mill owners and they have agreed to donate the leftover wool from the spools… end of runs, I think they call it."

"Yes, I'm familiar with that term."

"Lucy… Hamilton has been most influential. She has many contacts among the mill owners, I am sure we will get more."

Thursday, December 10th, 1914. Arthur and his pals had been in the Belgian town of Poperinghe for almost two weeks waiting for the call to go up the line. Having been kept in reserve, they knew it was only a matter of time before they took their turn in the trenches. The population of the town had more than trebled with the arrival of Allied troops.

The historic Town Hall had been requisitioned as the Divisional Headquarters and the town square was now a hub of vehicle traffic. Supply trucks ferried goods from the station to the various storage depots. Ambulances passed through on the way to the casualty clearing hospital, where the wounded were assessed and either patched up and returned to the line or sent on to a hospital for further treatment. Some of the streets showed evidence of enemy shelling. A house in Vlamingstraat had been completely destroyed by a direct hit, and the ruins boarded up. Nevertheless, the troops felt a sense of calm here during their 'rest' time.

The segregation between officers and the ranks remained sacrosanct. Most officers were billeted at Talbot House. They even had their own coffee house, the '*A La Poupee*' café. Other ranks made use of local estaminets for entertainment. As with other towns where there was a concentration of troops, a brothel was provided. Arthur and his pals were frequent visitors to '*L'Esperance*', a café-bar not far from the town hall and popular with resting soldiers. Just outside the town, a camp was being constructed to house the growing number of troops. It was where the lads of hut forty-three were based for their duty time, helping with the construction.

On a drab, cool morning, the sergeant major had lined up the men in the town square at six-thirty as usual, ready for their normal march and duty allocation. Lieutenant Hoskins appeared from one of the officers' huts and walked towards the assembled troops. A shiver ran down Arthur's spine as the news was read out.

"Gentlemen, it's my duty to inform you that tonight the battalion is being deployed up the line."

Movement to the trenches would be carried out at night; it was far too dangerous during the day. The men were excused duties for the remainder of the day.

"Eh up, Arthur, what shall us do for the rest of the day, do you reckon?" asked Henry.

"'Appen we'll go into town," Arthur replied.

Arthur, Henry, Samuel and Wilfred, the four pals from the Malt Shovel, had remained almost inseparable since their arrival in France. They knew each other well and a close bond had been formed between them, a real band of brothers. The four returned to their billet. Arthur decided to write a letter home. He had no idea when he would be able to write again. He took out his pencil.

'Dear Mam, I write to say we are being moved to the front later today and I do not know how long it will be before I can write again. For the moment, we are well and have nice billets in a house, me Henry, Samuel and Wilfred. We are in a town we call 'Pop' which is close to the front. It has nice cafés and some alehouses as well. They grow hops

near here and the ale is not bad but not as good as Knowle Spring. The weather here has been wet and the trenches will be muddy, I don't doubt, but it has to be done. Please say hello to the girls and to Ivy. Let her know I am thinking about her. Your loving son, Arthur'.

He would call in at the post office next to the headquarters. While he was composing his letter, he noticed Henry walking around. He seemed on edge, as if deep in thought.

"Eh up, Henry, tha looks bothered. What's up?" asked Arthur.

"Eh…? What… er, nowt, Arthur. 'Appen I need to post a letter."

Henry turned and left the billet. Arthur thought it a bit strange; he didn't appear to be carrying anything. He just shrugged it off. It was over an hour before Henry returned to the house to be quizzed by Arthur.

"Eh up, Henry, tha's been a while posting that letter."

"Aye, 'appen I stopped for a drink."

"'Appen tha's called in on the mam'selles, more like."

"So what if I did?" he said defiantly. "'Appen we'll all be dead in a week, and I weren't going to die without having been with a woman."

"What were it like?" asked Samuel.

Others in the room had pricked up their ears and joined them to hear of Henry's experience. They wanted full details, which Henry was only too willing to oblige. He had gone up in everyone's estimation. No-one else had had the nerve.

"Eh, Wilfred, 'appen tha should pay 'em a call, an' all. May change tha mood a bit," said Samuel.

"Leave him be, Samuel… Go on, Henry, tha was saying…," said Arthur. The room had gone quiet.

At seven o'clock, Arthur and the rest of the former hut forty-three contingent had lined up in the town square. There were about sixty troops moving forward to relieve those on the frontline. Most were from the Colsterdale camp and Arthur acknowledged several that he knew by sight. There was one in particular he had seen on a few occasions, and for some reason, he reminded him of his father. He had very similar facial features. He was with another group and Arthur had not thought to introduce himself. Many of the lads had formed small cliques, as Arthur had done, and they tended to stick with their own pals.

Sergeant Major Stafford, the once feared drill sergeant from the camp, was someone the men looked up to, someone in control, someone who protected his men; they had been through a lot together. He was once again at the front of the column and he marched the men out in pairs, led by one of the resting troops who had volunteered to take them to the trenches. As they passed the town hall, an officer stepped out from the shadows and joined the sergeant major. It was Lieutenant Hoskins.

The route from the town took them due north onto what looked like an old farm track which had been widened by the numerous vehicles and soldiers that had traversed it. As the troop moved forward, two ambulances passed them going in the opposite direction, followed at regular intervals by groups of soldiers returning to Poperinghe. Most were smoking cigarettes, and from the light, Arthur could make out their dishevelled appearance. There was no discipline or order in their march.

It was just over two miles to the start of the trench complex and an eight-foot-high wall of sandbags protected the entrance from sniper fire. It also obscured the view from the enemy trenches, so they were unable to detect troop movements with any clarity, they believed. The new arrivals were brought to a halt about two hundred yards from the entrance and sent forward in small groups in a stoop walk; any large concentrations were likely to attract a round or two of artillery, they were told.

There was a guard on duty, and as the groups approached, he gave them directions.

"Keep your heads down at all times if you don't want to get it shot off. There're bloody snipers everywhere."

There was a wide, stepped duckboard on a steep angle leading down into the trench. It was covered with mud and tricky to negotiate. It had been secured by more sandbags to deaden the sound of boots. The lieutenant and sergeant major led the group; Arthur and his squad were next. There was a corporal at the bottom of the ramp. Communication was in whispers.

"Officers' quarters are at the end of Shaftesbury Avenue, sir. Down to the right about a hundred yards, then left. You can't miss it; Captain Squires will brief you. Sergeant Major, if you can take your men past the officers' quarters and onto Piccadilly, someone there will tell you where to go."

Arthur followed the officer and sergeant major along the trench, stooping lower than was necessary. Immediately his boots were submerged in the mire; the firmness of the wooden duckboard flooring gave some foothold but it was still hazardous. The way was lit by small alcoves containing candles which gave enough light to see but not enough to attract the enemy. Every few yards part of the trench wall had been hollowed out; some were empty, others contained men sleeping.

They reached the end of a straight section; there was a wooden sign with the words 'Shaftsbury Avenue' painted on it attached to a post. The sound of distant shellfire was unsettling for the new arrivals. As the corporal had said, the trench had widened, and on the left a sand-bagged doorway was visible, again illuminated by candlelight. There was a sackcloth curtain acting as a door.

"Right, Sergeant Major, hold the men here and I'll report in," said the lieutenant and he went inside.

Arthur looked up. The stars were shining as bright as he could remember; it was a cold night and for the first time, Arthur started to feel the chill. His feet were soaked and his fingers stiff from holding his rifle.

Lieutenant Hoskins looked around the quarters. It was spartan but functional; it would have taken a number of men several days to construct such a place. There were four bunkbeds around the outside walls which had been shored up with timber joists and horizontal planks. There was also a desk and chair. The flooring had been raised and strengthened above the quagmire and was reasonably dry, just the evidence of visitors' boot-prints on the duckboard. After the darkness of the trench, the room was much brighter, illuminated by three hurricane lamps placed around the room.

A captain was seated behind the desk examining a map with a sergeant stood behind him. He stood up as the lieutenant entered and returned a salute. He was a tall man with dark hair and clean shaven, as was the requirement in the trenches, apart from the ubiquitous 'officer's moustache'.

"Lieutenant Hoskins, reporting for duty, sir."

"At ease, Lieutenant. Welcome to paradise… We'll get you fixed up with a bunk and I'll get Sergeant Acores here to brief you. Your men will be in Piccadilly. Would you like a drink? I've managed to acquire some rather nice coffee."

"Thank you, sir. I'll get the men settled and join you."

The captain got up and went to the corner where a coffee pot was brewing on a small primus stove on a shelf.

"Very well, Lieutenant. You can have that bunk there with the two blankets."

The lieutenant acknowledged and followed the sergeant out of the officers' quarters back into the darkness.

Arthur and his squad were blowing into their hands to get some semblance of warmth. Acores approached them; Hoskins listened while he briefed the team.

"Right, lads, listen up," said Sergeant Acores in a whisper. "Find yourself a spot along Piccadilly; that's this line here." He indicated with his hand. "Space yourselves out... There're two blankets each, help yourselves. There's a pile over there on those pallets. They came in today so they should be dry if the rats haven't started eating 'em. There'll be no duties tonight but stand-to's at five-hundred hours; that's when the Boche tend to be active. Any questions?"

"Where are the latrines, Sarge?" asked Arthur.

"About halfway down, you can't miss 'em; just follow the bloody smell."

"Right, I'll be briefing your sergeant major here about duties. Get some rest, you're going to need it."

Arthur led the squad down the dark trench; the sound of scurrying seemed to follow them. There were candles giving a modicum of light, and as they walked along, each soldier was allocated a spot vacated by a previous tenant. It was either a raised indent which allowed enough room to sit or an actual sleeping area about six feet long, which had been dug out of the side of the trench. There was about enough space to hold one man; it resembled a large rabbit hutch.

It took a while, but eventually, the men were settled. There were continuous movements up and down the trench as other units from further up the line went about their duties. The name 'Piccadilly' was apt.

Five a.m. the next day, the sergeant major went down the line rousing the men; most were already awake, many had not slept at all. The conditions were frequently called 'hell on earth', although many would argue it was even worse. Arthur was stood at his 'hutch'; he had placed his two blankets inside. Wilfred had joined him and was stood shivering.

"What'll us do when it rains?" he said to Arthur.

Henry was on his second cigarette of the day and had joined them. "'Appen we'll get wet," he interrupted.

The orders of the day were passed down the line in whispers. It seemed strange not having the sergeant major balling out the commands. It was 'stand-to', which meant battle readiness. Each man was carrying his loaded rifle with bayonets fixed. The men just lay against the parapet, the side of the trench facing the enemy, waiting for whatever orders came.

At five-thirty, two squaddies trudged down the line distributing the daily rum ration, which at least warmed up the men. The stand-to lasted until after daybreak. It was quiet. All the candles had been extinguished ready for darkness to return. Arthur noticed Wilfred, who seemed to be staring at the trench wall. Then more scurrying, and Arthur saw his first rat, the size of a cat. Someone threw some mud at it and it disappeared down below the duckboards.

As the light started to improve, he checked his surroundings. The parados, the opposite trench wall, was constructed higher than the parapet that faced the enemy to avoid presenting an outline to German snipers. Along the line, he could see someone with a box periscope checking any movement from the opposing trenches from a gap in the sandbags. An hour later, with no movement from the Germans, the stand-down was ordered.

"What'll us do now?" asked Henry.

"I'll find out," replied Arthur and walked down the trench to find the sergeant major.

He was briefing another team and acknowledged Arthur as he approached.

"Ah, Lance Corporal, there you are, standing orders of the day. The Boche are quiet, so get your men fed, then cleaned and shaved, ready for inspection at oh-nine-hundred. This morning there are some repairs to be done, Sergeant Acores will allocate duties."

"Right, Sergeant Major."

Arthur walked back down the trench and briefed the team.

A few minutes later, two men walked down the trench distributing breakfast. The catering staff had put the food into pretty well anything they could find. Cooking pots, petrol cans, or even old jam jars, and carried it up the trenches in straw-lined boxes.

"What's this?" asked Samuel as the food arrived.

"Maconochie, it's stew. Very good, too," said the soldier as he ladled a helping into Samuel's mess tin.

The rest of the squad received their ration and the two soldiers continued up the line.

"Bloody hell," said Henry, who was stood alongside. "'Ave tha tasted this? It's bloody cold... it tastes like someone's spewed in it."

"Try it with a couple of biscuits, that might help," said Arthur.

Wilfred had hardly touched his stew.

"Eh up, Wilfred, are tha not eating?" asked Arthur.

"'Appen I'm not hungry," he replied.

"Aye, but tha will be, come midday. Tha's got to eat summat or tha'll be poorly."

"Aye, 'appen I'll be poorly, alright, if I eat this shit."

"Try it with a biscuit or two like Henry. 'Appen it won't be so bad."

By ten o'clock, there was a queue for the latrines. Maconochies were renowned for their purgative qualities.

Arthur and his team were given repair duties; there was a trench collapse in Saville Row, the next trench after Piccadilly, following a hit by a German whizz bang or *minenwerfer* to give them their proper name – an artillery shell with devastating capabilities.

Just after midday, the feeding regime was repeated, this time with bullied beef, which was marginally better than the stew they had received earlier. There were also urns of tea, although by the time it had reached the line it was almost cold. The pals used it to soften their biscuits.

A little later, Sergeant Major Stafford sought out Arthur. "Lance Corporal Marsden… C.O. wants a word."

Chapter Eighteen

Arthur trudged his way to the officers' quarters where the C.O. was based. His boots were caked with mud which had dried into a hard crust overnight, but with his footwear now submerged again in the quagmire, they were soon soaking wet. He pulled open the sackcloth curtain and went inside. He stood to attention and saluted.

"Lance Corporal Marsden reporting as ordered, sir."

The captain looked up from his desk where he appeared to be writing in his personal War Book. He acknowledged the salute.

"At ease, Lance Corporal... Ah, yes, Lieutenant Hoskins tells me that you're a bit of a dab hand with the old Lee Enfield."

"Aye, sir, 'appen I am."

"Won a competition, I hear."

"Aye, sir."

"Well, you might be just the man I'm looking for. Private Jenkins, our last sharpshooter, was killed last week; took one in the cheek, unfortunately. I'm looking for a replacement. Do you think you can do it?"

"Depends, sir... what do you need me to do?"

"Keep their heads down... the Boche. Stop them throwing bombs over."

"Aye, I can do that."

"You'll need to work with a spotter. Report to Sergeant Acores, he'll introduce you to Corporal Blythe. He's on his own at the moment. You'll be excused all other duties, Marsden... Any questions?"

"No, sir."

"Very well, dismissed... and good luck."

Arthur saluted and left with mixed feelings. Before the war, the thought of shooting soldiers from a discreet advantage point would go against his own instincts and beliefs. However, since joining the army, Arthur's conditioning had changed his views, and his pre-war pacifist ideals had been replaced by the resolve to serve his country in whatever capacity was required. After all, the Germans were experts at this practice and had killed many Allied soldiers, not least poor Private Jenkins, his predecessor.

Sergeant Acores was just outside and Arthur joined him.

"Captain Squires said to report to you for sharpshooting duties, Sarge."

"Aye, Corporal, follow me."

Arthur followed the sergeant back down Shaftesbury Avenue and reached his squad, who were keen to know what was happening. Henry was holding a shaving brush and had lather around his chin.

"Eh up, Arthur," he said. "What's tha up to?"

"'Appen they want us to shoot a few Germans."

"Aye, well, shoot a couple for me, an' all," said Henry, and he continued with his ablutions.

At the end of the trench, there was an indent and the parapet had been raised. A soldier was stood with a box periscope.

"Corporal Blythe," said Sergeant Acores as they approached. He turned around.

"Eh up, Sarge, who's this?"

"Lance Corporal Marsden, seems he has a reputation for being a sharpshooter."

"Good, tha's some activity over there. They're up to summat."

"Right, keep your eyes peeled and call me if you see anything I should know about."

"Actually, Sarge, I need to be excused duties for a while, I think me guts're dropping out of me backside, and the pain's something rotten."

"I know a good replacement, Sarge," interrupted Arthur. "If the corporal's not fit."

"Who's that?"

"Private Dace, Sarge. He's a fair shot."

"Very well... Corporal Blythe, get yourself off to get it seen to. Marsden, get Private Dace up here."

The sergeant waited while Blythe, rather gingerly, waddled his way down the trench towards one of the medics. A few minutes later, Arthur returned with Harold Dace, the one-time bully of hut forty-three.

"This is Dace, Sarge."

"Right, you better listen up. One of you will be the shooter, the other the observer. Take it in turns about thirty minutes each, no more or you'll lose concentration. Shoot on sight; you have complete discretion. Anything that moves is a target. Any questions?"

"Aye, Sarge; what'll us fire with?"

"It's that rifle there," he said, pointing to the said weapon. "There's a special sight on it which one of the Germans kindly left behind at Ypres. There's some ammunition too," he added, pointing to a large wooden box to the left of the indent.

The sergeant picked up the rifle and Arthur examined the customisation. Telescopic sights were not in regular use in the British Army at this time and the addition was a curiosity. Arthur looked down the barrel through the lens.

"Eh up, 'appen we'll be able to see the spots on their arses with this." He passed the rifle to Private Dace, who did the same.

"Aye, well, make sure you look after it, and make every

round count. And remember, keep your heads down at all times. Once they've worked out your firing position, you'll become a target. We'll move you tomorrow to keep 'em guessing. Don't forget, tell me if there's anything I should know about… Carry on, Corporal." The sergeant left them.

"What do tha think, Harold? Reckon we can bag a Boche or two?"

"Aye, Arthur, don't see why not."

"Here, tha better have this and let us know what tha sees. I'll get used to the rifle." Arthur passed him the periscope.

Harold took it and peered towards the German trenches less than two hundred yards away.

"What do tha see? The other bloke said there was summat going on."

"Can't see owt. Looks quiet."

Arthur stood on the raised platform, which at least was out of the mud. The firing position had been constructed by two columns of sandbags with a gap in the middle wide enough for a man to stand. At head height, there were more sandbags with a slit to take a rifle barrel.

Arthur took his position and peered down the sight at the German positions. It was the first time he had looked over the parapet. It was like nothing he had seen before. A tangled terrain of posts and barbed wire. Tree stumps twelve feet tall, shorn of their branches and foliage. Boulders and craters, hundreds of them, most about eight to ten feet wide, all filled with stagnant, fetid water. Then he spotted other things… human remains, crows feasting on the carcases. He looked away for a moment.

"Eh, Harold, have tha seen this?"

"Aye, Arthur, I have. If tha's a hell on Earth, that's got to be it."

"Aye, Harold, tha's not wrong there."

Twenty minutes had passed without any sign of life, then Harold noticed some movement.

"Did tha see that?"

"Aye, what was it?"

"Don't know. Is it worth a shot to let 'em know we're about?"

"We need to get a better look, 'appen they may be looking for us."

"It's a periscope," said Harold.

"Aye, tha's right." Arthur took aim and pulled the trigger.

"Good shot, Arthur. I think you got it; it's gone anyhow."

That was the sum total of their morning's work.

After another distribution of the dreaded Maconochies, it was down time. Men would try to sleep or write home before the next stand-to just prior to nightfall. Arthur and Harold had been relieved with just a scout, who would call Arthur if there was any further activity from the enemy trenches.

Arthur was in his rabbit hutch trying to sleep when Sergeant Acores approached.

"Marsden, you awake?"

"Aye."

"Just to let you know, Corporal Blythe won't be returning. He's been sent back to the casualty station; looks like dysentery."

"Oh aye? That's bad news for him."

"Aye, it is… I'm here to tell you there's going to be a party going out tonight. You've been ordered to watch and report."

Arthur sat up and cleared his head. "What does that mean?"

"You and Dace keep an eye on our lads, and if they come under attack, you're to return fire until they can get back."

"Aye, Sarge."

"There's more ammunition if you need it." The sergeant was carrying a heavy wooden box which he passed to Arthur. He placed it on the ledge beside him for easy access.

"Operation will start at twenty-one-hundred hours. I'll be back just before it starts."

Arthur found Harold and briefed him. Henry, Wilfred, and Samuel had joined them, and Arthur explained what was happening. He also told them what he had seen in no-man's land.

Sending small parties into no-man's land was a fairly regular occurrence and always carried out under the cover of darkness. The objectives varied, sometimes to repair the defences following an artillery bombardment, sometimes to gather intelligence on enemy positions, and, very occasionally, a snatch squad to capture enemy soldiers in order to gain information. These were particularly hazardous.

Tonight it was a repair job, and the squad of six would be ferrying rolls of barbed wire across no-man's land enabling them to fix a large breach in the wall of wire and other obstacles designed to stop a frontal infantry attack by the enemy. The barbed wire was loaded onto large spools with a bar through the centre for carrying. The group would go out in pairs, each holding an end of the carrying bar. It was heavy as well as dangerous work.

At twenty-one-hundred hours, Arthur and Harold had taken up positions at their observation post. Their only illumination was the light of two candles set in small alcoves out of the wind. They were joined by Sergeant Acores and Lieutenant Hoskins who had been sent by the C.O. to observe and report back.

The night was dark and bitterly cold; it was starting to spit with rain. Harold was on the periscope and could make out the shapes of the soldiers stoop-walking towards the gap in the cordon of barbed wire. It was about halfway between the two sets of trenches. Arthur was following proceedings through his rifle sights. It was a harrowing experience for the 'volunteers' who had been selected for this duty. Rotting human carcasses littered the craters; it was far too dangerous to collect the bodies and give them the dignified burial their bravery deserved. Instead, they decomposed in the mud, food for carrion and rats. Stealth was the order of the day; any extraneous noise would alert the ever-watchful enemy.

All was going well when suddenly a flare was fired from the German trenches. The light only lasted about ten to fifteen seconds, but it had two effects; it lit up the area but also impaired the squad's ability to see by disrupting their night vision. Before the men could recover, a withering burst of machine gun fire opened up. Arthur and Harold watched in horror as the men were cut down. Then it went quiet.

"What's happening, Corporal?" asked the lieutenant.

"'Appen lads were spotted,"

"Can you see anything?"

Arthur started shooting at the German position where the machine gun fire originated. He stopped after ten rounds to check; there was no movement. He scoured the area where the maintenance party had been through his telescopic sight. It was difficult to make out anything; he was sure they were all dead. Then he saw something... a hand; it appeared to be beckoning.

"'Appen one of them's alive, Lieutenant, what shall us do?"

"There's nothing we can do. We'll just lose more men if we try and go over the top. It's just what the Boche want us to do."

"But one of them's still alive, I can see him moving," said Arthur. "We can't just leave him there."

Without waiting for a response, Arthur made a decision. Being in a raised position, Arthur was close to the top of the parapet either side of his protective enclosure. He handed his rifle to Harold and before anyone could stop him, Arthur had hauled himself over the top of the sandbags and rolled down the other side. He could hardly see a thing. He could hear the voice of the lieutenant calling him back in a shout-whisper but ignored it.

Arthur waited for his eyes to become accustomed to the dark. He was at least a hundred and fifty yards away from where the squad had been effecting the repairs. He was laid flat and started to pull himself along with his elbows. The rain was coming down more quickly now and aiding his propulsion. The area was like a swamp as he slithered forward on his belly like a snake.

There were all manner of debris scattered on the ground, shell fragments and shrapnel that tore at his uniform and into his skin, but he could feel no pain. He reached a large crater full of water and dropped into it. For a moment, he was submerged; the crater was at least four feet deep. He managed to haul himself out of the other side and continued towards the stricken soldier.

He was about fifty yards away and he could hear the man groaning. He wanted to shout to tell him to keep quiet but the Germans would be listening for any survivors and open fire again. Suddenly, another flare went up. Arthur played dead and hoped the injured soldier had done the same. Any movement would be met by a burst from a machine gun.

Fifteen seconds, then the darkness returned. Arthur was laid in the quagmire, his face covered in mud and muck. He suddenly felt a sharp pain on his earlobe. Instinctively, he put his hand up to the side of his face to be met by slimy fur. He rolled over in shock and fell back into another crater;

he could see the enormous rat move on in search of more amenable food.

He pulled himself out of the putrid pool and slithered forward. He stopped for a moment; he could feel an object underneath him. He was lay on top of a rotting corpse that had been swallowed by the mud. He gasped in horror then vomited. He composed himself, listened and watched. There was no response from the German machine gunner. Ten yards and Arthur could see the wounded soldier.

"Ah do, can tha hear me? I've come to get you back. Where're tha hurt?"

"Eh up, thank God… it's me legs, happen they've both been hit. I can't move."

"Is there anyone else alive?"

"Nay, I've heard nowt."

"Right, I'm going to have to drag you; try not to make any noise."

Arthur negotiated himself to the back of the soldier and took hold of his tunic collar and started to pull. The rain was coming down in torrents now, which he hoped would deter the enemy. It also helped slide the soldier along but it was exhausting work. Pull, stop, pull, stop, this time avoiding the craters which would almost certainly mean the death of his compatriot; Arthur would never have managed to get him out again.

Another flare went up and Arthur held his breath.

"Keep very still," he whispered.

It went dark again and Arthur continued. Thirty yards, twenty, then Arthur noticed a figure climbing over the parapet.

"Eh up, Arthur, let's give tha a hand."

"Thanks, Harold."

Harold Dace was as strong as an ox and managed

to manoeuvre the soldier to the lip of the trench, then he jumped down and took the weight. Other soldiers had heard what was happening and between them they helped the lad down onto a stretcher. The medic was waiting and quickly assessed his injuries. Both legs had taken hits; a bullet had passed through his right leg but his left had been shattered.

"We need to get him to the aid station as soon as possible. He needs urgent treatment."

"We can take him," said Arthur, "Me and Private Dace."

Lieutenant Hoskins arrived having been briefing the commanding officer on events.

"This man needs urgent medical treatment, Lieutenant," said the medic.

"Very well, see to it."

"Permission to take this soldier to the aid station," said Arthur.

"Permission granted… Lance Corporal, did you not hear my order, before you went over the top?"

"What order, sir?"

"Hmm… it doesn't matter, let's get this man away. While you're there, get yourself cleaned up. Be back here before first light."

"Aye, Lieutenant." It would mean a two-mile trek to the clearing hospital at Poperinghe.

It took nearly an hour to reach the aid station, and as they approached, an orderly, who was waiting at the entrance, went to meet them.

"Lad needs help," said Arthur.

"Right, take him through."

They carried the soldier into a corridor, a waiting area, to be assessed. There were several other men being treated. A nurse went immediately to them.

"What's the problem, Lance Corporal?" She spoke in

English with a French accent.

"He's been shot, both legs."

The nurse looked at Arthur and in different circumstances would have laughed. He seemed as if he'd been dipped in chocolate from head to toe. His face and uniform was caked with mud, his hair matted with all manner of things.

"This man's a hero, ma'am," interrupted Harold. "Crawled across no-man's land to get him back."

The nurse looked at Arthur. "Is that true? Then we better make sure we look after him then. You need to get yourself cleaned up. We'll see to the patient. Er, go to Talbot House, there's a bathing unit there."

"But that's for officers, ma'am?"

"I think maybe they'll make an exception for you."

"What about us uniform?"

"I'll get someone to find a replacement. Call in here on your way back."

Arthur and Harold walked back to the town square and reached Talbot House. It was gone midnight and only a couple of officers were in the bar. They knew the building well but hadn't ventured inside. There was a reception desk and a man in advanced years approached. He could not believe what he was seeing.

"*Mon Dieu,*" he said and put his hand to his face.

"Er, un bath," said Arthur and made gesticulations indicating washing.

"*Suis-moi,*" said the man.

Harold waited for Arthur in the bar.

Arthur managed to wash off most of the mud and muck and returned to meet Harold. He gave the manager a sixpence; he was still using English currency. Given they were still on duty, neither had partaken in an alcoholic drink. They returned to the clearing hospital where the nurse recognised them. Arthur was still wearing his soiled uniform.

"How's t'lad?" asked Arthur.

"He needs to go to hospital in Calais tomorrow."

"Can we see him?"

"Of course... he is there..." She looked at Arthur more closely. "What have you done?" She touched Arthur's ear. He winced.

"'Appen it were a rat."

"We need to treat it. Bites from rats... they are very bad."

Arthur ignored the comment and went to his compatriot he had just rescued from no-man's land.

"Ah do... how's tha legs?"

The soldier had his eyes closed but detected the informer. He opened his eyes and winced; speaking was an effort.

"Eh...? Oof... They bloody hurt, but at least I'm alive... Thanks for getting me out... Doctor were saying they're going to send me to the hospital... What's tha name?"

"Arthur... Arthur Marsden."

The lad looked at Arthur closely, his eyes focussed on his saviour. "Where's tha from?"

"Keighley."

"A baker?"

"Aye, how did tha know?"

"Tha has a sister... Grace?"

"Aye."

"I'm Freddie Bluet... 'Appen I'm tha brother."

"What tha on about?" replied Arthur, not really taking the reply seriously. The ramblings of a deranged man.

"Aye, it's true enough. I thought Grace would have told tha."

"Nah, she's said nowt. How do tha knows our Grace?"

"'Appen we were friends; she came to have a dress made by me mam."

"Aye, I remember the dresses. They all had one, me mam an' all."

"Aye, me mam said she worked for tha da in t'bakery when she were a lass. It were him that's me father, she told me."

Arthur was stunned into silence, trying to take in this revelation.

"If tha writes to Grace, don't tell her what happened. I wouldn't want to cause her no bother."

"No, aye." Arthur suddenly remembered the soldier and his resemblance to his late father. "Does me mam know?" he asked.

"Aye, 'appen she does."

"She never said owt neither," replied Arthur.

Just then, the nurse arrived with a bottle of liquid and a sphagnum bandage. She was also carrying some clothing under her arm.

"Let me see," she said. She lifted Arthur's collar and started cleaning his rat bite, then looked at the wound closely. "Your ear, some, er… it has gone, but it will heal."

Harold took notice. "Aye, 'appen rat's eaten tha ear." He started to laugh.

"I hope it bloody chokes it," said Arthur, then winced again as the nurse applied the disinfectant.

She finished attending to Arthur's ear and picked up the bundle. "I have new, er… clothes for you. You can leave those that you wear and collect them when you return for, er… rest. I will have them washed."

The nurse handed Arthur a fresh pair of trousers and a tunic. He didn't like to ask where they had come from, but there were no bullet holes he could see and they were free from lice. He turned to Freddie.

"I'll just go and put this lot on."

"Aye, I ain't going nowhere."

He took off his pattern webbing equipment, puttees and boots, then found somewhere private to change just along an adjacent corridor. The uniform was on the baggy side and short in the leg, but fashion was not high in importance. He transferred his personal items from the tunic pocket, including his pay book and Small Book, and his father's fob watch which he carried everywhere. He would need to replace his cap; he had no idea where that had gone.

Arthur returned to Freddie; he'd had time to think. The doctor had cleaned and bandaged Freddie's wounds, but he was still in a great deal of pain and was going to need an operation to save his left leg.

"We need to get back to t'line, Freddie. Stay strong, eh? I'll see tha when all this is over."

Freddie raised his arm; Arthur took his hand and squeezed it.

"Take care, Arthur. Tha keep safe."

Arthur and Harold left the clearing hospital and headed back; Arthur had a lot on his mind.

Friday, December 11th, 1914. In the hospital at Lamarck, time had passed quickly for Grace. Immersing herself in her work had lessened the pain of being away from her, now fiancé, Captain Keating. It hadn't stopped the letters; it had become a routine, and every two days, Grace would sit down and read the latest news whilst having a break or just as she was about to sleep. She had sent a letter to her mother to let her know of her recent engagement; she was awaiting a reply. Hetty, in her indomitable way, thought it so romantic.

There had been more trips to the forward base at Ramscapelle to collect the 'blessés' and distribute medical supplies. The route was now familiar to the pair, as was the scale of devastation, which seemed to get worse at every visit.

Just turned eight o'clock, Grace and Hetty had finished breakfast and were at the ambulance. Grace had opened the bonnet and was checking the mechanics; she had become an expert in the inner workings of the Wolseley. Hetty, meanwhile, was cleaning out the inside. Lieutenant Ashley-Smythe appeared from the main building and walked across the compound to the vehicle.

"Marsden, Mallender, I have a job for you."

Grace wiped her hands with a rag and looked up.

"Yes, ma'am," she replied. Hetty heard the conversation and joined them.

"I need you to go to Poperinghe. There're some men there requiring urgent hospital treatment and need evacuating; I said we would help. You can take some supplies with you while you're there."

"Of course, ma'am, where is it?"

"It's near Ypres." There were looks of concern from the two girls. "Don't worry, it's quite safe now, it's under our control; you shouldn't run into any problems… You can take Sister Belpair with you, she's been before. Come up to the office, I'll show you on the map."

The pair followed the C.O. back to her office. Hetty would be navigating and needed to check the route. In the meantime, two orderlies started loading the ambulance with bandages and other medical supplies, supervised by Sister Belpair, as well as a consignment of woollen socks and scarves.

An hour later, Grace had started the ambulance and it was soon bouncing its way over the cobbles towards Dunkirk. Sister Belpair had joined them in the front, which made it uncomfortable, but was manageable.

It was around fifty miles to Poperinghe, the journey continuing over French '*pavees*' filled with soldiers and military vehicles. Having made several trips to the front, they had become used to the battered terrain and the sight of beleaguered troops.

They were about ten miles away from their destination, chatting quite merrily, when Grace's worse fears were realised. There was a line of soldiers which she had to manoeuvre around and hadn't noticed a break in the cobbles. The ambulance lurched off the track, the driver's side front wheel slowly sinking in the morass which bordered the road. Grace leaped out without thinking and found herself knee-deep in the clawing mud.

The onlooking soldiers appeared highly amused and curious seeing women dressed in uniform. Hetty and Sister Belpair got out on the passenger side. The nurse immediately berated the men in French. Within moments, a group of about twenty were around the vehicle. After much debate, they managed to construct a solid base in front of the stricken wheel with boulders and cobbles that were lying around the damaged road. They encouraged Grace to get back behind the wheel.

"*Lentement, missy, lentement,*" one of them shouted as she pressed the accelerator.

With some pushing at the rear and others lifting the side, gradually Grace managed to move the ambulance back on the road to hoots of encouragement from the soldiers.

Hetty and the nurse got back in and waved to the men.

"*Merci, merci,*" shouted Hetty as they slowly pulled away.

"Goodbye, missy, *bon chance,*" they shouted back.

Grace's trousers and boots were caked with mud and the remainder of the journey was uncomfortable. As they got closer to the town, she was struck by the featureless terrain; brown, ugly even, with just the occasional hop-poles to break up the landscape. Half an hour later they were trundling towards the town square. Grace looked at the buildings, which were in far better condition than Ramscapelle and had mostly escaped the same devastation. The difference was quite marked.

Sister Belpair knew the way through the town and directed Grace.

At this time in this sector, the clearing hospitals, as they were known, were still mostly run by Belgians, but with British troops now in proximity, some staff from the Royal Army Medical Corps had arrived including the resident doctor in Poperinghe. Most of the nursing and support staff were local.

The building was formerly a Carmelite convent and had been commandeered by the army to be used as a forward medical base. A red cross flag was hung over the entrance. One of the orderlies had heard the ambulance pull up and alerted one of the nurses.

"*Dieu merci,*" she said as she walked towards the vehicle.

"Hello," said Grace cheerily, as she got down from the driver's seat. "I'm Grace, this is Hetty and Sister Belpair from Lamarck Hospital."

Her companions had joined Grace and they shook hands with the nurse.

"It is, er… very good to see you. I am Veronique Heymans; I am a nurse here. Follow, please…" She looked at Grace. "What happened to your, er… *pantelons*?"

Grace explained the earlier mishap as they entered the building. The nurse led them down the corridor, where the initial assessments took place, to a large room beyond. Grace's boots were making a squelching sound as she walked. A couple of soldiers were seated on the floor with bandages around their heads, smoking cigarettes. The hall was probably where the nuns would congregate for communal prayer; it was austere with stone walls and high windows, which let in minimal natural light.

Grace gasped as the scene unfolded in front of her. There were about fifty men scattered around the room, most on stretchers, some seated with their heads bowed. One or two were managing a cigarette. Grace and Hetty just stared.

"My, there are so many," said Grace. "What will happen to them?"

"*Oui*, er… yes, some they send back, some they die, and some we save," said the nurse.

"But we can only take four."

"Five," interrupted Sister Belpair.

"Five," confirmed Grace.

"Yes, that is good; we have prepared those who can travel. I will show you."

There were ten men separated from the others; all were on stretchers and seemingly unconscious. The four walked over to them.

"These, we think, will be safe to leave. They have, er… arms and legs injured."

Just then, a captain in uniform approached them from an anti-room.

"Hello," he introduced himself, "Captain Longmore, Royal Army Medical Corps, very good to see you. You've come to take some of our patients, I believe."

"Yes," said Grace and made the introductions.

"I have to say how much we appreciate you people; you're tremendously brave, you know."

Grace looked at Hetty. "Not really, we just drive ambulances."

"Ah, yes, but in dangerous places."

"Well, if it's good enough for our boys, it's good enough for us," replied Grace.

"How many can you take?"

"I was telling your nurse we can manage five... Sister Belpair here will look after them."

"Excellent, excellent. We'll be getting most of them away by train but not until nightfall, I'm afraid; it's just too dangerous during the day. There are some here who won't survive that long, unfortunately." He directed them to the separated men. "These here are strong enough for the journey; they have damaged limbs but otherwise they're in reasonable shape. I've treated them as best I can; we're so short of equipment."

"We've brought bandages and some medical supplies... oh, and some woollens."

"I'm most grateful, I'll get the orderlies to help you unload."

They walked towards the ravaged soldiers. Grace looked at them with overwhelming sadness. It would be something that would never leave her, how young; their broken bodies, life changing. One had clearly lost an arm, another a hand, while the others had leg injuries. She reached the third soldier and stopped, stared, checked and gasped.

"Oh my God... Freddie!?"

The soldier was barely conscious. His eyes flickered then opened slowly. His face still bore traces of mud, his hair matted and tangled despite being cleaned up by the medical staff. He tried to focus; the voice was distant.

"Freddie!" There it was again. He looked in the direction of the voice.

"'Appen I've died," he said falteringly.

"No, Freddie, it's me, Grace."

"Grace, nay, it can't be."

"Aye, it is, Freddie Bluet."

His focus became clearer. "Grace... what tha doing here?"

"I've come to take tha to the hospital." She looked at his legs. "Oh dear Lord, what has happened?"

"'Appen Boche took a liking to us. It were your Arthur that got me away."

"Arthur!?"

"Aye, he's in trench. Dragged me off no-man's land. Saved me life, make no mistake."

"How is he?"

Freddie winced with pain. "Aye, he were well enough... I never knew who he were till he told me his name. I told him I were his brother."

"Oh dear, how shocked he must have been."

"Aye, that he were."

She took his hand. "Don't worry, Freddie, we're going to get you back."

"But what I don't understand is, what are tha doing here?"

"I volunteered for the FANYs."

"Fannies...?"

"Yes, I drive an ambulance."

Freddie was lost for words and closed his eyes, his face screwed into a grimace.

Hetty joined Grace. "You know this boy?"

"Yes, he's my brother... well, half-brother, at least," replied Grace.

"My goodness, we better look after him then."

"Yes, we must head back soon. Can you and Sister Belpair get the patients ready? I need to see to the ambulance and refill the petrol."

The resident nurse was showing Sister Belpair the injuries

of the other four men to be taken back. The doctor had been attending another soldier and called out to Grace.

"You must have some food and a drink before you return. It's a long way."

"Yes, thank you, Captain."

Within half an hour, Grace had checked the ambulance and emptied the four petrol cans into the fuel tank, or at least one of the orderlies had. There was much excitement at the supply drop; the woollens were particularly welcomed. Although there was a fairly primitive stove in the hospital which served to boil water, it gave off little heat to the building.

The five patients were carefully loaded in the back, which left little room for Sister Belpair. She was just able to sit at the rear with her back to the cab facing the five stretchers. She handed out cigarettes to those who were able to smoke. They were given some bread and cheese to keep them going until they reached Calais.

Grace checked on Freddie, who appeared to be sleeping courtesy of the drugs the doctor had given him, then she started the ambulance. She and Hetty waved to the nurse and doctor as they pulled away for the journey back to the hospital, which would be completed in daylight as long as they did not run into problems.

They were just leaving the town square when in the distance another artillery barrage started; it made Grace jump. She turned to Hetty.

"Thank goodness they're ours."

Grace was in deep thought as she drove back. She couldn't believe meeting Freddie like that. She still had feelings for him, but as a brother.

Chapter Nineteen

Sunday December 13th, 1914. It was still dark when an orderly called at the billet on the *Rue Marivaux* that Grace and Hetty called home; it was five o'clock. He opened the door to the shop. Sleeping arrangements weren't comfortable but there were no complaints. It was nothing compared to the hardships being endured by Arthur and his pals in the trenches. The orderly peered through the dark, just making out the shapes of the makeshift beds scattered around the room.

"Missy Marsden, Missy Mallender… to hospital… you come… now." It was more a shout-whisper as if not to disturb the other sleeping residents, which failed miserably.

There were a few not very polite shouts in French for him to go away. Grace stirred and then focussed.

"Pierre…? What are you doing here?" Her first thought; it was something to do with Freddie.

"You come, er, the train, *c'est arrivé*… You must help… come, please."

Grace breathed a sigh of relief, then raised her head. "Yes… *oui, attendez*. Wait a moment… Hetty, are you awake?" She turned to her friend in the next 'bed'.

"I am now."

"We need to go; it sounds like the train's arrived from Pop, at last."

It was bitterly cold; it was not uncommon to find icicles on the top of the blanket where condensation had frozen. There was an old oil stove in the corner which would boil a kettle and did give off some heat, but due to the scarcity of fuel, it was not lit during the night. Grace and Hetty slept in their uniforms.

The orderly waited while the two girls put on their boots. "*Vite, missy, vite*," he encouraged.

It was only a ten minute brisk walk to the hospital, their footsteps echoing on the shiny cobble stones. There had been a frost and the puddles had frozen; their breath was visible in the early morning air. As they reached the compound, they could see a great deal of activity. Many of the wounded had arrived from the station on horse-drawn carts. Some were still in the yard where the two ambulances were parked; the horses nodding anxiously while they waited for their passengers to be off-loaded. Orderlies were ferrying the patients into the building on stretchers.

They went inside. It was mayhem as over-stretched staff tried to deal with the influx of the wounded soldiers from the clearing hospital. Hurricane lights were the only source of illumination, creating eerie shadows. Sister Belpair saw Grace and Hetty arrive.

"*Merci*, er, thank you for coming. We are trying to, how you say…? *Prioriser*."

"Prioritise," corrected Grace. "Of course, tell us what you need us to do."

The sister gave the instructions but Grace had a question. "How is Freddie?"

"I think he will be well; he needs to go to England."

"Can I speak to the doctor?"

"Of course, but he has been working all night. They are sending someone from the, er, *corps médical* today to help."

Grace could see the doctor on the far side of the waiting area where the soldiers were being assessed. She waited for him to finish with a patient who seemed to have lost most of his face.

"Hello, Grace, you have come to help? Thank you." He looked at the soldier he had just been attending. "Can you find Father Dominic? This boy won't live for much longer."

"Yes, of course, Doctor. How is Freddie, one of the boys we brought in from Pop, last night?" She described his injuries.

"Ah, *oui*, I think I have saved his leg, if it does not get infected, but he needs to go back to England. There is a boat going to Le Havre at midday."

"Can I take him to the port? He's my brother."

"*Mon Dieu*, but of course. I did not know this."

"No, you were very busy when we brought them in."

Out of the fifty-five men that arrived by train from Poperinghe, ten had died on the journey and another three since arriving with five more critical, the doctor explained. He bowed his head in frustration.

"*Pourquoi combattons-nous ces guerres? C'est un tel gaspillage*"

Grace translated for Hetty, whose French was not as good as Grace's. "Why do we fight these wars? It is such a waste." Grace put her hand on the doctor's shoulder as a gesture of comfort.

It was a hectic and distressing time. Grace had managed to see Freddie who was in a smaller room being used as a ward, but he was asleep. With the boat due to depart for Le Havre at midday, Grace and Hetty supervised Freddie's transfer to the ambulance around ten o'clock.

Freddie was awake but weak. The doctor had managed to repair the shattered bone in his left leg. Everything depended on containing infection, which was more of a threat than the original injury. He was hopeful rather than certain that Freddie's leg could be saved. Two orderlies carried Freddie to the ambulance on a stretcher and Grace watched as they placed him carefully on board. There were four other patients being transported to the harbour.

An hour later, Freddie was safely below deck of the S.S. Walmer Castle, a small packet boat occasionally used for transferring patients to Le Havre. From there he would be transferred to a hospital ship for the journey to Southampton. Grace had managed to say goodbye to Freddie before embarkation, but whether or not he was able to comprehend, she was uncertain.

While they were in town, Grace and Hetty decided to make use of the bathing facilities; there were none at the billet. A temporary bath had been set up at the *Gare Central* in a specially converted railway carriage. The procedure was, as normal, bureaucratic. It required obtaining a *'bon pour un bain'* from the ticket office and a porter would carry buckets of hot water from the engine until the bath was full. There were just four cubicles which meant they were always in demand and queues would build up at peak times.

As Grace lay soaking, she reflected on the events of the last few days. She thought of Freddie and Arthur. Pictures of broken men, the same age as herself, lying in the hospital, their lives changed forever. Then she thought of Matthew; she couldn't bear it if anything were to happen to him. The war was real, brutal, frightening, and not the glamorous crusade she envisaged when she had volunteered to help.

Sunday, December 13th, 1914. Arthur and Harold had returned to the trench around four-thirty, just before 'stand-to'. Most of the men were awake and there were whispers of acknowledgement as the pair walked down Piccadilly towards the officers' quarters. Arthur's sergeant major saw them approach; he had been checking on the men.

"Well done, Lance Corporal… C.O. wants a word."

"Aye, Sergeant Major," acknowledged Arthur. There were no formalities.

"Best wait here, Harold," said Arthur, then lifted the flap covering the entrance to the officers' quarters.

Captain Squires was seated at the table with Lieutenant Hoskins, a hurricane lamp providing a modicum of light. Two other officers lay on beds trying to sleep. The C.O. stood up as Arthur entered. Arthur saluted.

"Ah, Marsden, come in. At ease... I've been hearing all about your exploits earlier. Lieutenant Hoskins has given me a full report."

"Aye, sir."

"It doesn't need me to tell you that we can't have men jumping over the top willy-nilly. It puts other's lives at risk. You could have been killed, and I would have lost my best sharpshooter."

"Aye, sir, beg pardon, I weren't thinking, just instinct."

"Well, in future, you must curb your instincts; we have protocols to follow." He looked at Arthur. "What's happened to your uniform?"

"'Appen I left it in Pop at the hospital. Mine were caked with mud, sir; they gave me these."

"I see... and where are your stripes?"

"On my old uniform."

The C.O. looked at the Lieutenant and smiled. "Well, you need to get two more from the stores; I'm promoting you to Corporal."

Arthur looked at the captain in astonishment; he thought he was being reprimanded.

"And I'm recommending you for a medal... Despite my earlier comments, you showed remarkable courage." He smiled. "Have you eaten?"

"Aye, sir."

"Good, very well, it's stand-to in ten minutes. Get to your post... and well done, Marsden... Dismissed."

Lieutenant Hoskins followed Arthur out of the officers' quarters.

"Congratulations, Corporal. Your family will be very proud."

Arthur didn't voice a reply. Harold Dace was waiting, chatting to one of the lads.

"Harold, looks like we're up."

They walked down Shaftesbury Avenue to their positions. They hadn't been moved from the previous day, despite the sergeant's assurance.

As Arthur and Harold were about to take up their sniping duties, Henry and Samuel approached them. Arthur noticed Wilfred further down the trench; he appeared to be squatting next to his 'bed'.

"Hey, Arthur, how's t'lad tha got away?" said Henry in a whisper.

"Eh up, Henry, aye, 'appen he'll live," replied Arthur.

Sergeant Acores arrived. "Stop talking, lads, Germans will hear ya."

Arthur took the rifle and stepped up to the platform, then peered through the observation slit; Harold was observing through the box periscope.

Despite the sergeant's concerns, the stand-to passed off without incident and the trench returned to normal duties.

After the morning rum ration, the catering team arrived with breakfast, handing out unidentified food; the lads were assured it was bacon, with loaves of bread and a brew.

Harold was on rifle duty and Arthur with the periscope.

"Get thaself some breakfast, Harold, I'll keep watch," said Arthur.

Harold handed over the rifle and stepped down from his raised position.

Then, without warning, the world changed. Arthur was

pinned against the sandbags by an unseen force. Other sandbags flew through the air like leaves on a windy autumn day. Dirt, rocks, planks of wood, large splinters, pieces of corrugated iron used to shore up the trench sides, projected at the speed of sound in all directions until they found a landing point. Then the noise, eardrum bursting; the compression followed, carrying hidden missiles, metal fragments designed to inflict the maximum damage.

The shockwave sent Arthur sprawling; the periscope wrenched from his hands. Then darkness.

"Marsden, Marsden."

Arthur heard the voice calling from somewhere in his subconscious. He slowly opened his eyes; the brightness caused him to blink.

"Marsden, thank God."

There was mud in Arthur's mouth, his head covered in grime, bits of rock and dirt. He could feel fingers touching his face as if dusting a piece of furniture.

"Marsden, can you hear me?"

Arthur's senses started to return. He turned his face to the right in the direction of the voice.

"Ah do, Lieutenant." Not strict army protocol.

"Can you sit up?"

Arthur was covered in debris. He could feel a pain in his shoulder. Instinctively he touched it; he could feel something protruding from his chest and wetness. His legs were trapped under a mix of sandbags, planks and dirt. A splintered post lay across them. He flexed his feet and ankles; he could sense movement and gradually his mobility improved.

"Can you move your legs?"

More movement. Arthur felt a weight removed from his lower body as the post was tossed aside. He moved his legs then felt a searing pain. He winced sharply.

"Arghhh… Aye, 'appen I can."

Slowly, Arthur sat up. He had been knocked to the ground by the explosion and was covered in clawing slime. Rats were scurrying everywhere, disturbed from their hiding places behind the sandbags.

"What happened?"

"A whizz bang, probably targeting your position."

"Aye, looks like they've succeeded, an' all. Where's Harold?"

Arthur looked along the trench that was Piccadilly. To his left, the evidence of the devastation caused by the explosion was all too apparent. The parapet and parados had collapsed inwards. He could see soldiers digging frantically in the mud. Then he spotted a face protruding from the debris about ten yards away.

"Eh up, Harold, 'ow be tha?"

The lieutenant went over and started digging with his hands then made a terrible discovery. It was all there was – just Harold's head, nothing else remained. Pieces of bone, skin and entrails were mixed in with the dirt and rubble surrounding it. He immediately vomited.

Arthur was trying to free himself from the detritus covering his legs and hadn't seen it. He was being helped by other soldiers. Stretcher bearers arrived wearing red cross armbands. Further along, more soldiers were being extracted including the catering team; there was more bad news. Henry and Samuel were buried under a mound of earth and barbed wire from the parados behind the trench. They started tugging at a pair of legs protruding from the morass but they were not attached to a body.

Arthur watched the activity.

"Eh, help us up, I need to help me pals," he said to the attending soldiers and tried to get up.

The lieutenant had given up his fruitless rescue attempt, his fingers bleeding from the digging, and returned to Arthur.

"Stay still, Corporal, you're in no fit state." He turned to the stretcher bearers. "Get him to the medical centre."

Arthur was helped to his feet by the two men, and with his arm around each soldier, was drag-carried back along the trench towards the officers' quarters. Outside there was more space and it was being used as a reception area. Two other soldiers wearing red cross armbands took over Arthur's care while the stretcher bearers returned to the carnage along Piccadilly. The C.O. was watching events with some concern. Lieutenant Hoskins followed shortly after and brought the captain up to date.

The stretcher bearers returned a few minutes later with another casualty covered in mud and grime. He was still alive but there was a piece of shrapnel sticking out of his head. Arthur recognised one of his pals.

"Samuel!" he exclaimed. Again, Arthur tried to get up but was prevented by the attending soldiers who were dressing the wounds to his legs.

One of the first aiders went to Samuel. The stretcher was lay on the ground. The soldier looked at his colleague and shook his head. Arthur put his head in his hands.

After half an hour's frantic digging, the sergeant major returned from the collapsed trench, his hands also red raw from digging, and approached Lieutenant Hoskins.

"Six dead so far, two injured, then there's Private Stonehouse."

Arthur had been made comfortable and was sitting on a straw bale, frustrated at being unable to contribute to the rescue efforts, and heard the comment.

"Wilfred…? What's wrong with Wilfred?" shouted Arthur to the sergeant major.

"He's not well," replied the sergeant major.

"I've got to see him." Arthur tried to get to his feet.

"Let the medics deal with it, Corporal," said the lieutenant.

"Who's dead? I need to see my pals."

"Just stay still."

The trench doctor arrived. "What's the matter with this man, Lieutenant?"

"It's Corporal Marsden."

"*The* Corporal Marsden?" asked the medic.

"Yes."

"What seems to be the trouble?"

"'Appen I've got something in my shoulder."

"Let me see."

The medic examined Arthur. There was a piece of shrapnel about four inches long embedded in his chest, just below his shoulder. Blood was seeping from the wound.

"How about the rest of you? Is there pain anywhere?"

"Nay, 'appen that's about it. They've patched up me legs." He shook his head and hit the right side of his face with the palm of his hand. "Can't hear owt from this ear... Help us up, I need to see me pals."

"Stay still for the moment, let me check your legs."

The medic checked each leg in turn. There were no breaks and circulation was normal, but there were a lot of cuts which had been bandaged, as well as the heavy bruising.

"Any pain, Corporal?"

Arthur winced. "Nay, 'appen I'm alright."

"Let's see if we can get you to stand up. I'll leave the shrapnel where it is for the moment; it won't do any more damage."

The lieutenant and the medic lifted Arthur to his feet. He put an arm out against the parapet to steady himself and moved his legs one at a time. Sergeant Acores approached.

"Sir, we need to get the men away from Piccadilly; the Boche could fire another over any minute to get the rescuers... We'll have repair teams out tonight. We've done all we can."

"Yes, very well, Sergeant."

"What about me pals?" said Arthur, hearing the comment.

"Don't worry, Corporal, we'll see to it. We need to get you to the clearing hospital."

A full assessment of the incident was carried out.

It was the unfortunate Henry King, the life and soul of the group and one of Arthur's best pals, whose severed torso had been discovered; the rest of his body was found buried some distance away. Samuel was also now dead from the piece of shrapnel that had taken away the side of his head. His flimsy cap was no match for a speeding metal object. Harold Dace, the collier from Skipton who had helped Arthur with Freddie, had been decapitated. Another from hut forty-three, Eric Shipton, the hill farmer who had helped Arthur with the map reading in the camp exercise, had also been killed, as well as the two catering lads.

Wilfred Stonehouse, Arthur's long-time pal, was incoherent, shaking violently and talking to himself. Three others had been injured and would require hospital treatment, one seriously. The damage to the trench was considerable but would be repaired that evening.

The C.O. was assessing the situation and looked at Arthur.

"You better get yourself over to Poperinghe and get patched up, old boy."

Arthur suddenly collapsed and two stretcher bearers were called.

"Get this man up to the clearing hospital as quickly as you can. We can't afford to lose good men like this," said the captain.

An hour later, Arthur was at the makeshift hospital in Poperinghe.

Sunday, December 13th, 1914. For some reason, Mildred couldn't settle; she had a strange feeling that wouldn't leave her. She had just returned from church with Molly and Freda. Ivy was in the kitchen and was helping with the cooking as it was the housekeeper's day off. Ivy's condition was now plain for everyone to see and she was keeping out of sight from all but the close family.

Mildred was in her bedroom. Beside her bed was a decorative box with a red ribbon holding the lid in place. She undid the ribbon and took out the latest letters. She sighed as she read them for the umpteenth time; Grace working in a hospital in Northern France, Agnes in London performing in her first West End production, and then there was Arthur; he was her greatest concern. She had no comprehension of what his life was like as his letters were always brief. Daily reports in the newspapers didn't help; they were sanitised for the masses, the reality not deemed conducive for public morale. She would write back and send him one of her parcels; it must be dreadfully cold in those trenches, she thought.

Sunday, December 13th, 1914. Arthur had been carried by stretcher to the clearing hospital in Poperinghe and had been assessed; the injury to his chest would require surgery. The doctor had removed the piece of shrapnel and cleaned the wound. Arthur was also suffering from concussion and he couldn't hear out of his right ear. There were deep lacerations and severe bruising to his legs but were, mercifully, not broken and seemed to be moving satisfactorily. He was classified as a 'walking wounded'. The doctor had concluded

Arthur would need to return to England for further treatment before he would be fit enough to return to the trenches. He would be sent to Calais on the evening *'blessé'* train.

He lay on one of the beds and noticed someone, an officer, at the entrance talking to one of the nurses; she pointed in his direction. As the man drew closer, Arthur immediately recognised Lieutenant Hoskins. He raised himself and winced as the pain in his chest and legs hit him.

"Don't get up, Arthur, the C.O.'s sent me to see how you are."

"Aye, Lieutenant, ta."

"You can call me Norman, we're off duty now."

Arthur winced as the pain seared from the top of his shoulder and down his arm. He looked at the officer.

"Do you know, I reckon our Agnes took quite a shine to tha. Tha's a good man, I can understand why."

"Thank you, Arthur, yes, I still think of her fondly."

"Too wrapped up in her singing to see common sense, to my mind."

"Yes, you could be right, but I would never begrudge Agnes her dreams. I still have hopes that we will be together one day. Her letters express affection for me."

Arthur tried to sit up again but was met by an excruciating pain in his chest and he lay back down.

"How're me pals, er, Norman? I've not seen 'em brought in."

"Hmm." Norman bowed his head. "I have some bad news, Arthur; we lost… umm, Dace, King, Tanner, Shipton… and three others."

"What…? All of them?"

"Yes, I'm sorry, Arthur."

"What about Wilfred?"

"Private Stonehouse is in a bad way, I'm afraid. The

medic doesn't know what to do with him, but he's in no condition to fight. It's up to the C.O. but as you know, we can't afford any malingerers."

"He's no malingerer, sir… 'Appen he's sick."

"Well, that's up to the doctors to decide, but he's not injured. The sergeant major told him to pull himself together, but it doesn't seem to have made the slightest difference."

"What'll happen to him?"

"It depends on what the doctors say. At the moment, he's been struck dumb and he's shaking violently. The medic thinks a few days rest and he'll be himself again. The C.O. will decide what will happen to him. If he is malingering, he could face a court martial."

"No, no, that's not Wilfred, 'appen he's sick," Arthur repeated. "I need to see him. Let me see him; I can sort him out."

"You can't go anywhere, Arthur, not in your condition. If you start bleeding again, you'll be another one on the casualty list."

He gave up his feeble attempt to sit and lay back down, unable to say anything. Arthur was trying to absorb the news. Four pals with whom he had shared good memories and bad, gone, and Wilfred, his best friend since schooldays, goodness knows what has happened to him.

He suddenly remembered the times in the estaminets of Poperinghe where, despite the looming danger, they had enjoyed many boisterous evenings; the humour, much of it morbid, caused fits of laughter. Then there was Henry's trip to the brothel. How the lads teased him about his experience, but it looked as though he had had the last laugh.

"I believe they will get you away tonight," said the lieutenant, breaking Arthur's ruminations.

"Aye, so they say."

"Anyway, I better be getting back… Good luck, Arthur, I hope you make a quick recovery. If you do manage to speak to Agnes, give her my fondest wishes."

"Aye… Norman, 'appen I will."

Lieutenant Hoskins turned and Arthur watched as he walked out of the room. Then he was swept with another pain, nearly as brutal as the affliction in his chest. All his closest pals had gone; he was trying to absorb the news but there was just… nothing, a void which was once filled with companionship and bonhomie.

Lieutenant Hoskins arrived back in the trench and immediately reported to the C.O. As he reached the officers' quarters, he could see activity along Piccadilly where the incident had happened. Men were clearing the way despite the dangers of a further shelling. The bodies of the dead soldiers had been removed, or as much of them as they could find.

"Ah, there you are, Lieutenant; what's the latest on Corporal Marsden?" acknowledged Captain Squires as the lieutenant entered the room.

"Hmm, I'm not sure. The doctor's hopeful he'll make a good recovery as long as there's no infection."

"Quite, quite, well, that's something. He's a good man, we need him back here as soon as he's fit enough."

"Well, he's lost a lot of blood; they're planning to get him away to Calais on tonight's train."

"Good, good… Why wasn't the observation post moved?"

"I don't know, sir; I will speak to the sergeant major."

"Yes, yes, if you wouldn't mind. We need to keep the Boche on their toes; we can't afford to give them easy targets."

"No, sir."

"Very well… We do still have Private Stonehouse to deal with. What do we know about him?"

"He's a butcher by trade, sir; in fact, he has a shop a few yards away from Marsden's bakery. They were quite close, I understand… A good family, by all accounts."

"And you don't think he's malingering?"

"No, sir, I don't."

"Good, because I have the reputation of the regiment to consider."

"Of course… There was something that Corporal Marsden said. He mentioned that Private Stonehouse had not been himself for some time."

"Not made of the right stuff, you're saying."

"Hmm, possibly, but he's not fit to fight, that much is certain. He'd be a liability to himself and those around him, and I don't think he should be near a rifle."

"That bad, eh?"

"Yes, sir."

"Very well, I'll authorise his release to the medical people, see what they can do with him. But we need to keep this quiet, bad for morale and all that. Pass the word round he's got a concussion, that should do it."

"Yes, sir."

"Right, get someone to escort him up to the hospital… No, wait, I don't want him mixing with men who're properly injured. Make sure one of the doctors sees him outside."

"Yes, sir."

The lieutenant found Sergeant Major Stafford and the pair walked along Shaftsbury Avenue to the Piccadilly trench entrance where Wilfred had been taken. They couldn't believe the sight of him. He was in the corner being restrained by two stretcher-bearers and appeared to be hallucinating, trying to swot away imaginary objects. He was shaking uncontrollably and judging by the stains on his trousers had lost control of his bowels.

"Can you hear me, son?" enquired the sergeant major.

Wilfred looked at him, his eyes blank and lifeless. But for his movement, he might as well be dead.

"Right, you two men, can you escort Private Stonehouse to the clearing hospital and get one of the doctors to have a look at him? But stay outside, on no account should he be allowed to mix with the proper wounded... understood?" ordered the lieutenant.

"Yes, sir," replied the men in unison.

The stretcher-bearers managed to coax Wilfred up the ramp and along the track back to Poperinghe. The movement away from the trench had, at least, appeared to have had a calming effect.

They reached the clearing hospital and one of them went inside and summoned a nurse.

"What is wrong with this man?" asked the nurse.

"We're not sure, he's not saying owt," replied one of the soldiers.

The nurse looked at Wilfred. His eyes were unresponsive and he started waving his arms about again.

"This man is sick."

"Sick of being in the trench, more like. 'Appen he's a coward and a malingerer," said the soldier.

"No, no, he needs to be treated."

"Aye...? Well, he can't go in there, Lieutenant's orders."

"We will see. It is not for you to decide. What is his name?"

"Private Stonehouse, miss."

"Er, no, his, er, first name?"

The two men looked at each other. "We don't know, miss."

"You can return to your posts; I will look after him. I know what to do," the nurse replied.

"But what if he becomes violent?"

"No, no, he will not be."

The two men looked at each other and shrugged their shoulders, then headed back to the trench. The nurse waited for the men to leave and then led Wilfred down the corridor of the convent. There was a room to the right leading to an annex.

"Come, come, Monsieur Stonehouse, you are quite safe." Her voice was soft and reassuring.

Wilfred bent his head and started crying in convulsive sobs. The nurse put an arm around his shoulders.

"Come, Tommy, you are safe," she repeated.

His cries gradually eased, and he followed the nurse like a child would its mother.

There were two orderlies on duty and the nurse explained Wilfred's circumstances and the symptoms she had observed. One of them led Wilfred to a large room where other soldiers were housed and showed him to a bed. It was remarkably quiet.

The decision to segregate soldiers with mental illnesses was nothing to do with upsetting the morale of those with physical injuries; in fact, it was the opposite. Seeing more wounded being treated had a significant adverse effect on those 'wounded in mind'.

Just after dark, a train arrived at the railhead in Poperinghe. The wounded soldiers who were deemed fit to travel were transferred in ambulances shuttling back and forth from the clearing hospital. The train's carriages had been adapted to cater for the injured and a nurse was allocated to each compartment. Arthur was one of those loaded onto the train for the two-hour journey to Calais.

It was nine o'clock when the train arrived at the *Gare Central*. Grace and Hetty were waiting at the station in the ambulance. The area was alive with people and vehicles, including some horse-drawn, assisting with the transfer of the wounded for treatment at Lamarck and other hospitals in the town. This was now a daily routine; such were the numbers arriving from the front.

Grace watched as the injured were being carried from the carriages. There was little in the way of organisation; it was a case of random selection. She noticed some stretchers being moved to the side of the platform with sheets covering their heads. It was dark, the only illumination was from hurricane lamps being carried by the orderlies. There was an officer wearing a white armband with a red cross and Grace approached him.

"We're from Lamarck, we can take five in the ambulance and then come back for more. If you have any walking wounded, I can take more."

"Yes, there are one or two."

Grace and Hetty lifted the nearest stretcher and slowly placed the patient in the back of the ambulance. The pair had transferred four more patients onto the ambulance when the officer approached with a 'walking wounded', although that term would be loosely applied; the soldier was moving with no more than a shuffle. He appeared to be in a great deal of pain and was clutching his chest.

"Hello, can you manage to get on or would you like some help?" asked Grace.

"Aye, if tha don't mind," said the soldier. The voice was familiar.

Grace grabbed a hurricane lamp and lifted it up so she could see the soldier properly.

"Arthur…? Is that you?"

Arthur's eyes focussed. "Grace…? What tha doing here?"

"Oh dear Lord, what's happened?"

"Nowt too bad, bit of shrapnel, that's all."

Grace turned to Hetty. "It's our Arthur… my brother. Here, help me get him in the back."

There was a small wooden ladder in the ambulance just big enough to reach the cobbles. Grace positioned it, then, slowly, she and Hetty helped Arthur climb into the back.

With a full load on board, Grace returned to the hospital chatting animatedly to Hetty about Arthur. Orderlies were waiting to help unload when they reached Lamarck. Grace immediately went to Arthur and helped him down the steps.

"Come on, Arthur, let's get you seen to."

Arthur winced again as he tried walking to the door supported by Grace and Hetty. She spotted the duty doctor.

"Doctor McFarlane, can you look after this man? He's my brother."

They managed to get Arthur to a bed.

Grace could see her brother more clearly, albeit with the benefit of a hurricane lamp. His face was almost unrecognisable; it seemed he had aged by several years. He looked gaunt and dishevelled. His hair was matted and caked with mud, dirt and lice. His tunic was soaked with blood from the middle of his chest to his shoulder. There was a six-inch split in the fabric above his breast pocket. His vest underneath was visible and also stained. The doctor removed his tunic while Grace looked on; Hetty had returned to the ambulance to supervise the unloading of the remaining patients. Grace couldn't believe what she saw. His wound had been cleaned and bound by the team at the clearing hospital, but the bandage that was wrapped around his body was soaked red.

"We need to bandage this again; he's losing blood."

"Are you injured anywhere else?" asked the doctor.

"'Appen me legs're not right… and I can't hear owt from this ear." He pointed to the afflicted appendage which was still showing the evidence of the rat bite; the wound was weeping a translucent goo.

"Let's have a look," said the doctor and Grace helped him take off Arthur's trousers. His long johns were stained and dirty. The doctor checked Arthur's legs. They had gone a yellowy-purple colour and were covered in deep scratches.

"Hmm, I don't think either are broken, but you may have ligament damage. Your right knee is very swollen."

"I were a bit lucky, all me pals are dead," he added.

Grace looked at him. "Who's dead, Arthur?"

"It were all me pals from the Malt Shovel, and our Wilfred… he's lost his mind. It were a whizz bang."

"A whizz bang…?"

"Aye, 'appen the Boche took a liking to us. Blown to pieces they were." Arthur spoke without any emotion.

The doctor finished the examination. "I'll get the nurse to clean your ear; it looks like it may be infected."

Grace helped re-dress Arthur. "You must rest," she said and lifted his hand. "The doctors here are very good. We'll get you back to England."

Arthur lay down and just stared at the ceiling. "Aye."

Chapter Twenty

Monday, December 14th, 1914. Hetty had returned to their billet; Grace had decided to stay all night at the hospital with Arthur. She was on the floor with her back against the wall and a coat wrapped around her; it was bitterly cold. Arthur was asleep and seemed to be comfortable enough.

Sleep had eluded her. The shouts of the wounded and dying, pitiful, pleading cries for release from their anguish, kept her awake. It was a sound she would never forget. She watched the padre as he tried his best to give some comfort to those in their dying moments. It had been a busy night.

Hetty arrived from the billet at six o'clock.

"I've made you some tea, old thing," she said, handing Grace a tin mug. "How is he?"

Grace sat up and stretched. "Thanks, he seems peaceful enough; he's sleeping."

"What about you, did you get any sleep?"

"Not really, I wanted to be here for Arthur."

"What's going to happen to him?"

"Well, that's the good news. There's a packet steamer heading for Dover with an escort to take the wounded away, it's leaving at two o'clock. If all goes to plan, it means they can get him into a hospital in England tonight. They seem to be more organised now."

It was another two hours before Arthur began to stir.

"How are you feeling?" asked Grace.

He turned his head. "'Ow do, our Grace, what tha doing here?"

"I work here, Arthur..." Arthur appeared confused. "You're in hospital."

He blinked a few times, screwed up his face and tried

to sit up, then winced as his wounds complained at being disturbed.

"Lay still; I'll get one of the doctors to check on you," said Grace with concern.

Arthur was immobile; any attempt to move resulted in a searing pain in his chest and legs. A few minutes later, Grace returned with the duty doctor. He examined him and was satisfied that the wound was stable. Gradually, Arthur regained his mobility, and with Grace's assistance, he managed to get out of bed just as Hetty appeared. She looked at him sat on the bed his shoulders slouched, his head down on his chest.

"Hello, I'm Hetty," she said, cheerily.

"Hetty works here with me," clarified Grace. Arthur raised his head and slowly focussed his eyes.

"'Ow do," said Arthur, then winced again at the effort from speaking.

"I'm going to get you cleaned up and later we'll take you down to the boat. They're going to get you to a hospital in England," said Grace.

"What about me pals? 'Appen they'll not be seeing England."

"No, Arthur, but you can; remember that."

At midday, Grace and Hetty took Arthur and five other patients down to the harbour and saw him safely onboard the steamer acting as a hospital ship. There was an emotional farewell.

As she drove back to Lamarck, Grace's mind turned to her fiancé; she couldn't bear the thought of anything happening to him. She would write to him again as soon as she returned to her billet.

At the Allied clearing hospital in Poperinghe, in an

annex in the convent that was being used to house the 'wounded in the mind', a great deal of discussion was taking place between the doctor in charge of the facility and Major Hampton, commanding officer at the divisional headquarters. No-one quite knew what was to be done with them. The major considered them to be malingerers and not worthy of the uniform; the doctor convinced him that they were ill and needed medical help.

"Well, if it were down to me, I'd line them all up and shoot the lot of them. No use to man nor beast," the major told the doctor. That was the view among many officers.

With the C.O. more or less washing his hands with those suffering the misnomer 'shell-shock', the doctor made contact with the hospitals in Calais to arrange transportation away from the clearing station. With more men being brought in suffering severe mental trauma, the Poperinghe facility was in danger of becoming overwhelmed. The only treatment being administered was sedation with copious doses of laudanum.

The following day, Wilfred was transferred to Calais with several other sufferers, but despite the medical care, his condition deteriorated. He was mute and displayed involuntary shaking; he was also incontinent. After several days, he was finally sent by boat to England where he was admitted to a special hospital just outside of London.

It was opening night at the Trouville Theatre. Agnes was in her house in Bloomsbury, feeling a mixture of excitement and nervousness. She had the leading female part in a musical comedy and there had been a great deal to learn. The rehearsals had gone well and the director had been full of praise for Agnes's singing and dedication.

Mid-morning, she received two letters. She made herself

a cup of coffee, her hot drink of choice, and then opened the mail. The first was on fine vellum with the crest of the Earl of Harford at the top.

'*My dear Agnes, I am sorry for the tardiness of my writing to you but my circumstances have changed. After your fine recital, Mama and I had a long talk and the upshot is I have been accepted for a commission and have already started my service at the officer's training facility in Cranfield. I am looking forward to playing my part to free our fine country from the threat of tyranny. Mama has also agreed to help the war effort, and as I write, she is offering Harford Hall to the military to be used as a hospital. My father suffered greatly during service in the South African campaign and was not the same man when he returned and Mama thinks the Hall can be used for soldiers who have been similarly afflicted. I hope this letter finds you in good spirits and the rehearsals for your show have gone well. When I have some leave, I intend to come down to London and see a performance. I do hope you will be able to receive me. I will write again when I know a date. With fondest wishes, David*'.

The content was not what she was expecting. Then she turned to the other envelope, which was smeared with what looked like dirt. The letter had been written in pencil and dated before the devastating incident in the trench.

'*My dearest Agnes, As I sit here, it is thoughts of you that make my life bearable. Conditions are appalling, but we remain in good spirits. Your Arthur and several of his pals are here, but as an officer, it is not appropriate for me to fraternise with them, but they seem well enough. It is, however, bitterly cold and many of the men are without warm clothing. I do have a favour to ask; knowing your passion for campaigning, please consider telling your audience to send woollen clothing, or anything that might make life more comfortable for the men in the trenches. I do hope your rehearsals are going well and you will be a tremendous success; I know how hard you work. I will write again in a few days. With fondest love, Norman'.*

Both letters made an immediate impact on Agnes. She would contact Cameron and mention the need for clothing to be sent to the troops. She was sure he would support such an initiative.

That evening, Agnes was in her dressing room surrounded by flowers. She was drinking a honey and lemon cordial to ease her throat, as recommended by one of the more seasoned cast members. Cameron had already visited her and Agnes had explained her desire to promote the winter clothing initiative, which he endorsed immediately, and would mention it to the other productions he was promoting.

To everyone's delight, the production was a resounding success and there were roars of approval from the audience when the curtain came down. On her third curtain call, Agnes addressed the audience and told them of the need to send warm clothing to the soldiers at the front. She received another rapturous round of applause.

Back in her dressing room, she was removing her makeup when there was a knock on her door.

"Hello, Cameron, come in."

"Can I just say, I thought you were excellent, my dear. I am sorry to disturb you, but I have someone who wants to meet you." Cameron stepped to one side. Recognition was instant.

"Hello, I'm Marie Lloyd, you can call me Marie. I've been looking forward to meeting you."

Agnes was momentarily speechless.

It had been just over three months since the start of the war, and from the initial hundred thousand troops that were sent to Flanders as part of the British Expeditionary Force, less than ten thousand were still fighting. Almost ninety thousand had died and many thousands injured. These figures were not reported in the newspapers.

From the hospital ship, Arthur had been transferred by train to a clearing hospital in London before being moved to the Royal Infirmary in Leeds. Such was the demand for beds, as soon as he was strong enough to walk unaided, he would be allowed to be discharged into the care of his family. He would, however, need to report to the hospital for assessment at regular intervals to determine his readiness to return to the front and avoid any charge of desertion.

Saturday. January 2nd, 1915. Mildred was in the kitchen with Molly, Ivy and Freda. They were baking when a ring at the doorbell alerted her. She always shuddered when an unexpected caller arrived. Many mothers had received telegrams; they were never good news. Molly went to answer.

"It's alright, Molly, I'll go," said Mildred and wiped her hands with a towel.

"Ah do, Mrs Marsden. Letter for tha." The postman handed over the pencil-scribbled envelope.

Mildred thanked the man and he left. She returned to the kitchen, still clutching the letter.

"Who was it, Mam?" asked Molly.

Mildred sat down and started to open the envelope with a knife. "It's from Arthur," replied Mildred.

Ivy looked up from her mixing bowl with an anxious expression. "How is he?"

She scanned it and then paraphrased it for the girls.

"Oh dear Lord, he says he's been injured... he's in hospital."

"Injured...? Injured?" said Ivy. "How bad?" Her face was etched with concern.

"He doesn't say. He says not to worry."

"Where, Mam? Does he say?" asked Molly, who was trying to look over her mother's shoulder at the contents.

"He's in the infirmary... in Leeds. I must go and see him."

"Can we come?" said Molly anxiously.

"Better not, until I find out how he is. He says he's well enough... Can you look after the girls, Ivy? I'm going to call a cabbie."

Mildred had been pacing up and down wondering about her son. Ivy had taken the letter from Mildred and re-read it but was none the wiser. Mildred heard the crunching gravel as the cabbie arrived; it had taken nearly an hour since she had made the call. She put on her winter coat, shawl and hat. It would be a cold journey to Leeds; there was no heating in the taxicabs. The temperature was marginally above freezing with a threat of snow. Grey clouds were building from the west.

They reached the hospital complex at just after two o'clock; it had taken over an hour and a half to get there. She was directed from the reception desk to the third floor. As she walked through the wards searching for Arthur, Mildred couldn't believe her eyes at the number of men being treated. Then a nurse walked towards her.

"Can I help you?"

"Yes, please... I'm looking for my son, Arthur Marsden."

"Marsden...? Oh, yes, he's in the end bed." The nurse pointed down a long row of what must have been thirty beds or more.

Mildred walked past the injured men. Some were smoking, just staring into space, and made no acknowledgement of her; others were sleeping. Bandaged heads, missing limbs, crutches; she was trying to take in the images around her. Then she spotted him. The sight of her only son, laying in the blue uniform of the injured, was heart-breaking.

"Hello, Arthur," she said as she approached. There was barely enough room to shuffle towards the top of the bed. Arthur opened his eyes. "How are you feeling?"

"Eh… what…? Is that you, Mam?"

"Yes, Arthur."

His eyes fluttered as he was trying to focus. "'Appen… I'm well enough… They say I can go home." His voice was low and guttural. He was trembling.

Mildred instinctively held his hand. "Who's in charge?"

"There's… a doctor." Arthur winced and closed his eyes.

"I'll find him." She inched around the bed and went in search of the medic. The nurse spotted her.

"Nurse, my son says he can go home; I want to make arrangements," Mildred said, assertively.

"Yes, of course. I can do that for you," replied the nurse.

The following day, Mildred, Ivy, Molly and Freda were waiting anxiously for the taxi that Mildred had arranged to collect him.

"I must warn you, Ivy, he's not himself at the moment," said Mildred.

"Mam, he's here," shouted Molly excitedly at around eleven o'clock, the crunching gravel heralding the arrival of a vehicle.

Mildred opened the door and watched as Arthur struggled to get out of the taxi. Instinctively they rushed to help him.

As the cabbie departed, Arthur stood in the drive in the same uniform he had been wearing when he had left France, complete with his blood-stained, ripped tunic. His 'hospital blue' would be used again.

"Oh dear Lord," said Mildred seeing him struggle. "Let's get you inside."

Molly and Mildred helped him into the house; he was dragging his right leg. Ivy was in the hall and gasped as she saw him. Arthur felt overwhelmed; it was as though he was in a dream state, unable to process the events around him.

"I've made you some cakes, Arthur," said Freda, unintentionally incongruous.

Arthur looked at her but his eyes were not focussing. "Ta," he managed to say.

"Come on, Arthur, let's get you out of those clothes and into a bath. That'll make you feel better."

"Let me bathe him," said Ivy.

Mildred looked at her. "Yes, very well."

They helped Arthur upstairs.

"I've made you a bed up, you can have this room," she said, showing him one of the spare bedrooms.

Mildred and Ivy took him to the bathroom and helped him undress.

"I'll burn these, Arthur, we can get you some new." Mildred pointed at his uniform and underclothes piled next to the bath. Arthur didn't respond.

Arthur's injury was still bound and Mildred removed the bandage. Ivy gasped as the gaping wound in his chest became visible. His ear was a strange colour and was badly scabbed; he seemed to have lost his earlobe.

"I'll get some more bandage," said Mildred.

Ivy removed Arthur's underpants and helped him into the bath.

"We'll soon have you back with us, Arthur," she said as she gently started sponging his back. "You have your child to think of."

Arthur looked at Ivy as she pulled her skirt tight,

emphasising her growing belly.

"'Appen I'll not see t'child if they send me back." His speech was slow and measured. He still couldn't hear out of his rat-bitten ear.

"Best not to think that way, Arthur. 'Appen war'll be over soon, you'll see."

Arthur didn't respond.

It took almost an hour before Arthur was clean. Ivy had spent several minutes removing lice from his hair. Mildred had fortuitously brought Arthur's clothes from the bakery and presented him with a shirt, trousers, socks and underclothes. They re-dressed his wound and helped him with his clothes, then led him downstairs to the kitchen where Molly and Freda were desperate for him to try the cake they had made.

"Can you make some tea?" said Mildred; a command, not a question, as they sat at the kitchen table.

Ivy was holding Arthur's arm, trying to provide some comfort.

"It's so good to have you home, Arthur," she whispered.

The bathing had had a cathartic effect on Arthur but his dream-state continued.

"'Ave you heard owt about our Wilfred?" said Ivy with a concerned look.

Arthur's face seemed to crumple and suddenly weeks of emotion came to the surface. He cried like a baby, deep fathomless sobs causing his body to convulse. Mildred joined Ivy in trying to console him. Molly and Freda just looked at him in sadness. Their brother, strong, resourceful, and opinionated, head of the family, now a shell of the man he once was.

He gradually calmed down and composed himself. They managed to help him drink some tea, Ivy lifting the cup to his mouth as if feeding a child.

"Let's get you to bed, you should rest for a while," said Mildred. "I'm going to telephone Doctor Adams and ask him to call."

With Arthur comfortable, they returned to the kitchen.

"What's wrong with Arthur?" said Freda.

"He's not himself, dear," said Mildred. "But with our care, he'll recover."

There was the sound of the doorbell ringing.

"Kitty, how lovely to see you," said Mildred as she opened the door. "Come in."

"I've come to see how Arthur is. It was around the church that he was coming home today."

"That's most kind of you," said Mildred. "Yes, I spoke to the vicar last night to cancel one of my committee meetings and told him… Arthur's sleeping at the moment."

They went into the kitchen and greetings were exchanged with the girls.

"Is there any news of Freddie?" asked Mildred.

"Yes, I had a letter from him yesterday, that's the other thing I wanted to tell you. He's in a military hospital in London somewhere. He told me not to worry. It seems he's injured his legs."

"I wonder if they'll transfer him to Leeds as they did with Arthur."

"I don't know, I hope so. I've written back but not had a reply as yet." Kitty's face was one of concern.

"Maybe Arthur may have more news. Can I speak to him?"

"Yes, of course, but not today, why not call again tomorrow? I'm hoping he'll feel more himself then."

Kitty relented but was unable to hide her disappointment. She was desperate for any information about her son.

After Kitty had left, Ivy went upstairs to check on Arthur

and decided to lay with him.

Mildred had Arthur's uniform and started emptying the pockets. His father's fob watch was still there, his pay book, Small Book and an envelope. Mildred took it out and opened it. It was from the commanding officer of the Bradford regiment and addressed to Corporal Arthur Marsden.

'It is with the greatest honour I confirm the recommendation of the Conspicuous Gallantry Medal to Corporal Arthur Marsden for conspicuous gallantry and devotion to duty during operations at Poperinghe on 11th December 1914. Showing complete disregard for his own safety, he selfishly recovered a wounded comrade from no-man's land, saving his life.'

It was late afternoon before Arthur and Ivy returned to the sitting room. It was dark outside and the curtains were drawn; the wall-lights and the roaring fire in the sitting room made it homely and cosy. Arthur and Ivy sat on the sofa. Mildred was reading the newspaper and immediately looked up.

"How are you feeling, dear?" asked Mildred.

"Aye, fine enough, ta." There was a degree of uncertainty in his reply.

"Molly and Freda are making dinner; would you like some tea?"

"Aye, ta."

"I'll go and make it," said Ivy and left for the kitchen.

Mildred had so many questions but recognised she would have to tread carefully.

"Do you feel up to telling us about how you got injured?"

Arthur paused for a moment and put his head in his hands. "Aye, t'were a whizz bang."

"What's a whizz bang?"

"Summat the Germans chuck at us… 'Appen me pals are

all dead."

"Oh dear Lord, I'm so sorry, Arthur; there're no words of mine that will give you comfort." She looked at him; his pallor was still ghostly white. He winced as the pain in his chest returned.

She spoke softly. "I believe things happen for a reason, Arthur. You were saved to be with your family and be a father to your child."

"Aye, but I can't see no reason. Why were them killed and not me, eh? And what about Wilfred?" There was venom in his reply.

"What about Wilfred, Arthur, you've not said?"

"Aye, 'appen he's not right in the head; he's gone mad wi' all the shelling. He's not the only one either."

"Who's gone mad?" said Ivy as she entered the sitting room carrying a tray with three cups of tea.

Arthur put his hands to his face then looked at her.

"It's thar Wilfred, he were in a right bad way; I don't know what they'll do wi' 'im."

Ivy put down the tray on the table, sat next to Arthur and held his hand. "But he's alive?"

"Aye, if tha can call it that."

Mildred interrupted. "Don't worry, Ivy. We can make some enquiries and see if we can find out anything. We need to tell your mother as well; she'll be worried. I'll go and see her tomorrow."

Mildred had Arthur's letter and handed it to him. "I found this in your tunic. It says you're going to get a medal." She passed it to Ivy, who started reading it.

"Aye, for what use it be. It won't bring me pals back."

"No, Arthur, nothing will, but it says you were very brave."

"Not really, I weren't thinking."

"It says you rescued someone," interjected Ivy. Arthur looked at her.

"Aye, turns out it were Freddie, me brother that I didn't know I had."

"What…? Freddie?" said Mildred.

"Aye. He were in a bad way; may lose a leg… I heard they put him on a boat. 'Appen he'll be in England by now, I reckon."

"Yes, Kitty called round to see how you were. He's in hospital in London somewhere. I must tell her."

"Yes, it's what our Grace said would happen."

"Grace…? Grace…? What… your sister, Grace?"

"Aye, t'were her who took me to the hospital in France."

"Well, I don't know what to say, I'm speechless… How is she?"

"Aye, she were well enough. Driving ambulances about, day and night. Got herself engaged, an' all."

"Yes, she said in her letters… Do we know anything about him?"

"She never said owt. Mind you, I were asleep most of time."

Mildred was trying to take in these revelations.

There was another caller. It was Doctor Adams, who had taken a cabbie from town to answer Mildred's call. Mildred took the doctor's coat and hat and escorted him into the sitting room. She and Ivy left to allow the medic to complete his examination.

Doctor Adams, the family physician for two generations, checked the wound to Arthur's chest and re-dressed it, then examined the bruises on his legs and his damaged ear.

"I think you may have burst an eardrum, Arthur. It should heal by itself in the next few weeks but make sure you keep it dry. If you get an infection, you may lose your hearing permanently."

Arthur seemed to take in the advice. The doctor completed his work.

"Your injuries appear to be healing well enough, but it will take a while for you to be completely better... How are you sleeping? Are you getting, er, haunted by any bad thoughts or memories at all?"

"Aye, all the time."

"Yes, I've had a number of patients sent home with the same affliction. They will fade over time, but I will leave you with some laudanum to help you sleep, but please use it wisely."

"Aye, ta, doctor."

The doctor left Arthur in the sitting room. Mildred approached, with Ivy in close attendance.

"How is he, doctor?"

"He should recover, in time. His wounds appear to be healing well enough and he should regain his hearing if he doesn't get an infection; I've told him to keep his ear dry. It's his mental state which will need careful managing. Many of my patients who have been injured experience significant trauma. I have here a bottle of laudanum which will help him sleep."

He took out a small, brown, glass container from his Gladstone bag and gave it to Mildred. 'Trauma' was a new term for Mildred but she understood the context. She escorted the doctor to the front door, pondering his words. The cabbie was still waiting to return him to town. His account would reflect the additional cost.

"I'll call again on Tuesday afternoon, if I may, and check on progress," said the medic as he straightened his bowler hat.

In normal circumstances, Mildred would never have

countenanced Arthur and Ivy sharing a bed before they were married, but these were not normal circumstances, and she made no complaint when Ivy announced she would sleep with Arthur in case he needed anything.

As they lay in bed together, Arthur felt wracked with turmoil. His body ached all over, his legs restless and unable to get comfortable. When he closed his eyes, he could see the trench, the bodies, the injured in the infirmary. He remembered his pals with whom he had enjoyed the best and worst of times; why had they been killed and not him? Tears started rolling down his cheeks. Ivy consoled him.

"Shh, shh." She stroked the tears away. She reached for the bottle of laudanum next to the bed and poured a measure into a teaspoon. "Here, Arthur, drink this, it will help you sleep."

She gently tipped it into his mouth. Five minutes later, he was asleep. It was going to be a long road to recovery.

The following morning, Arthur woke with an opiate-based hang-over. It was still dark as he staggered out of bed and searched for the chamber pot. Ivy sensed his movement and also woke.

"Where's piss-pot?" said Arthur, still disorientated.

"There's a proper lavvy, Arthur... you remember?"

"Oh... aye."

"Here, let me help you."

Ivy went around the other side of the bed and helped Arthur to his feet. A searing pain ran through his knees as he tried to bear weight. She helped him along the landing to the toilet.

As he returned from his ablutions, he turned to Ivy.

"'Appen we need to get back to t'bakery."

"Ney, Arthur, this is your home until you're well again."

He got into bed and immediately fell asleep.

By nine o'clock, Molly had left for work at the seamstress's but the rest of the family were having breakfast in the kitchen. This was Arthur's first proper look at the family house he had so vehemently reviled in the past. His head was still muzzy and he needed a shave. He was dressed in his bakery clothes with his shirt collar undone. Ivy sat next to him. Mildred served eggs and bacon and placed a plate in front of Arthur.

"I can't be eating all this," he protested. "Not when lads are living on Maconochies and tack."

"What's that?" asked Freda as she helped herself to a slice of bread.

"Tha don't want to know," retorted Arthur and scowled.

Mildred was about to say something but Ivy intervened.

"Now then, Arthur, tha's not there now, tha's at home. You need to get tha strength back." She held his arm in a consoling way.

"This is no home of mine. 'Appen I should be in bakery."

Again, it was Ivy who provided the voice of reason. "When tha's well again. For now, tha can't look after thaself."

"She's right, Arthur, you need to be here with your family. Now eat your breakfast," said Mildred firmly.

Arthur had lost the energy to fight back and started eating.

The girls were washing up, and Arthur had hobbled into the sitting room and was seated at the table reading the previous day's edition of The Times. The doorbell sounded and Mildred went to answer it. She returned to the kitchen holding an envelope.

"Who was it, Mam?" asked Freda.

"It was the postie." She showed Freda the letter. "I think it's from Grace, though it doesn't look like her handwriting; it's from France." Mildred opened it.

'Dear Mrs Marsden, This is Hetty, Grace's friend. I am

sorry for the brevity of this letter but I wanted to let you know that there's been a terrible accident, the ambulance came off the road and turned over. Grace is in the hospital here and being looked after as best we can. I have stayed with her all night but she remains unconscious. I am sorry that I don't have better news but I will write again as soon as I know more. Yours sincerely, Hetty Mallinder'.

Mildred dropped to a chair, her face white with shock.

"Oh dear Lord," she said and handed the letter to Arthur.

"What's happened?" asked Freda.

"'Appen our Grace has had an accident," replied Arthur.

"What…?" said Ivy, who was now also reading the letter.

"I need to know what's happening; this letter was posted a week ago," said Mildred, who was deep in thought. She had an idea and went to her telephone. She clicked the switch hook several times.

"Hello… hello… can you put me through to Lady Garner at Coltswood Manor, please?" There was a delay, then a voice.

"Jane Garner."

"Lady Garner… thank goodness, this is Mildred Marsden, Grace's mother from Springfield Hall."

"Yes, I remember, Mrs Marsden, how are you? Nothing wrong, I hope?"

"Well, there could be. I've received a letter this morning from her friend at the hospital… in France, saying she's been involved in an accident… I wondered if you knew anything?"

"Goodness, how awful. No, I haven't heard anything. I've had several letters from Grace, she writes so well, but nothing recently… Look, leave it with me; I have some contacts over there. I'll try and find out what's happened."

"Oh would you? That's most kind."

"I'll be in touch as soon as I have some news."

"Thank you."

Mildred dropped the call and went back into the kitchen.

Chapter Twenty-One

It had been a week since the accident. Hetty had hardly left Grace's bedside for the first three days as she drifted in and out of consciousness; at last, she was beginning to recover. Her left arm was broken and her face looked like she had been in a boxing match. The doctor had diagnosed a possible hairline skull fracture but, luckily, the ambulance canopy had cushioned the impact of the blow as the vehicle tipped over and had almost certainly saved her life.

Hetty had sent a further letter updating the family on Grace's improved condition but, of course, it would take at least a week to arrive. She was in the outside yard helping to load one of the ambulances when she noticed a smart-looking young man in an officer's uniform looking slightly lost; he was staring up and down at the building. It was a chilly morning and the puddles were iced over. She walked over to the soldier.

"Hello... can I help you? You seem a bit lost."

"Ha, yes, I am. I'm looking for Grace Marsden... Captain Keating."

"Are you Matthew?"

"Yes, I am."

"Oh, I'm so glad you're here. I'm Hetty, Grace's friend. She keeps talking about you. It's this way."

She started walking towards the entrance, the officer tagging alongside.

"Is she here now? Only I've just been transferred to Étaples so I haven't been able to get my letters. I managed to get a ride with one of the ambulances and thought I would surprise her."

Hetty stopped and looked at him. "You won't have heard then?"

"Heard what?" said the officer with a concerned look.

"Well, there was a terrible accident about a week ago; the

393

ambulance turned over."

"What!? God, no… How is she? Is she alright?"

"Yes, she seems to be on the mend now."

"On the mend?" He looked at Hetty quizzically.

"Yes, come with me, I'll take you to her."

Matthew followed Hetty through the hospital; he couldn't take in the sight of so many wounded troops. Grace was in the corner away from the main hubbub. She appeared to be asleep. The pair approached the bed.

"Hello, old thing. Are you awake? I have a visitor for you."

Grace's eyes flickered and then slowly opened.

"Hello, Hetty," she wheezed. Then her eyes focussed on the man standing next to her. "Matthew…? Is that you?"

"Grace, darling, yes, it's me." He knelt beside the bed to get closer to her. "What happened? How are you? I had no idea…" He reached for her hand.

"I'll leave you two to catch up. I'll be along later," said Hetty and returned to her duties.

"I'm feeling much better… They're sending me back to England to recuperate." Her voice was slow and laboured.

He looked at her face, still bruised. He leaned over and kissed her forehead.

"What happened?"

She attempted to sit up but was still weak. "I was taking the ambulance to pick up some *blessés*… the road gave way; we tipped over. Luckily, Hetty was able to jump clear, but… I was trapped. Some soldiers managed to lift the ambulance and got me out… They brought me back here."

"Where are you hurt?"

"Just my arm; it's broken… It got caught in the steering wheel." She lifted her right arm which was encased in a white plaster cast. "I was unconscious for a couple of days…

Mm, I don't remember anything, only what Hetty told me."

"You said they were sending you back to England. Do you know when?" Grace shuffled uncomfortably and winced as she changed positions.

"Mm… Monday or Tuesday, the C.O.'s arranging a passage for me," she replied, her eyes now more focussed. "Anyway, what are you doing here…? I can't believe it's really you… I thought I was dreaming."

"Well, I've been moved up to Étaples; the unit transferred from Le Havre last week. Unfortunately, I've not been able to write, so I thought I would drop by and surprise you. I'm only about thirty miles away."

"Aye, you did that, alright… It is wonderful to see you… I've missed you so much."

"Yes, I've missed you too."

He held her hand and squeezed it gently, and for a moment, there was silence. It was broken by Grace.

"And you are in Étaples…? We have been there a few times… for supplies; it is so big."

"Yes, it is. I'm still trying to find my way around… Wait, I have an idea; I have some leave due to me. Why don't I travel back with you? You shouldn't be on your own."

"Is that possible?"

"I don't know, but I get on very well with the C.O., I can ask."

"Oh, Matthew, that would be so wonderful… In truth, I don't want to leave; there's so much to do here, but I'm no use to man nor ornament at the moment." She raised her right arm again.

"I'll try and get up here again tomorrow when I'm off duty and I can let you know. I'll get one of the drivers to bring me." He leaned over and kissed her on the forehead. "I love you," he said and left.

Friday, January 8th, 1915. Midday: Mildred couldn't control her excitement. Daisy Jessop was in the kitchen cooking while mayhem surrounded her. Ivy was lending a hand as Arthur was still in bed. Kitty had given Molly the day off and she was helping Freda with the chores. Mildred was trying to keep calm but the thought that Grace would be returning today was causing summersaults in her tummy. It was a chilly morning but bright with a scattering of clouds; rain was forecast for later. She checked the letter for the umpteenth time.

'Saturday, January 2nd, 1915. Dear Mam, I am writing to let you know that I am returning to England to recuperate from my accident. Please don't concern yourself, I am getting better every day. If the sailings go as planned, I should be back next Friday, but I can send a telegram when I get back to England...'

That telegram arrived yesterday sent from a hotel in London: *'Have reached London – STOP – will catch train tomorrow – STOP – arrive afternoon – STOP – Grace'.* Lady Jane had also been in touch keeping Mildred updated and had confirmed Grace's pending arrival with a promise of a visit once Grace had settled back in.

Mildred heard the sound of the crunching of gravel outside as a vehicle pulled up.

"Grace!" she exclaimed to herself. She walked to the front door followed by Molly and Freda.

She watched the vehicle pull up to a halt. It was not your usual cabbie but a much grander affair. The driver, dressed in chauffeur's livery, walked around to the passenger door, and opened it. The occupant emerged.

"Agnes!" squealed Freda. Mildred couldn't believe her eyes.

There was Agnes, dressed in the finest clothes Mildred had ever seen. A fur stole was wrapped around her shoulders, a stylish hat on her head, her makeup vivid but tasteful, her hair coiffed in the latest style. She walked towards the house with the poise of a model, her elegant shoes coping with the gravel drive. Mildred went to greet her.

"My, my, Agnes, you look so different, so fine… so grown up," she said as she stood and admired her daughter.

The driver was collecting packages from the back seat. The two girls made a fuss of Agnes, firing questions nineteen to the dozen.

"Can you bring them inside," ordered Agnes. The driver was stood holding six white cardboard boxes with the name 'Harrods' in bold lettering on each and was trying to peer over the top.

"It's so lovely to see you… It's such a surprise," said Mildred as they walked back to the house.

"Yes, I had a letter from Grace telling me about her accident and that she was returning home. Cameron has given me the weekend off. I've not had a break since we started the run. I wanted to see Grace."

"Oh, that's wonderful; we are expecting her this afternoon."

They went into the house followed by the chauffeur with the boxes. Then, having deposited the items in the hall, he went back to fetch Agnes's luggage. Agnes thanked the man and arranged for the return journey.

"It's Cameron's chauffeur, he's going to call for me on Monday and take me to the station in Bradford."

Inside, Arthur had dressed and was standing in the hallway with Ivy. Agnes was momentarily taken aback at his appearance.

"Hello, Arthur, how are you?" said Agnes.

Ivy interjected before he could reply. "He's feeling a lot better, aren't you, Arthur?"

Arthur looked at Ivy. "Aye, 'appen I am."

"I've bought you all something to make up for not being here at Christmas," said Agnes pointing at the boxes. "They're all labelled."

Agnes took off her topcoat which revealed a stunning dress.

"You look so beautiful, Agnes; like a real lady," said Molly.

"Thank you, Molly," replied Agnes.

Arthur was watching the proceedings; he shrugged his shoulders, turned, and went to the sitting room.

"Is he alright?" asked Agnes.

"'Appen he's not himself yet," said Ivy. "I'll just go and see to him."

The presents were duly distributed. Arthur's box remained in the hall while Mildred, Molly and Freda excitedly opened their gifts. There was another box labelled 'Grace'.

"Grace can open hers when she gets here," said Agnes.

A new hat for Mildred from one of Harrod's top milliners and dresses for Molly and Freda. They went upstairs to try them on. Mildred, Ivy and Agnes were in the sitting room catching up. Arthur had gone back to bed. Molly and Freda returned wearing their new dresses.

"My, my, they look so fine," said Mildred as they modelled their garments.

A few minutes later, the bell sounded in the hallway.

"Grace!" said Molly.

Mildred went to the front door. "Kitty… How are you? Come in."

"I won't stop. I just wanted to tell you the news. Freddie's in the infirmary in Leeds. I've just had word."

"Oh, that is good news… How is he?"

"Well, he didn't say a lot. Not much of a letter writer is Freddie, but at least he's alive."

"When are you going to see him?"

"I don't rightly know; they're not allowing visitors at the moment, so they said."

"Well, when you hear anything, be sure to let us know."

"Yes, of course. I do hope it's soon, it's such a worry."

They exchanged farewells and Kitty headed back down the drive to catch her train.

The house was alive with chatter; Freda and Ivy were helping Daisy in the kitchen preparing a meal for the family. Oswald Jessop had delivered a large joint of lamb which was cooking in the range. With the meadow having produced a good crop of vegetables, there were several wooden crates filled with potatoes, carrots and cabbages stacked in the scullery.

Just before two-thirty, the sound of a car arriving outside the house prompted Mildred to walk to the front door. Molly and Freda joined her. She watched as the cabbie stopped and the door opened. A handsome-looking man in the uniform of a captain walked around to the passenger door and opened it. He held the arm of the other occupant and helped her out of the taxi.

"Grace!" squealed Freda and rushed to greet her sister. Mildred and Molly followed.

The officer paid the cabbie and carried Grace's luggage in one hand whilst aiding Grace with the other.

Mildred held her hand to her mouth seeing Grace's condition. Her head was slightly bowed against the weather. She was wearing an officer's greatcoat around her shoulders; her right arm was in a sling and her face showing evidence of bruising.

"Quickly, Grace, let's get you inside out of the cold," said Mildred as she went to her daughter.

The party entered the house where Ivy and Daisy were waiting; Matthew followed behind with the two girls.

"Are you going to marry our Grace?" asked Freda mischievously.

"Yes, I am," replied Matthew.

Freda giggled; Molly gave her a playful slap on the arm.

"Don't be cheeky with the captain."

They got inside and Mildred closed the door. It was much warmer and Matthew helped Grace with the coat.

"This is Matthew," said Grace. Greetings were exchanged.

Mildred extended her hand. "Very pleased to meet you, Matthew. Come through to the sitting room, it's warmer, the fire is on. You must be freezing after that journey," she said.

Grace and Matthew made themselves comfortable while Daisy went to make some tea.

"You have a lovely house, Mrs Marsden," said Matthew.

"Thank you… I'll just go and help Daisy with the teas."

Mildred left the sitting room, smiling to herself. For the first time since the war broke out, all her family were back together; she felt a sense of peace.

That joy would be short lived as significant challenges lay ahead which would affect every member of the Marsden family as the Great War continued. The end of the bloody conflict was nowhere in sight.

To Be Continued

The Last Poppy – the final instalment of the Marsden trilogy - to be published by Fisher King Publishing 2022

Alan Reynolds

Following a successful career in Banking, award winning author Alan Reynolds established his own training company in 2002 and has successfully managed projects across a wide range of businesses. This experience has led to an interest in psychology and human behaviour through watching interactions, studying responses and research. Leadership has also featured strongly in his training portfolios and the knowledge gained has helped build the strong characters in his books.

Alan's interest in writing started as a hobby but after completing his first novel in just three weeks, the favourable reviews he received encouraged him to take up a new career. The inspiration for this award-winning author come from real life facts which he weaves seamlessly into fast-paced, page-turning works of fiction.

Alan R. Wolf